This one's for Bels. I can't thank you enough! You're the best.

Breaking

Legacies

Contents

Appendix

Part 1

The Crow

Chapter 1

neeling on one knee, I peered through the long, frosted blades of grass in the meadow, clutching the bow in my hand and watching the dense trees at the other end of the clearing. The forest around me was blanketed in a thick sheet of snow, but I was wearing enough fur to double my weight. So far, this had been a rough winter, and I'd been tracking an elusive deer for the last few days. Just the thought of him was making my stomach cramp hungrily.

"Tch!" I clicked my tongue at my wolfhound, which was crouched at my side but beginning to rise. I didn't want him giving away our position, so I gave him the hand command to lie down. He obeyed, lowering himself to his stomach so completely that his pure white fur disappeared in the deep snow.

While he all but vanished, I discovered why he'd been rising. I had to steady myself when the first point of the deer's antlers poked through the trees, because it excited me so much that I almost rose too. The animal took another cautious step, and then stopped to look around. Kneeling like I was, the grass around me almost reached my forehead, and its frozen gold color was camouflaged to the pale brown of my furs. I was well hidden, and after giving Albus the signal to stay motionless, I began to reach for an arrow at my back. The movement was so gradual that I'd let out three long, foggy breaths before my hand even brushed the quiver.

The deer took a few more steps into the meadow. I placed the arrow against my bowstring. The deer paused after another step as its head turned my direction; it was aware of danger, but it didn't matter. The vibrations of my bowstring shuddered in the frigid air, and the arrow sailed perfectly into the creature's heart. Albus knew that when I let loose my arrow he could move. He sprang up, prepared to make chase if I'd missed, but I never miss. The hart took one leap, and collapsed when its hooves touched down again.

I ran toward it, my left hand ready on the knife at my hip in case it was still breathing. We would *finally* eat – my mother and ten-year-old brother and me. We'd get to have something other than deficient vegetable stew.

The deer was dead the moment I shot it. As was my religious custom, I knelt at its side and placed my hand on its head to whisper, "Thank you for your sacrifice. May your spirit rest within me." Then I stood. "Eyes," I told Albus, motioning to our quarry.

While he was protecting our sustenance, I sprinted back to where I'd left my dark brown horse, Brande, and returned with him at a gallop even though I could hear the cart he was pulling beating against roots and the sides of trees. I detached the cart and pushed as much of it as I could underneath the deer, though I couldn't do much since the animal weighed far more than I did. There was a rope hanging from Brande's saddle, so I looped one end around the saddle horn and the other around the deer's antlers. Then I led Brande forward a few steps, until he'd successfully dragged our kill completely onto the wagon.

After reattaching Brande to the cart, I mounted, and we started back toward home with Albus trotting at our side. I was overcome with excitement in anticipation of presenting my mother with the deer, eager to see the smile on her face and the small dance Nilson did whenever I brought home food. That is, until I reached our farm and saw a group of horses outside, all clad in the king's red and gold. I'd known my brother to steal a sweet roll, or occasionally pickpocket to pay for said sweet roll. My only conclusion was that he'd been caught, and they were here to fine my mother for money she didn't have, and thus take Nilson to the prison in Guelder.

"What's happened?" I asked, already near a panic as I burst into the cottage.

There were soldiers standing around, but my eyes searched the small room for Nilson. He was sitting at the table with our mother, looking rather comfortable for a prisoner. When he saw me, he waved, with a sweet roll clutched firmly in his other hand.

"What've you got to look guilty about?" laughed a familiar deep voice.

2

I'd been so frightened that I hadn't tried to make out the faces of the soldiers. Now I looked at the one who'd spoken – a tall young man, bulky in his armor, with long brown locks and facial hair to match. I knew him to be twenty-one years of age, just two years older than myself. It was him who'd brought Nilson the sweet roll he was eating.

"That's a rotten trick," I scolded as I strode over, and when I got there I swung myself onto his back. "Coming here with all these men."

"Your eyes," he laughed, wrestling me off of him. "Look, look." He motioned for me to watch, and then mockingly exaggerated an expression of horror.

The soldier's name was Silas. Our fathers had been old friends, and we'd grown up together, hunting and tracking, even brawling when there wasn't anyone around to scold us for it. Silas's fortune and skill with a sword had led him to knighthood in the king's guard. My lack of fortune and sword-skill led me to the woods.

"Take off your armor," I challenged, rapping my knuckles against his steel chest. "I'll give you something to be frightened of."

"Kiena," my mother uttered, brown eyes giving me a similarly sharp review. She hated it when I didn't act formally in front of officials, even if it was just Silas.

I ignored the rebuke, finally taking off my heavy coat and then sitting myself right on top of the table, knowing she was still glaring at me. "Did you come for supper?" I asked Silas. "Just shot myself a hart of eighteen."

He squinted his eyes at me. "No you haven't."

"Come and look, then." I got up and stepped toward the door, leading him outside so he could see that I wasn't lying.

Some of the other soldiers had trailed along out of curiosity, and they stood by the open door of the cottage while Silas counted the tines of the deer's antlers. "Eighteen," he mumbled to himself when he finished, laughing in amazement. "Eighteen!" he repeated to those of his men who'd stepped out. Then, to one in particular, "I told you she was the right one."

"Right one?" I echoed, following Silas back into the cottage while my mother and Nilson passed us to take care of the deer. "For what?"

He waited until both he and I were seated at the table. I'd never seen him so suddenly serious, and sitting there with him, surrounded by five other soldiers, I was growing a little bit nervous too. "Princess Avarona has run away," he told me after a minute. I nodded, though that bit didn't particularly mean much to me – I lived on the edges of a forest over twenty miles from the castle. "The king wants her found before the Ronan Empire hears of it." I nodded again, this time in understanding. Our kingdoms had been at war for decades. If Ronan spies found her before King Hazlitt did, it would be over. "I got word to him that there was no better tracker in the kingdom than you."

"You did *what*?" I asked as my heart sank. "Silas, why?"

"Because it's the truth," he answered. When I offered no reply but the shaking of my head, he added, "If you bring her back safely, he'll reward you with more gold than could fill this cottage. You could move into Guelder. Nilson could have a sweet roll with every meal."

"And if I can't find her?" I asked. I'd never even seen the king, but everyone in Valens knew that the reputation of his temper preceded him. "Or if she gets hurt? Then he'll have my head, is that it?"

"You could find a fox in a blizzard," he said. I scowled at that, but to emphasize his point, he motioned toward my dog. "Even without Albus."

I don't know why I was even still thinking about it. I didn't much have a choice now. If the king had decided he wanted me, then I had to go. But what would Mother and Nilson do while I was gone? What if I *never* came back? They'd starve. "Silas," I prompted reluctantly, and I leaned in closer to him, casting a suspicious look around at the soldiers before whispering, "does the king know who I am?"

Before my father's execution, he'd been labeled a traitor to the kingdom. He'd fought for years to put King Hazlitt on the throne, and then one day he stopped fighting for the king. People said it's because my father had gained just enough support in the ranks to want power for himself, but that it wasn't enough to actually win, and for that, they said he was mad. If the king knew who I was, if he knew my surname and my family history, there's no way he'd hire me to find his daughter. He might even throw me in prison just because he could, because I had a traitor's blood.

Silas gave me a long look at the question, and though I knew him well enough to recognize the hesitation in it, he wouldn't risk my life to lie. He was my best friend, and I trusted him.

"No," he answered, "I only told him that I know the best hunter in the kingdom." He watched me for a long moment after that, studying the continued reluctance on my face. "We've lost brothers to this war," he said,

4

breaking my intense gaze at him and looking around at his soldiers, all of who mumbled 'no man is an island' in response. "Good men. Honest men. We can't lose on account of a reckless princess. For the sake of the realm, Kiena."

"Have I got to go to the castle?" I asked. Part of me thought if this ended badly, if the princess got hurt before I could find her or if she was able to avoid me, then it might be easier to run if the king had never seen my face.

"It'll be alright," Silas assured me, sensing my concern. Then he added, "You always wanted to go to the castle." But we both knew I'd never wanted to go to see the king. Silas studied me for a minute while I thought about it. Still, I don't know why; the choice wasn't mine. "You should like to go before word gets out."

I met his eyes with my own, staring while I took in his warning. Once word got out, there would be others searching for her, and I might be killed so someone else could return her for the reward. This job wasn't an opportunity. It was a death warrant. I didn't want to be upset with Silas, but I felt as though he might as well be here to take me straight to the gibbet. Regardless of that, I stood.

"Let me gather my things," I told him, and he filtered out of the cottage with the rest of the soldiers.

I'd been on the hunt for days, and though there was no time to bathe, I could at least try and make myself look presentable and capable to the king. I took off my leather vest and dirtied beige tunic, wrapped my bare chest in the binding linens I'd left at home the last few days, and then put on the only fresh long-sleeved tunic I owned. I put my vest back on and pulled my dark red hair out of its braid, threading only my long bangs together to one side so they were out of my face. None of it made much difference in the end, but at the very least, I felt more presentable.

I pulled my heavy furs back on for warmth as I strode outside, where I made sure everything I'd need was strapped to Brande's saddle – my bow and arrows, my sleeping furs, some food. Then I strode to the quartering rack to explain it to my mother.

"Can't you clean up a bit?" she asked, scrutinizing my hunt-tarnished leather trousers, my fur boots, and my hooded fur coat.

"He wants a hunter," I told her with a defeated chuckle, because I *had* tried to clean up. "Not a lady."

My mother's eyes grew watery, and she pulled me into a tight embrace. "Come back," she sniffled. "With or without the gold. Come back."

"I will," I assured her, pressing a kiss to her cheek. When she let me go, I ruffled my fingers through Nilson's long, sandy hair. "Keep your hands off things you haven't paid for."

He giggled, but he hadn't been paying attention to my conversation with our mother, because he peered up at me and asked, "You're leaving already?"

"I've got to help find a princess," I said, squatting down to be more at his level.

"A princess?" he repeated, hazel eyes widening with fascination. "Is she pretty?"

"I imagine so," I said, my lips curling with a smile. "Ain't princesses always pretty?"

He leaned in closer to me, cupping his hand to the side of his mouth and whispering as though it would keep our mother from hearing, "Are you going to kiss her?"

I couldn't help but laugh, especially when I heard my mother chuckle behind me. "Not if I can help it," I told Nilson with a sly wink, and he returned it like he truly thought I'd ever kiss a princess, and we were sharing that secret. Not having anything else to say, I poked him in the ribs, reminding, "Behave yourself."

All he did was giggle again and shy away from my hand, so I pulled him close and kissed the crown of his head. After a final, loving look at the both of them, I returned to the soldiers.

Silas was watching me from his horse as I reached them, and while I mounted Brande, he said, "She's just a girl." I assumed that was supposed to be reassuring. "Barely older than you. You could find her before the sun sets."

"She's educated," I argued. Maybe she'd outsmart me. Foxes weren't educated. Then, knowing she could bribe people to help her, I added, "And rich."

"Tutors and books can't teach someone what you know," he observed. He tugged his reins to the side, telling me with a smirk before he kicked his horse, "Think about the gold."

"Albus!" I called for the dog so he'd know to follow, and then took off after the retreating soldiers.

6

I tried to think about the gold. The whole twenty-mile gallop to Guelder, through war-barren farmland and poverty-stricken towns, I tried to think about it. Really, all I could think about was the icy wind whipping through my hair, tingling my nose and ears and making my eyes water, and hope I'd get to feel it for years and years to come.

The sun had gone down by the time we reached Guelder, and I thought to point out to Silas that I wouldn't find the princess by night after all. It was the first time I'd ever been to the stone city, but it was too dark for my eyes to explore. We trotted right up to the castle gates, and then beyond them to the massive royal stables. I didn't even have time to make sure Brande was properly taken care of because we were in such a hurry. Silas knew me well though, because while he led me into the castle, he assured me that Brande would be spoiled compared to usual.

The brick walls of the narrow passage we were tramping through were completely bare, except for the occasional torch outside of a door. The only source of constant light was another single torch, carried by the soldier at the head of our caravan. The knights' armor made an obnoxious clanking on the stone floor with each step. It was so loud that after winding through hall after hall, we came to a massive door, and it was opened before the lead man had a chance to knock.

"Enter," permitted the Chamberlain, richly dressed in red and gold garb. Following Silas, I began to walk through, but the man sneered, "Not the beast!"

I turned to see that he was talking about Albus, who'd been loyally on my heels. Or... at my back, I should say, seeing as the dog's head almost reached my chest. "Stay," I told him, though it was more of a nervous whisper. I was going to meet the king, and suddenly I didn't feel presentable enough in my dirtied hunting clothes. So I tugged off my coat, laying it over Albus's back so I wouldn't have to hold it, and could greet the king in what was practically my best attire.

The door closed between Albus and me, and after receiving an impatient glare from the Chamberlain, I followed Silas farther in. It wasn't just any threshold we'd crossed. We'd walked straight into the throne room, the king and queen visible at the long end of it. The high walls were decorated in brightly colored tapestries. Moonlight shone in through tall windows near the ceiling, the strength of it muted by the torches and candles scattered throughout the room. It took everything in me not to turn and run. I'd lived in the country all my life, no one ever taught me how to act in front of a king. All I knew was to call him 'Your Majesty,' and what I had of common sense told me to kneel. Kneel I did, as did Silas, at the foot of the throne.

"A girl, Silas," were the king's first words, spoken in gruff annoyance. "Is this a joke?"

I couldn't blame him for it, even if it was insulting. I *was* female, young and thin, some might even say gaunt, though I was taller than most women. I was fair featured too, with my dark red hair and plain brown eyes. I couldn't have looked like much, especially without the bulky fur I'd been wrapped in.

"No, Your Majesty," Silas said, rising. I stayed down. "She's the best in the kingdom, I assure you."

There was a momentary silence, during which I was afraid to take my eyes off the floor. "Get up, girl," the king demanded.

I did, and also lifted my gaze. The king was a massive man, almost filling the seat of his immense throne. The hair on both his head and his face were a deep black, like the pure onyx raven set in his crown. His eyes, too, were dark as coal, a stark contrast to his light complexion. The queen was in a smaller throne at his side, but she was more pleasant looking than her male counterpart. While her hair was a similar shade of black, her skin was dark, and her dark brown eyes were kind. It appeared she'd been crying, as even if the redness behind her eyes didn't give her away, she sniffled.

"Name," the king instructed, a command so harsh it made me flinch out of my sympathetic study of the queen.

"Kiena, Your Majesty," I answered, purposefully leaving my surname out of it and giving something of an awkward curtsy.

"You'll find my daughter, Kiena," he said in his rusty voice. Every word he spoke resonated like the deep growl of a bear. "Tie the brat up and throw her over your horse, if you must. The stable boys know to keep it saddled for you." I couldn't help but glance toward the windows, through which I could hear the faint whistling of the cold wind. He wanted me to start searching tonight. "Don't let her bribe you with gold, or horses, or kisses." At the last, his eyes narrowed at me, and he burst into laughter. "What am I talking about? Her charm won't work on a girl." He chuckled

8

to himself. "Good thinking, Silas. Bringing me someone immune to her beauty."

My eyes turned in their sockets to pass a side-glance at Silas, and the smirk on his face almost caused me to snort. I fancied women, and we both knew it.

There was a short pause, after which the king asked in irritated expectation, "Well?"

I flinched once more. "If it pleases Your Majesty," I began, listening to the whistling wind. "I should begin searching with the aid of sunlight." My horse was tired, Albus was tired, I was tired, and it was beyond freezing outside.

"In the morning?" he asked, and I almost cowered at the red tint his face turned. "You'll start tonight! Or I'll have your head on a bloody spike!" Temper was an understatement. When he saw that I wasn't taking leave of myself, he asked again, "*Well?*"

"To track the princess, Your Majesty," I said, afraid he'd tire of me the next moment and have me hung, "my dog must know her scent."

"Silas!" the king nearly yelled. "Take her to the princess's chambers, and get her whatever else she needs. You won't bother me again."

"Yes, Your Majesty," Silas said with a bow, and then elbowed me to do the same.

Once we'd left the throne room, I took a calming breath and, for comfort, set my hand on the coat on Albus's back as he lumbered at my side. "Won't bother him again," I mused when it was just the three of us, and I scoffed. "As if *he's* doing *me* some kind of a favor? Just because he's the king-"

"Mind what you say next," Silas whispered, but his face betrayed his appalled amusement. "The walls have eyes, and talk like that is treason within the castle."

I gave an apologetic smile in response, but I was impatient to be out of here. Out of this place that had turned Silas into a cautious wuss. Where I was afraid to breathe too loudly because the walls could see and hear, and probably sprout legs and drag me straight to the chopping block. Albus felt it, too. He was stalking silently at my side, head down, floppy ears cropped warily forward.

"Does anybody know why she ran?" I asked, following him down another dark corridor.

"She knows," he answered, finally stopping at an elaborately carved wooden door. "That's all I can say for sure."

"Maybe she has a good reason," I told him, and shut the door behind us after we crossed the threshold. The king did seem a careless man. "Perhaps she shouldn't be found."

Silas shot me a look when I said that, and I could've predicted what it meant. Mind what you say. I wasn't accustomed to so carefully guarding my thoughts, but it might suit me to learn. I was on the king's payroll now, and he wasn't going to pay me to ask questions.

I was surprised to find the chamber already lighted when we entered. Warm too, with a blazing fire in a decorated pit at the center of the room that made me push my sleeves up to my elbows, and take my coat off Albus's back to drop it on the floor near the entrance. The entire chamber was larger than three of my cottage, and decorated with silk-upholstered furniture big enough for a giant. There were three women in the room, seated close to the fire. Two of them were older than my mother, the other about my age, all of them plainly dressed.

"Kiena," Silas said, motioning to the women. "The ladies-in-waiting." They all stood to greet him with 'sir' and curtsies.

I ceased my surveying of the chamber to study the women. The older two were stern looking, and they appeared rather irritated at the day's events. The younger one's eyes darted about the room, avoiding me completely. She seemed rather afraid. Nilson always looked that way when I caught him with a stolen sweet roll – guilty.

Despite the observation, I ignored the women to make a round through the room. Part of it was to indulge my curiosity – how lavishly the princess lived, and maybe what she was like – the rest was to look for evidence. My exploring revealed a painting on one wall, and I assumed it was the princess. She was very much unlike both her parents in features, with long, dark brown hair, and sapphire eyes. She had, however, inherited her mother's dark skin, and some of her father's strength, it appeared, being that she didn't look as fragile as the queen. She looked lively, clearly energetic, and the 'charm' I'd heard of previously didn't do her justice. The king was right to be worried about bribery with kisses.

Nothing was out of place in the room; if she'd been threatened or even kidnapped rather than running away, it didn't happen in here. I strode to the princess's clothing drawers, a large dresser taller than me, and rummaged around for something useful. I pulled out a white underdress, and held it up to show the ladies-in-waiting.

"She wear this often?"

When they all nodded, I set my hand on the dagger at my waist and glanced at Silas. He knew what I was asking, and tilted his head in consent. I couldn't take the entire dress with me. It was much too bulky. Instead, I used my blade to cut a strip from the torso, where the princess's scent was sure to be the strongest. I almost laughed when, at the ripping sound it made, all three women cringed. It must've seemed so crude to them.

After I stored the strip in a small pouch tied near the dagger's sheath, I trod to the youngest of the women. "Might I ask your name?"

"Ellerete, Miss," she answered, still too guilty to even look me in the eyes.

I assumed she was the only one who knew anything, given the stern appearance of the other two. They were too motherly. Surely the princess would confide in the youngest one, one closer to her own age, before she would the others. "I'd like to converse with Ellerete," I said aloud, and when nobody made a move for the door, added, "singularly."

The other two women filtered out of the room, but when Silas remained near the door, I raised my eyebrows expectantly and nodded for him to leave too. It wasn't just that I thought Ellerete might be more talkative if nobody else was present, but I wasn't sure what to make of Silas right now. I trusted him with my life, but as a knight for the king, he was bound by different loyalties than myself.

"King Hazlitt has charged me with finding the princess," I told the girl when we were alone. I'd never questioned anyone before. This was new territory.

"Yes, Miss," she said.

"I suppose she's out there now, in the cold." I made a deliberate glance toward the chamber's closed window, and Ellerete looked too. "I wonder why she left," I mused, even though Silas had nearly told me not to wonder aloud. This was how I thought to earn the lady's trust.

The young woman didn't say anything until I looked at her, searching for a response. "As do I, Miss."

"Please," I practically begged, "don't call me Miss." King's errand or not, I was merely a peasant. If anything, we were only equals now because

11

I was under royal employ. Otherwise *I* might be calling *her* Miss. I sat down at the fire, near enough to the girl that she'd be more likely to confide in me if she could whisper. When I did, I noticed for the first time that her eyes kept darting to Albus, who was on the opposite side of her, watching me protectively. "Does he frighten you?" I asked, but before she could answer, I pointed to a far corner of the room. "Albus, go lie down."

She relaxed a little once the dog was farther away, but she still appeared tense. It only confirmed that she knew something, as she had to be as frightened of the king as I was. It was smart to be afraid.

"Ellerete," I asked, not bothering to give her a chance to deny some sort of knowledge, "did she tell you where she was going?" I did add, "No one but myself will hear if you were involved, you have my word."

She finally looked up into my eyes, staring for nearly a minute like she was trying to decide whether or not I could be trusted. "Ellie, if you please," she said eventually, and I smiled gratefully at the discarding of formalities. "She was in a panic," she confessed. "All she'd say was that she'd heard something she shouldn't have, and I was better off not knowing." I hummed, and Ellie continued. "She said her life was in danger should she stay." At that, tears sprang to her eyes, and I could tell she wholeheartedly believed the princess was in danger.

In earnest, I leaned forward. "Where was she headed?"

Ellie used the opportunity to take my hands up with her own. "You have to help her."

I pulled away, worried that the wall's eyes were watching. Listening. They'd hear if we got too loud. "I've got to bring her back."

Maybe Ellie knew about the walls too, because she scooted closer, whispering with the same frantic energy. "Not if it means her life. Please, Miss, promise to hear her out."

"If I can find her," I murmured in response. "Where was she headed?"

"You'll promise?" she asked. "Swear an oath? And I'll tell you?" I was under employ of the king. That was as good as an oath, and here Ellie wanted me to swear another, perhaps conflicting one. I should never have come, but there was a stirring of excitement inside me. I nodded, and she said, "South."

The stirring was gone. I stood, more than disturbed by what I thought she was implying. "South?" I repeated in a huff. "Toward the Ronan Empire?" What have I gotten myself into? "Why?"

12

"I don't know," Ellie said, trying to pull me back down. "You promised," she reminded.

I resumed my seat, leaning forward to put my elbows on my knees, and I buried my face in my hands. Eventually, I sighed and lifted my chin. "Why do you think the princess will trust me with details when I find her? I've been hired to bring her back. I work for her father."

Ellie's face assumed an expression of deep thought. We both sat there for a couple of minutes in silence, the only sound the still-whistling wind and the crackling of the large fire before us. "I know!" she exclaimed, shooting up. "I'll write a contract, with my own name in it too." She paced to the large desk at one end of the room. "And when you find her, you present her with your written promise to hear her account."

I strode over, watching from behind Ellie's shoulder as she scribbled out the contract with a quill. The letters didn't present themselves to me; I couldn't read. But I refrained from making it known, that way Ellie wouldn't get any ideas to put anything else in. When she was done, she signed her own name on the bottom, and passed me the quill to do the same. I didn't even know how to sign my name.

Returning the quill to the inkwell, I pulled my dagger from its sheath. "A blood oath," I told Ellie, and pricked my thumb against the pointed tip. "With the gods as my witnesses." I pressed my bloodied finger against the page, successfully signing away my fate. My life or my honor, if the princess were truly in danger, from here on out, one was at stake.

"She bribed a stable boy to have her horse ready," Ellie informed me while we waited for the ink and blood to dry. "And I don't think she'd have left without her falcon."

"Falcon?" I asked, watching her fold up the contract. I knew the royals occasionally hunted with falcons, but I wasn't sure whether to be pleased or distraught that the princess wasn't as helpless as I'd believed her to be.

"A peregrine," Ellie confirmed, melting red wax to seal the note and then pressing the princess's emblem to it. "Princess Avarona called her Maddox. She loved that bird even more than the hunt." She put the contract into my hand, but refused to let either go. "Don't let anyone but the princess open it."

I nodded my assurance. "Thank you, Ellie." When she let go of my hand, I shoved the note into a pocket of my vest, and then turned for the door, grabbing my coat to pull it on as I paced out. "Albus." The dog followed, and when I reached Silas, I asked, "Will you take me back to the stables?"

"Did you find anything out?" he questioned, immediately beginning to lead me.

"She took her horse," I answered, unwilling to disclose anything that might reach the king's ears. "Albus will need its scent as well."

Silas didn't say anything else until we reached the stables, as he seemed to be able to tell I was keeping things from him. It appeared, however, he knew it was with the best intentions. He showed me to where the princess's horse was kept so Albus could get its scent, and then to Brande. Before I mounted, he put a hand on my shoulder and gave it a fond squeeze.

"Be safe," he said, and then pressed a pouch into my palm. The coins in it were heavy, and they rattled together when I shook the bag. "An advance, for any trouble on the road." But before he let it go, he warned, "Without the princess, the king will consider it a debt."

I could tell that he was somewhat uncomfortable with the situation he'd put me in, and he wasn't the only one. I couldn't say 'thanks,' nor could I assure him that I'd return safely. I settled for, "Goodbye, Silas," and to let him know I wouldn't hold it against him, I swatted his face. He smiled and retreated a few steps while I mounted. "Albus, track," I instructed. The dog took off on the trail, and I followed without looking back.

Not surprisingly, the horse's scent led us out of the castle walls, and then completely out of Guelder. Albus slowed when we reached the fields surrounding the city, if only from the depth of the snow. It was almost hard to keep sight of him in the frost, the way he and everything else white glowed a pale blue in the moonlight. He continued south, for miles and miles until we reached the Black Wood.

There were three ways to cross from the Valens Empire to the Ronan Empire, and visa versa. One was by the Balain Sea, along the eastern coast that ran from the north to the south. Another was the Amalgam Plains in the west – it was an endlessly mixed stretch of mountain, marsh, and desert tundra – technically in the kingdom of Cornwall. The third was the Black Wood – a hundred miles of dark, dense forest; home to the supposed ghosts and goblins of folklore; refuge for bandits and highwaymen who robbed the tax envoys from the forest's villages to Guelder – escape

route for the dear Princess Avarona. The northern half of it rested in Valens, the southern half in Ronan.

I followed Albus into the woods, through trees so thick I had to keep
my elbows in and squint to make sure I wouldn't ride into any branches.
It wouldn't have done me any good to put my fur-lined hood on. The wind
would have only knocked it off. Eventually, Albus tracked the scent all the
way to a cabin – I could tell what it was by the way a dim firelight shone
out from the inside. He ran beyond the dwelling to the back, where behind the cabin was a small fenced garden, barren in these winter months.
In the place of plants was a large horse, which Albus stalked right up to,
and which whinnied when, as he was trained to do, he trapped it in a corner of the garden.

"Down," I called him off, dismounting my own horse and giving the
dog a congratulatory pat on the head. "Good boy." The horse reared when
I reached it, but I grabbed at its reins to steady it. "Easy," I said, stroking
the beast's muscled neck. "There, there."

The horse relaxed under the ease of my touch, and I proceeded to examine it. It was still wearing its saddle, which was made of a fine-polished
leather and embroidered in silver threads. The horn and stirrups were
plated in silver, and by the aid of moonlight I could just make out the
king's ensign branded into the animal's flank. This was the princess's
horse, there was no doubt in my mind, and so I strode back to the front
door of the home.

"Hello!" I called, knocking on the wooden door and gripping the handle of my blade, just in case the owner wasn't friendly. "I call on behalf of
the king." The door creaked on its hinges as it eased open, but there was
nobody to greet me on the other side. "Hello?" I repeated, this time while I
stuck my head through the entrance.

Nobody responded, and from the door I couldn't see a single soul in
the one room of the cabin. There was a lit fireplace on the far left end,
heating the pot that hung over it. I took a step in, making sure Albus was
at my side, but still nobody appeared, so I strode forward to examine the
tables that lined the edges of the home. They were littered with jars, each
one filled with something different. Some of them contained plants, others
bugs, dead or alive. Here, chicken feet. There, the tooth of a wild cat. The
cabin stank, and was thick with the smoke of burnt incense and herbs.
Magic was against kingdom law – it was feared and dangerous and for-

15

bidden, an offense of the highest degree – and I'd just stepped foot into the dwelling of a witch.

"Not a knight," came a soft voice from behind me, but it was so unexpected that I almost tripped over myself turning to face it. "Not a duke, or a baron, or a lord," continued the woman, so concealed in the black cloak she wore that all I could see was the glittering of the fire in her eyes. "Who is it the king sends in his place?"

After the question, she hobbled to the table at the center of the room and lowered her hood. She was old, with frazzled silvery hair like the witches in every terrifying story my mother told me as a child, but her nose wasn't long and pointed, and she didn't have any warts. I imagine in her youth she was radiantly beautiful, a beauty the remnants of which were still quite apparent.

"Is that the princess's horse outside?" I asked, backing myself as far as I could against the table behind me. Witches and sorcerers weren't to be trusted.

She placed a plant into the crucible in front of her, followed by what looked like a butterfly wing and a pinch of dark sand, and then she mashed them up for a minute before finally looking at me. "The princess is not here."

I was too intimidated to be demanding, too afraid of the stories to know how to approach the situation. "That's not what I asked," I whispered.

"Who else but a hunter," the woman observed, pouring the contents of the crucible into a small iron pot. "The blood of a warrior. The heart of a lover. The warrior sacrifices the lamb, while the lover thanks it."

She took the pot to the cauldron over the fire, and ladled a tiny scoop of the cauldron's boiling contents into it. I stared after her in shock. She could easily have deduced I was a hunter by my wardrobe, or my dog. But how did she know I had the blood of a warrior? My father had been a soldier. Nor was my religion standard practice in Valens. I didn't bow to the sole Valenian god at his totems around the kingdom, and those who did didn't thank their quarry for sacrifice.

"Do you know who I am?" I asked, taking a curious step toward her as she returned to the center table.

She bent herself over the mixture she'd created, mumbling to it too quietly for me to decipher any words. Before she was even finished, she raised one arm, and with a long, thin finger, motioned me closer. I stepped forward, if only because of my curiosity. Still murmuring, she flipped her palm to the air and motioned again, and this time I set my hand in hers.

"The blood speaks," she said, finally addressing me, and once she had my hand, she pressed a long nail to the spot I'd pricked with my dagger earlier in the night, reopening the wound. "Traitor." Before I could react, she'd moved my hand over the iron pot, and by the time I pulled away, I'd lost a drip into it.

"What have you done?" I asked in a panic, sticking the pad of my thumb to my lips before she could harvest any more of my blood. Then her words registered. "Traitor?" I repeated. I was no traitor, not like my father. Everything I'd ever done, I'd done to escape that label. "I beg your pardon!"

The witch was ignoring me again, busily stirring my blood into the mixture. I didn't know whether to be terrified that after one turn of her handle the mixture began to boil and smoke on its own, or whether to be angry about the words she was or wasn't saying.

"Why do you have the princess's horse?" I demanded, setting my hand on my dagger in an attempt to be intimidating.

"She asked for a trade," the witch answered calmly, as though she'd been cooperating the whole time and couldn't account for my displeasure.

I watched her pour the steaming mixture into a vial, fearful of losing a single drop. "What did you give her in return?"

She blew over the opening of the glass, and then pressed a cork into it to close it up. "A potion," she answered, extending it to me. "To help her hide."

"What's this?" I asked, almost afraid to reach out and take it for fear this was another trick.

"A potion," she repeated, holding it before her until I took it. "To help you seek." She pulled the hood of her cloak back up over her head. "Best to return home, hunter."

"I can't," I said. I examined the crimson fluid within the vial. "I have nothing to give you for this." Truthfully, I had the coins Silas had given me, but I wasn't going to use those unless I absolutely had to, especially not on something I hadn't asked for in the first place. The witch smiled at me, a crooked smirk that revealed the top row of her surprisingly straight teeth. She moved toward the door, as though she was preparing to leave, and opened it. "What do I do?" I asked before she stepped out. "Do I drink it?"

She didn't appear to have heard me, but when she disappeared in the darkness outside, there was a voice in my ear that said, "Cursed long before this night."

The voice caused me to shiver, because even though there was no one beside me, I could feel the breath against my skin. I looked down at Albus, and he let out a whine when his big brown eyes met my own. Not wanting to spend another minute in the eerie cabin, I paced outside and around back to where I'd left Brande, and I stored the vial in a saddlebag. The princess had obviously continued on foot from here, so I pulled out the strip of cloth I'd cut from her dress and knelt in the snow beside Albus, holding it to his nose.

"Get a good whiff of that," I told him, and after a few moments, I put it back into the pouch at my hip. "Track."

While he searched the immediate area for the beginning of the trail, I mounted Brande, and, at the signal of a declaring bark, we were racing through the woods again. We weren't riding for nearly as long as we did the first time. In fact, it seemed as though we'd hardly gone half a mile before Albus stopped at his next find. I jumped down to examine what looked like a dark patch in the snow. Upon closer examination, however, I discovered it was an expensive silk gown, some riding leathers, and jewelry. All were the princess's, I knew, but I wasn't sure what to make of it. Nobody in their right mind would shed their clothing, especially in weather like this. And what about the jewelry? It was like she'd vanished into thin air.

I was about to ask my canine companion what he thought – a habit I'd gotten into since he was one of my only two friends while I was out hunting – but he wasn't at my side. He'd crept a few paces away, and now stood on his hind legs, stretched up the length of a tree and growling at something perched in it. When I got to him, I squinted up into the branches, and I wouldn't have been able to see anything if it weren't for the gleam of one tiny eye. It was too small for a human or a wild cat, but too large for any kind of rodent.

Suspicious, I retraced my steps a few feet away from the tree, and then I stuck my arm straight out. "Maddox!" I called.

Sure enough, there was the soft flapping of wings from the tree, and moments later a large falcon landed right on my arm. There was a metal ring around one of its ankles. After angling it toward the moon, I could see it was imprinted with the royal mark, and there was a long, thin leather lead tied to the same leg.

"You're Maddox," I mused, venturing to stroke the bird's back. Ellie had to have been right about the princess's love for the bird, because it allowed me to pet it as though it were no stranger to being fondled.

I opened my mouth to ask the falcon if it knew what became of the princess, but before I got a word out, there was a shout in the distance. "It went this way!" Albus began to growl, but I shushed him just in time to hear the next yell of, "Get the pasty ghost!"

At the first shout, I'd thought maybe they were after Maddox, but by the second, I knew they weren't, and I'd grown curious. "You stay here with Brande," I told the bird, setting it atop the saddle and securing its leather leash around the horn.

I pulled my hood over my head, as I was accustomed to do when I was being sneaky, and with Albus on my heels, I sprinted through the deep snow toward the noise. The male voices led me up a hill, and when I reached the top of it, I hid behind a tree to see down the other side. There were three torches, but I could see additional movement against the white of the snow, indicating there were five men in total. That was, until there was a light behind me, one I hadn't noticed until it was too late.

"Oy!" shouted the man, in front of me now that I'd turned, and I glanced over my shoulder just long enough to see some torches starting up the hill to come to us. "You after our Will-o'-the-wisp?"

"No," I answered, trying to ignore the knife he was holding toward me, and Albus's menacing snarls. "I heard shouting. I was curious, is all."

"I won't have you lying!" he growled, advancing so far forward that I stepped too far back, and I lost my footing at the steep edge of the hill.

I went rolling backward, head over heels, and the snow did nothing to cushion my fall. At least I managed to avoid hitting any of the trees on the way down, or any of the men, who just watched me roll by. The hill was so steep that I didn't come to a stop until I reached the bottom of it, and only then because it was flat for hardly six feet before it turned into a large wall of ice. It was the glacier that stopped me, and I smacked into it with a painful 'oomph.' Albus had run down after me, and he nudged me with his snout when I came to a halt.

"Get her!" one of the men hollered.

I sat up, frantically searching for an escape route through the whirling in my head. An inconsistency in the ice caught my attention, and before I could think about it, I darted into the cave. It wasn't as dark as I imagined it to be on the inside. The moonlight reflected from the outside off of every glassy surface, creating a mysterious glimmer in the cavern. But I didn't stop to enjoy it. The men were on my heels, and the paleness of the walls only made it more difficult to avoid detection. So I kept running, taking one turn after another until I spotted a small crevice at the bottom of a wall. I slid for it feet first, disappearing with Albus behind me just as the men turned down the branch we were in. There was only enough room for Albus and me to lie down flat, but I sank deeper into the cleft, watching the blur of torches through the ice and hoping the men wouldn't be able to see me through it as they sprinted by.

"Where'd she go?" one of them asked, his voice echoing off the damp walls.

"Forget her," complained another. "Let's find the Will-o'-the-wisp."

The footsteps sounded closer and closer, until they passed me once again. Instead of heading for the exit of the cave, however, they ventured down a different branch, probably to search for the wisp.

Frustrated at getting myself in this situation, I buried my head in my folded up arms. "Stupid."

In response to my scold, there was a soft pant, but it hadn't come from Albus. It was too melodic. So musical, in fact, that it sounded more like a hum. It was a cute sort of noise, like I'd imagine a beautiful girl to sound when she let out a lovelorn sigh. I lifted my head, and had to stifle a cry of surprise even though I scrambled back into Albus. It was a little glowing ball that made the sound. A pale blue energy, small enough to hold in my hands if I put them together. At my fright, the little ball made another series of tones, this time like the ringing of tiny bells, and I knew it to be the equivalent of laughter.

"Are you the Will-o'-the-wisp?" I whispered, poking it with my finger. It was warm, and more solid than I thought it would be. The energy floated into the air a couple inches, and then shook up and down in confirmation. "Do you belong to the witch in that cabin up the hill?" This time side to side in a no. "Are you hiding from those men?" Again up and down. I put my hand out hoping to hold it, but when I did, it retreated. "It's alright," I assured it. "I don't want to capture you. I'm not interested in treasure."

This time I set my open hand on the ground, and waited until the blue wisp decided to put itself in my palm. Eventually, it did. It was vibrating rapidly, something I assumed at first was on account of its being a ball of energy. But it was inconsistent. Vibrate, stop, vibrate worse, stop. Like it was shivering. It was just a little blue glow, but in an impossible way it was kind of cute.

"Are you cold, tiny ghost?" Again the orb completed that up and down nod. "Albus could keep you warm until those men are gone," I told it, and then added with a chuckle, "he drools some." That adorable bell chime of laughter, and I couldn't help but poke it again in an attempt to tickle it. "You're a happy thing, aren't you, Little Will-o'?"

More delicate chiming, and to escape my wiggling finger, it floated again into the air. Chuckling to myself, I once more rested my head against my folded up arms, and scooted closer to Albus for warmth of my own. I couldn't continue my search for the princess tonight. I was too tired, and with those men out there it was too risky to leave the glacial caverns until morning.

I'd been lying there for a minute before the Will-o'-the-wisp decided to wedge itself between the crook of my arm and my neck. What with the ice on every side of me except for where Albus was, I couldn't complain about the additional warmth of the affectionate blue orb. So I made sure to pull my hood over to the side to cover up its glow, just in case the men went by again, and then I fell asleep.

Chapter 2

woke the next morning to a cold wetness on my face. It wasn't the first time Albus had licked me awake. "Stop it," I mumbled with my eyes closed, raising a hand to push him away, but his head wasn't there. I started to roll over to investigate, but I rolled onto something warm, and that let out a pained squeak. Then I tried to push myself up off the warm squeaky thing, and ended up bumping my head on the icy ceiling above me. "By the gods," I groaned, wiggling myself out of the crevice.

Albus scooted out after me, and right after him, that little blue glow. That's what had made that sound, and after I rubbed out the spot on my head, I bent over to pick up the energy. "I'm sorry, Little Will-o'. Did I hurt you?"

It lifted itself into the air, moving side to side. "Good." I smiled, dropping my arm to let it hover before me. "Thanks for keeping me warm. You should be safe now, I think the men are gone."

Pulling my hood back over my head, I started for the entrance of the cavern with Albus at my heels. It wasn't until I could see daylight clearly that I realized our new friend was following too. "Don't you have a home to go to?" I asked the blue glow. "Or a treasure to guard?" It answered in the negative. "Well," I mused, "I'm looking for someone, if you'd like to help."

When the wisp gave me that up and down nod, I started up the hill. At the top of it, I put my thumb and index finger into my mouth and let out a loud, shrill whistle. I did it again after a few seconds, and I could hear the faint thud of Brande's hooves in the snow. One more hoot was all it took for the horse to find me.

"Hey, old boy." I greeted him with a pat on the neck, and checked him over to make sure he'd survived the night just fine. While I did, I heard a happy hum, and when I looked up, my new friend was nuzzled into a perplexed falcon's breast feathers. "You like birds, Little Will-o'?" I laughed. The wisp must have been embarrassed, because it retreated immediately. "That there's Maddox," I told it, so it wouldn't think I was upset about it disturbing the bird. "She belongs to the princess. That's who I'm looking for." Will-o' made a noise that sounded like shocked curiosity. "Last night Albus and I tracked her to a witch's cabin. We lost her, but I have it on good authority that she's heading south."

The blue glow fell to the snow. It worried me for a moment before it started rolling around, and I realized it was drawing letters. I was impressed that it could write, but disappointed that it wasn't helpful. "I'm sorry, tiny friend." I strode over and scooped it off the ground while my cheeks tinted. I don't know why I was embarrassed to admit this to a ghost. "I can't read." Then, thinking it was trying to tell me something informative, I asked, "Have you seen someone that looked like a princess?" Will-o' shook side to side. "You sure? She's very beautiful. With brown hair, and sparkly blue eyes." And I pulled up a sleeve of my tunic and coat, "Darker than me, too." Again, a negative shake. "That's all right. We'll find her."

Before continuing our search for the princess, it was important we had a proper breakfast. I didn't have time to set traps, hunting could take hours, and I wanted to save the dried food I'd brought for an emergency. While I considered my options, my eyes wandered to Maddox, and I grinned.

"What would the princess say," I began to ask the bird while I unwrapped its leash from the saddle horn, "to get you to bring her a rabbit?" At the word 'rabbit,' the bird's head twitched, as though it recognized the sound. "Is that it?" I asked with a chuckle. With the bird in my hand, I threw it into the air, shouting as it took off in flight, "Rabbit!"

I watched Maddox soar beyond the tops of the trees. In the clear blue sky, she circled, round and round for minutes. Soon enough, she tucked her wings into her sides, and with her beak pointed toward the ground, she dove. I watched the sky for a couple minutes more, but the bird didn't appear.

"You think she'd keep it for herself?" I asked Albus, and began a search for any dry wood.

It took a while before I'd gathered enough and put it in a pile, and then I pulled out my flint rock to start a fire. I had it blazing by the time I looked up again, and Maddox was in the sky, once more soaring in circles. I huddled near the flame, Albus and the wisp at my side. We sat like that for a little while longer before something hit Brande's saddle, and there was Maddox, a brilliantly fat rabbit clutched in her talons.

"You queen of a bird!" I praised, standing to retrieve the hare. "You see that, Albus?" I asked the dog, and mumbled 'thank you for your sacrifice, may your spirit rest within me' before I began to skin my meal. "If you could do that with deer, then we'd be dining fat every night." I made sure to reward Maddox with some of the meat before I cooked it. "And half for you, you spoiled hound," I said, tossing half of the rest to Albus. "I imagine you've been grazing on plants all night," I said to Brande while I stuck my portion of meat on a stick to roast in the fire. "With that gut, I reckon you never have problems finding food."

At my last comment, the blue glow made that chiming laughter sound, and I couldn't help but giggle at myself. "Do I talk too much, Little Will-o'?" The wisp had been hovering near the flames, and, worried it might be freezing, I motioned it over and then set it in my lap, where it would keep us both warm. "It gets lonely while I'm always out hunting," I admitted. "Albus and Brande make decent company. They don't argue with me." When I said that, Brande huffed, causing me to chuckle. "Well, Brande's got a bit of an attitude, but between you and me," and I leaned closer to my new friend like I was relaying a secret, "he's not the favorite anyway."

My tiny friend was amused, and after laughing a little myself, I stayed silent to eat my breakfast. Talking as much as I did was normal, but Albus and Brande never completely knew what I was saying. Even though my wisp couldn't speak, it was nice that it could understand me, and its tolling giggles and melodic hums were enough by way of response.

Once I was done eating, I put out the fire and mounted Brande, ready to begin the next day's worth of searching. Maddox couldn't stay perched on the saddle horn while I was riding, so I moved her to my shoulder with the hopes that she wouldn't take to nipping at my ears. Just in case, I kept my hood up. Little Will-o' floated along at my side, while Albus did his usual thing trotting along around us.

24

The princess's scent had ended at the clothing she'd left behind. It wasn't normal, and it didn't make any sense, but it was the way things were. Without being able to track her by scent, I had to try and think. There was no way she could survive in the woods without weapons or Maddox, and she wouldn't last in the cold without her clothing. The only thing that did make sense was that she'd started toward one of the forest villages in an attempt to find food and shelter. She wouldn't have a difficult time of keeping her identity hidden. I'd lived nearer the castle than the foresters my entire life, and I'd never known what she looked like until yesterday.

I explained all this to the wisp, which chimed along with appropriate responses as we headed for one of the main forest roads. Clopping along the trails of the Black Wood, it wasn't difficult to tell where it got its name. At night, of course, everything was black. But the same was true for the daylight hours as well, all except for the snow. The trunks of the thick, old trees were black. The branches that bent and twisted into each other so that only small beams of sunlight made it through to the earth, those were all black. Even the leaves, and pine needles, and the tops of the shrubs sticking out of the snow – all black.

"You know why everything here is black, Little Will-o'?" I asked eventually, to distract myself from the fact that the air was colder under the shade of the wood. It answered no. "My mother always told me it's because most of the wars have been fought in the Black Wood, instead of by sea or the Amalgam Plains. Over time, the plants soaked up all the blood spilled here, and it's turned them all black." A hum of acknowledgment. "Of course, there are those that say it's because the woods are haunted," and I reached out to give the wisp a playful poke, "with ghosts more frightening than you, Little Will-o'." Then I added with a shrug, "Maybe it's both."

Finally, we reached a wooden signpost back near the area I'd found the princess's clothing. I couldn't read words, so I didn't know the names of the villages it was pointing to, but my mother had taught me to read the numbers, which indicated distance. Being in the state I figured her to be, it made sense that the princess would have headed for the closest village, one the post told me was only three miles straight into the forest.

I occupied the ride to the village with telling my wisp and animal companions more stories. I never was exactly sure why I talked so much sometimes. Out hunting, there were periods I'd lie in wait for hours, so concentrated on not making a sound that I feared to even breathe too loudly. It seemed to me the words just built up, and when I wasn't hunting they all came pouring out. Of course, I also explained this to my friends, though the only response I got out of any of them was a chiming giggle.

The village we reached was a small one, the largest building in it being a sort of inn. The inn only had one bedroom, but I wasn't interested in renting it. I asked the keeper if he'd seen a girl that fit the princess's description, only without mentioning who she was. The last thing I wanted to do was alert the foresters to the fact that the princess was in the woods. Instead, I told the keeper she had a debt to settle with my family, and if he happened to see her, I'd be much obliged if he kept her here. I made sure to let him know to keep her well fed and comfortable, and that I'd reimburse him for any trouble. That's exactly what I told every villager I asked, after each one of them said they hadn't seen her.

Even though most of them assured me they'd keep an eye out, I didn't expect them to remember. But I refused to be disheartened by it, and I continued to the next closest village to further my search. It took all day for me to discover nothing of importance, and by the time the sun was about to go down, I was exhausted and hungry. Reluctant to use the gold the king had given me to stay at an inn, I lit a fire a ways outside of the last village I'd searched, and sent Maddox into the air to find food.

She returned more swiftly this time with an ermine in her grasp. The small rodent didn't have much meat on its bones, but it would suffice until morning. I whispered my usual thanks, and after making sure Maddox and Albus were fed, I cooked my own portion over the fire. I was quiet while I ate, lacking the energy to speak too much until after I'd finished my meal. What I did instead was observe my two newest companions, Maddox and Will-o'. The wisp seemed to enjoy the bird's company a curious amount, even if the falcon appeared mildly irritated at having its feathers so often ruffled. It was an interest to me why the wisp seemed so fascinated with Maddox, as it paid little mind to any of the wild birds we encountered, but it was a fascination I couldn't account for, no matter how closely I studied.

My energy returned soon after I'd eaten, but for some reason I wasn't in the mood to talk for the rest of the night. The whole situation was troubling, but mostly it was that I didn't know what had become of the princess after she left the witch's cabin. I could track anything that left behind a scent or a print, but the princess had left nothing. Maybe she'd disappeared into thin air and ceased to exist. Or maybe she'd been transformed into a bird, and was out there somewhere, just a tiny sparrow that didn't know who it really was. I spread out under my sleeping furs with these queries in mind, unable to completely rest easy even after I removed the tight linens around my torso. Albus could sense my discomfort, because while he always stayed at my side, tonight he set his head right on top of my chest. Even the attentive wisp knew it, because it nuzzled against my cheek until it got a laugh out of me, and then it stayed perched at my shoulder for warmth the rest of the night.

By morning, most of my vigor had been restored, and I picked up telling my companions stories while we headed farther south to the next village. There was the love story about the giant and the star. There was the horror story about the skin walker in the mountains of the Amalgam Plains. Will-o's favorite, however, was the comedy about the sea dragon that played jokes on fishermen. All of the stories I communicated I'd either heard from my mother or from the permanent minstrel who nested at the inn nearest my home, and all of them I knew by heart.

I got something resembling information at the second village I reached that day. The inn here was larger, with a handful of rooms down a hall connected to the main area where there were dining tables, and a massive fire pit at the center of it all. I made sure to leave Albus outside, and greeted the innkeeper amicably enough, but the first thing he did was point to Little Will-o'.

"What's that?" he asked gruffly.

"A Will-o'-the-wisp," I told him, and trying not to make much of it, continued, "I'm searching for someone, and perhaps you've seen her."

All he did was glare at me through his squinty eyes. "You a mage?" His hair was cropped close to his balding head, and his teeth were a revolting combination of yellow and gray. "Magic's against the law."

"I'm a hunter, I don't do magic," I assured him, but motioned for Will-o' to hide away in the hood of my coat, out of sight. The innkeeper grunted in acknowledgment, and would have walked away if I didn't stop him. "The girl I'm looking for," I said, and then described the princess. He only gave me a sort of half answer that he hadn't seen her before beginning to turn away again. "Perhaps, kind sir, you could point me in the direction of the next southernmost village?" The only option I could see was to keep heading south.

"Next village isn't for thirty-five miles," he answered in annoyance, but returned to me to give me his full attention. "Along the border of here and Ronan. 'Til then it's all forest tribes." He narrowed those squinty eyes at me again. "You Valenian?"

"Yes," I responded, furrowing my eyebrows and wondering why he wanted to know.

"From Guelder?" he questioned, and I began to worry that he knew I was searching for the princess. I told him I was from somewhere near Guelder, and he gave another grunt, thoughtful this time. "I might've seen a girl, if you've got the gold for it."

Previously, I'd refrained from offering gold for information because I knew the ways of country folk. I'd known plenty of people who'd make something up if there were money in it for them. I would've said no to this man if it weren't for the fact that I hadn't offered in the first place. He suggested it, leading me to believe he really knew something.

The man watched while I pulled a gold coin out of the pouch at my waist, and at the same time Will-o' came out of my hood and bumped me on the side of the head. "Get back in," I whispered to the glow, ignoring its protest when it drew nothing but a hard glare from the innkeeper, and then I handed him the gold piece.

"There's a cave," he supplied, putting the coin into his pocket. "Less than a mile eastward and just on the other side of the river from here. You'll know it by a crooked tree. The branches hang down and nearly cover up the opening. I heard tell someone saw a girl there."

I gave him my gratitude and returned outside to where I'd left the rest of my caravan. Out of sight of the man, Will-o' left the cover of my hood, and when I mounted Brande, it pushed against my chest to try and stop me from going forward. It didn't do much to prevent my motion, and when Brande started forward, it carried Will-o' along at my breast. Still the little wisp tried, until I let go of the reins to grab it with my hands.

"What's the matter with you, Little Will-o'?" It wiggled until I let it go, and then tried to bring me to a halt again. "I've got to find the princess. She could be in the cave." The orb made that 'no' motion. "You don't think she's there?" Another no. "And why not?" Will-o' made a frantically loud ringing noise, and I sighed. "I can't understand you, tiny friend. If she isn't at the cave, do you know where she is?" I continued to let Brande carry me toward the river despite the wisp's protests, but to answer my question, it nudged the falcon on my shoulder. "That's not the princess. It's her bird, Maddox."

I knew the bell-like chatter was an attempt to get me to stop, but I was growing impatient. I finally had a lead on the princess's whereabouts, and unless Will-o' had a better idea of where to search, I had to follow it up.

"We're searching the cave," I said with finality, but to try and keep the blue glow from being too disappointed, I pulled at my hood. "Come on, get in for warmth."

It did as I said, but not before letting me hear what sounded like a very discouraged sigh. We reached the river after less than a mile, just like the innkeeper had said. I dismounted Brande a little ways from the bank, and, while I tethered Maddox to the saddle horn, Will-o' left my hood to float near Brande's head. Before crossing, I crouched in the snow to have a look at it from a distance. Sure enough, there was a tree on the opposite side of the water, with low hanging branches that nearly concealed a small cave in the uphill bank.

Albus was at my side, so once I got his attention, I motioned to myself. "Eyes."

He stayed put when I got up, but I could feel his brown eyes on me as I crossed over some rocks in the river. He was so perfectly camouflaged I could barely see him from the other side. In order to not feel so alone, I put my hand on my dagger, creeping up the small incline toward the cave.

"Hello," I called when I reached the opening. It was only a few feet tall, and not much wider, but it appeared to extend more than a body's length on the inside. Perfect shelter for a fugitive like the princess.

There was no answer, and so I crouched down to have a peek inside. "Hello," I said again, even though I could see nobody was home.

Right when I straightened up again, something pressed against my back, and something else much harder and colder reached around to touch my throat. Whoever had the blade against my neck let out a whistle, and a man left his position behind a shrub farther up the hill. Perfect. A set up. Surely I wasn't the first to fall for this scam. Who knows how many people the innkeeper had scouted for gold and led straight into this trap. I wondered what his take was.

"Hand over any money you've got," commanded the man holding me. "Jewelry too."

I began to reach for the pouch of coins at my hip, right beside my dagger, but the man in front of me growled, "Slowly!"

I slowed my hand, knowing if Albus wasn't in mid air already, he was on his way. Sure enough, the moment my hand brushed the pouch, there was a snarl, and the man holding me screamed. I pushed away from him while I pulled my dagger from its sheath, ignoring the pain in my neck that resulted from him nicking me with his blade. I launched myself at the man in front of me, taking us both to the ground, and before he had a chance to grab his own weapon, he had to take hold of my armed hands to keep me from plunging my knife into his chest.

I forced my entire weight against his arms, trying to stab him, but he was much larger and stronger than me. He shifted both of my hands to the side just long enough to hit me in the face. His fist got me so hard that I rolled off of him, but I kept a hold of my knife, pointing it straight up when he tried to get on top of me. Instead of being able to strangle or hit me, he had to continue wrestling with me for the dagger. I wished I was stronger, because he began to twist my hands inward, gradually turning the point toward my chin. Toward my neck. Toward my chest.

I thought I was done for, all he had to do was push, but then a blue glow smashed into the side of the man's head. My tiny wisp was too small to do any damage, but it startled him enough that he momentarily released his hold on my hands to swat at it. It was just momentary enough for me to force my point upward into his breast, and I wiggled out from under him as he collapsed. After glancing up to make sure Albus was all right, I lay near the bloodstained snow for a minute, panting for air.

The wisp bounced on my chest a couple of times, clearly concerned, but I wrapped my arms around it in a tight hug, so grateful that I kissed it when I let go. "You saved my life, Little Will-o'." I couldn't help but chuckle, "I'm glad you can't say 'I told you so.'" It ignored my remark and nudged my chin upward, bringing my attention back to the cut on my neck. I touched my fingers to it to assess the amount of blood. It was bleeding, sure, but the wound wasn't deep. "I'll be fine," I assured the orb.

Once I'd recovered enough to breathe, I sat up with purpose, and paced back to Brande with equal determination. I had a score to settle. Before I could do that, I had to make sure we had somewhere to camp out

30

for the night, seeing as the sun was setting by now. Unsure of how often the river was frequented by people who lived near the village, I built a fire a little ways away from it, where the light was sure to be hidden from anyone at the water's edge. When that was done, I removed Maddox from the saddle, and perched her in the safety of a tree nearby.

"Albus," I said, kneeling down by the dog at the fire. "You stay here. I'll be back before you know it." When I said that, there was a concerned hum, and I knew immediately where it had come from. "You stay here too, Little Will-o'. Make sure Albus behaves himself."

I could tell the wisp didn't like it by the way it floated with me a few paces after I mounted Brande. But where I was going, I needed to stay hidden, and that charming blue light would be difficult to conceal. Besides, I didn't plan on being gone for too long.

I rode Brande at a gallop until I could see the faint lights of the village, and we came to a stop just outside of it. By this time, the sun had gone down, so I pulled on my hood and crept through the shadows of the various edifices until I'd reached the inn. There was a back door in the ground outside of it, which, after pressing an ear to it to listen for movement from the inside, I crept into. It opened to the food cellar beneath the tavern, and I was pleased to find it was completely dark. Above me, I could hear the faint laughter of villagers drinking and eating, and I knew it was only a matter of time before someone wandered down into the cellar for more ale or food. Judging by the homely size of the village and the inn, I imagined the innkeeper to be one of the only people with access to the cellar.

I tucked myself away in the darkest corner, and there I waited. It felt like nearly an hour before the inside door that led to the tavern was opened, and light footsteps sounded down the stairs. The man who descended was carrying a torch in his hand, but he strode right to the opposite corner of where I was, and he hadn't so much as suspected someone else was down here. It was just the man I wanted to see.

In a few swift, silent strides, I crossed the length of the cellar, and from behind I reached around and pressed my dagger to his neck. "Scream and I'll cut your throat."

The man gasped, but kept from making any loud noises. He recognized my voice. "The hunter?"

"Didn't expect to hear from me again?" I asked, pressing the blade harder against him in case he was thinking of trying anything. "You have something that belongs to me. That's all I want."

"I-i-it's already been spent," he stammered, holding his arms out. "Check for yourself."

I felt around in his pockets with my free hand, and at finding them empty, I sighed with frustration. There was no honor in me killing him, not in cold blood like this. But he owed me.

"Give me my life, my lady," the innkeeper pleaded during my thought-ful silence, clearly afraid I was intent on ending him, "and my service is yours."

"I'll be back for breakfast," I told him. "I expect your debt to be paid in meals."

"I won't forget this mercy," he sighed with relieved gratefulness when I removed my knife from his throat. "Thank you, my lady."

I nodded toward the tavern for him to retreat, and once he was gone, I disappeared through the outside exit. When I got back to the fire I'd made, both Albus and Will-o' appeared happy to see me. I removed the saddle from Brande's back to give him some rest of it, and after I set it on the ground near the fire, I spread out my sleeping furs. I brought Maddox closer, letting her resume her normal spot on the horn, and then I collapsed backward onto my sleeping furs, resting my head against the seat of the saddle. Albus put his own large head into my lap, and at the same time, the wisp hovered over my face.

"Were you both worried?" I asked the blue glow. "Don't fret, I didn't kill him. I only wanted what was mine. Or... what was the king's, I should say, since I haven't found the princess yet." I put my hands out for the wisp, and brought it down onto my chest for some warmth while I explained in more detail what happened at the inn.

"You know something, Little Will-o'?" I said a minute after I'd finished my explanation. "I'm starting to worry about the princess. I don't care for the king's gold, wouldn't you believe it. I didn't even want to come looking in the first place." My tiny friend made a hum of interest. "But when I was at the castle, the princess's lady-in-waiting, Ellie, she told me the princess thought her life was in danger. Now I'm starting to fear the Ronan Empire's somehow got a hold of her." I paused to let out a weary sigh.

"We're at war, my kingdom and the southern kingdom, Ronan. If the Ronans kidnapped the princess, then they could ransom her to win the war. That's one of the reasons I have to bring her back to the king, you see." Will-o' gave the smallest up-down nod of understanding. "Did I tell you my father was a soldier? And then he was a traitor. He lost his life trying to keep King Hazlitt off the throne. Now maybe I'll lose mine trying to keep him there. What's that called, Little Will-o'?" While my mind searched for the word, I stroked the side of the blue orb with the backs of my fingers. "Is that irony?"

I could feel Albus's warm breaths as he snored against my lap. Even my own eyes were beginning to droop tiredly. "Am I boring you with all this talk?" I asked my tiny friend. "I really should learn to reflect silently." I inhaled deeply and closed my eyes so as not to keep bothering the wisp, but when I did, it nudged me as though it wanted me to continue talking. "Anyway," I complied, "I'm not sure the king deserves to keep the throne. The people have been taxed to death. We eat so little. I don't even know what the war is about anymore. But I'm supposed to bring the princess back, and her lady-in-waiting, Ellie, she made me swear that I'd hear the princess's side first. Even made me sign a contract." I patted the pocket of my vest where I still had the note. "But I can't write, so I made the oath with blood. I'm supposed to give it to the princess if I find her, that way she knows she can trust me."

I sighed again, and out of remembrance, I reached above my head to pull the crimson-filled vial from my saddlebag. "But I saw the princess's clothes in the woods, and I don't know what's become of her. I thought maybe the witch turned her into a bird, like Maddox here." I pulled the cork out of the vial, and tilted it until some touched my finger. The fluid disappeared almost instantly into my flesh, but I felt no aftereffect. "The witch gave me this to help me find the princess. Maybe if she's a bird, it will turn her back."

Out of curiosity, I glanced at Maddox, who was perched with her face buried in her feathers above my head. I stretched the vial above her, and spilt a couple little drops onto her back. She shook and looked at me like she was irritated I'd woken her, and I sighed that she hadn't magically transformed back into the princess. Although... Maybe the princess *had* been transformed, only not into a bird. At that thought, something made me pass a suspicious glance at my tiny friend. Was it coincidence that I'd found Little Will-o' shortly after finding the princess's clothing? Or that it took such a liking to Maddox? Or that it knew we wouldn't find the princess in the cave? Perhaps my Little Will-o' was the princess.

"May I?" I asked the orb, extending the vial over it. It made no sign of protest or retreat, so I tilted the potion until some poured into its glow. The crimson liquid absorbed into the wisp as rapidly as it did into my own skin, and I held my breath in anticipation. But nothing happened. Will-o' didn't turn into the princess either. "Well, I tried," I mumbled, severely disappointed because I'd thought I had it. Thought it all made perfect sense, and that I'd finally found the princess when she'd been right in front of me all along. I couldn't keep my eyes open much longer after that, and I fell asleep hugging Little Will-o' to my chest.

Chapter 3

long, piercing howl cut through the air, startling me out of sleep and upright. There were no wolves around me, but the sound had been close. It was a familiar sound, too. One I'd heard many times in the forest at home, and one that let me know wolves were on the hunt. I generally didn't worry about the canines. What with myself, Brande, and Albus, they usually left us alone, except for an occasional brave one that would try to steal my kill. But I couldn't see Albus or Will-o', and I was baffled by the fact that one of my sleeping furs was missing.

"Albus!" I called.

The response to my shout was another ear-splitting howl, and then a female voice screaming, "Help!"

Without hesitation, I sprang up, removed my bow and quiver from where they were tied to my saddle, and sprinted toward the noise. My speed was so swift that I hardly made a print in the deep snow, and after only a few paces I could hear the snarling of the pack. I kept running until they came into view. There was no time to react to who the woman was. She was backed against a tree, fending off three wolves with a stick. Albus was there too, clashing with two others.

My feet never stopped as I pulled the first arrow out of my quiver, and I let it fly at one just as it leapt for the woman. Only ten paces from Albus now, I sent the next arrow flying at a second wolf near the girl, and then I tossed my bow aside and equipped my dagger. Albus had the slight advantage of size, but he couldn't fend off two much longer. So I dove head first into the skirmish to save my hound, plunging my knife into the deep chest of the first wolf.

The final canine near the woman had taken her stick in its jaws, and while it tried to wrestle the wood out of her hands, she struck it on the head with her fist. She made a move to strike it again, and right as I stabbed the second wolf Albus was fighting, the girl's canine released the stick to snap its teeth around her wrist. She screamed in pain, but smashed the stick so hard across the wolf's snout that the wood splintered. The wolf yelped and let go of her, and before it could recover and lunge to attack her again, I jumped onto its back and buried my blade in its heart.

"Princess!" I exclaimed, turning to the woman while I shoved my dagger back into its sheath. There was still so much panic in my chest that I couldn't stop to breathe, but I took in her condition. Blood had already run down her wrist to her hand, and was dripping off her fingertips into the snow. She was smaller than I'd imagined, at least five inches shorter than me, and she was *completely* nude. In defending herself she'd let fall the sleeping fur, *my* sleeping fur, which she'd wrapped around her shoulders. "Your wrist. Your feet!"

In a rush, I returned the blanket to her shoulders. Then, knowing she could get frostbite if she kept her bare feet in the snow, I scooped her up and started running back toward my camp. When I got there, I dropped her onto the other sleeping furs. My mind was in such a state of agitation that I didn't know whether to tend first to her wrist or her feet. The fire had died overnight, and now it was nothing but glowing embers, but she needed warmth. *Stop the bleeding first*, I thought, and, falling to her side, I took her arm in my hands.

She pulled it away. "Tend Albus," she instructed, and I would've been surprised at the worried tone to her voice if that didn't further my panic.

Albus! He'd followed us back, and was lying in the snow nearby already licking his wounds. I flung myself to the dog, and my hands ran over every inch of him to assess the damage. He had bites all over his body, but though they were all bloody, most of them had already stopped seeping. The only one that looked serious was an open gash down the left side of his muzzle. Given its location, it wasn't a wound I could bind, but it was as good a spot as any. A dog's muzzle never took to bleeding long.

Comforted about his condition, I left Albus to take care of himself, and dashed back to the Princess. She'd taken to cleaning off her arm with snow, but every time she wiped away the blood, it was replaced by a fresh flow.

"Is it broken?" I asked, knowing a wolf's jaws were easily capable of such a thing.

I was finally beginning to breathe again, so I knelt at her side to examine the bites more closely. She shook her head in response to my question, wincing a little when I touched near the lacerations. It was fortunate that I always kept supplies in my saddlebags for emergencies like this. Occasionally, Albus got himself slashed by a deer's antlers, or I underestimated the amount of fight left in a wounded animal. It wasn't just binding injuries I'd become good at, but I'd taught myself to stitch them too, even if the end result wasn't as sophisticated as a surgeon's would be.

"What are you doing out here?" I reached behind the princess to pull my things out of the saddlebag – the surgeon's needle and silk thread, that had cost me an arm and a leg's worth of pelts; the roll of covering linen; and the decanter of antiseptic I'd brewed myself from herbs. "Why'd you leave your clothes behind? Are you trying to lose your toes?" Maybe it was the muddled rush of fear and fight, but until my last question, I'd forgotten who I was talking to, and I'd abandoned the necessary formalities. Now, my cheeks flushed red, and I bowed my head. "My deepest apologies, Princess. I've spoken too plainly."

She was quiet for a few moments, but I was too afraid to look up and see whether or not I'd offended her. "Surely you know how I've come here," she said eventually. I hesitated insecurely, but then, seeing as she wasn't upset, I reached for the decanter. She watched me pour some over her wounds, only wincing again just slightly. I thought she might be waiting for a response, but I didn't know what to say. "I've been with you the last couple of days."

I'd put the bottle back and was reaching for my needle and thread, but when she said that, my movements slowed with concentration. I was still too unsure to look her in the eyes, worried it might be brazen, but I squinted at the sleeping furs thoughtfully. The tone of her voice was so familiar. Soft and sweet, like the agreeable chiming of a melodic bell, reminiscent of my tiny wisp.

"The potion worked then, Princess?" I asked, trying to remain calm while I threaded my needle.

"Yes." I could hear a smile in her voice when she answered, but when I passed the first stroke of the needle through her skin she whimpered, and her other hand landed on my shoulder to squeeze it for a diversion from the pain. "I hadn't thought it did when you used it last night, but then I woke up this morning with you, and I had flesh again."

She sucked in a pained breath of air the next time her hand tightened on my shoulder. In the momentary pause of her explanation, my eyes passed over what was exposed of her bare body, still wrapped in the fur blanket, and at thinking that's how she'd woken up, *with me*, my cheeks tinted a dark red once more.

"The witch didn't tell me I wouldn't be able to change back on my own," she said. "I tried to yesterday, but I couldn't. I had begun to worry I'd be stuck like that forever." I moved on to the next tooth mark with a nod. "I thought I could run to the village before you woke and steal any clothing someone left on a line, but the wolves..."

I wanted to ask if she'd have come back after finding some clothes, or whether she'd have been on the run again, but I'd never spoken to royalty so freely. I didn't know my boundaries. "You're safe now, Princess," I told her in assurance, and nodded toward my dog, "thanks to Albus."

"And you," she added. She took in an inquisitive breath, and bent over enough to get in my line of sight. "Who are you?"

I straightened up to meet her gaze, because that's what she wanted. The painting in her chambers was nothing compared to her true beauty. It could never have captured the brilliant twinkle of her deep blue eyes, or the perfect shine of her dark hair, or the energetic glow of her russet complexion. I felt my face burn all over again, and I resumed concentrating on my work.

I hadn't mentioned my name to the wisp because it couldn't have said it, so I answered her question with, "My name is Kiena, Princess."

"Of house?" she asked.

"No house."

"Right, you said your father was a soldier, and then a traitor," she recalled, removing her hand from my shoulder now that I'd finished her stitches. "Who did he fight for?"

"My father fought for Lord Tithian, Princess," I answered, and in a way far more gentle than I bound any of Albus's or my own wounds, I began to wrap linen around the princess's wrist. Out of the corner of my eye, I could see that she recognized the name, even though both of us had just been infants at the time. Lord Tithian's township, Ocnellio, had been decimated after my father turned. It was a rough time during the war; Valens had been crippled by civil unrest that King Hazlitt was supposed to fix. No more Ocnellio, no more house Tithian. "My mother's just a cottager. Myself, a hunter."

I didn't tell her that my father was the infamous traitor who *started* the rebellion that *added* to that civil unrest. That he fought to keep King Hazlitt from the throne for reasons he never told my mother, and thus she'd never told me.

"What about a surname?" asked the princess, examining her finished bandage with a pleased smile. "You at least have a surname."

As much as I'd wanted to, I couldn't keep from answering her. She was royalty, and she'd just asked me a direct question. "Thaon," I answered, waiting for her to be appalled when she recognized it.

"There we have it. Kiena Thaon," her smile widened instead, and she extended her uninjured right hand to me, "Avarona Gaveston. Well met."

I was shocked, and entirely unsure of exactly what she wanted. Her hand was angled for a shake, but I'd been to one tournament my entire life, which was my only experience witnessing those of higher class, and the royals and ladies were made acquaintance with a kiss on the hand. I wasn't a knight, or even a boy, but if Avarona had any remnant of her father's temper, I wasn't going to disrespect her by shaking her hand, even if that's what it looked like she expected.

"Princess," I said, though I was blushing again, and I gave the best bow I could since I was on my knees, while I took her hand to press my lips to it. After the greeting, I studied her for a long moment, and though the princess looked thoroughly amused by my blushing, I was still in awe. "Do you really not know who I am?"

She thought about it for a minute. "Kiena Thaon," she deliberately repeated my surname with a look of complete understanding. "You've mistaken my apathy for ignorance."

My eyebrows furrowed at that, because it didn't make sense that she wasn't the least bit troubled about being in the presence of a traitor's daughter. However, I wasn't about to argue with her. I also needed to get the fire going to keep her warm before I could go to the village and find her some clothes, so I walked away to begin gathering firewood.

39

"If you didn't ask for the task of finding me," started the princess, "and given your family's reputation, how'd you come to work for the king?" I could feel her eyes on me as I strode farther away to search for some dry wood.

"I was recommended by Sir Silas Leventhorp," I called back to her, and so she'd know how I knew him, I added, "formerly of House Tithian. Now, of House Gaveston."

"Ah, Sir Silas," said her voice. "Your fathers fought together?"

Since I'd gathered enough wood, I waited until I'd walked back to her to answer the affirmative. With the embers still glowing, it didn't take much effort to get a flame out of the timber, and once it was blazing, I sat back on the sleeping furs, in front of the princess since she was sitting sideways to the fire. She was huddled up with a fur pulled tight around her, but her feet were sticking out the bottom, and her toes were almost blue with cold. I shouldn't have waited so long to get the fire going, but Avarona didn't make nearly as much fuss as I expected for a princess, and at that, a wounded one.

"Are your feet numb, Princess?" I made a reach for one of them, and when she made no protest, I pulled it into my lap to try and rub some life back into it. If I brought her back to Guelder without any toes, the king would have my head.

She watched me for nearly a minute in thoughtful silence before responding. "You needn't so much trouble yourself over me."

"You're the heir to the throne I serve," I told her with a shrug, wrapping my hands around the front end of her foot and trying to instill some heat into the icy flesh. "I'd trouble myself more, Princess." Speaking of troubling myself, I still had that pouch of gold, and I was almost ashamed at letting the princess sleep under the stars, even if I did think she was just a Will-o'-the-wisp. "I should take you to the village inn. You'd have a hearty meal, and a warm bed to sleep in."

"You'll do no such thing," she protested, but her movements were gentler when I motioned for her other foot. "The inn is the first place they'll look if the king has sent any of his soldiers to find me."

"I respectfully doubt that's so, Princess," I said, and tried not to look at her when she wiggled the toes I'd just finished warming under my thigh to keep the warmth in them, because I didn't want her to see me blushing again. It was fortunate I didn't work in the castle. It would be torture in-

40

teracting with royalty all day, especially royalty that looked like her. "I believe I was the only one Ellie told that you were heading south. The king should be searching north of the Black Wood."

"Dearest Ellie!" the princess exclaimed. "Do you have the contract she had written?" I pulled it out of my vest and handed it over, continuing to rub at her foot while she read it. When she'd finished it, she said, "You have to keep taking me south."

"Princess!" I blurted. "I made an oath to hear you out. I cannot keep taking you south."

"But you must," she begged, leaning forward and taking my face in her hands to make me look at her. "My life depends on it." She must have known I was going to ask why, because she answered before I could. "I can't tell you yet. I will tell you, I swear it, but not yet."

At the thoughtful expression on my face, she removed her hands and sat back patiently, retightening the fur around her shoulders. "Let me take you to the inn," I requested, and glanced deliberately at her wrist. "You'll be in pain later, and while I cannot remove it, I can at least make sure you're comfortable. And well fed."

Her blue eyes scanned mine. "Will you take me south?"

I didn't know yet whether or not I was going to keep taking her south. I should have said no already, but part of it depended on when she'd tell me why she ran away. So I kept from giving a direct answer. "*If* I take you south, you'll need your strength." She studied me again in thoughtful silence, and then nodded. "Albus," I called as I stood, and when he trotted over I told him to lie down where I'd been sitting. "You can shove your feet under him, if you'd like," I told the princess. "He's warmer than I am."

She smiled gratefully, and I took Maddox off the saddle the princess was leaning against and perched her in a nearby tree. Then I bent over at the princess's side to grab the saddle, so I could replace it on Brande's back. "If it's no inconvenience," I requested, motioning to it. She leaned forward so I could take it, but before I could pick it up to carry it away, she put her hand on my arm and pushed herself up enough so she could kiss me on the cheek. "What was that for, Princess?" I asked, straightening up to look at her while my face flushed. I couldn't figure her out. She didn't act like any royalty I'd ever heard about. She wasn't uptight, or quick of temper. She didn't even seem aware of her own title.

"For being so kind," she answered. "I imagine anyone else the king sent would be treating me like a child."

Again, because I couldn't figure her out, I wasn't sure how to respond. There was the fact that she was my princess, and treating her like anything but royalty would be punishable, even if the king did give me permission to throw her over the back of my horse like a criminal. There was the fact that her life might be in danger, and as a human being she deserved to be listened to. Then there was the fact that she was slightly older than me, according to Silas. So, instead of saying anything, I gave a small bow, and proceeded to fasten the saddle on Brande's back.

When that was done, I made my way back to the princess, kneeling at her side one last time. "I'm going to get you some clothes," I told her, and I pulled my dagger from its sheath and held the handle out to her. "Hold on to this, Princess, in case there's any trouble. I'll be back shortly."

I started to stand, but she grabbed my arm again, so I stopped. "I think I see a thought in there," she said, a slight smirk on her face as she pointed to my head. "I may be a princess, but don't come back with a dress. Bring me something practical."

That made me chuckle, because I very well would've come back with one. "What would you prefer, Princess?"

She shrugged. "Some trousers I could ride in. Warm boots. Perhaps a tunic, like yours." I nodded and pulled on my coat while I paced to my horse, but as I mounted Brande, she stopped me one last time. "Kiena, about the incident at the river yesterday, with the bandits..." I nodded once more, and tilted my head in wonder of why she was bringing it up. Her lips pursed with a mischievous grin. "I told you so."

"Yes, Princess," I laughed, and what I felt was becoming a regular blush darkened my cheeks. "Yes, you did."

On my way to the village, I stopped where the corpses of the wolves were so I could get my bow, since in my panic I'd left it. I'd also have to come back later to collect the pelts, which I could use to trade as an alternative to spending the king's gold. Then I galloped to the village. There were no shops that sold already made clothing, especially in a place as small as this, so I searched around for the wealthiest looking person. Seeing as the princess wanted something practical, naturally it was a male I was looking for. From him I offered to purchase some clothing, and it was fortunate he wasn't too large a man.

After securing the items for the princess, I made a short stop at the inn. The innkeeper looked almost terrified to see me, which was a comforting fact. I told him he'd be paying his debt in the form of a room as well, and gave him notice to have one prepared.

I was happy to find everything as I left it on my return to the fire. The princess was curled up under the furs, sleeping with Albus at her side. I gave her the clothes I'd bought, and while she got dressed I took my skinning knife from a separate sheath in Brande's saddle, and carried it back to the wolves to collect the pelts.

"These fit better than I expected," the princess said when I came back carrying the skins. "Thank you."

I bowed my head as a humble 'you're welcome.' Truly, the clothes were still large on her. The white tunic hung loose around her shoulders, and she'd had to roll up the sleeves past her elbows so they wouldn't hang below her hands. The same immensity went for the linen trousers around her waist. Not even her voluptuous curves could fill them out, though the curve of her hips at least kept them on.

"And the boots?" I asked.

"Uncomfortably big," she admitted, shrinking back one corner of her mouth apologetically and clicking her heels together. I had an idea of how I could fix that, but first, my stomach was growling. So I untethered Maddox from the tree and sent her out for something to eat. "Maddox has taking a liking to you," the princess observed as the falcon flapped away. "She's normally quite unsociable."

All I did to respond was give an awkward smile, still unsure of myself in her presence. The princess seemed friendly enough, but I didn't want to let my guard down completely in case she decided to run away again. Nor did I want my big mouth to get me in trouble. At the castle, Silas had warned me to watch what I say. The princess might not have owned the throne yet, but she still had authority to make decisions regarding my life, and I'd already said things worth of landing me in the gallows.

When Maddox returned, I said my thanks and began cooking up the food she'd brought, making sure the princess had enough to be satisfied. While I handed her a portion, she said, "Can I ask you something?" I nodded, sitting nearby with my own scrap of meat. "That prayer you say... I'm not acquainted with it in Valens's Caelen religion."

"I'm not Caelenian, Princess," I confirmed.

43

Her eyebrows furrowed curiously, and I could see the thoughtfulness in her blue eyes as she fell quiet for a minute. "Who are you praying to?" she asked eventually.

"The gods of the earth," I answered, noting how her eyes narrowed with even more curiosity. It wasn't entirely surprising. I'd never met another person who knew what I was talking about. "It's, um," I began timidly, "it's a family tradition, I suppose. An old religion." The princess nodded with interest. It seemed like she wanted conversation while we ate, so even though I wasn't necessarily comfortable with speaking, I continued. "I was taught that when we're born, our spirit is a gift from the earth gods, and when we die, we return to them. How we're received then depends on how we live, how and what we take from and give to the earth."

"Do they have names?" she asked, swallowing down a bite of food. "The gods."

I shook my head, feeling my cheeks begin to tint at the level of attentiveness she was showing. "They're older than names." All she did was hum, but she continued to watch me for long enough that my face felt like it was on fire. "And you, Princess?" I asked. "You bow to the Caelen god?" She pursed her lips with decisiveness while she shook her head, but that caused my own curiosity to spike. That was the religion of Valens, though I knew her mother was from Ronan. "What about the Ronan god?"

"Goddess," she corrected with the hint of a smile. "And no." She gave a soft shrug, tossing the cleaned bones from her meal aside and then reaching down to trace the outline of her toes through her boots. "I've never seen results from the application of diligent practice."

Had I been more comfortable with her, I might've joked about her fortune at there being no lack of religions in the world to practice. However, seeing as I was far from at ease, I simply smiled and rose to continue my chores. The first thing I did was clean the wolf pelts. Originally I'd been planning on using them to trade, but I figured it was more important that Princess Avarona was properly dressed. It seemed she was comfortable enough at the fire and with Albus's added warmth, and it didn't appear she was in a hurry to get to the inn. So I spent almost the entire day crafting better attire. I whittled a sewing needle out of a bone from the rabbit Maddox had brought, and after tearing out the soles from the boots I'd purchased from the villager, I shaved them down to size and created fur boots that fit the princess's feet. The plain tunic I'd bought for her wasn't nearly warm enough, so with the remaining pelts I made a pair of gloves and a hooded cloak to throw on over it that would do a more thorough job of keeping her warm.

The princess was pleasantly surprised with my first presentation of the boots, and later on, when I gave her the cloak and gloves, she was so grateful that she bestowed on my cheek another kiss. I thought to tell her she needn't reward me, and that I was only doing what was within my power to keep her safe, but I far from minded how she took to rewarding my efforts. I also didn't mind making efforts because, while I'd been gone, I noticed she'd torn some cloth from the linen I'd wrapped her wrist in, and she'd done what she could to clean the wound on Albus's muzzle.

Needless to say, this princess perplexed me. So much so that while I walked along at Brande's side as the day approached sunset, guiding the horse while she sat on his back, I kept peering at her out of the corner of my eye.

"You haven't talked as much today," she pointed out as we journeyed toward the village. She was right. I'd hardly shut my mouth when she was the wisp, but now I was afraid of saying the wrong things. "And why do you keep looking at me like that?"

This time I met her gaze, and my cheeks flared as I tried to think of how to explain myself. "If I'm honest, Princess, I'm not sure what to make of you."

"What to make of me?" she repeated with a chuckle. "Do I intimidate you? You hadn't seemed frightened of me this morning."

"This morning I was worried enough that I forgot my wits," I told her, and added while my cheeks tinted, "and my station." I glanced up at her awkwardly. "And you're awfully comfortable in the presence of a traitor's kin."

"Are *you* a traitor?" she asked, but that ringing playfulness never left her voice.

"No," I answered, trying not to be upset that she'd even ask.

"Well then," she said, "why should I be uncomfortable?" I didn't have an answer for that, and when she spoke again, she finally sounded serious. "We are more than the legacies of our fathers, Kiena, remember that." I met her eyes, and it was so encouraging, such an extent of trust that I couldn't help but smile gratefully. "And you won't offend me," she added, but I offered no reply. "If I act helpless," she started saying, regaining the amused tingle to her voice, "or if I fall off Brande and pretend to be hurt, would you forget my title and speak freely again?"

She seemed to sincerely want me to be more at ease, so I gave in, and tested the waters by saying, "Not now that you've told me you're a faker, Princess."

"Ah, touché!" she laughed. "Though I don't think you should keep calling me 'Princess.' If someone were to hear, it could get us in trouble."

"What would it please you to be called?"

"Ava," she said readily, and when I looked up at her, she had another smirk on her face. "I also happen to think Little Will-o' has a nice ring to it, don't you?"

My cheeks burned a bright red, so that I was almost tempted to pull my hood up and hide my face. But, growing more comfortable with the princess's light humor, I couldn't help but smile. "I happen to think you're a relentless tease, Ava."

"I can't help myself the way you color, Kiena," she responded, copying my tone exactly. She'd taken to giggling at the way I blushed again when she said that, but too soon her smile faded, and her eyebrows scrunched unhappily.

"Is your wrist beginning to hurt?" I asked, squinting through the trees to see if I could spot the village. A small sliver of a cabin was visible between the breaks.

When the princess answered in the affirmative, I picked up my pace, leading Brande more quickly toward the village. We reached the inn shortly after, and I made sure the fire was going in the room so Ava would be comfortable while I went back out to secure Brande in the stables. I took my sleeping furs and saddle back into the inn with me, and before returning to the princess, I got a loaf of bread, some cheese, and a cup of wine from the tavern. I carried all this back with some difficulty, the hardest part being not spilling the drink. The princess was sitting under the covers of the bed when I returned, and she flinched with surprise at my opening the door.

"It's just me," I offered, dropping my furs and saddle onto the floor so I had a hand to close the door with, and I made sure to secure the latch. Upon turning around, I saw that Albus had made himself comfortable at her side, and, of course, my cheeks turned rosy. "I'm so sorry," I mumbled while I set the rest of the things down on a small table in the room. "He's used to sleeping on the bed with me at home," I explained. Albus was treated like a king at my house, when I knew most people didn't even let their dogs indoors. "Albus, get down."

The wolfhound began to rise, but Ava put her hand on him in protest. "It's fine," she said. He resumed his comfortable position, even going so far as to put his head in her lap, and I tried not to chuckle at the gloating look in his eyes. "I feel safe with him here. And more so, now that you're back."

I took off my coat and vest to settle in for a comfortably warm night, and then carried the food to the bed and handed Ava the cup of wine. "For your wrist," I told her when she glanced into it. "To take the edge off." Then I ripped off a piece of bread and handed it to her. "You're truly afraid for your life, Princess?" At my question, her lips curved into a frown, though I couldn't be sure whether it was her fear or the fact that I'd called her 'Princess.' In case it was the latter, I added, "There's no one around to hear it."

"I wish you wouldn't say it at all," she sighed, picking at the bread and putting a tiny crumb into her mouth. "Now that you don't treat me like a Will-o'-the-wisp, I feel as though I've lost a friend."

My eyes dropped gloomily. It hadn't occurred to me that the princess might be lonely, and I couldn't imagine what it was like feeling as if no one was on your side. Even *I* had Albus and Brande when things got lonely. In an attempt to cheer her, I nudged her chin up so she'd look at me. "Are you royalty, Little Will-o'?" I asked in feigned surprise. "By the gods, I'd hardly noticed." It was bold touching her like that, and even as I did it, the action made me nervous. But then she grinned, and I was instantly put at ease.

"Will you tell me another story?" she asked, avoiding my question about the danger she was in. "I rather enjoy your stories."

"What kind would you like?"

Ava took another gulp from the cup of wine, and smiled gratefully when I offered her a cut of cheese. "Tell me one with you. I want to know what kind of a place you come from, or what your family's like."

"Me?" I repeated. She nodded with interest. "Alright, uh, well, my father died before I was born, you know, but I have a little brother. Nilson. He's adopted, of course. My mother's a cottager, she only has a few acres, but a friar was going around with this little infant he'd found on the side of the road, and no one would take him in. She's got more heart than she does money, so she saw fit to look after him." I'd been picking at a spot of fur on the blankets, but here I glanced up to make sure Ava was still interested. She nodded me on. "You know the kingdom, I'm sure," I said, thinking she'd have had tutors that would've taught her geography. "So, our land's only a few miles out of Wicklin Moor, near the edge of the Rockwood Forest."

Ava nodded again, so I continued. "Nilson's always had a particular enthusiasm for sweets," I paused, knowing this was a story about thievery, and pointed at Ava with a smile, "now, you can't tell another soul this story. Swear it?"

"You have my word," she swore, giggling at my tone.

"We're too poor to be wasting money on sweets, you see, so when he was just a tiny boy, he got it in his head that he could pinch it. Usually it was just from the neighboring farms, and he was so small that he actually made a fair thief." I paused to take a bite of food. "Every once in a while, however, he'd want something fresh. So he'd hike the two leagues to Wicklin Moor, and come home with his pockets full of still hot pastries. Mind you, Ava," I said, already pleased by the amused grin on her face, "we hadn't given him any money. Not even the most charitable baker's going to give him that many sweets for free, but we just couldn't get it out of him how he happened upon so many.

"The furs I don't use, I take into town to sell. This particular time I'd hunted a bear, and since I had more coins in my pocket than usual, I thought I'd come home with a sweet roll for Nilson." I was already holding back laughter because I knew the part of the story that was coming up, and at my merriment, Ava's face was lit up with expectation. "So I walk into the baker's shop in Wicklin Moor, and the baker's standing there, waiting on me to make a selection. I look up from staring at the baskets of goods, and you know what I see behind the baker?" Ava shook her head. "There's Nilson, dangling from a rope through a fresh hole in the roof, reaching for the pastries the baker had just taken off the fire." Ava snorted with laughter and covered her mouth with her hands. "He'd made friends with one of the beggar boys in town, so this boy's at the other end of the rope, holding on for dear life so Nilson could get them their sweet rolls."

"Did he see you?" Ava asked, struggling to hold back her amusement.

"Aye, he saw me all right," I told her. "And my eyes were so wide with shock that the baker noticed, and he turned around and his eyes went wide at seeing Nilson. When the beggar boy noticed the baker, he panicked and let go of the rope, and Nilson dropped straight into a barrel of flour." At this point I was struggling to even keep telling the story because I was laughing so hard. "So the baker grabs his wooden roller and lets out this angry yell, and Nilson shoots out of the barrel all covered in flour from head to toe. The baker takes a swipe at him with the roller and misses, and Nilson comes running toward me and keeps on going out the door, leaving a trail of flour footprints behind him. And the baker turns around and his face is all red because he's so angry, and he starts running toward the door to chase after Nilson."

"What did you do?" Ava asked.

"I'll tell you what I did," I chuckled. "I stuck my foot out as the baker was going by. Got him so good he tumbled through the door head over heels and rolled into the street. By the time he even knew which way was up, I'd run out the back door of the shop." It was a fond memory, made fonder by the way the princess was enjoying it. "I wasn't too pleased, you know. But I got home long before Nilson did, and when he came trudging up the road still caked in flour, I couldn't stay mad. We laughed about it for days, even though I had to sneak past the baker's every time I went into town after that."

I let Ava laugh it off for a minute, and, noticing that she was done eating, I moved the food to the small bedside table. "May I check your wrist?" I asked, holding my hands out. She put her arm into them, and I removed the bandage to have a look at her wounds. "Is it still painful?" It was puffy and red, and surely tender to the touch, but the antiseptic I'd brewed was powerful, so I wasn't scared of infection.

"The wine's helped some," she answered, and at the concerned look on my face, she chuckled, "I'm not as delicate as you seem to think I am."

I smiled warmly and replaced the linen around her wrist. "Well, sleep is important."

I got off the bed to grab the sleeping furs I'd dropped near the door, feeling the princess's gaze on me while I did. "What are you doing?" she asked eventually, when I'd begun to lay them out on the ground near the bed.

49

"I was going to sleep on the floor," I answered. "Albus tends to spread out at night."

She watched me adjust them for a few moments, almost as though gathering the courage to say, "I'd prefer it if you slept with Albus and me."

I looked from the furs to her. "You needn't be afraid, Ava."

"What I needn't be and what I am are quite at odds," she admitted, and I could tell it wasn't easy for her to ask. She may be a princess, but it didn't appear she felt entitled to what she wanted. How could I decline? I sat back down on the edge of the bed to take off my boots, and then I slipped under the covers in compliance. "Thank you, Kiena," she said, and she gave my cheek another of her tender rewards before turning around to throw an arm over the hound.

Don't let the princess bribe you with kisses, that's what the king had told me. That was a joke. Here I was already, nearly prepared to keep taking her south, just like she wanted. It was only an intuitive pull in my gut that kept me from calling it bribery. She was genuinely afraid. She was genuinely grateful. And, best of all, she seemed to genuinely enjoy my company.

"Goodnight, Little Will-o'."

$\mathscr{C}$hapter 4

 woke early the next morning knowing there were things to be done, but the bed was warm with Albus and Ava, and it was much softer than the one I slept on at home. The shutters of the single window were trembling in their frame, agitated by the wind outdoors. Years and years of experience had taught me to feel the weather in my bones. I could hear the direction and strength and intention in the whistling of the wind. I could smell the collecting moisture in the air. A snowstorm would be here by mid morning, and it put me on edge.

Instead of abandoning the heat of the princess at my side, I lay there with my eyes open, thinking. The paths available to our situation were limited so long as Ava wouldn't tell me why she'd run. Taking her south was too treacherous. On the road to Ronan, spies were a possibility, bandits a probability, and danger a guarantee. The princess hadn't revealed her destination in the south, but I'd heard stories of how the Ronan capital was so far south that the woods grew denser and hotter and wetter until you reached the Emerald Sea. It was a long distance to travel, and in land unfamiliar. I couldn't take her south.

Had the castle not been the safest place for her? If a spy had infiltrated the ranks and threatened Ava's life, were there not hundreds more of the king's soldiers to find them? Yet, she'd run. She'd left her father and mother and the safety of their home because something made this journey less of a threat. I couldn't think she'd leave them without a word should their lives also be in danger. Though I knew so little of her, that much I was certain of. I could see it in her sincere care for Ellie, and how she'd tried to bandage Albus's muzzle. She was caring and kind. Life was important to her, and her own was at risk; I very well couldn't take her north.

The fire had died during the night, and the sharpening bite of the air outside was piercing through the room so that my ears had begun to tingle. Though Ava had her face buried in Albus's fur, I wouldn't wait for her to complain of the cold, so I slipped out of the heavy covers, careful not to stir her or the dog. I put on my boots for warmth and knelt at the dead coals, resurrecting the ashes with fresh logs and tinder. Afterward, I gathered the sleeping furs I'd laid out the night before, rolled them back up, and then tied them to the saddle. By the time I was finished, I noticed Ava had shifted, and her eyes were following me across the room.

"I tried not to wake you," I told her while I tested the latch on the windows, making sure the wind wouldn't push them open.

Ava sat up, dropping her head back against the headboard. "I woke at your absence."

Her arms rose high above her, stretching as she yawned, and her wide mouth and sunken eyes and disheveled hair created such an uncouth look for a princess that I couldn't help but smile just a little. She still looked beautiful, but in a delightfully graceless way. I was about to ask how her wrist was, but then she yawned again, and finished the action with a tired sigh.

"Are you accustomed to sleeping in?" I asked, doing little to mask the tension in my voice because of the storm, and by it, the unintended implication that she was spoiled.

"Kiena," Ava said with a smirk, all sarcasm even if she was still waking up, "if you think princesses have the luxury of sleeping until midday, then I'm afraid you are terribly mistaken."

"I wouldn't know what princesses have the luxury of," I told her, moving back to the saddle to grab the antiseptic. I carried it over to the bed, and sat down at Ava's side to motion for her hand.

"Study, practicing my studies, studying some more." She gave me her arm so I could remove the bandage from her wrist. "It's rather tiresome, really."

I poured a small amount of antiseptic into my hand so it wouldn't spill on the bed, and massaged it over her wounds. "If I'm honest, Ava, it sounds rather simple." She didn't have to worry about eating every day, or providing food for anyone else, or what would happen if she got sick. She didn't have to worry about a lot of things.

I could feel her eyes on me as I worked in the last of the liquid. "I've sounded overindulged," she realized.

However, my immediate worry wasn't that she'd given me the wrong impression. I'd been too tense to take in her playfulness, and I'd likely been offensive in doing so. "I shouldn't have-"

"Don't," she interrupted, putting her hand on mine to make me look at her. "You've spoken your mind, and I quite prefer it that way." But when I finally did look at her, her brow softened with concern. "You're troubled."

"No." I removed my hand from hers so I could rebind the linen around her wrist. It wouldn't do for her to see exactly how troubled I was. I was supposed to be protecting her, or returning her to her father. Either way, I couldn't seem vulnerable. Only, I knew she was watching me, waiting for more of a response. So I added, "It's just the storm."

"What storm?"

"The one that'll be here in a few hours." Finished with the bandage and reluctant to discuss it more, I asked, "How are you feeling?"

"Well," she answered, and pressed a grateful kiss to my cheek. "Thank you."

"Albus," I prompted, and when he picked up his tired head to look at me, I reached across Ava to rub some antiseptic into the wound on his muzzle. He started pulling back halfway through, so when I finished I gave his snout a teasing nudge. "Go back to sleep, you lump." He dropped his head inelegantly.

"May I?" Ava asked, holding out a cupped hand.

I wasn't sure exactly why she wanted some of the antiseptic, but I tipped the decanter over her palm and spilled a few drops into it. Before doing anything with it, she reached up with her other hand, setting the backs of her fingers against my chin to angle it away, exposing that small cut on my neck. She dipped her fingertip into the liquid I'd given, raising it to paint a careful stroke over the knick.

Though my chin was turned up, I could glance sideways just enough to see her out of the corner of one eye. It was hardly a wound that needed looking after, but she was being so careful about it. Every touch was bare, like she was afraid of hurting me, and she was diligent about making sure every drop of the fluid was fully absorbed, as though she wasn't sure she trusted the antiseptic's efficiency. She seemed mesmerized by the task, and in turn I was mesmerized by her intense focus. So entranced by her tenderness that I'd completely forgotten about the storm, and I'd begun to relax. But all too soon she'd rubbed it all in, and her finger left my neck in a long, slow graze.

"Better?" she asked, a concerned crease between her eyebrows.

It hadn't hurt in the first place – I'd nearly forgotten it was there – but I nodded gratefully. "Aye. Thank you, Little Will-o'."

"Pleasure," she said with a smile, making sure to meet my eyes with her own.

And she didn't look away. She held my gaze, and though she no longer had her hands on me, I was still so entranced that I couldn't break my stare. She had the most gorgeous sapphire eyes I'd ever see a thousand lifetimes over. They were big and round, and their deep blue glimmered like a sea of gems. And they were gentle like her touch, so full of thought and emotion and wit, appearing altogether incapable of any semblance of a glare. It felt like an entire minute before my eyes wandered to her mouth. To her full, soft lips, and I found myself wondering what I could do to earn another kiss on the cheek. Or maybe I could…

A gust of wind slammed into the shutters, creating a bang so loud that I nearly fell off the side of the bed. It immediately reminded me of the storm, and at the same time I realized what I'd been about to consider while looking at Ava, and I felt my shoulders and back go rigid. I stood, stiffly making my way back to the saddle so I could return the decanter to the bag.

"I should make sure Brande is settled before the storm rolls in," I said, and though Ava had opened her mouth to say something, I grabbed my coat and left before she could.

Don't let her bribe you with kisses, I reminded myself as I paced out in-to the gusting wind, crossing the empty distance to the stables. Three days and I was already vulnerable to bribery – and for two of those she hadn't even been human! Was Ava doing it on purpose? She teased, and smirked, and made me blush for sport, but to what end? If she didn't trust me, she could've snuck away in the night, any night, but she'd stayed, knowing my errand. If it was protection she wanted, if that's why she stayed… I'd promised to hear her out long before I'd even met her. She needn't make a game of earning my affection.

54

"Hey, old boy," I greeted my horse, and when he extended his head over the gate, I pressed my forehead to his. "You're awfully calm about this storm coming," I told him, patting the side of his jaw. "How about you teach me the trick?" I strode back to the entrance of the stables to grab the stiff brush, and then carried it to Brande. "I think I might be in trouble with this girl," I told him as I hopped over the gate and began to run the brush down the length of him. "Charming, isn't she?" In his usual way, Brande huffed his end of conversation. "She's almost perfect."

With the next huff, Brande whipped his tail, cutting it against the edges of my ear.

"Oy! Alright, I said *almost*." I flicked him in the flank for slapping me. "It's her only flaw, isn't it? That she's royal. Her father's the reason we haven't got a copper for food." I strode around to the other side of Brande. "And why there ain't food even if we had a copper. And why Hodge's boy got conscripted and killed. And why Mother's scared next time the soldiers come around they'll think Nilson is old enough for a war job. And why old man Nickles got thrown in the prison at Guelder on suspicion of being Ronan." I stopped brushing and dropped my arm to my side thoughtfully. "Ava's half Ronan, isn't she?" I asked, and then added, "lot of peace her parents' marriage brokered. Bloody useless."

Outside, I could hear that the wind was picking up speed, and so, as much of a relief as it was being able to vent to Brande, I was too afraid to stay out here much longer. "I'm going back in, old boy."

Before I left, I made sure he had enough food and water to last him a while, and I nodded to the stablehand on my way out. I hurried back into the inn and to the room. When I pushed open the door, Ava was sitting at the small table at the far end near the window, and had just given Albus something to eat – probably a bit of bread from the half loaf on the table. It startled her when I walked in, and her eyes widened guiltily as though she wasn't sure if she could feed him bread. I tried to hold back a smile at the display, though a small one cracked my lips.

"You shouldn't leave the room without my knowing it, Ava," I told her, knowing she'd had to leave to get the meat and cup on the table, and after I closed the door behind me and shed my coat, I went to sit across from her.

"Got to keep an eye on me?" she asked with a smirk. Though I was safely indoors, I couldn't ignore the way the shutters were shaking in their frame only feet away. Had I not been so tense at their shivering, Ava's smile might have been enough to make my cheeks tint. "What if I ran?" she asked before I could come up with a response. "What would you do?"

I didn't want Ava asking about the storm, so in an attempt to hide my discomfort, I teased, "Your father gave me permission to tie you up and throw you over Brande's back."

"Would you?" she giggled.

I considered it for a long moment, noting her joy at that being one of the boldest things I'd said to her. I'd have to watch myself. I couldn't guard so well against her charm *and* my tension. "I don't suppose I would," I answered, and she cropped her eyebrows with interest. "I'd follow you, make sure you were safe." I'd try to convince her to come back to Guelder with me too, though I didn't say so.

"For the king's content," she asked, but her playfulness was gone, "or yours?"

I considered that too, even more carefully than her previous question. That sounded like a test. Like she was judging my motive or my resolve to doing the right thing. I'd sworn two oaths. She knew it, and she was trying to figure out which I'd choose. "Your father's content is my freedom, Ava," I told her, "and my freedom is my content." However, I knew what she was *really* asking me. Did I care about her more than the king? Did I trust her enough to chance it? "But I've always thought a clear conscience is a freedom none can take."

"And the risk to you?" Her big, sapphire eyes met mine. "It's worth it?"

"No matter what I do, my life is at risk," I said, setting my hands on the table to lean forward with focus, "it has been since the moment you ran." It hadn't been my intent to make an accusation of that fact, but Ava still glanced away with a stinging amount of remorse. I didn't want her to feel guilty for running, not if her life was in danger. She had every right to protect herself. "It's the risk to you now, and yes, it's worth it."

She looked at me again, staring at me for such a long, silent moment that I started to feel weak under her gaze. "If the king was the risk to my life," she said, barely a whisper, "what then?"

My eyebrows furrowed at that. Was it another test, pitting my two oaths against each other? Or was she finally trying to tell me something? "Then our risk is the same, and my life is yours."

Ava took in a deep, thoughtful breath. Her hand moved across the table, so slowly that there could've been time for me to move mine if I'd wanted to. But I didn't want to. I let it land on top of mine, and it was inappropriate, but my cheeks colored. "The witch," Ava said quietly, seriously, "she said my life was intertwined with another's. I think she meant you."

"Perhaps," I agreed.

I paused for a silent minute to consider my options. What I truly should have done was taken my hand out from under hers because I enjoyed it too much. The warmth of her skin was contrarily comforting and stirring all at once, like every time her lips touched my cheek. But this conversation was an important one. It appeared she was so close to telling me why she'd run from the castle, and if I removed my hand from hers, it would be like removing a promise. There was safety in the contact of skin; I felt it, and I was sure she did too. So I left it.

I even clasped my free hand over the top of hers, so it was cradled between both of mine. "It's all the more reason for you to trust me, and tell me what this is about."

I don't know if she saw through it and knew that I was trying to make her feel more at ease, but she blinked at me for a second before removing her hand and sitting back. "You should leave, you know," she said, but every bit of it was full of genuine concern. "You should go home, and abandon this. You've been so kind to me... I can't see you hurt."

"I *can't* go back without you," I told her, "you realize this?"

Once more, her gaze fell. "I'm sorry."

"I don't blame you. I blame whoever's threatening your life." This time, I reached across the table to set my hand on hers, and her eyes met mine when I did, and there was a building brim of tears beneath their brilliant blue. It was torture to see her like that. "Ava, is it your father?"

Her watery eyes watched me, taking me in with due consideration before she blinked away the tears, sniffled, and motioned to the food. "You frightened the innkeeper something fierce," she said with as much cheer as she could manage.

I sat back and removed my hand, and though I felt defeated that she wouldn't entirely trust me yet, I tried not to let it show. I gave a small smile. "He earned it."

The shutters hadn't ceased their shaking, and I'd been so caught up in talking to Ava that I'd nearly forgotten about it, but now a gust of powerful wind hit them so hard they broke open. It startled me straight out of my seat, and I stood there, frozen as snow pierced into the room. Only a moment passed before Ava hurried over, struggling against the wind and the pain in her injured wrist to shove the window closed. Seeing the wince on her face snapped me out of it, and I rushed over to help her. Together, we replaced the shutters, and while I sat back in my seat, frustrated that I could no longer hide my worry, Ava secured the latch to keep them closed. Still, they rattled violently, and I sheltered my hand over my eyes as if that would shield me from the stress.

My heart kept hammering away in my chest, and now I was embarrassed because I could feel Ava staring at me. *It's only a blizzard*, is probably what she was thinking. *How could Kiena protect me if she's frightened of a simple blizzard?*

If it's what she thought, she didn't say it. She strode over, knelt at my side, and set a hand on my thigh. "Are you alright?"

I made an irritated motion toward the shutters. "If only they'd stop their bloody shaking!" I could handle the wind if it didn't constantly sound like it'd break into the room.

Ava stayed there for a moment, and after casting a long look around the room, she stood and strode over to the small pile of firewood in the corner. She picked up a log and peeled off a thick piece of bark to carry to the window. There, she jammed the bark into the small crack between the two shutters. It took an obvious effort for her to wedge it in tight enough, but when she did, there was no more room for them to go about their racket. The noise ceased altogether.

She watched my shoulders slump, exhausted from the tension, but I was still too rigid and ashamed to express the gratitude I felt. When I said and did nothing, she walked back over, took my face in her hands, and leaned to press a slow kiss to my cheek. I closed my eyes against the warmth of her lips, and in spite of myself, I let out a revealing sigh.

"You needn't be afraid, Kiena," she told me, reaching for my hand and taking it across the small table with her so she could sit down again.

And that comfort in the contact of skin – which had been so useless when I tried to get a confession from her – worked wonders on me. "What I needn't be and what I am are quite at odds." She didn't say anything, but

I could see the question in her eyes: *why*? Instead of answering that question, I took my hand back and folded my arms on the table, groaning as I dropped my head onto them. "I hadn't wanted you to see my weakness."

"If fear is weakness," Ava said, "then everyone is weak."

"Your life is in danger," I replied, lifting my head and blushing at the fact that there wasn't a bit of amusement in her expression. I don't know why it was more awkward for me that this wasn't funny to her, but the last thing I wanted her to do was worry. "Your fear is reasonable."

"I have others," she said, her head tilted almost scoldingly. "I have many. My greatest is never finding somewhere to belong."

My eyebrows furrowed. "But this entire kingdom is yours."

"Is it?" she asked with a skeptical chuckle. "Were it mine, it wouldn't mean the entire kingdom should be home. I belong at this inn no more than you do."

"And the castle?" I asked.

"The castle has many parts, and is thus many things," she answered. "I've yet to find a part that feels like home."

I'd been speaking to Ava so freely, and so without formality this entire morning, that it didn't cross my mind to watch what I said until now. "What about Ellerete?" It was a personal question – the implications of which could be wildly offensive – but this was as good a time as any. "Might a soul feel like home?"

Ava's eyes narrowed the slightest bit with concentration, as though she weren't sure I meant what I really did. "Indeed," she began, the hint of a smile reaching one corner of her lips, and for the first time, her cheeks shaded. "Ellie was a stability amongst the castle's commotion, and, when privacy permitted, a dear friend." I don't know if it was intentional, but Ava's gaze fell and lingered at my mouth, so that by the time she met my eyes again, I'd colored furiously. "But I've yet to share that depth of the soul's intimacy."

I hadn't the inkling of a clue now what to say. She hadn't expressed a single displeasure at the nature of the question, or even the smallest of disapproval at my suggesting she might share that intimacy with a woman. She was making it increasingly hard to mind my station, and to keep from thinking of her as a friend rather than my princess. But she *was* my princess, and it wasn't my place to be asking those kinds of questions, or to be thinking the kinds of things I was to make me want to ask those questions. It was so clear to me that she already considered me a friend, and, as she'd considered Ellie one of her dearest friends, she didn't mind my lack of title. The truth of the matter was, however, that once my task was seen through, whether I took her north to her father or south to her own destination, it was likely I'd never see her again. I don't know why, but I felt the pang of that thought in my chest.

"Kiena?" Ava prompted, breaking my silent reflection. "Why snow storms?"

I glanced toward the motionless shutters while I took in a deep breath. "I taught myself to hunt as a child, out of necessity," I began to explain, feeling far too vulnerable to meet Ava's eyes. "Albus was just a pup the first time we went out on our own. Mother was sick, she needed something of substance, but I hadn't learned to read the weather yet, not like I can now." Having heard his name, Albus finally got off the bed and trotted over, setting his head on my lap as if he knew the story I was telling. "A storm came only shortly after we'd gone out, a bad blizzard that lasted days. I couldn't see more than a couple inches before my eyes, and Albus was too young to know the way home. We got lost."

"For days?" Ava asked in concerned understanding.

"Aye," I answered. "I knew not to wander, so we curled up beneath a fallen log. It was so cold. I held Albus to my chest to keep us warm, but we were both wet and frozen and shaking." I scratched behind my dog's ear. "By the time the storm ended, dear Albus was stiff. I thought I'd lost him." Ava reached out to stroke Albus's back, like she felt the immediacy of the danger all those years ago. "I hardly had the strength to run home, but I did. I warmed him back to life." I laughed at myself, my cheeks tinting while I admitted, "I cried so many apologies into his fur it was hard to dry him by the fire."

Ava smiled at that, the warm kind of smile that eased my bashfulness. "You know better now," she offered. "You won't be caught off guard again."

"No, I won't," I agreed, leaning back in my seat and feeling strangely comforted having shared my discomfort. "But the cold is a glutton, and its greed chips at me whether I permit it to or not."

"Your fear is not ill-founded," she said. Albus turned away from me to meet Ava's loving hands, and ran his tongue up the side of her face so that she giggled her bell-chime laugh. "And Albus seems to have forgiven you."

"I'm grateful to you," I told her, but her eyes met mine with confusion. "For your concern."

"You needn't thank me," she said, pushing Albus's face away when he tried to lick her again.

"Still," I said.

At the tone of my voice, she looked at me with a somber understanding. "You're welcome." After a moment's pause, she grinned and picked up something else on the table that I hadn't noticed until now. "A traveler had parchment," she said, holding up the paper, "I got him to part with some."

"I don't suppose you should be making the acquaintance of travelers." I tried to narrow my eyes in rebuke, but I couldn't help smiling at how excited she looked. "And educated ones at that." She was more likely to be recognized by the educated.

"What's done is done." She set her teeth in a grin in response to the look on my face. "May I borrow your dagger?"

My eyebrows rose at that. Ava stood and walked to the fire, picking a long, cool piece of charcoal from the edges. It became apparent to me that she wanted to sharpen the charcoal to a point, so I removed my knife and handed it to her as she sat back down. She held the charcoal over her knee and proceeded to carve over one end, and I managed to watch her calmly for a minute before she nearly skinned herself.

"Be careful!" I exclaimed, wincing at how close the blade had been to slicing through her trousers. Then I realized my protest had been too forceful, and added, "If you'd please."

Ava smirked, and I'd seen her smile enough by now that I knew she was about to tease me. "Tell me, Kiena, how many times have you cut yourself with this blade?"

I reached out to take it when she handed it back, answering, "Too many to count."

"Alas," she said, doing what she could to hold back that smile. "Here you are, alive and well." I pursed my lips as though I wasn't amused in the slightest, though truthfully, even Ava caught the entertained glimmer in my eyes. "Perhaps I should be a bit more reckless to prove I'm not so fragile."

"Is it your goal to suffer me an early death?" I replied. "By the gods, you're well on your way."

Ava laughed, testing the point of her charcoal at the corner of a parchment. "You weren't so uptight about me a couple of days ago."

I stood to walk to the saddle on the floor, reaching in one of the bags for my sharpening rock. "I hardly knew you a couple of days ago."

"Are you saying you've grown attached?" she asked playfully.

Though I blushed, I refused to look at her so she wouldn't see it. "Mind yourself, Ava," I said with just as much jest, though at the recesses of my mind I was hoping she'd heed my warning, "or a subject might forget the true height of your title."

"Maybe *that's* the goal," she said without a hitch.

"To what purpose?" I asked, suddenly suspicious and serious despite the fact that Ava was still almost maddeningly smug.

"The comfort of both."

I glanced down at the stone in my hand so Ava wouldn't notice my confusion. "That's a broad answer."

"Indeed," she agreed, and when that's all she said, I felt my eyebrows furrow. "I've frustrated you," she observed flawlessly.

I paced over and resumed my seat in the chair across from her. "No."

"Liar," she stated. "What's upset you?"

"It won't do to have me forgetting where you come from," I told her, and at the same time I glanced up at her, I felt myself *wanting* to forget.

"Why?" she asked. All hint of playfulness had abandoned her expression, and now she was leaning forward against the table, watching me with sincere interest.

"Where I'm from," I said, meeting her gaze, "royalty's not associated with a subject's comfort."

"But we're not where you're from," Ava said, "and we're not where I'm from. Might comfort be associated with whatever we'd like?"

I just couldn't figure her out. She wasn't being direct, and though I'd kept up with her banter thus far, it was getting to the point of losing me. I thought I knew what she was trying to tell me, but I couldn't let myself get too comfortable with her. If I did, I'd risk feeling things I shouldn't be feeling, or doing things I could be killed for. I was already walking a fine line in being so friendly and informal with her. It was dangerous, but she seemed determined to guide me over that line.

"I suppose it remains to be seen," I answered, and Ava's lips curled with approval.

Chapter 5

hile the storm raged outside, Ava had been working over her parchment, and I'd cozied up on the floor in order to groom Albus. Usually I didn't fret so much about the state of his fur, or what he felt or smelled like, but Ava insisted that she didn't mind him sharing the bed. The least I could do was make sure he was clean. So I spent a better part of the day picking pine needles and brushing dirt from his fur, and even trimmed his nails with my knife – a task he hated and for which I had to reward him with a handsome sum of meat. I took off my chest wraps to have some rest of them while I sharpened my knife, made repairs to my clothing, poked at the fire, anything to keep my mind occupied. Ava seemed well equipped for the stagnation of the storm, but I wasn't accustomed to sitting still or having no tasks, especially in the midst of a blizzard.

By the afternoon, I'd exhausted myself of things to do, and so I stood and strode over to the table where Ava was sitting, curious about what she was working on and desperate for a distraction. I'd previously refrained from exploring my curiosity because I'd thought she was writing, and I wouldn't have been able to read it anyway. When I got there, however, I found that she'd been drawing. The one she was working on now was an exact representation of Albus, so I picked up another she'd set face down to admire it too.

"That's not finished!" she protested, immediately standing and making a reach for the paper in my hands. Having no desire to upset her, I handed it over without protest before I got to really look at it. But she didn't look satisfied when I did. "You gave it up too easily."

I let out a confused chuckle. "Is that not what you wanted?"

"Not really," she said, gaining her playful smile as she held her arm out to dangle the paper away from me. "It's just a drawing, nothing to get serious over. If you want to see it, you can wrestle it from me."

"If you think I'm about to wrestle a princess," I began, glancing from her glimmering eyes to the parchment.

"See, that's just the problem," she said matter-of-factly. "You've stopped calling me Princess, but you haven't stopped treating me like it. Not completely." She wiggled the drawing in front of my face, daring me to make a grab for it. "I can tell you're still afraid of offending me. You joke, and you laugh at my teasing, but you don't tease me back."

"I don't refuse to wrestle for fear of offending you, Ava," I told her, too amused and comfortable to worry much about verbal banter. "I wouldn't want to embarrass you when I win too easily."

Ava snickered delightedly. "Only one way to prove it." She held the paper away from me again, and playfully pushed my shoulder with her other hand. "Come on, stand up for yourself." And with a smile, she pushed me again. "I'll gladly show you the drawing if you can take it from me." Another delicate nudge. "Have at it."

I made a grab for the parchment, but she was waiting for it, and swiftly pulled it away. When I took a step toward her to get my reach closer, she blithely jumped sideways. I laughed, shaking my head in defeat and completely giving up my cautious ways. If she wanted bold, that's what she was going to get. I darted at her, and before she could turn around to dash away, I grabbed her by the waist and threw her over my shoulder. She shrieked with laughter, dangling the paper in front of my eyes because she knew I couldn't grab it without dropping her.

"Kiena," she giggled, "you've got something on your face." And she swiped her charcoal-smeared fingers across my cheek.

I laughed so hard it was difficult not to drop her, so I hurried a few paces and dumped her on the bed. Now she was cornered. She made a move to jump off the bed one way, but I would've been there by the time her feet touched down. She feigned the other way, but the result would've been the same. I was the victor of this round, and I held out my hand triumphantly.

"Give it here, you clever minx," I teased.

Her eyebrows rose with surprise at my playful name-calling, but a mischievous smirk let me know that she enjoyed it. "As m'lady commands," she assented, giving a sporty bow and extending the paper to me.

I grabbed it hastily in case she was planning on teasing me further, and held it in my hands to look at the drawing. She was a great artist, and the image of myself that met my eyes was beyond flattering. "You do me a compliment with this portrait, Ava."

"On the contrary. You underestimate yourself, Kiena." She scooted back until she was leaning against the headboard. "You're very beautiful." My eyes involuntarily darted up to meet Ava's, and when my face burned red, I shyly looked away. "Why do you blush so much when I say and do things?"

"I'm not accustomed to anyone like you," I admitted, holding the portrait in my hands for a distraction even though I was done looking at it.

"What am I like?" she asked, the hint of a smile in her voice. She took pleasure in making me blush, I was certain of it.

"Intelligent, *and* kind, *and* funny, *and* beautiful," I listed honestly, mentally adding confident to that list. "Near impossible to find a person that's all four. It's a rare combination."

"Rare," she mused thoughtfully, and when I glanced up from the drawing, I saw her eyes look me up and down. "Yet here we are."

"Here we are," I repeated, looking away from her again, and when I realized she was calling *me* all of those things, I colored once more.

I didn't mind calling her all that, I was sure it wasn't unusual for people to attempt flattering her. But she wasn't doing me any favors by flattering me. No favors by continually making me complacent to her royal title and treating me like an equal. No favors by tempting the desires I knew already existed within me. I cleared my throat uncomfortably, and turned to set the drawing back on the table.

"Smells like venison," I said distractedly. "Should I go and fetch supper?"

So as not to give her the chance to say something flirtatious, I turned for the door immediately. Albus knew the word 'venison,' but when he made an attempt to follow me out directly to the food, I made him stay with Ava. The innkeeper recognized me, and even though he looked somewhat indignant about the fact that I was there for more food, he gave me a healthy portion and a large cup of mead. I carried the plate and cup back to the room, where Ava was waiting for me at the table.

She'd brought Maddox over and perched the bird on the back of her chair, so after I'd sat down, I cut a strip of meat from the steak. "Here," I said, handing it to Ava, who then fed it to Maddox. I also pushed the entire cup across the table to her. "You can have all this too."

Ava glanced into it, and then cast me a suspicious stare. "You're the one's been on edge all day."

"I don't like mead," I told her, cutting a larger piece of meat for Albus, who'd been pawing at my leg ever since I'd sat down. "It's too sweet."

"Mead?" she asked in shock, and tilted the cup to her lips to take a reassuring sip. "Too sweet?"

"Aye," I laughed in response to the look on her face. "I'm not fond of sweet foods."

"What are you fond of?" She ripped a piece of stale bread from the loaf from this morning, dipping it in the mead to soften it. "This is very good though," she said, pushing the cup back toward me as though she wanted me to be sure.

I shrugged and answered her question with, "Salt."

Ava made a face, but watched amusedly while I took a gulp of the mead. Sure enough, it still had the aftertaste of honey, which caused my tongue to turn over in my mouth and successfully made Ava burst into laughter. "I love sweet things," she told me, taking the cup back. "My mother used to tell me stories of the sweets they have in the Ronan Empire."

I tried not to let my surprise at that show. It was the first time Ava had talked about that side of her. "Did she?"

"Indeed," Ava confirmed enthusiastically, chewing and swallowing a piece of meat before continuing. "It's always warm there, so they have an abundance of fruits." She washed down the venison with a swallow of mead. "Fruit pastries, and pies, and wines, and candies."

"Is Ronan blood made of sugar?" I chuckled.

She glanced down at her arm, as if to see the blood beneath her own skin. "It very well may be," she agreed lightheartedly.

"Perhaps it accounts for your delightful personality," I said teasingly.

"Was that sarcasm?" Ava asked, squinting one doubtful eye at me even though her lips curled with amusement. "Or did you just call me sweet?"

My bottom jaw dropped awkwardly, because that was a trap no matter which way I answered. If I said it was sarcasm, I risked being rude. But if I admitted to having called her sweet, it would land me in another kind of trouble. My cheeks started shading at the conflict, and Ava looked thoroughly pleased by it. "There you go, blushing again."

But I was getting bolder about her teasing me, and about teasing her back. "It was sarcasm," I stated flatly.

Ava laughed at that. "No need to get sour."

"It might be my lack of Ronan blood," I said.

"Maybe," she agreed with a smirk, "we can't all be perfect." Before I could come up with a decent retort for that, Ava asked, "How did you know they were cooking venison?"

"The exquisite smell of a hunter," I said with exaggerated pride.

"Honestly?" she asked in disbelief. I nodded. "I want to test you."

I huffed amusedly, but nodded a second time. "Alright."

Ava jumped out of her seat, excitedly grabbing my hand and pulling me out of mine. She dragged me to the furs I'd set out to sit on earlier while grooming Albus, and plopped me down on them. "Close your eyes," she said, already glancing around the room for something to test me with. "And cover your ears."

I did as she said, laughing the entire time until I felt something touch beneath my nose. I inhaled, and had my eyes been open, I would've rolled them. "That's the mead," I chuckled. Even with my fingers in my ears, I could hear her gorgeous laugh, and she removed the cup to go and find something else. A few moments later, I felt the presence of the next item. I inhaled, and my nostrils were flooded with a sharp smell that made me pull my head back. "The antiseptic," I said.

Ava muttered an excited praise, and pulled one of my fingers away from my ear just to lean in and say, "Keep your eyes closed."

I laughed, returning my finger to my ear to wait. She brought something else, and though it was a bit harder to identify, it wasn't difficult. "I believe that's charcoal." Another proud exclamation, and I felt Ava's presence depart only to return a moment later. I inhaled the wonderful smell of the outdoors, the deep, comforting scent of pine. "Firewood," I guessed easily, and the conjecture was met with a giggle. Something was replaced under my nose shortly after, so she couldn't have gone far to get it. I inhaled deeply, involuntarily feeling one corner of my mouth turn up in a smile. I don't know if she'd simply stuck her arm under my nose, but I knew it to be her. "That's your scent, Ava. I'd know it anywhere."

The scent disappeared, and though I heard no mumble of praise this time, I waited patiently for the next test. Instead, her hands landed on my knees, and I was about to open my eyes to see how the game was being changed when something warm pressed against my mouth. I knew the very moment it happened that they were Ava's lips. Soft and careful, I'd never forget how they felt against my cheek, and when I recognized them, my breathing stopped and my face flushed.

Out of stunned awe, my fingers slid away from my ears and my arms fell to my sides, and I sat there, frozen. I hadn't done anything yet. I could still pull away, and it could be like I hadn't done anything wrong. But that was *so* far from what I wanted, and I'd already indulged in it by not pulling away immediately. So when Ava's delicate hand cupped my face, I parted my lips to indulge in it a little more. And I kissed back. I swayed with her every time she leaned forward to kiss me deeper. I matched every tender movement and parting of her lips with the movement and parting of my own. I met the careful caresses of her gentle tongue with the tip of my own and I got drunk off the taste of her.

Her other hand had joined its partner to touch my face, and now one slipped around the back of my neck while the other tangled in my hair. With the next forward sway she pushed us all the way over, and though the hand in my hair cushioned my fall, out of instinct to steady myself as I fell backward, my hands landed on her hips. I knew I should stop this, but now that my hands were on her, I had an overwhelming urge to indulge those too, and I didn't have the mind to stop them. They ran up the sides of her ribs and then back down, worshiping the gloriously full shape of her body. They slid up the middle of her back, pressing between her shoulder blades to bring her chest closer to me. They snaked back down, past her hips and her lower back to the plump flesh beneath it, and here I grabbed to bring that part of her closer too.

In response, Ava released an approving hum into my mouth, a sound as soft and sweet as any noise she made, her hips pressed seductively harder into mine, and I felt it in my heart and my stomach and between my legs. I was so torn between the feeling of her against me and the building tension in my chest. Between an extraordinary desire and knowing what satiating it would mean. Between sense and sensation. And sensation would've won out if it weren't for the fact that I was beginning to panic. I'd meant to indulge, but I'd indulged much too far. Before I could convince myself not to, I shifted Ava off of me and stood.

"Why'd you do that?" I asked frantically, wiping my sleeve over my lips because just the taste of her was too tempting.

The confused look on her face made me feel immediately guilty, and even worse was that she appeared somewhat hurt. "Wh-I... because it felt right," she offered as she got up, and it was the first time she'd ever looked that unsure of herself. "You didn't seem to mind."

"I mind," I countered frenziedly. "I mind very much." I took a deep breath to try and calm myself. There were *so* many conflicting feelings. "That's punishable by death, what I just did."

"You didn't do anything wrong," she said, and I couldn't meet her gaze because of the pained look in her eyes. The look I'd caused by being too informal.

"I kissed you back," I told her, trying to make her understand. There were laws; she should know that more than anyone. "I put my hands on you."

"You're welcome to do it again." She took an earnest step forward.

I took a frightened one back. "It can't happen again." I inhaled deeply once more, still trying to ease the panic. "It's improper."

"Because I'm a woman?" she asked, sounding mildly offended.

"Because you're a *princess*," I replied impatiently. I'd never met with anything more frustrating. I could let her treat me like an equal, and I could pretend like I believed it, but there had to be a line. And still the *only* thing I wanted was to cross that line. "And I'm..." I paused, sighing before I met her gaze. "I'm nothing. I'm a traitor's child."

"You're so much more than that," she whispered disappointedly.

I refused to look at her again for fear that I'd buckle. I had to hold my ground, but I *wanted* to lose this debate. "It doesn't matter," I started, thinking it would help my case, "and it won't convince me not to take you back to the castle."

There was such a tense, lengthy pause that I finally had to look at her. It was the first time I'd ever seen her look truly upset. "I don't care about my title," she said angrily. "Or the wealth you don't have." She took a couple strides toward the door, passing me and turning around to say, "I kissed you because I happen to admire who you are, and what you stand for." A couple more strides, and she reached for the handle. "But you know what? Nevermind." She huffed, opening the door. "To you I'm just a whore that would sell myself for a false sense of freedom."

"Ava," I pleaded hastily, instantly regretting that I'd said what I did. "That's not-"

She slammed the door behind her before I could finish. I groaned my frustration, pacing over to the bed and dropping face first onto it. Then I groaned some more before rolling onto my back.

"*Why*, Albus?" I whined to the dog curled up on the bed nearby. "Why did I have to open my stupid mouth?" Albus took in a deep breath, letting it out in one long, grumbling sigh. I took in a deep breath too, though as I sighed I threw my arms out to either side of me. "Gods take me, that was a kiss for the storybooks." Albus made another long-winded noise, and as if I could understand him, I slapped my hands against the bed with frustration. "I *can't* kiss her again. If the king finds out, I'll be killed." I buried my face in my hands, groaning again. "Why'd she do that? Why is she intent on torturing me?"

I bolted upright when the door was thrust open. Ava burst in, and by the look on her face, I was terrified she'd grown enraged in her absence and was back to yell at me. She was breathing heavily, her normally energetic complexion pale.

"Soldiers," she panted, slamming the door closed and plastering her back against it. "Soldiers in the tavern." And my heart plummeted.

Chapter 6

re you sure?" I asked, rushing to the sleeping furs to roll them hastily.

"Kiena," Ava said, and after she'd pulled on the fur cloak and gloves I made her, she came over and grabbed my shoulders, "*they saw me.*"

In reply to her claim, there was a pounding on the door of a room down the hall. "Open up!" a soldier yelled.

"We have to go," Ava muttered, pacing to the window and pulling out the bark she'd wedged there in the morning.

I hurried over to stop her. "Ava, *the storm*. You don't have proper clothing. You'll freeze to death." There was a crash as a nearby door was broken down.

"I'll chance the cold before I let them take me back to Guelder," she said in a panic, but when she remembered my intense fear of snowstorms, she paused, turning from the window to take my face in her hands. "Kiena, please, I am begging you." I took in a breath to ask a question, but she didn't let me get it out. "I'll tell you everything. The moment we're away from here, I swear it. *Please.*"

"We could die," I emphasized, glancing at the window with my heart hammering so hard that I could feel the pulsing in my skull.

"We'll die if we stay," she pleaded.

I studied her face for the span of a moment, taking in the fear in her eyes and weighing it against the terror in my chest. I couldn't get her caught, not yet, not when I didn't know what was waiting for her back in Guelder.

"Go," I said, motioning to the window.

She yanked it open to be met by an icy blast of wind. She grabbed Maddox before climbing out, and I threw on the vest and coat I'd shed in the warmth of the room and picked up my saddle. I gestured for Albus to jump out after Ava, and after he was clear, I threw the saddle out and followed. We ran in the direction I knew the stables to be. Once inside, I rushed to get the saddle on Brande's back, working the straps and buckles as best I could with my already frozen fingers.

"Up," I commanded when it was secure, and after Ava climbed on, I got up behind her.

I didn't hesitate to kick my heels back, and Brande took off at a gallop toward the exit of the stables. We burst through right as a third soldier dropped out our open window. The wind was howling far too loudly to hear what they said, but one pointed, yelling back at some still in the room while the other two sprinted for the stables to retrieve their own horses.

It didn't matter. It took less than ten paces before we were out of view. The snow whipping through the air was too thick to see much in any direction, and it blocked out the moonlight so everything that wasn't blanketed white was pitch black. We only galloped for fifteen minutes, dodging trees and changing direction often because getting ourselves lost in the woods was better than being captured. Then we slowed, because if the soldiers hadn't caught up yet then chances were they never would. The storm had likely already filled Brande's hoof prints with snow. Now I had to find somewhere to stop, but I didn't know if Ava would let me.

"Ava," I hollered over the sound of the wind. "Should we keep going?"

She was hunched into herself, arms wrapped as far as she could get them around her chest. She made no response.

"Ava?" I yelled, leaning forward to see her.

She was already shivering so fiercely with cold that she couldn't form words. I had to find somewhere to stop, but even if I did, there would be no dry wood to start a fire. Everything was frozen and wet – Ava's clothes, my clothes, the forest, and my animals. This was the worst thing we could have done. We should have found another way.

I pulled Ava back into me and wrapped my free arm around her to try and warm her. Even over the violent wind whipping through my clothes, I could feel her shaking. We had to find somewhere to stop, and then *maybe* we'd get out of this alive. I steered Brande blindly, squinting into the storm to look for some form of shelter. There was nothing. Ten minutes and I couldn't see a single thing, and Ava's shivering was getting worse by the second because my outer clothes were wet, blocking any body heat I could've given.

I leaned forward on Brande, as if the extra inches would give me a better view because I was desperate for something. Anything. There was nothing but snow. "Damn it!" I reached behind me and untied my sleeping furs, wrapping them around Ava even though I knew they'd do little to help. She was already soaked and cold. "Think, Kiena, think," I told myself.

I couldn't let it end here. My blood was pumping too hard for me to feel fear or frost, but I felt the building sense of defeat. This was it. We never should have left because we had no idea where we were going, and now we were stuck in this storm and Ava was half frozen. It was so cold that I knew she wouldn't last another twenty minutes, not in the clothes she was wearing. I'd have given her my layers but, like the blankets, they wouldn't have done anything now, she was already too drenched. I should have given them to her at the start. I'd be half frozen instead of her, but what was my life compared to hers? I should have given her my layers.

I gave up. There was nothing to do, nowhere to find shelter or warmth, and I was about to surrender us to the cold. But then, just then, there was a flash of orange in the blinding white of the snow. I squinted harder, pulling Brande's reins in that direction. Again, a distant dot of orange firelight. A torch. I kicked my heels back to get us there faster. It could have been a figment of my imagination, or it could have been a soldier searching for us, but at this point, I didn't care. I'd get us captured. If they killed us, well, we were dead anyway. But maybe they'd take us in. They'd get us out of the storm and warm Ava back to life, and then I could think of how to rescue her and escape again.

The flame was getting closer, and nearby I spotted another, and we were nearly there. Brande was galloping as fast as he could through the drifts of snow, but it slowed him down considerably, and for a moment, I feared we'd never catch the lights. Then all at once we were upon them. We gained on the person holding the torch so unexpectedly that Brande almost ran them over. I pulled back on the reins as they dove to the side to dodge my horse, and when they realized they hadn't been trampled, they rose out of the snow. Their entire face was covered for warmth, and their clothing was so thick I couldn't tell if it was a man or a woman, but I could feel that they were shocked at my arrival.

"Please!" I shouted over the deafening wind. And I was so desperate, so out of options that all I could beg was, "Help!"

The person stepped nearer, holding the torch close to my face, and they just stared at me for a moment. I don't know what they were looking for, or what they found satisfying about me, but they grabbed the leather leads attached to Brande's bit to guide him. I released the reins to let the person take us, and wrapped both of my arms around Ava, for comfort mostly, because there was nothing I could do to give heat. It felt like it took forever, the person wading through the thigh deep snow, until we came upon a steep mountain. It appeared to be a dead end, and for a split second, thinking this person wasn't trying to help us after all, I nearly panicked. But they continued forward toward the sheer wall, and soon all the wind and snow ceased. We'd been led into the start of a cave.

"That's not Gibbons," observed a man inside.

Something went up at the entrance, so that we were blocked now from the outside world. The entire inside was lit with torches, and while there were a handful of people around now, I could see that the cave split off in a variety of directions.

Our guide removed their head covering, revealing a dark skinned man, his black hair tied at the back and his brown eyes full of careful concern. I trusted him instantly, if only because he motioned worriedly to Ava. "Hand her down," he said. I helped Ava off while he held his arms out, and he said to one of the entrance guards, "Go start a fire in an empty tunnel."

The guard hurried away, and I hopped off Brande, an entire layer of snow falling from my clothes when my feet hit the ground. "I'll take her now," I told the man protectively.

He didn't protest, and put Ava in my arms. "Follow me."

I carried Ava behind him as we headed off in the direction the other man had disappeared. There were a multitude of tunnels, some of which had wooden doors built at the start of them. I had no idea what kind of place we'd come to, but right now our situation was too dire for me to care. Our guide led us past some of these doors and farther into the cave, until we reached an open one, inside of which his companion had just started a fire.

74

"I've set out some extra furs," the man said, meeting us at the entrance of the short inlet.

"Thank you, Oren," said our guide.

Ava was still trembling in my arms, and I needed to warm her as quickly as possible, so I stepped through the open door, Albus following at my heels.

"You should-"

"I got it," I interrupted the man, "thank you." And I kicked the door closed, because I knew what I had to do and I didn't want them around. I rushed over to the fire and the sleeping furs on the ground beside it, and set Ava on her feet. "Can you stand?" I asked, gentle even though I was frantic to get her warmed before she was too cold for revival. She was shivering stiffly, arms stuck around her chest and her body tense, but she managed a nod. "Your clothes are soaking wet, I've got to take them off to get you warm."

Ava gave another nod, but made no move to take off her clothes. It only took a moment for me to realize that she couldn't; she was too cold to put much effort into moving. So I did it for her. I took off her cloak and then grabbed the hem of her tunic, sliding it over her head, careful not to look and careful not to do it too fast because I knew how frozen limbs could hurt when jostled. After I managed to get her tunic off, I did the same with her trousers, and then helped her down into the sleeping furs.

Albus had already curled into himself at the fireside, and though I would've had him lay atop Ava to help warm her, I knew there was no way I could get him to move. All I could do was tuck Ava in and make sure no heat escaped. It was only now that I began to feel the cold that had seeped into my own bones. My top layers were soaked too, so I removed my heavy fur outerwear and set it near the fire to dry, doing the same with Ava's wet apparel. Then I sat on the ground nearby in my damp clothes, wrapping my arms around my knees while I began to absorb the heat.

Though I'd begun to warm already, Ava was still shaking, so desperate that she scooted herself nearer the fire. "Not too close, Ava," I said. She was already as close to the flame as she could get, any more and she'd burn herself.

Yet she made no response. All I could hear was the loud chattering of her teeth. She wasn't warming fast enough. The fire was only able to reach the side she faced it with, and the air in the cave was so chill that it robbed her of whatever warmth she managed to get from the flame. There was only one other option, but I couldn't. Not after today. Not after she'd kissed me.

I sat there for another minute by the fire, but I couldn't tune out the sound of her trembling. She was frozen and miserable, and through the chattering of her teeth, I could hear that her breathing was stunted and shallow. She'd been too cold for too long, and if I didn't do something soon, she'd get sick. Or worse. I tapped my heel against the ground, struggling with the conflict while my eyes wandered over to Ava. She'd gotten even closer to the fire, so close that I could smell the hairs of her blanket singeing. I couldn't just sit here.

Resolved that I had to suck it up, I stood and pulled off the remainder of my damp clothes. As I lowered myself into the sleeping furs beside her, she turned away from the fire to face me. "I've got to get in," I told her apologetically, pulling the blanket up to my chin, "it's the only w-"

She didn't even let me finish. Her arm wrapped around my waist and she pulled herself into me so that even our legs were intertwined. She buried her face in my neck, and I sucked in a jolted breath at the frigid feel of her skin. Every bit of her was frozen. The arm around my waist and her feet wrapped around my calves and her entire torso pressed against the front of me. I could feel her icy flesh stripping my body of heat, but I didn't care as long as it helped. I wrapped both my arms around her to pull her closer, to give her as much of my warmth as I could.

And it did help. With me at one side of her, and the fire at the other, she had the heat she needed. Not long after I lay down, she stopped shivering so badly, and soon after that she stopped altogether. Her skin started to feel warm again, her breathing returned to normal, and we were both exhausted enough by the cold that we fell asleep.

I woke at what felt like early morning. My body was drained of energy and I could've slept longer, but it was heavy footsteps that had woken me. My eyes cracked open to see the same man from last night. He was putting fresh logs on the fire that had dwindled overnight, and when he saw that I was awake and noticed him, he passed me a simple nod and then retreated out the door. However, now that I was awake and realized Ava was still tangled up in me, I couldn't go back to sleep. Nor could I bring myself to move...

Though I couldn't see her, Ava must have woken too, because she released a laugh into my neck. "This is not how I imagined ending up naked with you."

"This is not the time for jokes," I protested, squeezing my eyes shut. How could she laugh now? When for me it was still sinking in that she'd been so near death only hours ago, and that I'd almost got her killed. "I'm sorry, Ava," I said, the full fear of last night finally making its loathsome appearance. I knew better than to go into storms like that. I'd almost lost Albus because of it, and I'd gone and risked Ava in spite of it. I swallowed hard as I felt tears sting my eyes. "I should have come up with something else, another way to get out of there. I never should have taken you into the storm."

She only squeezed herself tighter against me. "You have no need to apologize." And for a moment I allowed myself to hold her in return. I'd been trying for so many reasons not to touch her, but just this once I put my hand on her back to return her forgiving embrace.

"Ava," I breathed, pulling away from her because of what I'd felt at her back.

My hand had set on a scar, one I'd never noticed because I'd never seen that side of her bare – last night I'd tried not to look – and I'd certainly never caressed her flesh with my fingers. I met her eyes to make my concern apparent. She'd known what I felt, but she turned onto her stomach instead of saying anything, exposing her back so I could look at it, and I peeled down the blankets to see.

It was *massive*. An old burn scar as if she'd been branded, and it covered the entirety of her back, from her shoulder blades to the center between her hips. Like a brand, it was only the outline, but its workings shaped an intricate crow, wings stretched at her shoulder blades and talons extended down the length of her spine. But my heart didn't just sink because of what Ava had gone through. I recognized the mark. I'd seen this very shape before, though the last time I'd seen it, it was so small I'd mistaken it for a raven. That onyx bird set in Hazlitt's crown.

"I told you," Ava said humorlessly, "I'm not so fragile as you think."

"Did King Hazlitt do this to you?" I demanded, with every desire to stick my knife straight through the heart of whoever had put the scalding metal to her flesh, particularly if it was Hazlitt. "Is he the person threatening your life?"

77

"Why do you ask if it was the king?" Ava turned back to look at me, a fearful but curious crease in her eyebrows. "How would you know that?"

"I've seen that symbol, Ava," I muttered. "In his crown. Was it him?" Her shoulders bobbed with reply. "What do you mean you don't know?"

"I woke up one morning in searing pain," she said. "I have no recollection of who did it, or how." Her eyes filled with tears, as though she could still feel it. "I showed my mother, and she was terrified, but she wouldn't say if she knew anything."

I sat up, setting my elbows against my knees and burying my face in my hands because my head was suddenly spinning. A person didn't just forget how they came by pain like that. This was too much, and I knew already that I was in over my head. "You know what that sounds like?" I asked.

Ava was quiet for a thoughtful moment before whispering, "Magic."

I released a heavy sigh, trying to calm my racing mind. "The witch told me someone was cursed." I glanced back, and Ava's eyes fell because she knew what I was implying. "Ava... crows are omens of death."

Slowly, Ava sat up too. She left the furs and gathered her dry clothing from near the fire to begin pulling it on. "Get dressed," she murmured. "I'll tell you what I know."

I did as she said. She finished before me, and sat back down on the furs to be near the heat of the fire. Once I was dressed, I lowered myself next to her. I don't know if it was for warmth or comfort, but once I sat, she scooted into my side and linked an arm through mine. Though I'd been so wary of constant contact with her, and though I couldn't kiss her, or touch her, or tell her how I felt, I could allow this much. More than that, I *wanted* to allow this much.

"You know we're losing the war?" Ava asked, and though I knew nothing of the war's politics, I'd seen the broken state of my kingdom's people. I nodded. "King Hazlitt has been trying for years to negotiate with Cornwall in the West, to get them to send soldiers, but they've wanted nothing to do with our war."

"Smart," I muttered.

"Indeed," Ava agreed. "They see the king's greed for power, and know it to be his ruin." I felt Ava take in a deep breath, and heard her release it in a heavy sigh. "But the king is desperate. In the summer, he hosted the royal family from Cornwall to negotiate a different treaty." I hummed curiously. "A marriage between House Gaveston and House Tardin, to vow lasting peace between our kingdoms no matter the turn of the war with Ronan."

It took a long moment for me to realize exactly what she was saying. "You're betrothed?" I exclaimed, pulling my arm from hers and making to scoot away. I'd be put to death for sure.

"Kiena, please," Ava begged, but she let me retreat. "Hear me before making your judgment. I'd not have kissed you were I to marry another."

"Swear it," I demanded, terrified of the position I'd been put in. By the gods, I *was* a traitor. I'd crossed lines I could never uncross.

"On my life," she swore, and though there was still a large part of me that was panicking, I settled back down at her side. Ava was too unsure of herself now to take my arm back, but maybe it was for the best. "The betrothal was a rouse. The king made it clear to me that I was to win the affections of the prince, and I did. I played his game, knowing well that I was doing it and that King Hazlitt had some ill motive. I did it anyway, because the prince is a good man, and I thought even if I could never love him, at least I'd be somewhere happier." She hung her head, and I refrained from making my displeasure known. "The royal family went home to Cornwall while preparations were to be made for the wedding."

I dug the heels of my hands into my eyes from the sheer stress. I couldn't hear this, it hurt my head and heart and my very soul. But I *had* to hear it.

"There are secret tunnels in the castle," Ava continued. "As long as I do the few things Hazlitt asks, he cares very little how I spend my free time, so I explore them sometimes to keep busy. I happened upon the king's most trusted advisor, speaking with a mercenary." Ava glanced sideways at me, waiting until I met her eyes. "Kiena, he was an assassin."

"I don't understand," I whispered.

"Before the wedding plans were finished," she said, "the king would have me killed. He'd blame it on the Ronan Empire by saying they'd caught word of an alliance. I was meant to be a sacrifice, Kiena. My life for the rage of a prince whose affections I'd deceived."

"And Cornwall would lend soldiers to King Hazlitt's cause."

Ava nodded. "That's why I ran," she said. "I was afraid, and I couldn't let the king go through with it. He can't win this war. He shouldn't even keep the throne."

"Ava," I breathed stressfully. This was *way* over my head. What did I know of kings and politics and wars? Who was I to decide the fate of any of it? "Why are you going south? What's there for you that isn't death?"

There was a long silence, and eventually Ava mumbled, "My father."

My face set with confusion. "King Hazlitt i-"

"King Hazlitt is *not* my father," Ava interrupted. "I'm not a Gaveston by blood." I met her eyes, and she could read the inquiry in them. Who was her father? "By blood, I'm of House Ironwood."

Ironwood. "The king of the Ronan Empire," I whispered. "You're Ronan."

"Entirely," she confirmed.

"How?"

"My mother was pregnant when she married Hazlitt," she answered.

"But their marriage was for peace."

"A treaty Hazlitt betrayed when he found out," she said. "Or he simply used it as an excuse. Before Akhran Ironwood was king, he asked my mother's hand. She's originally of House Fysher."

Ava paused to see if I'd heard the name, but I shook my head. "I know nothing beyond kings," I told her.

"House Fysher carries influence in Ronan second only to House Ironwood," she explained. "On account of the treaty with the soon to be King Hazlitt, my grandfather disregarded my father's request, and negotiated with Lord Fysher for my mother's marriage to Hazlitt Gaveston." My head was swimming. It was so much to take in and understand, but Ava wasn't finished. "The Fyshers lent aid to put Hazlitt on the throne, and once he was there, he refused to end the war."

"So... my father, traitor to King Hazlitt..."

"He was right all along," she said. "I suppose he knew the king was deceitful." And I felt so validated by my father's refusal to fight for the king that I let out a relieved breath.

"And what of your grandfather?" I asked.

"My father wouldn't forgive him," she answered. "He died of grief shortly after, and my father took the throne."

"That's why Ronan continues to fight," I said, finally understanding. "For your mother?"

Ava gave a half nod. "King Akhran, my father, he's married now. But House Fysher needs to make up its betrayal to the Ronan empire. They and House Ironwood have the means to see this war to the end."

"And King Hazlitt?" I wondered aloud. "Why does he fight? Why are we at war?"

"I have only speculation," Ava said, folding her arms atop her knees and resting her chin on them. "Rumors I've heard amongst the castle." I hummed for her to continue. "Magic isn't against the law in Ronan like it is in Valens. It's monitored carefully, but it's practiced." She laid her head sideways to see me. "I heard of a book, locked away by Ronan scholars for centuries because it contains the darkest magic. He wants its power so he can conquer more than Ronan. He wants the continent: Ronan, Cornwall, the five other nations, The Amalgam Plains, all of it. He wants to establish himself as the first High King."

"So King Hazlitt has been doing magic?" I asked, feeling a shiver go up my spine. My mother had told me stories of dark magic, everyone in the kingdom knew of its danger, and I was starting to wonder about the truth in all the superstition.

"If he has, he's not been caught by the right person."

"And your back?" I suggested. "I suppose he *is* the one who did that?"

"It would appear so," Ava consented. "But it's been years, and I've yet to discover the mark's purpose."

I let out a heavy, stressed sigh, and sat there for a moment. I rubbed my hands over my face, massaged my fingers into my temples, and sighed again. "Going south," I said, revisiting Ava's destination. "What do you expect to happen when you arrive? Why are we going to King Akhran? Does he even know you exist?"

"I'm a love child. I was hoping..." Ava paused, huffing as though laughing dryly at herself. "I'm hoping he'll feel some affection for me, and finally give me a place to belong." And her eyes met mine, and her lips pursed in the smallest smile like she knew how wishful that sounded. "I know the castle at Guelder. Maybe I could help end this war, and get my mother back."

The sigh I let out now was the heaviest yet. "You're a citizen of Valens, Ava. That would make you a traitor to your kingdom." She needed help getting south; it was too dangerous for her to go alone. "If I take you, I'm a traitor by association." I'd never live with myself if I made her go alone and she didn't make it. I already felt strongly for her. Whether she'd been trying to or not, and whether I could act on it or not, she'd won my devotion. I wanted her to be happy, and to feel like she had a family even if it meant I'd never be able to see her again afterwards. "I've been trying my whole life to follow the law, to do what I've known to be right and escape my father's inheritance. Come to find, maybe it's not something worth escaping." I shut my eyes against the thoughts fluttering through my mind, trying my hardest to organize them. "It's a lot to consider."

"You have a mother and brother to care for," she said understandingly, and I nodded.

Mother and Nilson needed me. I put meat on the table, I took care of things Mother had grown too old for and Nilson had not yet grown enough for, I sold furs for things I couldn't make myself. They were my responsibility.

"Kiena, I couldn't let you regret this decision." Ava set a reassuring hand on my arm. "I couldn't bear it if something happened to them because you came with me."

But did I not have a greater responsibility? This war had been going on since before my birth. The king had conscripted every man he could to the farthest reach of the kingdom. It was only a matter of time before Nilson was old enough. He was small for his age, but the king was desperate. He'd take Nilson, and Nilson would be killed in his first battle. But I could help end it, for Nilson, and for every boy like him.

Nilson was nearly old enough to help mother, and to take over for me around the cottage. If I never made it back from this journey because I helped Ava accomplish what she'd sought out to do, my family would survive. If I went back, and Ava failed because she was alone, it was only a matter of time before the king drafted Nilson to fight, before Mother and Nilson were dead and I was alone in the midst of an unending war.

"I'll take you south," I told her, and behind the surprised look in her eyes was a building excitement. "I've already broken a few rules. What are a few more?"

Ava grinned, throwing her arms around my torso and squeezing me so tight I couldn't breathe. "Thank you." She also kissed my cheek, not once but a handful of times in rapid succession, planting the last one hard. "Thank you, Kiena, thank you."

"No need to thank me," I teased, "I couldn't let a fragile princess travel alone."

"Fragile," she huffed, giving me a sporty shove strong enough that I fell over sideways, and I couldn't help but snort with laughter.

Chapter 7

ot long after I decided to escort Ava south did we begin to wonder exactly where we were now. Every so often voices passed by outside the door to our small cave, but not once did someone try to enter; not since the man who had woken us. Though this place was clearly a secret – I'd decided so at the way the entrance had been hidden after our arrival last night – I didn't feel threatened at being here. They'd saved Ava's life, cared enough to replenish the fire this morning, and Albus was still curled up comfortably beside its warmth. Albus always knew when something was wrong.

So we decided it was time to see what was going on outside our chamber, and I gave Ava my dry fur coat because she still had fewer layers of clothing than I did, and I could handle the chill of the caverns. I opened the door, sticking my head out first to check for danger, and meeting the eyes of a young boy sitting on the ground across the hall. When he saw me, he stood, his shaggy brown hair bouncing with the motion. He couldn't have been much older than Nilson, eleven years of age, maybe.

"Morning, my ladies," he greeted, bending at the waist in a shallow bow, and I found myself wondering how long he'd been sitting there in wait.

Ava giggled at his enthusiasm, and leaned over to see him eye to eye. "Morning…"

"Oscar," the boy supplied.

"Willow," she told him, sticking out her hand, which he took and shook, an action I admired the bravery of despite the fact that he didn't know Ava was a princess. I also appreciated the fact that Ava gave him a fake name, even if she passed me a coy smile after she did. "Pleased to make your acquaintance."

"Pleasure," Oscar said, brown eyes beaming and landing on me.

"Kiena," I told him.

I don't know if he could instinctively tell the status difference between Ava and me, but his handshake with me was a lot sturdier. "Oscar. Well met." And Ava giggled again, causing Oscar to pass her a grin as if he knew he was being cute. Then Albus came out from behind my legs, and Oscar's eyes lit up even more. "Hello, pup!" The dog's nose was level with the boy's, but he boldly reached for Albus's head, rubbing behind his ears and down his neck, laughing when Albus licked the side of his face. "I'm to escort you to the dining hall for a generous meal. Best stew in all the kingdom, and a lamb leg for the hound."

"I do love a good stew," Ava agreed, sticking out her hand.

Oscar took it, and as he began to drag her in the direction of the dining hall, she tossed me a teasing look over her shoulder. I laughed, rolling my eyes and following after them. Oscar led us back to the entrance of the cave and down a tunnel on the opposite side. This one was taller and wider, but much shorter, as it seemed to end at a large door.

The door Oscar pushed open, revealing a massive hall with tables set throughout. We must not have been under a steep part of the mountain, because there was a hole above the hall, about as wide as I was tall, and through which a flood of natural light lit the interior. It provided good ventilation for the fires over which food was being cooked, and despite the clean smell of the crisp air coming from it, the fires kept the chamber rather warm. It was so warm that I could see snow blowing over the top of it, but by the time any flakes that made it in reached the floor of the cavern they'd melted over the damp floor.

There weren't nearly as many people in here as there were seats. In fact, only a handful were sitting at the farthest table, half men and women, all of them cloaked in light fur and each with a different weapon at their back or hip. One of them was the man who'd found us last night, and another was the one who'd prepared our fire. Both stood when they saw us come in, and left the group to walk over.

"Father," Oscar greeted the smaller man, who I remembered from last night as Oren. Oscar bowed his head in greeting to the other. "Sir Caedia." Then he motioned to Ava and me. "Ladies Willow and Kiena."

"A knight?" Ava asked.

Sir Caedia had been studying me ever since he'd walked up, but now he cast an interested eye on Ava. "Depends on who you ask," he said, mussing Oscar's fluffy brown hair. "Please, call me Kingston." And even though he directed his next question at Ava, his gaze wandered back to me. "Are you feeling recovered?"

"Very much," Ava answered, following his glance my direction. "Thank you."

Kingston nodded, and though I could tell he was trying not to stare at me, he wasn't doing a good job of it.

"What is this place?" I asked for a distraction.

He took in a breath, but if he'd been about to answer, he stopped himself and gave a small smile. "Eat something," he said, motioning to the nearest table. "Refresh yourselves. Once you're fed, perhaps, Kiena, you might grace me with conversation."

I studied him for a long moment, taking in his supposed hospitality and weighing it against the fact it seemed he was interested in speaking to me alone. It was a bit alarming – maybe he knew who Ava was – but I'd yet to see any sign of aggression, and I wasn't about to give reason for one. Not unless I had to. So I nodded in agreement.

"After you've eaten," Kingston said before walking away, and he gestured toward the wrapping around Ava's wrist. "There's an infirmary back at the main entrance; first right, second left. If you'd like new linens for that."

We both said our thanks and sat down at the table he'd motioned to. After he'd gone, a woman brought out two large bowls of stew, two mugs of ale, and as Oscar had promised, a large lamb leg for Albus. It *was* delicious, and quite possibly the best stew in the kingdom, though my experience was limited. Ava's appetite had been profoundly increased by the energy she'd expended shivering last night, and while we ate, I could hear Albus cracking at the bone of his meal. It was grand, and though I couldn't finish my own bowl, I'd still eaten so much that I grew heavy and tired.

"What is this place?" Ava mused like I had earlier, pushing away her empty bowl and glancing around the dining hall.

I shrugged. "I suppose I'll find out when I talk to Kingston."

"Do you trust him?" she asked.

"I don't distrust him," I told her. "But it makes little difference so long as they don't stop us from leaving. We shouldn't stay long."

Ava nodded. "The king will hear soon that I've headed south."

While I answered I stood, ready to find the infirmary and make sure Ava's wrist was still doing well. "There'll be more soldiers to avoid. We'll have to be careful, and I need to get you a weapon." We headed back out into the short hall, Albus trailing behind us with the large bone hanging out the side of his mouth.

Making the first right and the second left, it didn't take long for us to find the infirmary. I pushed open the wooden door, not seeing anyone immediately inside. "Hello?" I called.

But it was such a small part of the cave, and completely empty of whoever's job it was to care for the sick. There were only a couple tables at the back with supplies, an empty one in the middle of the area, and a sleeping cot off to the side. Still, I assumed it was fine if we made use of the supplies, so I wandered over to the stock tables while Ava leaned back against the one at the center. There was clean dressing linen, and a multitude of glass bottles of liquids. I grabbed only the linen, because I wasn't sure which decanters were for what, and I trusted my own antiseptic more anyway. I carried the roll of linen back around to Ava, and after I'd set it on the table and placed myself in front of her, she handed me her wrist to remove the old bandage.

"Does it still hurt at all?" I asked, unwrapping the last bit from around her hand. She didn't answer, and when I glanced up at her she was giving me a blank look that I knew the meaning of. "I know you're not delicate," I chuckled. "Does that mean I'm not to care?"

"No," she said, studying me closely and giving a soft smile. "I enjoy your care."

I'd be lying if I said I didn't catch the implications behind her tone, and it'd be an even bigger lie to say it didn't immediately make my stomach flutter. She was so close to me, and the warmth in her voice evoked memories of the heat of her lips. The recollection of how she felt and moved and tasted, the knowledge that she'd wanted it, that she'd *started* it. And I knew she was thinking about it too. I could feel it in the sudden silence and tension between us. I could see it in the way her eyes followed me as I leaned across her to grab the clean linen.

I tried not to meet her gaze while I wrapped the new cloth around her wrist. I tried not to let my touches linger, but my heart was beating hard. I could feel it in my throat, hammering at my chest, tingling in my fingertips

87

every time they made contact with her flesh. I finally finished, and I would've turned away and made my retreat before the temptation got worse, but her other hand came over and set atop mine. Then it slid under so she could press our palms together, her fingers slipped tenderly between my own and I could hear the request in the slowness of her touch. Look at me. Notice me. *Kiss me.*

"Ava, please," I whispered, but even as I met her gaze pleadingly, I could feel myself leaning in.

"I don't understand," she said, begging just as much as I was but for the complete opposite reason. "You want to." She set her forehead against mine, and she was so close that I could feel her breath on my lips. "I can feel it."

And gods, I *did* want to, more than anything. I had to shut my eyes because the beseeching sparkle in hers was too much. "It doesn't matter what I want."

"That's *all* that matters," she argued, and her lips brushed against mine in the most imploring way, but she wouldn't finish the action.

She wanted *me* to. Only, I couldn't, because just one kiss wouldn't be enough. If I did, I feared I wouldn't be able to stop myself this time, and I'd give whatever she wanted and invest myself wholly, and I'd end in ruin. But was it wrong if I just let her do this? The barest graze of her lips against mine. I was so tempted to allow it. To part my lips further so she could brush them more completely, so I could skim her with the tip of my tongue. The modesty of it wouldn't last if I did, and I knew it. I could hear it in the hitch of her breathing. I could feel it in the rushing of my pulse and the longing ache between my hips.

I pulled away and opened my eyes, and Ava looked so defeated that my heart nearly stopped. I didn't want to hurt her. "Don't make this harder for me," I begged.

"It doesn't have to be hard, Kiena," she said, and like that night at the inn, she looked so confused. She just didn't get it.

"It does," I countered, taking another step back. "We can't do this."

"*Why?*"

"*You're still a princess.*" I whispered it so nobody passing the door would hear, but it was harsh in my frustration.

Her eyebrows furrowed as if I'd wounded her. As if that was the worst reason I could've possibly come up with. "I told you I don't care about my title."

"The *world* cares, Ava," I muttered. "Ronan, Valens, Cornwall, it's all the same." I made a broad gesture with my arms, "When all of this is over," and I motioned between her and me, "this would end too. It's not our choice to make." Her eyes softened the slightest bit with understanding. "I'm not royal. I'm not even from a respected family. We don't get to be together, you understand? It doesn't matter what you want, and it certainly doesn't matter what I want." I sighed, and now that I'd said it aloud, my voice lowered with the defeat I felt. "I don't know if that's even what you wanted from me, but there you have it. Rules. One we can't break because you've already won my heart, and now I'm begging you to leave it be."

Ava took in a broken breath and held it for a long moment, swallowing down whatever emotion she felt before giving a soft nod. "I'm sorry."

I shut my eyes, because what hurt the most was that she felt she had to apologize. "It was me," I told her. "I never should've kissed you back."

She shook her head. "I know the laws. I know them, I do. I just..." She never finished, just let out a heavy sigh. "Will you still come south?"

In an attempt not to feel so dismal, I said, "I'm uptight about you. Someone's got to keep an eye." Ava managed a tiny smile, but it didn't look like she had anything left to say. "Should we go and search for answers?"

She nodded, and wandered to the back of the infirmary to grab a fresh roll of linen. She strode toward the entrance with it, but stopped when she reached me. "Kiena?" Even though I was already looking at her, I hummed curiously. "Yours is not the only heart that's been won." And as if to reassure me that she wasn't upset, she put the linen roll in my hand. "Here, you left yours at the inn."

She meant my chest wraps, and I hadn't thought for a moment she'd have been paying that much attention, but she *had*, and that was *painful*. If there weren't so much preventing it, I'd have given her my entire heart that very moment. Gods, she deserved it. But though her admission and her attentiveness changed nothing about our circumstances, it did change something, because I knew she was telling me what she wanted from me. Her motive was pure, and as thanks for that reassurance, I leaned over and allowed myself to plant a brief kiss to the side of her head. In response to it, she gave my forearm a fond squeeze, then retreated out the door without saying anything else.

I flattened the roll and put it into a pocket of my vest, following Ava out of the infirmary and back toward the main hall of the cavern. There were more people around now, so many that it seemed a small town resided within the mountain. Some of them looked at Ava and me curiously, but most didn't appear to notice we were outsiders. Those who looked like civilians continued carrying loads of supplies to different destinations or stood around talking amongst themselves. All the others, at least half of everyone we saw, looked like some kind of warrior. Though I hadn't felt threatened since we'd been here, I did find myself worried about just what kind of 'warriors' these were.

Kingston was nowhere in sight when we reached the main entrance cave, but I managed to catch a familiar face in a small group of children that were running by. "Oscar," I stopped the boy. His group of friends continued on while he waited for me to say what I wanted, and I could tell he was impatient to chase after them. "Do you know where I could find Kingston?"

"Probably at the armory, my lady," Oscar said, pointing straight down a passageway we hadn't explored yet. "All the way down." And he ran off after his friends before I could tell him thanks.

Ava and I ventured in the direction Oscar had told us, past more tunnels and chambers until we reached the end. There was no door that opened up into the armory because the cavern widened significantly the farther we got, until we were standing in an opening the size of the massive castle doors in Guelder. It wasn't just an armory either. This portion of the cave was immense, so large that there was a small army of men and women training with all kinds of weapons. Broadswords and rapiers right ahead of us, archers visible at the distant rear, and other areas for hand to hand and maces and pole weapons. There was a blacksmith just to the left of the entrance, and a stockpile of weapons and supplies on our right.

"What *is* this place?" I muttered once more.

As I studied the large training ground and armory, I caught the eye of a familiar man standing around the swordsmen. When Kingston saw me, he hurried over, giving a small bow when he reached us.

"My ladies," he greeted. He straightened up and looked at Ava. "How was your meal?"

"Delightful," Ava told him, but her normal cheerfulness had been replaced by a somber curiosity.

I couldn't take it anymore. "Is this a bandit hideout?" I blurted. "Are you thieves?"

Kingston laughed. "No," he answered, unsuccessfully trying to wipe the smile off his face while he glanced around. "Not necessarily." I didn't know how to respond to that, I didn't even know what that was supposed to mean, but I couldn't keep Ava in dangerous company, and Kingston seemed to read some of that concern on my face. "I'd be more than happy to explain."

He made a motion for us to follow, then walked over to the armory and sat down on a wooden box with the branded image of arrows on it. Ava and I did the same. However, Kingston didn't start to explain the moment we got comfortable. I remembered that he'd wanted to speak to me alone, but instead of saying it bluntly, he extended an incredibly polite apology to Ava.

"I am sorry, my lady," he told her, "but these secrets are best bestowed on one set of ears at a time." Ava glanced at me. "If you'd like to explore," Kingston told her, "Lady Kiena is more than welcome to tell you everything afterward."

Ava gave me a questioning look, as if to make sure I was fine with that. I nodded. "I'll be just here," she told me, and while I was still unexpectedly comfortable, she seemed to have grown rather suspicious.

I smiled at her to let her know I'd be fine, and as she walked away to explore the training grounds, I pointed to her, telling Albus, "Eyes." He followed after her.

Both Kingston and I watched her wander over toward the blacksmith, and then he turned on his box to face me. "It's brave business traveling with runaway royalty," he said. My hand immediately set on my dagger, because he knew who Ava was and I'll be damned if I was letting anything happen to her. "No need," he assured me, glancing down at my weapon, "she's in no danger here. Not from any of us, you have my word." I loosened my grip on the knife, though didn't remove it completely. "You're in no danger either." He offered me a toothy smile, full of a sudden excitement I couldn't account for. "In fact, Kiena Thaon, should word get out around here who you are, you'd be quite like royalty yourself."

I took in a breath to try and respond, but I was so incredibly shocked by his words and his knowing my full name that I choked on it. "Excuse me?" I asked with difficulty, clearing my throat as if that would help. "How do you know me? *What is this place?*"

"When you found me last night," he explained, "I would have sworn you were your mother. You look so much like her in her youth." I met his dark brown eyes, feeling my brow converge with confusion. "Kiena, this is your father's rebellion, stronger than ever."

That statement hit my ears, but it didn't fully sink in right away. I let out a dry, disbelieving laugh and stood. I took in another breath to try and say something, but shook my head because nothing would come out.

"We've met before, you and I," Kingston said. "You weren't even old enough to stand on your own, but your father and I were close friends."

"Caedia," I repeated his surname under my breath, trying to think if I'd ever heard it mentioned before.

He released a humorless huff of laughter. "Caedia was my mother's maiden name. My given surname was Tithian."

My eyes widened with recognition. "Lord Tithian's son."

Kingston bowed his chin in acknowledgment. "I chose to follow your father when he defected from the ranks, and was by his side as he built this rebe-"

I held up a hand to keep him from saying any more, because I needed to reverse, and I already had enough to process without focusing on who he truly was. "My father's rebellion was destroyed, along with him and my family's name."

"That's what we'd have the king believe," he said. "We masquerade as bandits and common thieves, building ranks and buying time. Searching for our moment."

"My father," I began to ask, thinking of everything I'd ever been told about him. "Did he want power? Was he mad?"

"Mad, no," he answered. "Power..." His lips pursed with conflict. "Yes and no." I took in another deep breath, releasing it in a heavy sigh as I began to pace in front of him. It was already so much so fast; part of me couldn't believe this was real. "Are you alright?"

"Just," I rolled my hand in the air, "tell me. Everything, please."

He didn't even try to ease me into new information, just went straight into saying, "Your father wanted power, but not the kind that comes with a throne." I nodded but didn't stop pacing, so he continued. "All he wanted was for the people of this kingdom to be cared for, and he knew once Hazlitt had the throne that wouldn't happen. Fighting an international war with Ronan whilst there was unrest amongst rulers was tearing this kingdom apart, and he wanted it to end." When Kingston paused, I made a hasty hum for him to keep going. Now I wanted him to say everything so I could process it all at once. "When your father recognized Hazlitt's greed for power, when he learned the true motive behind our king's desire for the throne, he deserted the infantry to start a rebellion."

"Motive?" I cued.

"I don't know what Princess Avarona has told you, or what she knows herself," Kingston said, and I finally stopped pacing to meet his gaze. "Hazlitt is a sorcerer, hiding it from all but his most loyal followers and close military because of this kingdom's profound fear of magic." He watched me for a reaction. "You suspected as much?"

"Aye."

"Good, you know more than I hoped." He stopped again, this time inhaling a slow breath before saying, "The power your father wanted was also magic. Well, *more* magic."

"More?" I repeated, feeling the blood ice in my veins.

"Because of kingdom law, those born with the ability nurture it under penalty of death should they be caught. For most his life, your father chose not to risk it."

I sat back down immediately, pulling one foot up on the wooden box so my knee was against my chest. "Magic," I whispered, staring straight at the cavern floor and setting my chin on top of my knee. I didn't know what to think or say or do, or how to feel. I didn't know what it meant for Ava, or for me, or the kingdom. "My father had magic?"

"But not enough experience to stop Hazlitt," Kingston said.

"The princess said Hazlitt wants a book from Ronan," I told him, wondering if he knew better. "A book of dark magic."

"It's not the book he wants," he replied. "It's a bottle of elixir hidden within the pages. There's a mage in Ronan history, a woman who discovered such deep secrets of magic that she could bestow a dark power greater than anyone could be born with, or that anyone could learn in a single lifetime. Before she was put to death so she could never give that gift, she made the elixir in an attempt to bribe the king for her life. It can't be destroyed, but the king knew the consequences of magic that powerful, and so he locked it away."

I nodded understandingly. "But Hazlitt doesn't care for the consequences."

"No," Kingston agreed. "He doesn't."

I let out a heavy sigh. "I need to sit on this a bit before you tell me any more."

"Of course," he said.

We sat there for a minute in silence, during which I searched the immediate area for Ava, because in the intensity of everything I'd just heard, I'd lost sight of her. I spotted Albus before I spotted her – he was sat with the group practicing at swords. My eyebrows furrowed at that, because I'd told him to watch Ava and he always followed my instructions devotedly. Then I realized he *was* watching Ava, and picked up my head with shock. She was in the middle of a ring of swordsmen, with a practice rapier in her uninjured hand and dueling with another warrior. I hadn't known she could even hold a sword, let alone know how to use it. But she was, and she looked to be having an incredible amount of fun doing it. All of them were smiling; Ava, the man she was dueling, the crowd around them. Meanwhile, all I could do was stare, entirely perplexed.

Kingston must've noticed it for the first time too, because he chuckled, "Your princess has skill with a sword."

"She's not so delicate as she looks." I couldn't help that my lips curled with an impressed smile, even though my cheeks colored darkly at the fact that he'd deliberately distinguished her as *my* princess. She was his princess too. "And she's not *mine*," I clarified, adding with a sigh, "she couldn't be."

But even as I said that, Ava finished the duel, skillfully tripping her opponent off his feet and holding the point of her practice sword to his chest when he hit the ground. Then she happened to glance our direction, and when she saw that we were watching, she grinned at me, bending at the hips and sweeping her arm in an unsubtly flirtatious bow.

"I think any woman," Kingston began, laughing as he nodded toward Ava, "especially one so bold as that, might be whatever she desired."

94

"I've never been one to challenge fate," I told him. The last thing I needed was someone else encouraging my affection for her and making me feel like it was possible. Fate was that she was a princess, and I was far from viable as a suitor in every way.

"Maybe not yet," he said. "But it's in your blood."

I ignored that and changed the subject. "What do you know of her situation?"

He knew I was talking about Ava, and was silent for a few thoughtful seconds. "Next to everything." My eyebrows rose at that. "With our numbers, Kiena, I have eyes everywhere."

"You mean spies?" I interpreted, and Kingston nodded. "You said you were searching for your moment. What did you mean?"

"Hazlitt is well guarded," he explained, "not just by soldiers, but his magic as well. We've expanded our support considerably, infiltrated his military ranks, but gaining a man's trust takes time. The spread of influence is slow."

"Is it only numbers you need?"

Kingston shook his head. "Hazlitt has an ability for magic like nothing we've seen. But though his abilities are diverse, few of them are powerful."

"You need magic to defeat him," I supplied.

"Indeed."

"Can you not use what influence you have to find someone from Ronan?" I asked. "Ava said magic's more common there."

"The Ronan Empire keeps a close watch on its abled. Sends them to schools, apprenticeships, and positions that they wouldn't abandon for a rebellion in another kingdom."

"And an alliance with King Akhran?" I suggested. "Your goals align." Instead of answering, Kingston smiled at me with an amused glimmer in his eyes. "Have I said something wrong?"

"Not at all," he assured me. "You so look like your mother, but you've much of your father in you."

"I'm not a rebel," I told him.

"Aren't you?" he asked, casting a deliberate look toward Ava.

"I'm going home after this," I said, meeting his gaze and shutting him down with determined earnestness. "To my mother and brother. Start calling me a rebel and I'll have nothing to go home to." I stared back ahead of me. "A Thaon can't work, or purchase land, or apprentice, or do anything but survive. No matter his intentions, my father still damages the life my mother tries to maintain after his death. I won't do the same."

Kingston studied me for a long, silent moment before saying, "My apologies, Kiena. I meant no offense."

"It's forgiven," I said.

"Do you not fear the consequences of assisting the princess in her escape?"

"I do," I sighed, dropping my foot off the box and leaning forward with my elbows on my knees. "But the king sent me to retrieve her. As far as he knows, hopefully, I'm still searching."

"The king sent you?" he asked in shock. "You've met Hazlitt?"

"Once," I answered. "You fought with my father in the war?" He nodded. "Leon Leventhorp, you knew him?" Again a nod. "His son, Silas, is a knight in the king's guard. We grew up together. He recommended me as a tracker."

Kingston laughed, and I couldn't help but raise an eyebrow at him. "Fate is a peculiar thing," he chuckled.

Before I could respond to that, a pair of warriors entered the armory and stomped right up to Kingston. "Commander," one of them greeted. Kingston bowed his head at them in response. "We've had a scuffle with Valenian soldiers, and captured one of them. He wears the armor of the king's guard."

Kingston made an intrigued face and looked at me. "An acquaintance of Silas's, perhaps. Would you care to accompany me?"

I considered it for a moment before agreeing, and waved to get Ava's attention. She hurried over with Albus at her heels, and together we followed Kingston and his two warriors to see who they'd caught. We strode halfway down the long tunnel before turning down a side one. The path declined deeper into the mountain as we traversed steps carved into the stone floor, lower and lower until we reached a single door. The warriors entered first, then Kingston, Ava, and I, and they closed the door behind us. There were a handful of others who'd brought the king's knight down into this small dungeon, and they'd tossed the prisoner into one of the few cells. But when I saw who the prisoner was, my face paled.

It wasn't an acquaintance of Silas's. It *was* Silas.

Chapter 8

I could see the evidence of the fight Silas had been in before the warriors brought him here. His face was bleeding, and his hair was matted with sweat and dirt. His hands were bound behind his back.

"Release him," I told Kingston. I didn't want Silas hurt, and I knew little enough about these rebels that I had no idea what they'd do with him.

"You know him?" Kingston asked.

"This is Silas."

Kingston studied Silas for a long moment, and then glanced at me. "I'm sorry, Kiena, I cannot. Not until I know what he does."

My gaze met Silas's, I watched him look from me to Ava, and I recognized the emotion in his eyes. He was angry. At me, I had no doubt. He'd had faith in me that I'd do the job I was sent to, and I failed him.

"What will you do?" I asked.

"Question him," Kingston answered.

"How?"

He didn't respond to that with words, but with a look that I understood as 'however is needed.'

"Let me do it," I pleaded. "Keep him bound if you must, but get him out of there and let me talk to him. Please."

Kingston took me in for a silent minute, so tense and thoughtful in his consideration that I wondered how little he trusted me. He was probably right not to trust me – not even *I* knew where my loyalties were at the moment – and I already felt the pressure of that conflict bearing down on my chest.

After another minute, Kingston nodded at two of his warriors. "Open it."

They did, and after they'd opened the cell door, they retreated with Kingston out of the dungeon. Ava had remained at my side, so I leaned into her a little to whisper, "It's best if I do this alone." She followed after the warriors without a protest.

Now it was just Silas, Albus, and me. Silas trudged out of the cell only to lean back against the outside bars, watching me silently as I approached him. Though I got close enough to hug him, I didn't, and I didn't know what to say to him either. He was upset with me and I didn't know how to make it right.

"Hello, Albus," Silas said.

Albus had always loved him, but now he *growled* – a deep, throaty rumble so unnerving that Silas pressed harder into the metal at his back while his upper lip curled with frustration. And that pressure on my chest grew painfully the moment Albus growled, because he always knew. He'd never threatened Silas a day in his life, but he knew what I couldn't.

"What are you doing here, Silas?"

"What am *I* doing here?" Silas asked sarcastically. "I got *special* permission from the *king* to be out looking for you, because I know how skilled you are, and I knew there was no way you hadn't found her yet unless something had happened to you. I'm here because I was worried for you, Kiena. What are *you* doing here? Who are these people?" That was the last thing I could tell him, and when all I did was watch him silently, he shook his head with displeasure. My secrecy hurt him because we'd always been honest with each other, and I could see that the hurt made him defensive. It made him angrier. "You ran from the tavern last night," he said, and my eyes widened with shock because he'd been there. I hadn't recognized him, I'd been in too much of a hurry and the snowfall had been too thick, but he'd been one of the soldiers. He'd seen me run with Ava, and he glanced toward the door of the dungeon with a glare. "What are you doing with the princess?"

"All is not as it seems," I said.

"You had one task!" he snarled, so suddenly it sent me back a step. "It wasn't to ask questions. It wasn't to make decisions or choose sides. It was to find her and bring her back! My men are dead because of you!"

"You must listen to me," I begged. This wasn't the Silas I knew. Not the lighthearted friend I'd grown up with. He was irritated and probably still riled up from being captured, and so on edge that I could *feel* his tension. "The king is not what he'd have you believe."

"Avarona's manipulating you to escort her," he murmured skeptically.

"He's a sorcerer, Silas," I said, growing desperate by his bitterness. "All he wants is more power." Silas's cold brown eyes locked on me, giving me a hard stare that lasted ten long, uneasy seconds. But there was nothing of what I *actually* expected. No confusion. No shock or fright. It was as if the realization had struck me in the gut. "You knew," I choked. I thought we'd always been honest with each other, but he hadn't just been lying to me. *He'd* just tried manipulating me.

"I'm on the king's guard," Silas mumbled. "Of course I knew."

"I don't understand." I shook my head like that would help, like that would force away the truth of what I was being told or ease my own building hurt. "Do you know what he wants with her?"

He knew I meant Ava, knew I was asking if he'd been aware all along that Hazlitt would kill her on account of the alliance with Cornwall. "We are so close to winning this war," he said, "we've all made sacrifices." And I took a horrified step back. All it did was offend him. "God have mercy, Kiena. He's willing to give his own daughter for the kingdom! And you have the gall to look at me like that?"

He'd been keeping things from me this whole time, and the last thing I was going to do was tell him that Ava wasn't Hazlitt's daughter by blood. For all I knew, Ava being entirely Ronan would only make him care less. "Silas," I breathed, "what have you gotten me into?" My eyes filled with tears at the betrayal I felt. "How can you stand there and act like this is right when you know what he'll do to her?"

"Because it *is* right," he answered, and when I let out a disgusted breath, he took an earnest step forward, lowering his voice to ensure that no one outside the door could hear. "This kingdom has been at war since before we were born. It's been falling apart for generations, it's steps away from ruin."

"Because of Hazlitt," I expressed in irritation.

Silas clicked his tongue. "You blame the king like every other commoner who hasn't a clue what we go through or how hard we try. You haven't seen the battlefields." He took another step toward me. "But you've

99

seen how the people starve. You've been wanting all your life; Nilson goes wanting. Hazlitt *still* stands against those who would usurp his throne, who see this kingdom's people in poverty and would start another uprising anyway, for their own selfish gain."

He was probably talking about lords throughout the kingdom who thought they had a better claim to the throne than Hazlitt, but my eyes dropped guiltily. We were in the hideout of rebels, of a capable group of people who *would* start another uprising, of a group of people who had been inspired by *my* father. It put an intense pressure on my chest, and I began to feel the magnitude of this conflict in my heart. Silas believed in his cause wholeheartedly – I could see it in his eyes and hear it in his voice – but now that I had the hope that my father wasn't a traitor, now that I knew Ava's fate should she return to Guelder, I couldn't just abandon this.

I could feel myself growing more confused and torn by the second. "And the answer is an elixir that will give him *more* power?"

He squinted at me, with obvious shock that I knew so much, and I couldn't deny I was slightly thrown that he already knew it too. "Yes," he said, recovering from his surprise. "We get an alliance with Cornwall by whatever means necessary and we can defeat Ronan, we can end this war and Hazlitt can get the power he needs to send this kingdom into a golden era." He paused for a long moment, watching me closely as my eyes filled with tears, making sure I was absorbing the importance of what he was saying. To see if I would understand the need for Ava's sacrifice.

"You could live comfortable," he added. "When this war finally ends, our kingdom will prosper, and you can stop worrying about whether or not Nilson will make it into his teens. You can see your mother grow old." I sniffled, and when a heavy drop slid down my cheek, I ran the back of my hand across it. "It's not an easy choice to make, I know that. I know the princess, and I know she doesn't deserve this. But it must be done. There are more lives at stake than just hers."

I took in a deep, quivering breath, because this was it. This was the choice. Hazlitt was terrifying, and powerful, and cruel to those around him, and I'd seen little fruit from this war that had plagued my entire life, but maybe that elixir was all he needed. Maybe it would set the kingdom straight and things would be good again, and all it would take was handing Ava over. All it would take was going home and forgetting about her, and I could trust the fate of the kingdom to the *king*, and I could go back home where I belonged and care for my mother and Nilson.

"You should have left me out of this," I whispered, wiping my fingers across my cheek as another tear fell. "I can't let you take her. Find another way."

Silas blinked his disbelief. "That's what you'd have me tell *the king*? To find another way?" When I nodded my brokenhearted consent, his brow furrowed with a newfound animosity. "You fancy her," he accused. I glanced away to try and mask the guilt on my face. "You stupid, brain-boiled halfwit!"

"Mind your tongue," I said sharply. He'd never talked to me like that, not in the nineteen years we'd been best friends. I wouldn't allow it.

"Did you lie with her?" he demanded.

"Silas," I warned, but my steel was broken by a teary sniffle.

"It's a death sentence, you know that?" He watched me for a brief second. "Answer the question!"

"I will not," I muttered.

"Why?"

"Because," I told him honestly, and saying this to him for the first time in my life was agonizing, "I don't trust you right now."

"You don't-" he began to repeat, but stopped short because his face burned red. "You don't trust me? After *everything* we've been through, you're defending one simple girl who's risking an *entire war*, one I've put my life on the line for, and *you* don't trust *me*?" He took in a deep breath, letting it out in a furious rumble. "All I'm trying to do is keep you alive! Is to care for you as if you were my own kin! I gave you an opportunity! I gave you a better life on a bloody silver plate and you're throwing it away like it's nothing! You know what the king would have given you for returning her?" He paused, only to breathe so he could keep shouting. "He would've given you your surname back! He would've cleared you and given you wealth to redeem the life your traitorous father stole!"

"Don't do this." My eyebrows furrowed pleadingly. I didn't want this. I wanted him to understand. "Please, Silas. Give me another option. *Any* other option."

"I can forgive this betrayal," he said. "I'll escort you both to the castle. The king will never hear of your mistake. It's the only way."

My eyes brimmed with fresh tears, because I could see the resolve in his gaze, and I knew he could see the same in mine. "I can't do that."

His face flashed with wounded anger. "Do you even understand the stakes? Can you possibly comprehend the lives lost? The lives you're risking!" I pursed my lips to hold back a dismal frown. "Damn you, Kiena!" he yelled. "All you had to do was keep your hands away from her royal cunt! And you couldn't even do that!" Even though his wrists were tied, he was so angry that I took a frightened step back, but he took one forward. "You're following in your father's footsteps, and that fool girl will get you killed!" He turned his head toward the door, shouting, "You hear me, Avarona! The king will find and kill you both! You understand! Get in here, you whore!"

Without even thinking about it, my hand sailed through the air, and I slapped Silas hard across the cheek. It quieted him instantly, and I was so conflicted by what I'd just done that I couldn't decide whether to apologize or to keep grinding my teeth out of anger or to slap him again. Though Silas stopped yelling, he straightened up, chest heaving as he squared himself before me. For a moment, I feared he was so angry that he might break through the rope around his wrists and strike me in return. Then Albus set to growling at him again, and Silas side-glanced at the dog before taking a step back.

"She's got her claws dug deep in you," he said with a disappointment so severe it cut me to the bone.

"You're wrong," I told him, unable to mask the sadness in my voice. "Hazlitt has poisoned the ranks and you can't even see it. The Silas I used to know wouldn't sacrifice an innocent life for anything." He said nothing, only stood there with his jaw working back and forth furiously. "I hope you'll come to understand."

When I started for the door, he snarled after me, "If you leave, it's done." I reached the exit and stopped, turning to face him one last time. "If I mean so little to you, then walk out that door. Leave and everything you've ever been to me is *nothing*."

"I'm sorry, Silas." I grabbed the handle and opened it. "Don't try and find us."

"Traitor!" he hollered after me, and even though I'd already closed the door behind me, I could hear him yell, "I'll hunt you both!"

I leaned back against the other side of the door, feeling multiple pairs of eyes on me. I shut mine and took in a deep breath, trying with everything in me to push down all the emotion I was feeling. It didn't help. Needing to do something to work out my frustration and pain, I hurried away without saying anything to any of them, not even Ava. The closest thing I could think of was the armory. I rushed to it with Albus on my heels, and headed straight to the back where the archers were. I must've looked as upset as I felt, because even though none of them knew me, they stepped aside, opening every practice lane while I grabbed a bow from the nearest warrior.

And I shot arrow after arrow in rapid succession, another thud landing just seconds after the previous one. Pull. Silas had lied to me from the very start. Aim. He was willing to sacrifice an innocent woman. Release. After all these years, he'd threatened to hunt me too. Thud. He called Ava a whore. Pull. Aim. Release. He called me a *traitor*. Thud. Traitor. Thud. Traitor. Traitor. Traitor. I fired shot after shot until I'd filled the bull's eye with arrows, so many I'd begun to split them down the shaft.

I pulled back on the loaded bowstring again, and the moment after I released it, a hand set on my back. "Kiena," Ava prompted.

Shooting had hardly helped either. I threw the bow down, and though I didn't know when Ava had arrived or if she'd been watching me the entire time, I gave the briefest apologetic pursing of my lips and then hurried back out of the training grounds. The only place to get some privacy was back in that cave Kingston had given us. Ava and Albus were both following closely, but the nearer I got to the cave, the harder it got to control how my emotions were shifting. Frustration and betrayal were fading, and more and more I felt the pang of heartbreak. By the time Ava shut the door behind us, tears had flooded my eyes once again. I kept my back to her and the door, wiping at my cheeks and trying my hardest to blink the moisture away.

The only sound for almost a minute was my sniffling, and then I heard Ava's footsteps approach me. Instead of coming around to look at me or saying anything to try and make me feel better, her arms wrapped around my waist from behind. She simply hugged me, resting her head against my upper back and just leaving it there. Silas had no idea how wrong he was, because this girl deserved it far less than he thought. I knew she'd heard everything he'd yelled, all of them had heard his shouting, but she wasn't trying to defend herself. She wasn't telling me how inaccurate or heartless he'd been, or trying to assure me that she wouldn't lie, or promising her affection wasn't bribery. All she wanted was to comfort me, and her honesty was apparent in her selflessness. It had been since the very beginning.

"He thinks I've betrayed him," I whispered. She removed her arms so I could turn to face her, and when I couldn't stop a final tear from falling, she reached up to thumb it away. "He's been my best friend my whole life, and he thinks I don't care about him. I've hurt him and he'll never forgive me."

"He'll see how much you care," she assured me, her big blue eyes full of concern. "Silas is smart. One day he'll realize."

I managed to offer a grateful smile, though truly I felt so uncomforted that I just wanted to forget about it. "We should leave soon," I said distractedly. "The longer we're here, the more soldiers are catching up with us."

Ava nodded in agreement. "And Silas?"

I let out a heavy sigh. I didn't even know if Kingston would give me a say regarding Silas's fate, but I had to try. "I'll request that he be released in two days time. We'll have a head start."

Ava watched me for a long span of thoughtful seconds, eventually saying, "He threatened to hunt us..."

"I will not allow him to be imprisoned," I said, and there was still so much residual tension and frustration that I was instantly irritated at what I thought she was suggesting. It wasn't even an option if I had a choice. I owed Silas that much.

"Kiena, I know you care for him." Her voice was so soft, almost pleading me not to take offense, but she said it anyway. "But he's an unnecessary risk."

"It's out of the question!" I growled. "Do not mention it again." She blinked at me, shocked by the force with which I'd spoken, and I was immediately and painfully aware of my mistake. "My sincerest apologies, Ava," I said, bowing my head. "That was out of line."

"You've got to stop doing that," she said, looking calm as ever. "Stop treating me like I'm better than you." And the understanding and patience in her eyes when I met her gaze was calming. So appeasing and full of forgiveness that I wondered how I could've gotten upset with her in the first place. "I'll respect your request in regards to your heart, but for this partnership to work you must accept your place as my equal. If you're angry, *be* angry."

Only, I was so unable now to be angry that I didn't know what else to do. My shoulders slumped as I strode over to the fire. It was little more than glowing embers by now, but it still gave off heat, and so I sat down, pulling my knees up to my chest and wrapping my arms around them. Ava followed and lowered herself at my side, folding her legs beneath her.

"I'm not angry with you," I told her. "I'm just... frustrated." And I was confused, because even if I couldn't let Ava be killed, I was no longer certain I was doing the right thing. There were too many people involved. Too many people for whom either decision was the right thing, and Silas had put me in this position by keeping things from me.

I paused to let out a stressed sigh, and while I did, Ava timidly traced her fingers down the length of my arm, until she'd reached my hand. Instead of protesting, I let her take it, because I knew she was trying to help me feel better. I let her fingers intertwine with mine and I let her pull my hand into her lap. Because I loved how comforting it felt to be in contact with her, because while my mind and emotions were all over the place, it tethered me to something real. And because I'd already crossed lines more grave than this one. I'd already kissed her, and put my hands on her, and Silas probably believed I'd done so much more. I'd *thought* about doing so much more. What sin was this in comparison?

"When I was sixteen," I began to explain, running my thumb over the back of her hand, "there was a girl I'd met in town, and I'd taken to sneaking out at night to go and visit her at her father's farm. We spent most of those nights in the barn."

"Naughty," Ava muttered under her breath, and the teasing glimmer in her eyes made my lips twitch with an almost smile.

"We were never particularly quiet, you see," I continued, "and one night her father came out. By the gods, he was furious. Chased me clear off his farm." I couldn't help but chuckle when Ava rolled her eyes. "He didn't get a good look at me, though, it was so dark. So he got it in his head that it was Silas who'd been there, because he'd seen us around so many times and couldn't fathom it'd been a girl with his daughter." When I paused again, Ava hummed for me to keep going. "He confronted Silas, attacked him. He was such a large man. Nearly castrated him too, the way

Silas tells it, but Silas never told it was me. He just took the beating, and you know what he did afterward?" Ava shook her head. "He snuck her over to my cottage the next night with some bottles of wine. All three of us got piss drunk." I huffed at the memory, which made Ava laugh.

"Silas bought that cottage," I said, feeling my laughter subside as the heartbreak resurfaced. "The one we still live in." And Ava's eyes widened with surprise. "Because of our surname, we can't buy land. My mother worked a lord's farm before then, but he treated her like dirt because she was a traitor's widow. So Silas pinched things from the castle during his squireship to buy us a cottage." Ava looked like she wanted to laugh at the fact that Silas had been stealing from the castle, but she didn't because I couldn't stop a single tear from falling, and she used her free hand to whisk it away. "I paid him back most of it with what I earned hunting, but he gave us a way out. That's the kind of friend he is... was... I don't know anymore." I closed my eyes and took in a slow breath. "He's like family. I owe him my freedom, and my mother's. I owe it to him that he not be kept in a cell."

Ava nodded. "You won't hear another word of it from me."

Though I didn't meet her gaze, I gave a grateful smile and set my chin on my knees. "Promise me," I begged after a minute of reflection, because even if she *was* lying to me, or even if these rebels were misguided, I needed something to believe. "Promise me that everything you've learned in the castle confirms Hazlitt wants power only for himself. That he doesn't care about the kingdom or its people."

Ava's deep blue eyes studied my face with concern. "There's so little anymore that I can promise," she said, "but I know Hazlitt, and that I *can* promise. You have my word." All I did was nod and fall quiet to collect myself. I could feel Ava's eyes on me in those silent moments, until eventually she reached up with her free hand to push some of my loose hair behind my ear. "I knew what you were risking in taking me south... but I hadn't considered the things you'd be sacrificing." She squeezed my hand for emphasis. "Kiena, you don't have to do this."

Selfless. But I could never leave her. Especially not now that we knew Silas had spotted us. That he and an unknown number of other soldiers knew she'd come south, and they'd be looking for her from here to Ronan. I no longer doubted that she could take care of herself – she was far from fragile – but it didn't mean I wouldn't do everything in my power to make sure she got to Ronan safely. If Hazlitt truly did have the kingdom's best interest in mind, he'd find another way to end the war.

I leaned across the space between us to plant a lingering kiss to her forehead, and I whispered against her skin, "It's done." Ava pulled back to look at me, and I knew that she was aware my feelings had something to do with it, and it was so hard with how close she was and the way she kept glancing at my lips to remind myself that she was still royal. If her true father accepted her when we got to the Ronan capital, she'd still be a princess. "You know something?" I said to distract myself from where my desires were heading, and even though Ava could clearly tell why I'd done it, she leaned sideways into me and put her head on my shoulder, and I didn't care to stop her. "The king's a right asshole."

"You've no idea," she replied gravely.

"How is it you were raised by him and turned out alright?"

"It's like I said," she answered, "we are more than the legacies of our fathers."

"Turns out I might not be," I said, and that was truer than ever, because in not telling Silas where we were, I was supporting this rebellion, and in taking Ava south, I was supporting Ronan. It also seemed like now was the appropriate time to tell her everything that Kingston had told me.

She listened intently, never letting go of my hand or moving her head from my shoulder while she gave appropriate responses and asked questions – not all of which I had the answers to. She appeared shocked when I explained what this cave system was and who it belonged to, and even more so when I told her about my father's magic. Though she was clearly surprised about the magic, it didn't seem to scare her. In fact, I think my father having had magic was far more frightening to me.

I'd just finished telling her all about Hazlitt's sorcery when there was a knock on the door, and then Kingston entered with Oren at his side. Ava lifted her head from my shoulder when they walked in, and her grip on my hand loosened like she was giving me the chance to take it back if I wanted. I really didn't want to, but I caught the hint of a smirk on Kingston's lips at the position we were in, and it made me self-conscious. I didn't want him encouraging me to give any more than I already was, and so I did remove my hand.

"Kiena," Kingston greeted, and bowed his head to Ava, "Princess."

"Ava, if you will," she corrected him.

He nodded in consent and then looked at me. "I wanted to consult you about our prisoner." I watched him silently so he'd continue. "He knows nothing of this place or its purpose. Therefore, I will put his fate in your hands."

Even though I'd told Ava where I stood on dealing with Silas, I still glanced at her to make sure she approved. Her chin dropped in a nod.

"We should continue traveling tomorrow morning," I told Kingston.

"I thought as much," he agreed.

"I would like Silas to be released two days after our departure. Take him to a nearby town and set him free."

"As you wish," he said easily. "I'd like to aid you in whatever ways possible. Would you require a second horse, I will spare one for you, along with whatever supplies you should need."

"We'd be forever in your debt, Kingston," I said.

"Just arrive at your destination safely," he replied, and then turned to Oren, telling him, "have Kiena's horse and another prepared come morning." Oren handed over the sword he'd been holding, and bowed to the two of us before retreating out the door. "May I join you?"

I motioned for Kingston to come over, and he crossed the cave to sit on the opposite side of me as Ava. "A gift for you," he said, handing Ava the sheathed longsword Oren had given him. "A woman with your skill should have a weapon of her own."

"It's wonderful," she said, pulling it halfway out of the sheath to examine it with a grin on her face. "I am eternally grateful."

He offered a genuine smile, appearing pleased that she enjoyed the gift so much. His eyes met mine soon after, and I recognized the sobering look in them. It was the same as when he'd asked to speak to me alone, only this time he was hesitating in telling Ava to leave, as though he wanted me to decide.

"I've told her everything," I assured him. "She's welcome to know what more I should learn."

"Very well," he agreed, reaching into a pocket within his coat, "I also have a gift for you." He pulled out something that was folded up in leather, and proceeded to unfold it until he'd revealed what was inside. "It was your father's."

It was pendant on a long chain necklace. A dragon made of some dark metal with its tail hung and twisted around a black opal, a stone so dark

108

that the red, blue, yellow, and green specks within it seemed to glow by some unnatural light. It was enchanting to look at. It called to me, attracted my attention as though it were saying my name. I reached out to accept it, but Kingston clasped his hand over it before I could touch it.

He gave me an apologetic smile. "Allow me to explain, before you take it." I nodded eagerly. "It was your father's, given to him by his father, and his father's mother, and so on." He carefully removed his hand to offer me another glimpse, for some reason watching closely to ensure I didn't make contact. "Nilan, your father, told me of a legend, of a small village deep in the mountains of the Amalgam Plains. So deep, Kiena, they lived alongside dragons."

I didn't say anything, intent on listening, but Ava took in a breath and leaned forward with interest.

"Dragons all over the world were being hunted," Kingston continued. "These were some of the last. Armies wouldn't venture so deep into the mountains, but dragon hunters would, and did. So the dragons communed with the earth gods to seek protection. In exchange for that protection, the gods were able to take some of the dragons' strength and offer it to the villagers as different kinds of magic. Skin walking, control of beasts or the elements or even humans, the ability to heal oneself or to disappear or move on a cloud of smoke."

Kingston paused to remove the necklace from the leather, and dangled it before me. "That magic was bestowed through these; pendants, warded against darkness and given each villager, compatible with their blood only. Thus, compatible with their bloodlines."

"This," I began, motioning toward the necklace, "is magic? Dragon magic?"

"It's what your father believed," he confirmed. "I've not put it in your hand because, once you touch it, there is no going back. You will have your bloodline's abilities."

"Which were?" I asked, my eyes fixated on the gemstone. I was so tempted to reach out and touch it, but there was an instinctive fear of magic that caused my heart to speed up and my hands to remain at my knees.

"The elements, mostly," Kingston answered. "Your father governed the earth and water, just like his father, and I tell you, until his death, he seemed almost immune to injury. His grandmother controlled fire and weather. The gods taught your ancestors how to control their magic, lessons that have been diluted and lost through the ages." He lowered the necklace back into the leather. "If your bloodline contained other abilities, your father didn't know of it." He extended the leather and pendant, setting it down in my hand so the necklace never touched my skin. "There is risk, Kiena, in any magic. Should you not be able to control it, you will be consumed by it. You will be a danger to yourself and others. Do not accept that gift lightly."

I stared down at the necklace in my hand, considering the risk Kingston spoke of. I had no desire to chance harming anyone I cared about, even if it was on accident. "How did my father learn?"

"His father taught him," he answered, with a twinge of sympathetic sadness in his voice.

"And you?" I suggested hopefully. "You can't help me?"

Kingston shook his head. "My apologies, Kiena, I know nothing of what it takes to practice magic."

I offered a small smile to let him know it was fine. "Thank you for keeping it safe all these years."

"I had hoped to find you someday," he said with a nod. "As it happens, you found me."

He paused for a thoughtful moment, eyes going wide as if he'd suddenly remembered something, and then he pulled two more necklaces out of his pocket. These were each made of glittering steel. The medallion was only the size of a copper coin and in the shape of an arrowhead, point downward and with such a large head of an owl in it that all you could really see was the eyes, tufts of its ears, and its beak.

"This is our symbol," he said. "If you ever see someone with this, you can trust them. We are the Vigilant. Your father chose that name." He gave one to each of us by putting it around our necks, and then reached under the neck of his own tunic to show that he was wearing one too. "You never know when you might need a friend." We nodded with understanding, and he watched us for a few seconds before rising to his feet. "I should go and see to preparations. Come find me if you need anything."

We both gave him grateful smiles as he left. Once he was gone, I took to studying the dragon necklace in my hands again, and I could feel Ava leaning into me to get a better look too. The idea that it would give me magic if I simply touched it was both exciting and terrifying. There were so many dangers attached to it, and, for now, I was convinced those dangers might outweigh the benefits.

"Would you like to see it?" I asked Ava with a laugh, because she was leaning into me so much it had begun to knock me over.

She nudged me teasingly for the sarcasm behind my tone, and reached out to take the pendant from the leather wrapping. She should have been able to touch it like Kingston had, but the moment her hand set on it, there was a flash of pale blue sparks, like lightning. They jumped at Ava's fingers, and even though she'd let out a yelp of pain and yanked her hand back, the sparks followed, biting at her for seconds until she'd shaken it out. But once the shocks were gone, she froze, as if petrified, for only a short second before she gasped and the brilliant blue of her eyes turned a swirl of dark, blood red.

"Ava?" I prompted, tossing the necklace aside in my intense worry.

She shut her eyes tight and pressed the heels of her hands to them. "My back," she muttered, sucking in a hard breath through her teeth.

I obeyed the implied instruction, and lifted the fur and her tunic up to expose her skin. The crow-shaped scar on it was glowing the same blood red her eyes had turned. Kingston said the pendant was warded against darkness. It had to be true. It had to have triggered whatever this mark was for, and that was concerning in more ways than I cared to think about.

Ava took in a slow, controlled breath, and as she let it out again the glowing faded, until once more, it was simply a scar. I let her clothes fall back down, meeting her gaze to find that her blue eyes were full of tears.

"Are you alright?" I asked, cupping her face in my hands and using my thumb to wipe away a tear.

"I *am* cursed," she sniffled. Saying those words caused a few more drops to spill down her cheeks. "I saw him. I saw Hazlitt." She reached up, taking one of my hands from her face to squeeze it hard in her own. "And he saw me."

"What do you mean?" I asked, my eyebrows furrowing with unease. "Does he know where we are?"

"I don't know," she said. "But I saw where he was, at the castle. So he might." She pulled away from my hand with a sense of urgency, blinking away the tears. "We must leave." She stood and buckled her sword's belt around her waist, and then began to roll up the sleeping furs so hastily

111

that she did a messy job of it. "I cannot allow something to happen to the people here should we stay any longer."

"Ava." I stood up too, but she ignored me to set the furs by the door, returning to roll the second set. After frantically setting those by the door too, she opened it, glancing out as though she expected Hazlitt to be here already. I strode over and grabbed her by the shoulders, turning her around to face me. "Ava," I insisted, "be still." And though it looked difficult, she met my eyes and tried not to move. "Are you alright? Did it hurt you?"

She took in the concern on my face, and that seemed to calm her more than anything. She dropped her head forward against my shoulder. "No. I'm fine."

"You're the smarter one of us," I told her, wrapping my arms around her for comfort. "I need you to keep your head." She huffed with slight amusement, and I gave her one tight hug before pushing her back enough so she'd look at me. "On my life, I won't let anything happen to you."

"I know." She stretched upward to peck me on the cheek. "And I'd do the same for you, but we owe it to Kingston to depart immediately."

I nodded my agreement, and now that she was a bit calmer, we gathered our things and went to search for Kingston. When we explained to him what had happened, he seemed to think it best that we leave right away as well. The horses were prepared, and after giving our thanks for their hospitality, Ava and I continued our journey south.

Chapter 9

e'd been traveling for days now since we'd left the Vigilant camp, following along the main road that connected Valens to Ronan. We were technically in Ronan now, and everything was changing. Though we'd been traveling uphill all day, crossing the last mountain range between here and Ronan's capital, it wasn't getting colder. It was getting warmer. There was still a chill in the air, but the snow had been thinning considerably since yesterday. By now, all that really remained was a frosty glow on the foliage around us. I was so accustomed to the bitter cold that I'd even shed my fur coat, and was starting to wonder what I'd do about the heat infamously related to Ronan.

Ava was traveling at my side atop the horse that Kingston had given her. Right now she was laughing: an infectious, open laugh that echoed in the thinning woods around us even though I wasn't finished with my story. I was telling her about how I'd dealt with some older boys who'd harassed Nilson a couple of years ago. Anytime Nilson got near town or went to the river outside it with any of his friends, they'd terrorized him. So I'd snuck down to the river and kept out of sight so Nilson wouldn't see me. Clearly I hid the boys' clothes, but even better was that I'd set Albus on them once they got out of the water.

"Completely nude?" Ava asked, still cackling.

"Aye," I answered. "Ran baring their pasty bums all the way back to town. Albus chased them at least a mile."

Ava snorted. "And what did you do with their clothes?"

"I let Nilson decide." As I replied, I peered ahead of us to see how the terrain was changing. We were almost to the top of this mountain. "He'd been plotting his revenge," I continued, "though he had little means to executing it." Ava nodded in anticipation. "He'd discovered where they all lived. So he cut out the back of all their trousers and we dropped the clothes off at their doorsteps."

"You Thaon's are a ruthless lot," Ava accused with a delighted laugh.

I hummed my agreement. "King Hazlitt had better be careful."

"I'm sure he has nightmares about seat-less trousers."

"Letting Nilson on the king will be a last resort," I teased.

Ava laughed off the conversation for a minute before saying, "I wish I could have met your brother."

"He would've liked you." I imagine Nilson and Ava would've gotten along very well. He was only ten years old, but I almost envied his charm when it came to girls. Almost. "What will you do?" I asked, following the direction my thoughts were taking me. "If you can't stay in Ronan?"

Ava considered it for a long moment without looking at me, and then shrugged. "Perhaps I'll go with you and meet Nilson after all."

She sounded so casual about it, in a way that made it seem like she wouldn't have minded if that was what really happened. But all it did was hurt, because it felt like she was joking when being with her was one of the few things I'd ever wanted out of life. I wanted it more every day. Every time she sat by me at the fire at night, every time she kissed my cheek and grabbed my hand and *smiled* at me.

"You shouldn't say those things," I murmured.

Though I wasn't looking at her, I could sense that she'd glanced over at me with surprise. "Why?"

"Because our fortunes could never align like that."

"Kiena," Ava said, with a sigh so soft that I almost didn't hear it. "Sometimes things are only impossible because you believe them to be." I didn't know what to say to that, so she added, "If my real father doesn't accept me, how many other choices will I have?"

I didn't answer, but I realized what she meant. She had no other choices. If King Ironwood didn't accept that she was his daughter, if he didn't decide to throw us both in prison for being from Valens, where would she go? She couldn't go back to Guelder, and she'd shown no interest in seeking out her mother's other family in Ronan. So why wouldn't she go with me? But the fact that it was so much more probable than I'd allowed myself to think was as exciting as it was terrifying. If she went with me, she wouldn't be a princess. No one would stop us from being together, and all it would take was a rejection in Ronan.

The length of silence had been so extended that Ava finally asked, "Would you not want me to?"

"No, that's not it," I assured her. "I just, I don't know what else I expected you to say." I paused with hesitation, weighing the consequences for a moment before saying, "I've been afraid to want."

"What is it you want?" she asked quietly, as if she already knew the answer and was scared of deterring me from saying it.

But I wouldn't say it, not directly. "What I want makes me selfish," I answered. "And that makes me incapable of being anything but afraid." I *wanted* Ava, but more than that I wanted *Ava*. I wanted her not once, or not from now until I left her in Ronan. I wanted her always, but hoping that she'd be rejected in Ronan simply so she'd be with me was wrong. It was hoping that the family she'd always dreamed of, that the home she so desperately wanted didn't want her, and I could never wish that. "Believing in something's impossibility is simpler than hoping for it when you shouldn't."

I finally looked over at her, only to see that she was watching me with an understanding sympathy in her eyes. "I used to feel that way about home," she said, and then let out an amused breath. "Hoping *is* terrifying."

I nodded my agreement. In the lull in conversation, I noted how we'd finally reached the peak of the mountain's incline. However, it wasn't like I expected. The mountain didn't descend after the peak. We'd reached a plateau, one that stretched for miles and miles and was our first break from the thick forest. There were scattered trees, but not enough to provide us with cover, as it was mostly tundra and boulders.

"Can I ask you something?" I asked, scanning around us as we began to traverse the lengthy top of the mountain, making sure there were no soldiers on the road because we now had a clear view of its entirety. Ava hummed her consent. "How did you find out King Ironwood was your father?"

"I've always known," she answered, much to my surprise. "My mother told me when I was a child. She used to tell me stories of Ronan, many were about him."

"You don't talk much about your mother," I pointed out.

Ava's lips pursed with a regretful smile. "Hazlitt is an even crueler husband and father than he is king. It broke her long before I learned to steel myself against it." Her shoulders slumped a bit, and I could already see why she never talked about it. "Where my mother learned complacence was the only way to lessen the heat of his temper, I learned that defiance was the quickest; his wrath was worse, but it didn't come as often. Still... it was hard to see my mother's complacence as anything less than making her an accomplice."

"Do you resent her for it?" I asked.

She shook her head. "The times I made him particularly furious, he took it out on her too, but she never once told me to stop fighting him. She encouraged my fortitude."

I didn't exactly know what to say now, but I understood why it was so important for Ava to get to Ronan, to put a stop to Hazlitt and to rescue her mother from him. It didn't seem like she wanted me to say anything either, so we rode along in silence for a minute. After that, I began to notice a changing in the tundra half a mile ahead of us. It had been getting darker, and now I realized why. The mountain was split, and there was a massive gap that we'd have to cross to get to the other side.

"Whoa," I muttered, kicking my heels back and not bothering to stay on the road in order to get to it faster, because I'd never seen something like this and was fascinated. I wanted to see how deep it went.

Brande picked up to a trot, carrying me forward to the massive chasm, and when we reached it, I dismounted to poke my head over the sharp edge of the cliff. And it was *deep*. It cut through all the way to the bottom of the mountain, and was so wide that I could actually see down to the ground below. Surely travelers traversed crossways through the mountain using the road at the base of the canyon.

"Kiena," Ava called, finally catching up and stopping a good thirty feet from me at the edge. "Please be careful."

I took a few steps back from the cliff, and turned to face her as she got off her horse. "Did you know about this?"

She strode over slowly, and I noticed that she appeared cautious. "Yes." When she reached me, she grabbed my arm with one hand, inching just close enough to the edge to see how far down it went. "Though it didn't sound quite so deep when I read about it."

I glanced in the direction the main road twisted off. "There's a bridge."

Ava paced away from the edge and all the way back to her horse before answering. "You know, it wouldn't be the worst thing if we found a way around."

My eyebrows rose with disbelief. We'd opted for going up and over the mountain because the entire range of it went on for over fifty miles. That was days of extra travel that would be doubled by now if we decided to go around. Not knowing how many soldiers were trying to find us or how far behind they were, that was a risk I didn't want to take if we didn't have to.

"Let's have a look at the bridge at least," I suggested.

It was with obvious reluctance that Ava got back on her horse and followed me the distance to the main road. When we reached it, I dismounted again to examine the bridge that spanned the canyon. It was wide enough for a carriage to cross, and multiple ropes that were thicker than my arm supported the wide wood planks of it. Sturdy seemed like an understatement, but just to be sure, I strode out onto it and jumped up and down.

"Kiena!" Ava protested. Once more, she'd stopped her horse a good distance from the chasm.

"It's perfectly safe," I told her, and to prove it I mounted Brande again, rode him out onto the bridge, and turned him in a circle. "See?" All she did was shake her head, refusing to so much as look at me like she was terrified I'd plummet to an early death. So I rode over to her, asking, "You're afraid of heights?"

"I thought I could do it," she said, "that's why I didn't say anything. But I can't."

"You can," I encouraged. "Close your eyes if you'd like," and I motioned to her horse, "she'll get you across."

"Are you *completely* mad?" Ava asked, and though she was entirely serious, it was so melodramatic that it took an effort for me not to laugh. "Trust the horse to get across on her own?"

"I promise she wants to die no more than you do." Despite my effort, I chuckled a bit, and Ava's brow furrowed pleadingly, because she truly couldn't do it and my amusement wasn't helping. It wasn't until I actually studied her, noticed how stiff she was while her hands' grip on the reins trembled, that I realized she was literally terrified. "Would you trust *me*?"

117

I got off Brande again, and Ava hadn't answered because she was so uncertain, and she hadn't tried to move. So I walked over to her, took Maddox off the rear of her saddle, and shifted the bird onto Brande's back. Then I slid Ava's foot out of the stirrup, put my own in and lifted myself up onto her horse, sitting directly behind her.

"We'll be too heavy," she argued, her voice shaky.

"Ava, see those tracks?" I pointed to the dirt below us, to a set of straight grooves in the ground that disappeared at the bridge. "Those are from a carriage, and the bridge is still standing. If they can make it, we can make it." I reached around her, taking the reins from her hands with one of my own. The other arm I wrapped around her chest to hold her against me. "Close your eyes."

I couldn't see her face from behind her, but I was certain she'd closed her eyes because she grabbed the arm wrapped around her chest with both hands, and leaned her head back on my shoulder. But she was still tense, especially when I kicked my heels and the horse started forward. Her grip tightened as she went rigid.

To distract her from it, I said, "Tell me something more about you." The horse took its first steps onto the bridge, and at the shallow clomp of its hooves against the wood, Ava's grip clenched again. "Tell me about your first kiss."

"My first kiss?" she repeated.

"Aye," I agreed, briefly glancing back to make sure Albus and Brande were following behind us. "I'm curious. How old were you?"

"Fifteen," Ava answered, and I hummed so that she'd continue. "It was a stable boy."

"How very predictable," I teased.

"Quiet, you," she giggled, and I was glad that I could feel her relaxing already. "I'd caught him looking at me many times, and I was determined to know what it was like." Ava's hold on my arm loosened, but she didn't remove her hands completely.

"Did you enjoy it?" I asked.

"Not at all," she answered, so at ease now that I actually peeked around her to see if her eyes were still closed. They were. "I didn't like his lips or his hands or the shape of his body."

I murmured my understanding, and to keep the conversation going so she'd remain calm, asked, "And the first time you kissed a woman?"

"A week later," Ava said, and we both laughed at that. "Hazlitt was entertaining the Duke of Geladria and his family. They stayed with us for almost a month... His daughter didn't seem to mind that I flirted when no one was around, so I kissed her."

"And you liked it better," I mused.

"So much better," she confirmed. We reached the end of the bridge, but Ava continued talking so she didn't notice, and I didn't want to stop her and, frankly, I didn't want to get back on my own horse. "Women smell different, and sound different, and feel different. They even taste different. It's better. More comfortable." She took in a deep breath, releasing it in a relaxed sigh. "I didn't love her by any means, but I figured out what I wanted, and what I liked. It was more valuable to me than anything I studied."

"How so?"

Ava opened her eyes, and glanced behind us to see that we were a safe distance off the bridge by now. While I pulled back on the reins to finally bring the horse to a stop, she turned just enough to look at me, and by the smirk on her face, I could tell she was entertained I hadn't told her we'd made it to safety.

"It had given me resolve," she finally answered, watching as I got off the horse, "to refuse suitors I knew could never make me happy." Once I stood beside her horse, she glanced back toward the bridge again, and then down at me. "Thank you, Kiena."

It was one of those circumstances she would've given me a grateful peck on the cheek. I could even see the desire for it in her eyes, and since she was too high on horseback to reach my face, I took her hand and pressed the back of it to my lips. "You're welcome."

There wasn't more than an hour and a half left of daylight, so I figured we could stop now. Especially because I wanted to get settled before dusk, as the lack of forest cover made it so I wouldn't start a fire for fear of being seen.

"We should make camp," I said, pointing to a large boulder in the distance that we could sleep behind. "I'd like to take your stitches out before it gets dark."

"It's time?" she asked, grinning. She'd never complained about them, but I knew how much of a nuisance they could be.

119

I nodded, and together we headed away from the main road and to the massive boulder. We stopped behind it, and before pulling out my medical supplies, I grabbed some of the smoked meat Kingston had packed for us. I gave some to Albus and Maddox while Ava set out our sleeping furs, and once she was comfortable on top of hers, I strode over, giving her some of the meat on a tin plate while I sat down to work on her wrist.

Ava handed me her arm, swallowing a bite of food before saying, "I was beginning to think you'd leave them in forever."

"To get in the way of your fearsome battle scars?" I asked playfully. "Not a chance." I clipped the first stitch with my knife, and noticed how Ava's fist clenched with pain when I began to pull it out. "You can take my shoulder."

She set her food down to grab my shoulder with her free hand. "Have you given yourself stitches?" she asked, hand tightening with the next thread I removed.

"Countless times." I nodded toward the dog curled up a few feet away. "Albus too."

"You're quite the careful surgeon," she complimented as I pulled out another.

I moved on to the final one with a soft laugh. "Albus might disagree."

She chuckled, but remained silent while I grabbed the disinfectant and rubbed some over the nearly healed wounds in her wrist. It was well enough that I probably didn't need to wrap it back up, but I did anyway because I figured it was better to be safe. As I was securing the end of the bandage, Ava's hand on my shoulder slid up to my neck, and she leaned forward to finally press a grateful kiss to my cheek.

It was no different than any other time she'd done it, except for the fact that now she didn't actually say thank you, and she didn't simply touch her lips to my skin. It felt like it lasted longer than usual. Like her lips hovered for a moment before touching down and were slow to draw away, and she didn't draw away completely. It was long enough for me to finish the bandage, and in spite of myself, I let my hands linger at her wrist. I let them slip down to her hand and settle on either side of it.

And I didn't know what to do. If she'd expressed her thanks in words I could've said 'you're welcome,' but she hadn't, and I realized she was hesitating to completely pull away because I'd leaned into her lips even before my hands clasped around hers. I'd closed my eyes against the feel of them, and, gods help me, I was so immediately tempted to turn and capture her mouth with my own, and she knew it. She could sense it. I was so near doing it too. After everything that had happened today, after the shred of hope she'd given about how she'd go with me if she couldn't stay in Ronan, I *was* going to kiss her. I turned my head, and lined my lips with hers.

"Just once," I whispered, a pleading breath that she'd stop me if I hadn't the strength to.

Her eyes met mine, full of a conflict I'd never seen in them before. "Our hopes are at odds," she said, and I knew what she meant. She hoped to have a home in Ronan, but she knew that I hoped otherwise. Shutting her eyes tight, she took in a deep breath before opening them again to let me see they were full of tears. "I'm sorry, Kiena," she said, dropping her forehead against mine in a way that let me know she wouldn't kiss me.

I pulled back, refraining from letting my confusion show as I set my fingers under her chin to tilt it up, to get her to look at me. "For what?"

"I told you that I'd leave your heart be," she said, sniffling and leaning away from my hand to wipe at the first fallen tear. "And I've gone and convinced you that there's a real chance." That *stung*. I couldn't tell if it was hurt or anger or the fact that I felt stupid for almost giving in, but it caused a pang in my chest. Ava noticed the hurt look on my face, and caught my hand in her own. "That came out wrong."

"How *did* you mean it?" I took my hand back as my brow furrowed with offense. "What do you want from me, Ava?"

"I want you to know that I thought it would be easy," she uttered. "Whether I had you or not, I thought it would be easy to know you'd leave me in Ronan because I'd have the family I always wanted. But it's not. Every day it gets harder, and the more I want you, the more I realize how much it will hurt to let you leave." She wiped at her now tear-soaked cheeks. "The more I want to kiss you, the more I understand why you want to resist." I wasn't angry anymore, but it still hurt worse than ever. "So I resist for you," she said, taking in a calming breath when I reached up to thumb a tear from her eye. "Because it's what you want."

I sighed, falling silent for a few moments to let that sink in. The worst of it was that no matter what happened, Ava would be disappointed. Either her father would reject her or I'd have to leave her. And I *did* have to leave. I couldn't stay with her because I had to look after my mother and Nilson. That wasn't a choice.

"So you know," I said, wiping away the last of her tears and trying to give a sarcastic smile to cheer her up. "You probably should've just kissed me. Don't know when you'll get another chance."

Ava gave a tearful laugh and rolled her eyes. "I'll try to remember for next time," she said, and pulled her knees up to her chest. "If only you knew how hard it was to resist you. I don't know if I could have stopped you after just one."

"I *do* know," I corrected. I brushed my thumbs over the remaining moisture on both her cheeks, and pressed a tender kiss to her forehead. "Don't cry." But she sniffled one last time, so I added, "I've never made a girl I fancied cry before."

"You fancy me?" she asked, like that was news to her even though she had that flirtatious smile at the corner of her mouth. And that smile combined with the dew still in her eyes made her look so righteously adorable that I was on the verge of kissing her again. I more than fancied her. I dared say I was falling in love with her.

Instead of answering directly, I narrowed my eyes. "You're terrible at playing stupid." At the accusation, she bared her teeth in a knowing grin, and I couldn't help but laugh, "Eat up."

I went back to Brande to grab my own food out of the saddlebags, and once I had it, I resumed my seat near Ava. We ate in silence as the sun began to set, but finished with the heavy gray of dusk remaining. Ava took both of our tin plates to put them away, and when she came back, she dropped onto her stomach on her sleeping furs, facing downward so she could dote on Albus, who'd curled himself at the foot of her blankets. He'd been sleeping, but the moment she laid down, he rolled onto his side, lazily exposing his belly just enough that she could rub it. It never got old watching the way she was with him. How she adored him as though she'd raised him herself. He certainly didn't mind either, given the way he scooted after a moment, turning in a circle so he could lay his head near her hands and she could rub behind his ears.

I watched them for a minute before curiosity caused me to reach into an inner pocket of my vest, where I'd stored my father's necklace. Just because I hadn't decided yet what I wanted to do about it didn't mean I couldn't sense its pull. Even before I unfolded it from its leather wrappings, it was like I could feel its power. A steady thrum of energy had been vibrating in my blood all day. Excited and calling, brimming with something I could only describe as a stimulated current that I knew would relent at my touch alone.

All it would take is a touch, and who knows what kind of magic I'd get. Control of an element is what Kingston seemed to believe, but which one? I'd never been particularly fond of any element over another, if that's even how it worked. Maybe I didn't get to choose at all. My thumb stroked the soft leather that separated the metal necklace from my hand, tracing around the pendant so dangerously close that I was nearly touching it.

All it would take... But if I couldn't control it then I could hurt Ava, I could hurt Albus or Brande, and when I returned home I could hurt Mother or Nilson. There was no one to teach me, and I had no idea how difficult it would be to learn. That terrified me. It was the only thing keeping me from actually meeting metal with flesh.

"What will you do?" Ava asked, turning back around so she was laying right ways and slipping under her blanket.

I folded the necklace back up and returned it to my pocket, then got situated within my own furs beside her. "I don't know," I answered. I turned on my side to face her, and it was getting dark enough now that I could barely see her. "Think on it more."

She folded one arm beneath her head, and reached up with her other hand to run her fingers through the fur at the edge of her blanket. "Are you afraid?"

Where I'd previously been so reluctant to let Ava see my fears, now I took comfort in sharing it with her, because I knew she'd do nothing but make it better. I hummed my confirmation. "I don't know how to make sure I can control it." I shrugged. "Or if I even have what it takes."

"There is greatness in you," she said, "I saw it the very moment I met you."

And she spoke with such confidence that I knew it to be nothing but what she truly believed. Like I knew she would, she made me feel better, and while I did blush at the compliment, it wasn't her words that were responsible. It was her faith in me. Effortless and firm although I felt I'd done so little to earn it. I reached over to set my hand on top of hers, and she rotated her own enough that she could run her thumb over the backs of my fingers.

"I think you're destined for incredible things," she continued. "If you decided to, I know you could do it."

It wouldn't have mattered how hard I was trying to fight how deep my feelings for her were getting, my heart swelled. So much that I pulled her hand across to my furs, just to hold it beneath my chin in both my own. "How is it you believe in me so?"

She was quiet for a minute, thinking to herself as if she truly wanted to give me the most genuine answer. "You've such a powerful sense of justice, Kiena," she said eventually. "You've compassion like I've never seen, it's in everything you stand for. Everything you do." She paused, and her thumb made a mindless stroke against my hand. "You believed in me when you had every reason not to, and you risked everything for me on blind conviction." Her eyebrows converged with an emotion I could only suggest was overwhelming gratitude. "I owe you the world."

I dropped my chin to kiss her hand, saying, "You owe me nothing, Little Will-o'."

It was too dark now to see her at all, but as she squeezed my hand, I could practically feel the smile on her face. Neither of us said anything after that. Soon my eyes began to droop closed, and not long after, I fell asleep. Not once the entire night did Ava take her hand back. I woke up the next morning with it in the same spot beneath my chin, clasped comfortably between my own.

I couldn't really help myself when I touched my lips to the backs of her fingers, and at the same time I caressed her arm. Her skin had been exposed to the cold air all night, and was icy when I touched it. The only explanation was that she'd braved the cold in order to keep holding my hand, and for that I planted another kiss while I began to rub some heat back into her flesh. I also didn't miss the fact that her lips curled with a smile at the start of my care, alerting me that she was awake.

"Did you sleep well?" I asked.

She blinked her eyes open, and had just been about to answer when Albus rose to his feet, letting out a deep growl. I turned to look in the same direction that he was, and when I saw what he was growling at, I let go of Ava's hand and rolled onto my stomach to push myself up. There was a group of horsemen, at least eight by the glimpse I'd caught, and less than a mile away on the other side of the bridge. And though they were wearing plain clothing, they seemed particularly interested in Ava and me.

"Get up," I said, springing to my feet. "We've been spotted."

Chapter 10

va bolted upright, scrambling to her feet as I hurried to gather my sleeping furs. The moment I'd stood, the men across the canyon kicked their horses to a gallop. They were nearly at the bridge, less than another minute and they'd have already reached us.

I was in such a rush that I gave up on trying to roll my furs, and threw them onto Brande's back in a messy heap as Ava did the same with hers. There was so little time to do anything else. The men were close enough that I could hear them yelling to each other, so I made sure Ava got onto her horse and then I slapped my hand against its flank. It started running, and as I vaulted onto Brande's back, one of the men shouted at four others to go after Ava. Their accents were Valenian. They had to be Hazlitt's men.

"Albus!" I hollered, and motioned to Ava as I kicked my heels back. "Eyes!" Albus chased after her, with Brande and me right behind him.

We took off, galloping across the start of the remaining miles of plateau with the men gaining ground behind us, hot on our trail. The four who'd been told to chase after Ava were entirely focused on her, but the other four were beginning to separate. I glanced back just in time to see one of the riders pull back on his bowstring, and steered right on the reins so Brande would cut across just as the man released. The arrow went sailing by me, but it was clear now that they didn't want me alive. I grabbed my own bow, letting go of the reins to steer with my feet while I twisted in the saddle, firing a blind shot behind me.

Our head start hadn't been great enough, and the men had to have come from healthy means, because their horses were quicker. Stronger. In a mere minute, four of them flew past me to get at Ava, and I knew they'd reach her in no time.

"Ava!" I shouted at the top of my lungs to warn her. She glanced back to see the four coming to her, and untied Maddox from the saddle so the bird could fly off and avoid injury, and then she urged her horse to push faster.

I'd been paying so much attention to the men going after Ava that I'd stopped watching what the men behind me were doing. The archer had wound up again, and the only reason I knew was because the arrow he released skimmed my shoulder. The tip of it tore through my tunic, ripping my flesh to the bone on its way to the ground ahead of us. I let out a yelp of pain and shock, but I didn't have time to dwell on the injury.

There was enough strength in my arm to still be able to fire an arrow, so I released another in the direction of my pursuers. But the men ahead of me were catching up to Ava and Albus. I watched one of them ride right up to her side, raising the blunt end up his poleaxe and preparing to strike her in the back. In the brief moments before he did, I worked another arrow into my bowstring, firing it so accurately that the tip pierced straight through the center of his back. As he collapsed off his horse, Albus sprang at the next nearest man. He jumped right in front of the man's horse, clamping his jaws down tight on the animal's throat.

I didn't get to see what happened next. The archer behind me had fired another arrow. The whistle and thud of it sounded at my back, but it hadn't struck me. It hit Brande in the hindquarters. My horse stumbled three paces before regaining his balance, and then he reared with pain. He rose straight up onto his back legs, and because I had my bow in my hands, I didn't have the grip to stay on him. I plummeted to the earth as the archer's next arrow pierced deep behind Brande's front shoulder.

Shooting to my feet, I wound up once more and fired, hitting the archer with such impact it knocked his body backwards off his horse. But one of the others reached me, sticking out his foot and kicking me in the chest as he rode past. I hit the ground again and rolled backward, choking and struggling for air while I came to a stop. As I wheezed, I heard the thump of feet hit the ground nearby, as though one of the men had jumped off his horse. His boots stomped over to me, but the moment his hand gripped the back of my neck, I grabbed my dagger and spun, slashing across his thigh.

He stumbled back, clutching at the gaping wound. It caused a lull just long enough for me to glance ahead at Ava. She'd been knocked off her horse too, and now she had her sword drawn a good thirty yards away with Albus at her side, though the men looked far more hesitant to fight her than they did me. They wanted her alive.

The other two men who reached me flung themselves off their horses, while the one I'd slashed unsheathed his massive broadsword. He wasn't the only one who was armed either. The second had an axe, and the third a war hammer that I imagined weighed at least half what I did. I scrambled sideways as I struggled to my feet, putting all three of them in front of me where I could see them. The one I'd cut was bleeding profusely, but I doubted it was enough to make him useless.

I reached my feet and held my dagger in my hand, watching closely to see what they'd do. They outnumbered me, and they were bigger and stronger, but each of their weapons was heavy. It would take them as long to wind up for a blow as it would for me to dodge, and that's where my survival lay. In dodging. If I got caught once, I'd be done for.

Just as that thought crossed my mind, the one with the axe lunged forward, gripping it and rotating his torso as he came at me. I ducked around him as he swung diagonal, the bit of his axe cutting deep into the dirt where I'd been standing. Not a split second later there was a grunt from behind me. The man with the war hammer raised it with both his hands, and I had just enough footing to dash forward. I rolled toward the man pulling his axe out of the ground, sticking my dagger out as I did so it sliced through his calf, and the man's shout mixed with the war hammer's metallic clank as it made a small crater in the earth.

At the forefront of my mind was the intense desire to glimpse behind me and see how Ava was doing, but I couldn't take my eyes off of these three for a moment. I had each of them in front of me again, my heart pounding as I prepared for the next attack. It came when the man with the broadsword ran at me, point of the sword first in such an unpredictable manner that I didn't know which way to dodge. Not until the last moment. He swiped left, only to gain momentum to swing it hard around right. The feign nearly caused me to make the mistake of cutting left and throwing myself right into the blow, but as my feet skittered left, I caught the trick. In mid-motion I couldn't change direction, so I dropped straight onto my back as the thick blade went sailing through the air above me.

The man used the momentum of his swing to heave the sword upward, taking it in both hands as it reached the apex above his head to bring it down with all his might. I rolled away from him, hardly avoiding the tip of the weapon as it struck the dirt, but the other two hadn't been standing idly. As I stopped rolling, the axe man's heavy boot stomped down on my arm, trapping it against the ground so that I couldn't make another swing with my dagger. The shadow of the war hammer appeared high above my head, and I was so trapped that even though I turned onto my side to hug the boot holding me down, trying to keep the hammer from landing straight on my chest, the dull edge of it scraped against my back as it met the ground.

I tried to ignore the agony as I reached with my free arm behind the boot and grabbed my dagger. I brought it back, slamming the point of it into the leg of the man keeping me pinned. He fell backward, but before I could recover the dagger from his leg or move out of the way, a different boot connected with the already bruised spot on my back. I arched out of sheer pain, only to see that the other man was raising his broadsword. From my side, I kicked my leg up, getting him in the stomach so that he dropped his heavy weapon. As the man with the war hammer wound up again, I grabbed the broadsword, scrambling out of the way as the hammer smashed into the dirt once more.

I reached my feet and raised the sword defensively, watching the man I'd stabbed pull my dagger out of his leg and toss it away. The man with the hammer roared in frustration. He rotated at the hips as far back as he could, and because he wasn't near enough to strike me, as he turned forward again he released the hammer from his grip. It came flying at me with such speed and force that I couldn't have dodged it if I wanted to. The weapon bypassed the sword and collided with my already cut shoulder. I spun in a full circle from the impact, dropping the sword, and I hardly got a chance to register the intense and crushing pain of the blow before the man whose sword I'd taken grabbed the neck of my tunic, holding me in place so his fist could catch me square in the jaw.

He didn't let me fall. He held me up, pulling his fist back again and sending it crashing into my stomach. Then he let me go, and I buckled over, staggered a few steps backward and fell to my knees. He picked his sword up off the ground while the other recovered his war hammer, and this was it. I was done for.

Unless...

Through the pain and the panic, my hand shot instinctively to the inside pocket of my vest. I didn't have time to be afraid of the consequences, because if I didn't do this now, I was dead. I grabbed the leather-wrapped necklace and pulled it out, undoing the bindings as fast as my fingers could. Right as the man with the broadsword began to wind up, I grabbed the pendant in my bare hand.

A cold spark shot up my arm, and it was so excruciating as it barreled across my chest and through the rest of my body that my hand clasped shut around the necklace. The pain traveled down my limbs, straight through to every end of my body and back again, and each direction it had gone reconnected at my chest. It felt like my heart was exploding. Every muscle tensed except my lungs, which released all the air I had in an agonized scream as the pressure built and built until I couldn't contain it anymore. Until, all at once, it burst.

A pale blue lightning erupted out of me. It shot into the three men around me, and they stiffened at the current for a split moment before collapsing into convulsions. What was left of the surge barreled into my head, settling in my mind like a thrilling static fog. I don't know how, but before I could even blink, I'd crossed the thirty yards to Ava on a bolt of lightning and without taking a step. I stopped behind the man dueling with her and grabbed the back of his head, releasing a fresh current and not even stopping to make sure it would kill him because I knew it would. Another blink and I was ten feet away at the second man that Ava had knocked down. I sent out a stream of sparks that wrapped around him, gripped him, and with a flick of my wrist I'd thrown him head first into a nearby boulder. The other one Ava had knocked unconscious, and I sparked to him in the span of a second and filled him with current. I looked around, examining the bodies to make sure none of them had any fight left.

"Kiena?" Ava whispered.

That fog was still in my head, and in this condition, everything felt like a threat. Again, without taking a step, I crossed the distance between us in a flash. It scared her when I reached her that quickly. So much that she fell backward onto her hands, wincing at the crash. Though I was still in some deeply instinctual, defensive state, something within me was worried about her pain. I dropped my pendant and squatted at her side, grabbing her hand and checking her palm to make sure she hadn't injured herself.

130

But something else caught my attention, something that consumed the entirety of my focus.

It was a deep, rapid beating. A chorus of gushing throbs like a heartbeat. It was *Ava's* heartbeat, thudding hard with exertion and fear. I could feel it pulsing in my ears and against my flesh and beating gently against that static fog in my mind. I brought her palm to my lips, planting an apologetic kiss to it to try and calm that frightened rhythm. Then I dropped lower to press an open one to her wrist, to that thin spot of skin where her heartbeat was strongest.

The beat faltered the moment my lips met her flesh. It caused an upset in the rhythm of her heart that met the swirling fog in my mind like a thickening intoxication. I closed my eyes against the feel of it, absorbed it like comfort after being in the blistering tension of battle.

"Kiena?" Ava asked again, and though she sounded confused and afraid, my eyes snapped open at the interruption. The primal force of my power still perceived danger, even though deep down I knew there was none.

I couldn't collect myself either, no matter how hard I tried; the magic was in control, and it felt threatened. I whipped her wrist to the side so it was out of the way, grabbing the neck of her tunic in my other fist and yanking her up to sit. It was my full intention to eliminate the threat I saw her as, but this time her heartbeat skipped with fear, and her eyes met mine with an intense mix of emotion. It was enough that the magic hesitated, and I could see my own eyes reflected in hers, because the fog in my mind wasn't a figment of my imagination. The current resulted in a pale blue static that swam amidst the brown of my irises.

"Kiena, stop," Ava pleaded, craning her face as far away from me as she could and trying to slip her wrist out of my grasp, but I held it tight.

And with the magic's hold just as powerful as my own deep desires, I was confused. I didn't know whether to kill her or listen for more of her heartbeat because I couldn't think over the clouding in my mind.

"Kiena," she said again. Her throat bobbed as she swallowed hard with fright. "It's me."

I let go of her wrist to create a lethal current of sparks in my hand. I tried to fight the overwhelming instinct, gods, I *tried*, but it wasn't enough, and Ava wasn't waiting anymore for me to control this on my own. The moment I let go, she grabbed the sword she'd dropped when she fell, and she brought it between us and pressed the sharp point of it beneath my chin.

It made me angry, being threatened like that. The *magic* made me so frustrated about it that I felt my upper lip curl, but her eyes met mine, a world of desperation in their brilliant blue as she whimpered, "Please come back to me."

And somehow the terror in her eyes and that plea reached what rational recesses were left at the back of my hazy mind. Like the retreating of water at the shoreline, that fog left me. I forced it away and clung to the thoughts and desires and instincts that I knew were *mine,* and mine alone. In the reflection of her eyes, I could see the sparks of blue leave my own, and all at once I was completely aware of what I was doing and what I'd done. I let her go, scrambling back a few feet and feeling my stomach turn with panic, because what I'd feared most about the magic had almost come true. When all Ava did was let the sword fall from her hand and drop back to lie in the dirt, my heart plummeted.

"Did I hurt you?" I asked, scrambling back over. I knelt at her side and leaned over her, reaching out to make sure she wasn't injured.

"Don't." She flinched, her hand shooting up defensively to ward me off. To keep me from touching her. "Give me a moment."

"Ava, I'm so sorry," I said, but I backed off because I'd almost hurt her, and the last thing I ever wanted to do was break her trust in me. "I'm so, so sorry. Are you alright?"

"I'm fine," she whispered.

Her eyes shut tight as she took in a deep breath, swallowing hard once more and letting that breath out again with deliberate slowness before opening them. I fell back to sit as she pushed herself up, so overwhelmed with how the magic had affected me, and what I'd almost done to Ava, that all I could do was bury my face in my hands.

After another few moments, Ava's hand set on my knee, and she began to say, "You're all beat-"

"Brande!" I interrupted, vaulting to my feet.

It wasn't until I rose that I realized Albus wasn't around anymore, and as I sprinted back to where Brande had fallen, I found him. Brande was lying on the ground with the two arrows in him, and Albus had left Ava and me to lie down near his head.

I raced over, falling to my knees at Brande's back when I saw the state he was in. The arrow in his flank was something I could have fixed, but the one behind his front shoulder... His ribs were heaving with the struggle for breath. I knew the arrow hadn't reached his lungs, but there was his heart, and his liver. It had pierced something, and Brande was in so much pain that every few breaths he let out carried a soft but pleading squeal. I reached for the shaft of the arrow and gripped it in my hand, preparing to try and take it out to see what I could do, but Brande threw his head back at me the moment I put pressure on it, snapping with protest.

I let go, dropping my forehead against his neck as tears flooded my eyes. There was nothing to be done. "I'm sorry, old boy."

Ava's footsteps stopped a few feet behind me, and I knew she wouldn't try to cut my grieving short, but our time was limited. Who knows how many other men were out there, or how close they were. I stood, pacing the few feet to where my dagger had been discarded and picking it up off the ground. The moment I tried to carry it back to Brande, knowing what I had to do, Albus rose to his feet, because he knew what I was about to do too. And he growled, placing himself directly between Brande and me.

"Move, Albus," I murmured. Only the consistent rumble from his chest met it. As if he could understand me, I implored, "I will not leave him to suffer." Albus did nothing but snarl harder, and my spirit was already breaking and he was making it worse. "Move, hound!" I hollered at the top of my voice, because I didn't have the heart to fight this right now. Albus's ears and head drooped, and he didn't just move, he trotted away from me and all the way back to where Ava's horse was standing.

I didn't so much as look at Ava as I strode past her and lowered myself to my knees behind Brande. I wrapped my arms around his thick neck, unable to keep a few tears from dropping into his hair with my face buried against him, and for him I said the soldier's prayer. "In life you fought. Need you fight no more. In eternal sleep find peace, strong warrior." I sniffled, kissed his neck, and ended his suffering.

I didn't want to dwell on it, so I straightened up, wiped the tears away, and gathered my bow. I took only my medical supplies out of Brande's saddlebags because they were too valuable to leave behind, but I didn't have the will to gather anything else. Before leaving, I strode to one of the men I'd killed, and tore open the breast of his outer shirt to reveal the layer underneath. The king's crest stared up at me, causing my lips to purse with fury. If Hazlitt kept this up, he was looking to make it personal.

"Let's go," I said to Ava, pacing past her to head over to where her horse and Albus were.

My father's necklace was in the dirt where I'd dropped it when Ava had fallen, so I picked it up and put it back in my inner pocket. The supplies I'd taken I transferred to a pouch of Ava's saddlebags, and by the time I was finished, she'd reached us.

"Up." I motioned toward her horse, instructing her to get on.

"You're bleeding," she whispered, but not even the low volume of it could mask the sadness in her voice. She felt the loss too.

The arrow wound in my shoulder was nothing compared to the throbbing pain in that entire region from being hit with the hammer. It would stop bleeding eventually, and right now the emotional pain in my chest hurt worse than the injuries to my shoulder, face, and back.

"Get on the horse," I said, and this time she obeyed.

When she was sitting comfortably, she stuck two fingers in her mouth and let out a shrill whistle, and Maddox landed on the rear of her saddle moments later.

Like I hadn't the heart to take anything else from Brande's saddlebags, I also hadn't the heart to ride. It would've felt like a betrayal. It would've been like all the years Brande had spent at my side meant nothing. So I walked. As we traversed the rest of the mountaintop and started our descent, the entire day I walked alongside Ava's horse. Albus wouldn't so much as look at me, and he trotted paces ahead of us with his head down like he resented me for what I'd done.

Maybe I resented myself for what I'd done too, but what choice did I have? Brande was dying. Suffering. I'd had him since he was a colt. I'd got him for free because the breeder couldn't break him. No one could break him so he'd been given away, and in the end all it took was respect and patience. A friendship. That's what broke him, that's what made him a companion to me for seven years. I owed it to him not to let him suffer. But really I just owed it to him to have kept him alive, to have kept him safe. I didn't. I failed him. Maybe if I'd taken the magic sooner we wouldn't have been in that mess, or I could've handled all eight of the men before anyone got hurt. Now here we were, walking with one less friend.

As we walked, I held my hand out in front of me, constantly materializing an unstable ball of sparks in my palm. It never lasted longer than a few seconds because I couldn't control it now, and the only reason I'd been able to do anything with it earlier was because it had controlled me. All day, I practiced, creating sparks and trying to keep them alive as long as I could. I couldn't keep anything alive, but at least it kept my mind off thinking of other things. It took all my focus, every bit of it but what I needed to keep my feet moving.

"Kiena?" Ava's voice cut through my concentration, destroying the thriving ball of sparks in my hand. I immediately created a new one. "Kiena," she said again.

I dropped the energy. "What?" I asked, my voice cracking because it had been so long since I'd said anything.

She made a deliberate glance around the lush green forest we were in. The trees overhead were thick, blocking out a majority of what daylight was left so that everything was covered in shadow. "It's getting dark."

I studied the obscurity of the wood, assessing the truth of her statement. "I'll gather firewood," I said, trudging away to collect the bit we'd need for the night.

It wasn't hard to find dry sticks. There was no more snow, and the woods were thriving and warm, and though the air was a bit damp, it didn't soak into everything like snow did. By the time I carried back the wood, Ava had already set out her sleeping furs – furs we'd have to share because I hadn't taken mine. I preoccupied myself with using my magic to start the fire, and it wasn't until the flames were lit and I sat down next to Ava on the furs that I realized we hadn't eaten since last night. It wasn't an abnormal thing for me to go a day without food, but surely Ava was starving. Still, instead of saying anything about food, the moment I sat down she got up to pull my disinfectant out of the saddlebags and then lowered herself again at my side.

"Will you let me care for you now?" she asked.

I said nothing, but made no protest when she reached for my shoulder. It had been so long that the blood had dried. It stuck my tunic to the wound so that when she peeled the fabric away, the edges started bleeding all over again. Ava unraveled the linen from her wrist and, along with the antiseptic, began to clean the dried blood and the open wound.

"Are you hurt?" I asked in a whisper, and I was so emotional from the day that the fact I hadn't so much as scanned Ava for injuries made me feel immensely guilty. "I hadn't asked."

"Nothing sleep won't fix," she answered. She draped the linen over my other shoulder to free up her hands, and reached for the small strings at the neck of my shirt. "May I see the rest of it?" I let her, and she loosened the highest ties just enough so she could push my tunic and vest off my shoulder. It exposed my entire collarbone and the topmost part of my chest, revealing to her the entirety of where I'd been struck by the hammer. "Kiena," she said, sucking in a sharp breath as she set her hand against my bare skin, "this is bad."

My eyes dropped to it. It was already black and blue, and still throbbing. Surely it was hot against her hand as well, but I didn't care. "It's just a bruise."

For a moment, she said nothing, just sat there with her eyes wandering back and forth between my face and the injury. Then she set her fingers beneath the part of my jaw that wasn't swollen to request that I look at her. "It's allowed to hurt."

I met her eyes with my own, and the caring in her expression was enough that I almost couldn't keep the tears at bay. "The only thing I feel, Ava..." But I couldn't finish. Just put my hand to my chest, to my heart so she'd know what I meant.

She pressed her hand over the top of mine, cupped my face with her other and then touched her lips to my forehead, and the gentleness of her hands and lips lingered for a long minute to offer comfort. All it did was make me weak to restraining the emotions I'd been forcing back.

"How far are we?" I asked, pulling away from her and trying to change the subject so I wouldn't start crying. And bless her. She let me avoid it.

"Close," she said. Though we were off the road and there were no signs to gauge our distance, Ava scanned the woods as if that would help. Truly, I think she was trying to calculate how far we'd traveled today. "I'd say thirty miles outside the capital."

I nodded, replaced my tunic and vest to my shoulder and then stretched out to lie on the furs. "We'll start early," I said, throwing my arm over my eyes so I could attempt to block everything out. "You should eat."

It was silent for a few seconds, as though Ava wasn't sure what to do. "Are you hungry?" she asked. "I'll fetch you something."

"No," I answered, turning onto my side to face away from the fire.

Ava didn't respond, but she got up and I heard her shuffling around through the remaining minutes of daylight. I imagine she fed Albus and Maddox, and then got something of her own to eat. It took a while before she returned to the sleeping furs, during which I hadn't been able to fall asleep. I'd simply lain there, focusing on the sounds she was making as she moved around and trying to imagine what she was doing. Anything but think about the pain in my chest.

When she did return, she slipped silently under the blankets, making sure to adjust them and drape them over me as well, because I hadn't put myself under them when I'd lain down. Though we had to share the furs and I was facing her, she turned her back to me once she got in, as if to offer me some privacy on account of how distant I'd been all day. However, now that she was lying down, the only sounds were the bugs in the night and the crackling of the fire. It wasn't enough to keep my mind from wandering. Not enough to keep from thinking of Brande or from finally feeling the severe aching in my body.

Hardly a few minutes after Ava settled, I felt the first hot drop force itself from my eye. I tried to be strong. I tried to be quiet so as not to disturb her, but a couple minutes more and salty tears were streaming sideways down my face. A sniffle broke through the silence, and I knew Ava hadn't fallen asleep yet because she shifted at the noise. When it happened again she turned to face me, and she couldn't see me and she didn't say anything, but she knew.

Her arm slipped around my waist, she scooted into me, buried her face in the crook of my neck, and held me close. There was no stopping it then. I could do nothing but release every bit of emotion that had been plaguing me all day. My own arms wrapped around her, pulling her flush against me and clinging to her tightly. In the safety of her warmth, I let myself feel everything.

The guilt at not doing a better job of keeping us safe, at having to do what I'd done to put Brande out of his misery. Guilt at how I'd acted under the magic's influence, at how quickly and easily and without remorse I'd taken the lives of those men, and almost taken Ava's. The pain in my jaw and back, and the violent throbbing in my shoulder. Most of all, the pain of losing Brande. The sting of losing one of my closest companions, and of knowing how Albus was upset with me because of it, it was torturous. It was a pain I'd never suffered before. A loss I'd never experienced in my life. So I cried until I couldn't keep my eyes open, and eventually fell asleep.

I woke the next morning still holding Ava, but there was a new warmth at my back as well. Untangling myself from her, I sat up, only to find that it was Albus. He'd come over to lie at my back in the night, and him being there and the fact that he looked at me when I sat up made me sigh with relief.

"Does this mean you forgive me?" I asked him.

He put his head in my lap, but after a moment rose to all fours to press his muzzle beneath my chin. I wrapped my arms over his shoulders in a grateful hug, sticking my face in his fur. As I let him go, Ava woke and sat up, and in my gratefulness to her I let my head fall on her shoulder, and nuzzled my face into her neck.

She set her cheek against me in reception. "How are you feeling?"

Better wasn't quite the right word, because it still hurt, but I did feel better than I had yesterday. Though physically I was sorer than ever. "I'll be alright eventually." I straightened up, stretching my arms before me and wincing at the pain it caused in my injured shoulder. "Are you ready to find your father?" I asked, "And hope we don't get killed the second we step foot in the city?"

"I'm ready," she said with a soft smile.

We ate a small breakfast and then packed up our camp, and before long we were traveling again. I still preoccupied myself with practicing magic as I walked alongside Ava's horse. I was getting better at sustaining the sparks in my hand, and had even learned to make them travel halfway up my arm. Ava must have been able to tell I was in a better mood too, because she asked me questions about what it felt like or gave me challenges about where to direct the current. It wasn't as frightening for either of us when I was in control.

As we journeyed during the day, it got drastically warmer. It wasn't hot by any means; being winter still, it could only have been as warm as our summers in the north, which were cool. However, through walking and the exertion of practicing magic, and being so accustomed to the bitter cold of my home, I'd begun to sweat, and eventually shed my outer vest and rolled the sleeves of my tunic up to my elbows.

We'd been traveling for at least fifteen miles when, toward the better part of the afternoon, something caused me to stop in my tracks. When Ava noticed I'd ceased walking, she brought her horse to a halt, but she kept from saying anything at the look of concentration on my face. At first, I didn't know what had caused me to pause; I couldn't see or hear anything out of the ordinary. But then I *felt* it. It was so much weaker, but I recognized the sensation of feeling someone else's heartbeat from when I'd sensed Ava's. This time, however, there were multiple.

"We're being watched," I whispered. Each beat was steady, each faint, but every one was distinguishable from another in their distinct rhythms. "There are five."

Ava's eyebrows furrowed as she scanned the woods around us. "How do you know?"

"I can feel them." I grabbed my dagger from my waist with one hand. In the other I prepared a current of sparks, and though I wasn't sure exactly how I'd attack with it, I'd figure it out. Prepared for our new assailants, I commanded, "Come out!"

For a handful of tense seconds, there wasn't a single sound. Then came a female voice. "Are you Avarona Gaveston?"

Ava looked at me with shock. "Perhaps," she called out blindly. "Who wants to know?"

From every direction around us, there was the cracking of footsteps in the foliage, and our five observers emerged from the woods. Two women and three men, all dressed in camouflaged green and brown, but each with the Ronan sigil on their breast. Though none of them had their weapons drawn, I raised my dagger and my other hand to a defensive level at my chest. At my movement, one of the women put her palms out comfortingly. She wasn't looking at me, however; she was watching Ava.

"Are you Avarona Gaveston?" she asked again.

This time Ava paused for a lengthy second, considering her answer before saying, "Yes."

The woman dropped her hands, straightening into a more relaxed posture. "King Akhran Ironwood is expecting you."

Chapter 11

va looked at me, and I at her, and the confusion was clear in both of our eyes. After a moment, she glanced back at the woman who'd said the king was expecting her.

"I beg your pardon?" Ava asked.

"The king," the woman repeated. "He's expecting you."

Ava shifted almost uncomfortably in her saddle. "I know, but… how?"

"I'm sorry, my lady," the woman, who I assumed was a soldier, said. She paused awkwardly, and then corrected herself. "Um… Princess. I don't know the specifics. All I know is we've been out searching for you for days now."

"We're supposed to go with you?" Ava asked, to which the woman nodded. "For what purpose?"

The woman's head cocked. "I'm sorry?"

"What are the king's intentions?" Ava clarified, clearly not ready to trust them completely. However, Albus hadn't growled at them once, and for that I was ready to follow, even if we kept our guard up. "Is it in our best interest to go with you?"

"I should hope so, Princess," the woman said. "His orders were to find you, bring you and any companions no harm, and to take you straight to him at the castle."

Albus trotted away from me, and I nearly called him back before I realized one of the other soldiers had knelt down and put his hands out, and Albus was comfortable enough to go and get his ears scratched. When Ava looked at me to see if I believed them, I simply shrugged. Whether or not they were telling the whole truth, they hadn't yet seemed threatening.

"Very well," Ava agreed. "We'll follow you."

We did follow them. Back to the main road, where just off it a sixth soldier was watching out for all of their horses. They all mounted when we got there, and their leader looked at me, hesitating for a moment.

Then her eyes fell on Ava. "I believe the king would appreciate if we made haste," she said, clearly wanting me to double up with Ava.

Ava hesitated too, but for a different reason. She knew me well enough that I was sure she knew why I hadn't ridden since yesterday, and I knew her well enough to know that she wouldn't force me. But this is what we'd been after since I found her. Meeting her father was what she wanted more than anything, and we were so near the castle that I couldn't look her in the eyes and deliberately delay it. Not when we were *this* close.

Before Ava could disagree, I stepped up to her horse. "Sit forward," I told her. She passed me an unsure look, like she didn't think this was a good idea, but I gave her a small smile to let her know it was fine.

She scooted up in the saddle to make room for me, and once I was comfortably behind her, we were off. The soldiers led the way at little more than a canter, but it only took a few minutes on the road before everything began to change. There wasn't as much forest because of all the farmland we were passing, and the miles between here and the castle were flat enough that I could actually *see* our destination. The capital city of Ronan, though I still didn't know what it was called, stretched out for miles beyond the farmland. It wasn't like Guelder, though, where the castle was situated at the heart of the city. The castle was visible across from the city, and was nearly half as large.

The sight of it seemed to excite everyone, as our pace increased to where I could tell Albus was working to keep up. At this speed, it took little less than an hour before we got to the massive stone castle. The gates opened as we reached them, and while the soldiers slowed our pace inside, they didn't stop until we'd ridden past a second gate and all the way to the rear of the large yard. We came to a halt in front of the stables, each of the soldiers dismounting and passing their horses to a stableman.

Once Ava and I were on our feet again, she began to pass her reins off, pointing to Maddox as she did. "Keep her with my horse."

The man nodded and took the horse and Maddox into the stables. While five of the six soldiers disbanded to go their own way, their leader motioned for Ava and me to follow. We trailed her into a tower with Albus

141

at my side, up a rounded set of stairs, and down a wide hall to a door where two soldiers were standing guard.

"Is he in there?" our guide asked one of them.

"Aye, Commander," one nodded. "But he's with council."

"He's waiting for this interruption," she said as she bypassed him for the door, opening it and stepping aside for Ava and me to enter first.

There were two men in the room. One was sitting at the end of the single long table at the center, with his head bent over a piece of paper so the only bit of it I could see was the crown. The other was a man in green robes, standing at the king's side and pointing to something on the parchment. When we walked in, both of them looked up to see about the disturbance, and by the gods I knew immediately that we'd come to the right place. King Akhran *was* Ava's father, of that I had no doubt. He had the same soft, dark skin, the same round nose and, best of all, the same brilliant, emotive blue eyes.

He leapt out of his seat the moment he focused on her, and without even being told, he knew who she was. "Avarona?" he asked, a slow smile creasing the corners of his mouth. The very next moment he was pacing across the length of the room, and it made me nervous for only a second before he wrapped his large arms around her, pinning hers to her sides as he lifted her in a tight hug.

In spite of everything I'd been through the last couple days, I couldn't help but smile at the fact that he appeared so happy to see her. By the time he set her down again, her eyes were full of tears, which she hurried to wipe away when he let her go.

"Look at you," he breathed in awe. "You're beautiful." He looked at the soldier who'd brought us here and repeated, "She's beautiful!"

"Yes, Your Grace," the commander agreed with an amused chuckle.

"Like your mother." King Akhran glanced back at the man in the robes. "That'll be all for now, thank you." The man nodded and left, and the king looked at the commander again. "Bring my wife." She did the same and retreated out the door, closing it behind her. Akhran stared at Ava for nearly a minute, speechless and with a sparkle in his eyes. Then his gaze softened and wandered from her to me, and I saw him take in the especially marred look of my shoulder. "You've had a rough journey," he pointed out.

Ava's mouth fell open, and though she clearly had so much to say, it took her a while to actually get something out. "How did you know I was coming?"

"I hadn't spoken to your mother in years. Fourteen to be exact." He gave a knowing grin. "Imagine my surprise at receiving a letter saying you'd run away."

"She got a message to you?" Ava asked in shock.

"Indeed," he said with a nod. "She suspected you'd try and make it here." He turned his gaze on me again. "Who is it that's accompanied you?"

"Your Grace, this is-" Ava seemed about to give him some title or position, but I had none, and she faltered for a moment over what to say. "Kiena. And Albus."

"It's a pleasure," the king said to me, and my only experience being addressed by a king was with Hazlitt. While this didn't feel like so formal a meeting as required me to kneel, I made a deep and respectful bow. "Please, no," the king chuckled, motioning for me to straighten up. "Ronan formality ends with a title. No need for grand gestures." He stuck his hand out to Albus, allowing Albus to sniff him before rubbing the top of his head in greeting. After he'd satisfied himself with petting my dog, he motioned toward my shoulder. "You're injured, Kiena."

"It's nothing, Your Grace," I said.

"She's being modest," Ava disagreed. I cast her an embarrassed glare, because the last thing I'd have is a king fretting over it, but she simply raised her eyebrows at me, challenging me to deny it.

The king's lips curled with delight at the exchange. "Come," he said, walking past us for the door. "I'll escort you to my personal physician."

He led the way out, and as we followed him down the hall, I heard the two soldiers who'd been guarding the door trailing behind us. "Did you find much trouble on the road?" he asked.

While Ava walked at his side, I stayed a couple steps behind them, too unsure of myself to engage in actual conversation. He was Ava's father anyway. I didn't want to get between them.

"Hazlitt had men after me," Ava answered. "They were responsible for Kiena's wounds."

"You've made your friend an enemy of her kingdom, I imagine," he accused, though his tone was so lighthearted it seemed like he hardly minded. He glanced backward at me as we turned down another hall. "An enemy of Hazlitt's is a friend of mine, Kiena." Then he turned with a smile and said, "And a friend of my daughter's is a much welcome guest." Even from behind her, I could tell that Ava grinned when Akhran called her his daughter. I nodded gratefully at him. "Will you be staying long?" he asked Ava.

"I had hoped to stay as long as you'd have me," she answered.

"Good!" he said, peeking back at me again. "And you?"

I refused to look at Ava as I answered, because I didn't want to know if it disappointed her as much as it disappointed me. "Just long enough to ensure Ava's comfort, Your Grace."

"Very good." He stopped at an elaborate door, opening it up and smiling at the middle-aged woman inside. "Sevedi, a patient for you."

The woman, whose height rivaled mine and who had long, curly black hair and bright brown eyes motioned us in. "Who have you brought me?"

"This is Kiena," the king answered. "See to her health. I'll send someone to bring her to us when you're done."

It was clear he meant to keep taking Ava somewhere else, but her face fell instantly. "I don't- uh-" she stuttered, and though she couldn't actually say it, the reluctance was written all over her expression. She didn't want to leave me. Either she didn't trust them with me or she didn't trust them with herself, but *I* felt comfortable. I doubted this place was anything but safe.

"I assure you, she's in the best hands," Akhran said.

She looked at me questioningly, and I nodded to let her know that I was fine with it. "Would you like to take Albus?" I asked. He'd keep her safe if she felt insecure.

She shook her head. "Keep him with you." And it told me where her concern was.

"Enjoy yourself," I told her, nodding to the door where the king was already retreating. "I'll be with you again in no time."

Ava disappeared hesitantly, and once she was gone, the physician, Sevedi, let out a laugh. "She's worried about your injuries?"

I followed the woman's silent prompt and hopped up to sit on the stone table. "More or less."

"I'm guessing more," Sevedi chuckled. She pushed the neck of my shirt over my shoulder so she could examine the wounds, noticing the one in my chin as well. "Any others?"

I pulled up the back of my tunic so she could see the bruise across my spine. Her hands felt around it for a minute before setting flat against the injury. I couldn't see what she was doing, but then it was like something cool touched against my heated flesh, and after being in pain all day, it was such a relief that I sighed loudly.

"Wait till I get to your shoulder," Sevedi said.

"What substance is it?" I asked, trying to glance behind me and see what she was using. If it was a brew of herbs that grew in Valens then I'd have loved to make a concoction like it.

"None," she laughed. "It's magic." It was such an unexpected answer that it took me a moment to realize she meant literally. She finished on my back and returned to the front of me, catching the look of surprise on my face. "Where are you from?" When I told her Valens, she made a noise of understanding at my disbelief. "Lie down."

I lowered myself onto the table, asking as I did, "Were you born with your magic?"

"Many are born with magic," she answered, setting her palm against my chin. At the same time as the cooling sensation started, her hand began to glow a soft orange. "It's only a matter of pursuing a specialty." I made a hum of comprehension. "Few are born with magic like yours though."

My eyebrows furrowed. "How do you know I have magic?"

She huffed with amusement, as though the question was absurd. "Are you joking?" But at the look on my face, she sobered. "You're rippling with it. Right powerful too. How long have you been practicing?"

"Well, I, um," I stammered as her hand moved to my shoulder. "I just got it yesterday."

Sevedi blinked at me like she didn't believe it, and laughed, "Like hell you did." I couldn't help but chuckle, nodding my assurance that I was telling the truth. "Show me," she requested.

I held my hand above me and built up a soft orb of sparks, saying self-consciously, "I can't really control it yet." And she snorted her entertainment for lack of a better response. "Can everyone with magic feel someone else's?"

"To an extent," she answered. "My specialties are detection and resto-
ration. I sense that if you learn to control your abilities, you'll be un-
matched by-" For a reason I couldn't understand, Sevedi stopped short
and her eyes narrowed with focus. I thought there might be something
more wrong with my shoulder, until she slipped a finger under the chain
around my neck, pulling the medallion up so she could look at it. It was
one of the necklaces Kingston had given Ava and me. "Interesting piece of
jewelry," she mused.

Though we weren't in Valens, and I doubted a Ronan would care that I
associated with Valenian rebels, Kingston had said he had spies everywhere. I was sure King Ironwood wouldn't be pleased to learn if he had
spies in his castle, and there was no way of telling if Sevedi knew what it
was without revealing that information.

"Gift from a friend..." I said.

Before I could say anything else, out of the corner of my eye, I saw
someone small run past the doorway, their footsteps echoing after them.
They stopped before getting too far though, and the soft patter returned
until a little boy stuck his head in the door.

"Who are you?" he asked. He looked about seven or eight years old,
and had tanned olive skin with ear-length black curls and dark green
eyes.

"Kiena," I answered, watching as he strode past Albus and right up to
the table to watch what Sevedi was doing.

He pushed onto his tiptoes to try and see, though it did little to help
because the table was at his nose. "I'm Akamar." Being unable to catch a
glimpse, he settled for resting the tip of his chin on the table beside my
head. He certainly wasn't shy. "What happened to you?"

"I got attacked by some men," I said.

His eyebrows rose high up into his hairline. "Were they frightening?"

"Aye," I chuckled. "They were."

"You sound funny," he pointed out.

Though that could have been rude or offensive, he was rightfully
adorable, and all I could do was laugh. "I'm not from around here."

Sevedi clicked her tongue. "Excuse the young prince." And to him, she
said, "Where are your manners?"

"I do apologize," the boy told me, dropping his chin sheepishly. "I always speak out of turn."

I blinked away my surprise at him being the king's son. Truly, I should've known by the lavish way he was dressed. "It's quite alright, Sir," I said, and he grinned a smile full of missing teeth.

"Is this your dog?" he asked, pointing at Albus.

Sevedi removed her hand from my shoulder and helped me sit back up. Before answering Akamar, I took a moment to look at what her magic was capable of, and my jaw nearly dropped. She hadn't just eased my pain. The wound was gone completely, and all that was left was an old-looking scar.

"Thank you, Sevedi," I said, rotating my shoulder to test it. There wasn't so much as an ache. She nodded at me, and so I pushed off the table and said to Akamar, "That's Albus."

"Will he bite me?" he asked.

Since he seemed afraid of how large Albus was, I wanted to put him at ease. "Where I'm from, we bow to royalty." And at the statement, I also gave Albus the hand command to 'bow.' He stretched his front paws out before him, lowering his chest to the ground while the back half of him remained in the air. I normally used that trick to woo a pretty girl, but Akamar jumped merrily. "Sit," I said next. Albus got up and then sat down. I squatted next to the prince, demonstrating sticking my hand out while I told him, "Hold out your hand." Akamar extended his hand before Albus, and I told the dog, "Be polite, shake with the small prince."

Albus put his paw in Akamar's palm, and it was bigger than the boy's hand, but Akamar shook it and giggled, "Pleasure to meet you, Albus."

Sevedi strode to the door to look out it, but she didn't see what she wanted. "The king said he'd send someone for you."

"I'll help you find Father!" Akamar volunteered. I glanced at Sevedi to make sure that was allowed, because the last thing I'd want is to get caught with the prince and have someone think I was a threat. Especially since even the young prince could tell I wasn't Ronan. But Sevedi shrugged with lack of concern, and so I followed the boy out the door. "Are you friends with my father?" he asked as he led the way down the corridor.

"My friend is," I answered, unsure of whether or not he was even aware he had a half sister. "I'm looking for her."

He gave a serious nod in acceptance of our mission, but the serious expression lasted only a second. "He's as big as a horse!" he mused, pointing at Albus again. I laughed and nodded my agreement at the exaggeration. "Can I ride on his back?"

Akamar was small, but still a bit large to be sitting on Albus's back. Reluctant to disappoint him, I suggested instead, "Would you like to sit on *my* shoulders? I'm taller than he is."

His face lit up, and he practically pulled my hand to hurry me as I knelt beside him. He was a bit heavy, but I managed to lift him over my shoulders and then stood back up. Normally I'd have been a bit concerned about acting so informal with royalty, but Akamar seemed to have gotten his friendliness from his father, and he was young enough that I thought few would mind his being treated like a child so long as I doted on him.

The prince steered me down another hall, and seeing as we hadn't found his father yet, he stopped a man passing by us. "Have you seen my father?"

"I have, Young Prince," the man answered. "He was headed toward the east wing with a young lady and your sister."

Akamar gave him a salute and pointed me in the direction of the east wing. It was a bit of a walk, and a part of me wondered after a while if he might be leading me in circles just so he could ride my shoulders longer.

"How old are you?" he asked as we traversed the halls.

"Nineteen," I answered. "And yourself?"

"Seven," he said proudly. "And my sister's seventeen. What about your friend?"

"She's twenty," I told him, and he made an impressed noise as he guided me down another corridor.

Eventually, we reached a dead-end hall, and he stopped me at the start of it. "I don't see Father..." he murmured.

Halfway down, an older woman came out of a room, and when she saw Akamar on my shoulders, she hurried over. "Your mother has been looking all over for you," she scolded, and I took the hint and put him down. "You must dress for temple."

"She's searching for her friend," he told the woman, pointing at me.

"Ah, my lady," she greeted. "The door I've just come out of." She grabbed Akamar's hand to drag him off.

"Bye!" he waved at me as they retreated.

I waved back, and then headed for the room the woman had come out of. When I reached it, I gave a soft knock on the door and then eased it open. "Ava?"

She was the only one inside, but was so preoccupied with exploring that she didn't notice I'd entered until I closed the door behind me. At seeing me, she ran over, throwing her arms around my neck so enthusiastically that she nearly knocked us to the floor.

"We made it!" she exclaimed, hugging me tight. And she was so joyful that I lifted her off the ground, twirling her in a circle just to hear her giggle. "I couldn't have done it without you and the king is so kind and I met his wife and my sister and-" She stopped, releasing me from the hug in a panic. "And I'm touching your shoulder, Kiena, I'm so sorry!"

"It's fine," I chuckled, pulling my clothing away so she could see.

She gasped, coming forward to run her hand over the entirety of my upper chest and shoulder. "That's *remarkable!*"

"It's magic," I corrected amusedly.

She grabbed my face to get a better look at my jaw. "Have you any pain?"

"Not a bit," I answered. Just because she could, she tugged me into another hug. "I met your brother."

She pulled away only enough to look at me, leaving her arms around my neck. "What was he like?"

"Delightful," I told her with a smile. "And the queen? Your sister?"

"Oh, they're spectacular," she cooed, so full of elation that she spun us around. Once more, she stopped short, ceasing our spinning with a horrified look on her face.

"What is it?" I asked.

"I'm being so insensitive," she whispered in dread, setting her hands on my shoulders only to bring me in again for an apologetic embrace. "You're grieving, and here I am going on and on about how wonderful this all is." She wasn't even really talking to me. It was more like she was muttering to herself, scolding herself. "I'm so selfish."

"Stop," I said, even though the reminder stung a bit, "don't think that for a second." And I took her face gently in my hands to emphasize it. "Seeing you so happy is... well... none of this has been in vain."

"Kiena," Ava murmured, and as if we'd both thought of the same thing at once, her face fell.

I'd be leaving. That's what all of this meant. My thumb stroked her cheek, and I was about to tell her not to think about that, because I didn't want to think about it either, but before I could, someone pushed the door open.

"Avarona?" a young woman called, and she came in before I could pull away from Ava, so that it was awkward and suspicious when I did. "Oh, hello." By the entertained smirk on her face, she'd certainly gotten the wrong idea about what was happening.

I stepped farther away, my face turning dark red as Ava cleared her throat.

The girl laughed at that, walking over to the large bed at the end of the room and dropping the clothing she was carrying onto it. Ava and I must have both appeared extremely tense, because the girl giggled to herself once more. "I assure you, there are many things in Valens considered taboo that are perfectly normal here." After she'd freed her arms, she came back over to us looking completely at ease. "You must be Kiena," she said. "I saw my brother on the way here and he was positively gushing about you. I'm Nira."

Of course she was the princess. She had the same shaped eyes as Ava and her father, though they were brown, and in features she was a little lighter – I imagine she looked more like her mother. She was also a bit taller, standing at least two inches above Ava. And gods help me, she did the same thing Ava did when we first met. Held her hand out like she wanted me to shake with her. They must've got that from their father too. I glanced at Ava for help, but she didn't respond fast enough and I didn't want to wait so long that I made it even *more* awkward. Because the king had told me not to, I didn't bow, but I took the princess's hand and pressed a brief peck to the back of it.

"Princess," I greeted.

Nira passed an impressed and amused look to Ava that only made me blush deeper. "Quite the charmer," she teased.

The Ironwood women would be the death of me... and on purpose, I imagine. "My apologies, Princess," I said stiffly. "I'm not experienced with royalty." And Ronan royalty, at that.

"You're doing quite well," she assured me, and then threw an arm over Ava's shoulders to lead her to the bed. "I brought a few for you to choose from." She spread the fancy dresses she'd set down, picking one out to hold it up to Ava. She studied the combination for a moment, then set it down and grabbed another. However, Ava had reached for one too, and when Nira saw it, she dropped her own and beamed about the selection. "Oh! That would be beautiful on you."

Ava held the dress up to herself, and turned enough to show me how it looked. I nodded my agreement. "It's perfect."

Nira waved for me to come closer, and she held a dress up to me when I reached them. It only took her a moment to spot my aversion. "That simply won't do," she said with intuitive understanding. "I'll call for the tailor."

"I assure you, Princess, that won't be-" I stopped short because Nira, already knowing what I was going to say, pinched the bloodied shoulder of my tunic. "Necessary," I finished with a laugh.

"Call for the tailor?" Nira ask Ava.

"Call for the tailor," Ava confirmed.

Nira looked at me. "Call for the tailor?"

"Aye," I chuckled.

Nira tossed the dress back on the bed, muttering to herself as she paced for the entrance, "Now where is my father? I swear he can't pass a soul without stopping to chatter for at least five minutes." She swung the door open and glanced out, but I guess she didn't see anything. "I'll return in a moment," she told us, and shut the door behind her as she left.

The second she was gone, Ava snorted with laughter, and she took my face in her hands when I gave her a confused look, giving it a fond shake. "If you get any more awkwardly adorable," she laughed, "I won't be able to take it. You must stop."

Even though I was failing at hiding my smile, I narrowed my eyes at her. "Forgive me if I'm uncomfortable around people with the authority to chop my head off."

Ava snickered, removing her hands as she rolled her eyes. "No one's going to chop your head off."

"Not if I'm polite," I quipped. While she laughed, I took a gander around the room – at the waist high dresser just inside the door, and the fireplace next to that. At the massive bed Nira had put the dresses on, and at the desk on the opposite side of the room as the fireplace. "Is this where you're sleeping?"

"Yes, um," she glanced away, "I asked that we be kept together, if that's alright with you." I nodded, but she explained, "It's wonderful here, and I feel safe, but... I don't know... I'd worry about you less if you were near."

I just couldn't resist teasing her, and said with a flat expression, "You're worried someone will chop my head off."

"Your head is staying right where it is," she smiled, but the smile faded a second later, and she shrugged. "Also, I guess if you're leaving soon, then I want to spend every moment with you that I can."

That felt more like the truth than her being worried about me. I nodded, but it was clear that neither of us knew what to say about it now. What could I say to her that would make it better? What could she want to hear other than that I was staying? I'd told her our fortunes could never align the way we wanted. It's why I'd been so resistant to giving her everything. In the end, I wondered if the pain could even get worse than this. Worse than the hurt look on Ava's face or the tears pooling at the edges of her eyes.

"You're not allowed to be sad," I said, wrapping my arms around her shoulders and pulling her into a comforting hug. "I'm not gone yet."

Ava buried her face against my collarbone, squeezing me so tight that it forced some air out of me. "Will you just," she paused and pulled away, and though she'd managed to blink the tears from her eyes, she still looked to be in an immense amount of suffering. "Will you stop being stoic for thirty seconds?" My eyebrows converged unsurely. "I'm not asking you to kiss me or to tell me everything about how you feel. But is all of this truly as easy on you as it appears? Do you not feel the same agony that creeps through my chest at the thought of losing you?"

She thought this was easy for me? "Will my grief make you feel any better about this?" I asked, for a moment allowing the ache I felt to show on my face. "Will it not make things worse?"

"It *will* make me feel better," she said. "Because I'll know that when you're gone, you won't just forget me, like I won't forget you. Because knowing you share my longing means I'm not alone in this." Her sad blue eyes blinked slowly. "Am I alone in this?"

I let out a deep, miserable sigh and hugged her to me again. "You've not been alone since I rescued you from the wolves." I set my forehead against hers, and though I could feel her looking at me, I closed my eyes so the hurt in hers wouldn't torture me any more. "I come from little means, Ava. I've been cold. I've gone hungry. I've known want, intimately. But I've never known want like this." I pulled away to cup her face in my hands, to show her *me* without the stoicism. "I've never known want as profoundly as I want you." She raised one hand to set against the back of mine, leaning her face into my palm. "If it was just me, if I didn't have to look after my mother and brother, I'd stay. In a heartbeat, I would."

"They're your priority," she said with a nod of understanding. "And they should be."

"Knowing something *must* be done doesn't make it any easier." My thumbs caressed her cheeks, but she reached up with both hands to take mine, guiding them to her lips. "That's what you needed to know, right?"

"Yes." She pressed a kiss to my knuckles. "Thank you."

"Good." I gave a small smile, and to try and lighten the mood, I motioned around the room. "Enjoy this. You can miss me when I'm gone. For now, show me what it means to live like royalty. You know this is my only chance."

Ava huffed with laughter, and I was glad that her expression brightened as she said, "Feel the bed!" I touched the top blanket with my hand, which made her giggle. "No, no, get on it!"

I sat down on the edge, but the second I did, I realized what she'd wanted me to feel, and I couldn't help but throw myself backward completely onto it. "Surely it's the softest thing in the world."

"Isn't it?" Ava asked, tossing herself to my side, and as if Albus finally thought it was an invitation, he jumped on it too. "It's one of the only things I missed about the castle."

As I chuckled at that, there was a knock on the door, and reluctant to simply open it like last time, Nira asked, "May I enter?"

"Of course," Ava called with a laugh, sliding off the bed.

Nira came in carrying some more clothes, though it was only two sets this time, and with an older woman following behind her. She strode right up to me as I regained my feet, and draped one of the articles over my shoulders. The other was a plain dress that she handed to Ava. "I brought you something simple to wear about the castle." While I removed the clothing from my shoulders to get a look at the fresh tunic and trousers, Nira motioned to the woman she'd brought, talking right to me. "Found the tailor as well. She'll take your measurements." No sooner had Nira

153

said it than the woman pushed my arms up so they were sticking straight out, and she began to take my measurements immediately. "We'll need a rush on it," Nira told the woman. "It has to be ready for tomorrow night."

The tailor nodded, but my eyebrows rose. "What's tomorrow night, Princess?" I asked, glancing back and forth between Nira and Ava, both of whom appeared to know.

"It's my uncle's fortieth birthday," Nira answered, "and Father's throwing him a party right downstairs."

"Ava," I nearly whined, "a party?" I'd never been to a party, and frankly, being around that many nobles sounded like torture. How was I supposed to behave? What was I even supposed to *do* at a party? Ava didn't get a chance to answer.

"It will be wonderful!" Nira said. She grabbed Ava's hands to begin twirling about the room with her. "There'll be dancing and music and food and *boys* to flirt with." I simply stood there, probably looking horrified because Nira stopped dancing with Ava, watching me while Ava giggled to herself. "You can't dance, can you?" she asked knowingly. I shook my head because I knew nothing of Ronan dances, and awkwardly adjusted for more of the tailor's measurements. "Well," Nira sighed, "I'm late for temple as it is and Father's probably losing his mind about it, but when I return, Ava and I will take care of that." She looked at Ava, who gave a nod of agreement.

The Ironwood women would be the death of me...

"Marka will be by shortly to take you both for a bath," Nira continued. "I truly must go." She paced toward the door, waving as she left. "Be back soon!"

I watched as the tailor also left without a word, and then told Ava, "You and Nira are very much alike."

"Are we?" she asked with a laugh.

"Aye," I confirmed, chuckling as I sat on the bed to pet Albus. "She's much more lively though."

"I never imagined my father's children would be so open to me," she admitted. "But I have yet to meet my brother."

"He'll adore you," I assured her. That boy was so friendly I couldn't believe he'd be anything but excited about meeting Ava. "I hope Marka comes soon..."

Ava knew what I meant, and her head bobbed with an eager nod. "A bath sounds incredible."

"It really does," I laughed in concurrence.

She tossed herself onto the bed next to me, but she did it so that she landed on top of Albus, and she wrestled with him while we waited for Marka. Though the knowledge that I'd have to leave eventually lingered at the back of my mind, and though the loss of Brande was still fresh, seeing Ava so overjoyed was revitalizing. Hearing her mirthful laugh and seeing her smile was what this journey had been all about. It was healing, and for the next few days before my necessary departure, I'd bask in it as much as I possibly could.

Chapter 12

he party had already started downstairs, and though the walls were too thick to really hear any of the music or noise, we'd been called on twice now because we were late. Nira had finished getting ready minutes ago, and now her ladies-in-waiting were fitting Ava into her dress as fast as they could. It appeared to be a tremendous task because of all the layers – layers fastened on by countless ties that looked like they'd be torturous to undo when Ava was ready to take the dress off. I'd stopped watching because of how constricting it all seemed.

It had been simple for me to get dressed in the brand new clothing delivered by the tailor. There was the dark brown pair of leather trousers that were a bit tighter than I was used to, fitting narrow down the leg so they could tuck into the matching pair of calf-high boots that had been crafted as well. The green tunic I was wearing had loose sleeves that reached just below my elbows. It was the rich shade of pine with gold colored trim around the neck and arms, and long enough to hang halfway down my thighs. Finally, there was a wide, decorated leather belt that went around my waist over the shirt.

Because Ava wasn't ready, Nira had sat me down on the bed, and posted herself behind me so she could do my hair. One of the ladies had volunteered to do it, but Nira insisted that she wanted to. She liked the simple braid I kept it in; however, now she was braiding the front of both sides, weaving them together at the back so they'd remain out of my face.

Even Albus had been groomed, though it took little more than a bath and a brief brushing of his wiry fur. It didn't seem like a common occurrence for dogs to attend parties, but someone in the royal family had paid mind to how inseparable we were. Albus had been included in the prompt the two times someone had been sent to fetch us.

While Ava finished dressing, the door of our room burst open, but instead of it being a servant who'd come to get us this time, it was Akamar. He sprinted into the room in a tiny outfit much like mine, though more richly adorned, stopped to pat Albus on the head, and then jumped on the bed to climb onto me.

"Are you four ever coming to the party?" he sighed, folding his legs to sit exactly as I was, and so he'd fit perfectly in my lap.

Finished with my hair, Nira slid off the bed to sit more comfortably at the desk on the side of the room, asking, "Who sent you up here?"

"I did," answered a female voice from the door.

It was the queen, Gwinn, looking like the most elegant woman I'd ever seen in her party dress. She had Nira's fairer skin, but her brown eyes were so rich that they appeared to glow behind the gold of her jewelry. Her black hair was pulled up into a sophisticated knot, and the smile she passed around the room was as inviting as her voice.

"We're almost finished, Mother," Nira told her.

Gwinn nodded, crossing the room to where Ava was while she cast a friendly look my direction. "Evening, Kiena."

"Your Grace," I said, bowing my head as much as I could with Akamar in my lap out of habitual instinct.

"I'll finish this," she told the ladies-in-waiting, who were tightening the laces at the front of Ava's bodice. They shuffled out of the room.

"I apologize for the delay," Ava said, offering a repentant smile.

"Your father should come apologize to you," Gwinn chuckled. "He's so eager to make introductions that he's being unbearably impatient." She tied the remainder of Ava's strings in a bow, allowing the ends to hang decoratively down the front of the dress. "You look darling," she praised with a grin.

"Thank you." Ava reached up, shyly tucking some of her hair behind her ear.

We'd interacted with the queen multiple times since we'd arrived yesterday, and no matter how generous she was, Ava remained timid. Out of all her father's family, I had no doubt she'd expected the queen to like her least of all. That not being the case hadn't seemed to sink in quite yet.

Gwinn nodded, and then glanced over at the boy in my lap. "Akamar, would you like to escort the ladies downstairs?"

Akamar jumped out of my lap to run to the door, saying instead, "Come on, Albus!" The queen laughed and rolled her eyes, following her son to the entrance.

Before climbing off the bed too, I took a moment to look at the finished effect of Ava's dress. And it was *stunning*. The silk gown itself was a mix of dark gray and a deep maroon, but what caught my attention more than anything was the bareness of it. I'd caught glimpses of Ava naked, more than once, but there was something about the teasing way her shoulders and collarbone were exposed, something about the way her long hair was draped over one shoulder to display her neck that made me gulp. Temptation was great enough when she'd been wearing the baggy tunic and trousers we'd found for her. A dress more fitted to her curves, one that reminded me that I *knew* what was underneath, might be a greater temptation than I could resist.

Of course I'd only meant to glance, but when I ended up staring, Ava's lips curled with a smirk. "You like the dress?" she teased.

I'd been so thoroughly staring that I hadn't even realized all the others had left, including Albus, and closed the door behind them. Though my cheeks tinted, as I got off the bed, I said with as much composure as I could, "Possibly." But when I actually reached where Ava was standing, that temptation flared. Just a touch couldn't hurt... right? I lifted one hand, and as innocently as I could, I traced my fingertips over her bare shoulder and down the length of her arm. "You look like a princess."

For some reason, that compliment didn't seem to make her as happy as I thought it would, but she caught my hand as it reached the end of her arm and slipped her fingers through my own, giving a small smile. "You're looking quite noble yourself."

"Good," I chuckled. "The less I stand out, the better." I brought her hand to my lips to kiss the back of it. "Let's not keep your father waiting." I'd begun to turn to head for the door, but Ava wouldn't let go of my hand, so it stopped me when I took a step. I faced her again, growing concerned at the hesitant look on her face. "Are you alright?"

There was a long beat of silence, during which her blue eyes ran over the entirety of my face. I couldn't tell what she was thinking or feeling. Maybe she was simply nervous about being introduced to new people.

Whatever it was, it took her a few more seconds to collect herself, and then she put on a cheerful smile and nodded. I wasn't dull enough to completely believe her, but I knew if she'd wanted to tell me what was going through her mind then she would have. So I led the way to the door, out it to the stairs, and down them to the party in the grand hall below.

The queen had wandered a few steps away from the stairs to talk to some other women, and Nira had done the same in the opposite direction. Amongst the dark and rich colors of the nobles' clothing, it wasn't difficult to spot the pure white of Albus's fur. He was with Akamar, being shown by the prince to a group of other young children and loving every moment of the attention.

We hardly reached the end of the stairway when the king spotted us. He hurried over, smiling at me and offering a rushed compliment about how I looked. Then, muttering assurances about bringing Ava right back, he all but dragged her off to make those introductions Gwinn had mentioned. It left me standing there alone, but to my relief, it wasn't for long. Nira graciously came over when she saw that her father had stolen Ava.

"Come on," she said, looping her arm in mine. "Accompany me in a dance." I wouldn't resist the princess physically, but my face portrayed my reluctance. Nira simply laughed. "You can no longer use the excuse that you can't. Ava and I made sure of it."

She was right. They *had* taught me to dance, just like she'd promised, though my confidence in it wasn't nearly as solid as I'd have hoped before doing it in public. Nira left me little choice, however. She took me straight to the large area where other guests were dancing, and started me on the simplest of Ronan routines they'd made me familiar with.

At first, neither of us said anything. Mostly I was trying to focus on not fumbling around. I still didn't make conversation right away once I got into the steps, because I found myself glancing at the other dancers. I'd remembered what Nira said about taboo things in Valens being considered normal in Ronan, and as I studied the guests, I realized she was right. Men and women were coupled together, surely, but so were men coupled with men, and women with other women. Though I had no doubt some of these were merely platonic, like Nira and myself, there were others that clearly weren't. It was simultaneously fascinating and encouraging.

159

"Tell me, Princess," I said, glimpsing my feet to make sure I was doing the dance correctly. "Was there a particular boy you were so interested in flirting with?"

Nira tried to contain the smile on her face, but she answered without even having to search for him. "To our left. In the blue tunic and black vest." I looked at him, and when it lasted more than a moment, she cleared her throat as if to keep me from appearing suspicious. "I won't be flirting with him though." My eyebrows rose at that. "I'm too shy."

I nearly snorted with disbelief. Nira was anything but shy, but she appeared serious, which could only have been telling about the depth of her affection for him. "Do you think me shy?" I asked, and Nira nodded. "If I fancied someone, shyness wouldn't keep me from flirting. *You* certainly have nothing to be nervous about."

"Were you forward with Ava?" she asked.

"Ava?" I repeated in shock. I don't know why it surprised me so much. Nira knew, and I was certain her entire family suspected something. "Ava and I... we're not..."

"Not what?" Nira asked, sidestepping in time with the music. "You're clearly fond of each other."

"Aye, but," I paused, trying to figure out how to explain it. "It's complicated." Nira didn't look satisfied with that. "I'm not highborn."

"I've known my sister nearly two days now," she said, "she doesn't seem to mind." It took her all of one second to catch the look on my face and figure it out. "It's not her who minds."

"I don't mind the consequences of her being royal," I answered. "Not anymore. But I have family that I cannot abandon for a castle."

"So then, Kiena," Nira began sarcastically, "why would I stop being shy about flirting with Vanick, when clearly affection is not a guarantee of acceptance?" My mouth fell open as I struggled for a response. At making her feel more confident, I'd failed miserably. "In spite of my reserve," Nira said, not looking the slightest bit defeated, "I'll approach Vanick, if..."

"If?" I prompted.

"If you ask Ava to dance," she finished. I sighed instantly, and Nira took my hands with excitement. "Come on," she begged, "don't you want her to remember it after you leave?" I glanced Ava's direction to consider it, and Nira made an indicative nod toward Vanick. "Or for the sake of young love!"

"You are wicked, Princess," I laughed. "Are you even shy? Or have you set me up?"

Nira's lips curled with a smug smile. "I guess you'll never know."

"Have I got to do it right away?" I asked. If I was going to ask Ava to dance, I needed some time to build up strength, that way I'd be able to resist any bursts of temptation.

"Whenever you'd like." Nira shrugged, gazing in Vanick's direction once more. "If you'll excuse me, I'll go uphold my end of the bargain."

I nodded and watched her stride directly up to the boy. "Yeah, right, she's bloody shy," I muttered under my breath.

Now that I was alone again, I looked around for something to do. Ava was no longer being dragged about by her father, and was at the end of the table full of food, conversing with a couple of young men. I strode over, working up the nerve to try and make conversation with the first noblemen I'd experience, but just before I reached them, they parted with Ava. It was actually somewhat of a relief…

"Making friends, I see," I said, leaning my shoulder against the wall beside the table.

"A few." Ava grinned, though it seemed to be more at my return than at the fact that she was making friends, and for that, I couldn't help but smile.

But despite her joy, this was the first time in a long time that I'd actually felt awkward with her. I still felt out of place amongst people like this, but at the back of my mind, I knew it was more than that I was out of my element. It was the conflict of leaving soon. The conflict between wanting to enjoy my last days with Ava and wanting to sulk about losing her already. The conflict between wanting her all to myself and knowing I had to share her with her family. Most of all, the conflict between how much I wanted my hands all over her, how much I wanted to be as *near* her as possible these last days, and how I knew doing that would make leaving all the more painful.

I didn't know what to say now, and when Ava noticed, she hesitated for a long moment and then took my hand. "You should try some of the food."

"The infamous Ronan sweets?" I asked, letting her fingers slip through mine as she pulled me along the length of the table.

She didn't let go of my hand when she stopped, and she reached for a single red berry with her other. "Try this one," she said. I must have looked hesitant, because she chuckled. "I promise it's not that sweet."

I let her put the berry in my mouth, and no sooner had I bit down than a burst of sour liquid from the center of it washed over my tongue. It wasn't just a little sour, either. It was so terribly sour that my face puckered and my eyes watered. So terribly sour that I couldn't even move my tongue to swallow the berry, so it just sat there getting more and more sour by the second, while Ava just got worse and worse at holding back her amusement. By the time I managed to swallow the fruit, she'd covered her mouth with her hand, but her shoulders were shaking.

"Thanks for the warning," I choked, my lips twitching with a smile at how pleased Ava was.

She burst into laughter, throwing her arms around my neck in a conciliatory hug. "Your face, Kiena!" She pulled back and planted a kiss to my cheek. "I'm so sorry, but that was so adorable I'd do it again." She kissed my cheek twice more and gave me a second hug.

I wrapped one arm around her waist when she released me, turning her toward the table with an evil grin as I grabbed another of the berries. "Your turn." She gasped and tried to make her retreat, but I had a firm grasp on her waist. "Come on now," I chuckled, "it's only fair." She whined, but held her hand out for the berry. I gave it to her, waiting patiently for her to eat it. All she really did was stare at it, and then at me, and she was taking much too long. "The longer you wait the wor-"

As I spoke, she reached up and shoved the berry into my mouth, and at the perfect moment so that it stuck between my teeth and broke open. She snorted with laughter at the immediate look of shock on my face. It wasn't nearly as bad as the first time now that I knew what to expect and my tongue was used to the taste, but I still cringed.

"I said I'd do it again," Ava giggled innocently.

"You," I said, swallowing hard, "are in a world of trouble." I grabbed her by the waist once more, but this time I pulled her right up against the front of me so she couldn't get away. I picked another berry and put it to her lips. "Open up." She snickered, and though it seemed hard because of the massive smile on her face, she pursed her lips together and shook her head. "Let's go," I laughed. "This is happening whether you like it or not." She struggled a bit more in my grip, trying desperately to keep her mouth shut through her laughter. "Avarona Gaveston," I scolded, "you open your mouth right this instant."

She couldn't help it then. She burst out laughing, her mouth involuntarily opening wide and allowing me to finally throw the berry in. Now that she had no choice, she bit down on the fruit, and the look on her face was without a doubt one of the funniest things I'd ever seen. Her eyes squeezed shut as tight as they could, her lips puckered horribly, and she shook her head back and forth as if somehow that would help rid the taste faster. It was clearly far worse for her than it was for me – I actually liked sour things – and through my intense laughter, I squeezed her to me in a hug.

"Are you quite satisfied?" she chuckled, swallowing and leaning back enough so she could look at me.

"Aye, extremely," I agreed, pressing a truce kiss to her forehead.

As I did, I glanced over her head and locked eyes with Nira. She saw the position Ava and I were in, and though she was completely across the room, she tapped her hands together in silent applause, then motioned to the dance floor as if to tell me now was my chance. But I wasn't *trying* to flirt with Ava, and I was so not ready to ask her to dance that it translated to me actually shaking my head. Ava noticed the action, and followed my eyes behind her. Nira caught her turning though, and returned to her conversation as if she hadn't been watching us.

"Who are you looking at?" Ava asked.

"No one," I said, offering an exaggerated smile because maybe if I acted adorable Ava wouldn't press it.

"Right..." She glanced behind her again, but unable to discover who, she let it go. "I made many promises of returning for conversation while my father was introducing me. Will you come along?"

"If you'd like," I said with a nod.

Ava took my hand once more, leading me to the first set of people whom she had to speak with. She didn't let my hand go once, not while talking to them, and not as we moved on to the next group. For a better part of the night, I followed her around the room. Fortunately, everyone we met with was far more interested in Ava than they were in me, and other than introducing myself or being introduced by Ava, I did very little speaking. It felt like hours of conversation, as we'd visited with at least six groups of people, before something caught my eye. Across the grand hall,

Albus had finally found his way to the buffet table, and was inches from being comfortable enough to snatch an entire roast bird.

"If you'll excuse me," I interrupted, because that had to be more polite than simply running off.

I slipped out of Ava's grasp and all but sprinted across the hall. "Albus," I whispered when I reached him, and wrapped my arms around his neck to keep him from biting down. "That's not for you," I scolded. A man beside me turned to see what was happening, and laughed when he realized. "Your Grace," I greeted the king, blushing at the fact that, despite my scold, Albus was still craning for the meat.

"Hello, Kiena," he said as he grabbed a fat bird leg, and gave it to Albus without even looking. "Are you having a good time?"

"Yes, Your Grace," I answered, and shooed Albus away. "Go eat in the corner."

The king chuckled at that, but instead of saying anything about it, he motioned toward the dancers. "I was hoping you'd do me the honor."

"A dance?" I asked in shock. He gave an amused nod, and though I couldn't think of a reason why he'd want to dance with me, I tried to rid my surprise. "Of course."

I followed him out, and since it had been a while, I focused on my feet to try and get back in the rhythm. He didn't give me much of a chance before starting conversation.

"Truly," he prompted, "are you enjoying yourself?"

Truly, I wasn't much for crowds, or parties, or nobles, but following Ava around, being able to be close to her physically without worrying about what anyone might think, it had kept me from feeling completely uncomfortable. "I've not thought I wasn't enjoying myself, Your Grace."

He smirked at the indirectness of that. "Good. I hope you've felt as welcome here as Ava."

"Aye," I said, and then, realizing how informal that must have sounded, I corrected myself immediately. "Of course, Your Grace."

"If I might ask," he began, "what is it that calls you back to Valens?"

"Duty," I answered, wondering why he wanted to know. He watched me curiously for a few moments, as though that wasn't as specific as he'd hoped. "A mother and brother. Both of whom I care for."

He nodded, blue eyes wandering away, and he danced for a minute in thoughtful silence. "You've done me a grand service, bringing Ava here," he said eventually. I hadn't done it for him, and surely he knew that, but before I could respond, he continued. "I've spent a great deal of time amongst the poorest of my people, taking them food and clothing." I nodded, completely unsure of where he was going with this. "I've come to recognize the struggle in their eyes." He made a lengthy pause, during which I tried to decipher his purpose. "I would very much like to compensate you for everything you've done."

"Compensate?" I repeated in utter shock. Did he mean what I thought he did? As in compensate with money. As in he wanted to send me home with gold for bringing Ava here safely. "Your Grace, I assure you, you need do no such thing. I've not brought her here for reward."

At first, he didn't respond, just kept moving in the steps of the dance, watching me for a few moments before his eyes were pulled elsewhere. "Ava loves you," he pointed out. "I'd be a fool not to see it." I didn't say anything to that, but the king met my gaze with a soft smile. "Your lack of noble title does not negate your noble heart, Kiena. If you won't allow me to pay you for your service, let me gift you a comfortable sum. For Ava." As the dance switched our positions, it turned me so I could see Ava, and I watched her fondly while I considered the king's offer. "Allow her to take comfort in knowing you've one less concern when you leave here."

It took me a long minute to think over. I wasn't comfortable being paid for what I'd done. It made everything I'd done simply because it was right feel like I'd done it for profit. Made me feel like I'd abandoned my kingdom and Silas for money. It didn't *feel* honest. But he was right about Ava. About how she'd take some small comfort in knowing that money wasn't as tight a concern. She'd never even met my mother and brother, but she'd put their needs before her own. She'd been more than willing for me to give up bringing her here if it meant danger for my family. For that, I knew it would make her feel better about my leaving if I accepted the king's gift.

"Yes, Your Grace," I agreed, dropping my chin in a small bow. "I don't know how to thank you."

"You've done more than enough already," he said with a sincere grin.

From behind him appeared Nira, and as she reached us, she linked her arm through his. "Father, I hate to interrupt," and she looked deliberately at me, "but the night is nearly over and Kiena has yet to fulfill a promise."

"Very well, then," he said, bowing deeply, and his adoption of the Valenian custom solely for me made my heart swell with gratitude. "Thank you for the dance."

I bowed in return, and after Nira dragged him away, I strode up to Ava. She was still busy talking, but my arrival to the company caused a pause in conversation.

I gave an apologetic nod to her companions as I offered her my hand. "Care to dance?"

Ava beamed, saying rushed goodbyes to her acquaintances and then following me. There were a few different dances that she and Nira had taught me last night. Though the rhythm of the music was upbeat, for my dance with Ava, I chose the steps that would put us closest. It was the dance for couples, and while we weren't necessarily a couple, I knew all that truly lacked was the calling us one. Plus, I knew Ava would like it. If I couldn't give her anything else, I'd give her this. Nira would be right pleased as well...

"I was starting to think you'd never ask me," Ava teased, lining her hands and body up close to mine to begin the routine.

"You could've asked me, Little Will-o'," I told her.

She shook her head. "I didn't want to force you."

"I took an arrow for you," I chuckled. "A dance is nothing." It seemed mindless when she put her hand on the shoulder in which I'd been hit with the arrow, but her face wasn't quite so mirthful. In fact, she looked suddenly pensive. "Have I upset you by waiting too long?"

"No," she said, and to make sure I believed it, she pushed up to kiss me on the cheek. "Not at all."

"What's bothering you, Ava?" I asked. It wasn't like her to be so downcast so often.

She looked me in the eyes, and as if that made it worse, she dropped her head forward against my shoulder so I couldn't see her face. "You know what's bothering me."

And when she said that, I *did* know. It was the looming of my departure, weighing on her more every hour. It was still two days until I'd decided to leave, but it seemed the closer it got, the worse Ava began to feel. Already knowing how much it was hurting her was near unbearable.

"Tell you what," I said with forced excitement. "You could write to me, tell me all about how much you miss being chased by soldiers."

She huffed a somber laugh into my shoulder. "Kiena, you can't read."

"So draw for me then," I suggested. "You're a spectacular artist. When the war is over, you can visit." Ava said nothing, just stayed there with her head on my shoulder and hardly even putting any effort into the steps. "Ava," I sighed, "I don't want to spend these last days with you in misery."

It took a few moments, but eventually she took in a deep breath and straightened. "You're right," she said. "But Kiena, I don't think I can-"

"That man kicked Albus!" I interrupted.

As she was speaking, my gaze had wandered briefly behind her, to where Albus had been following Akamar for lack of something better to do. But that moment was all I needed to see a man who was walking by, and like Albus was some inconvenience in the way, the man kicked him. It wasn't a forceful or even a violent kick. It was more of an impatient brushing aside, but he'd put the sole of his boot flat against Albus's flank, and pushed hard enough that Albus stumbled. And I didn't know or even care how highborn the man was. I wouldn't have it.

"What?" Ava asked, turning to see where I was glaring. "Who?" Her demeanor had shifted, and she seemed as upset as I was.

"That man with the disgusting rat hairpiece on his bloody bald head," I growled. I puffed up, and took an irate step in his direction, intent on giving him a piece of my mind.

Ava grabbed my arm to stop me. "Whatever you're going to do, re-think it."

"Why?" I demanded, nearly ready to pull my arm out of her grasp.

"Because." She took my face in her hands to force me to look at her. "Nobles here settle their squabbles with duels." I groaned, because I didn't have the slightest bit of skill with a sword, and I didn't know how to confront the man without ensuring I wasn't challenged to one. Besides, challenging a guest to a duel was no way to show the king gratitude for his hospitality. Ava studied me for a moment, and then glanced at the man. By the time she looked at me again, her lips had curled with a grin. "I have an idea."

She whispered it in my ear, and I snorted with laughter and nodded my eager approval. The first thing I did was fetch Albus, and posted him at the wall on the opposite side of the hall as the stairway up to our room. Then I followed Ava, who'd gotten herself a full cup of wine. She strode right up to the man, bumping into him and spilling the wine all over his elaborate tunic, but she'd done it so forcefully that wine flew up into the air too. Most of it landed on the floor and his shirt, but some of it splattered all over that disgusting hairpiece of his.

"Good Sir!" Ava exclaimed in feigned shock, grabbing a handkerchief from the nearest person and beginning to dab clumsily at the man. "I am so sorry, Sir!" He looked furious, especially as Ava began to swipe roughly up his face, and when she reached his hairpiece, she purposefully pushed it backward off his head. "Please, excuse me!" Ava continued.

I rushed behind the man before he could turn around, and grabbed his hairpiece off the floor. I had to run, but at this point I didn't care. I bolted across the room and put the hairpiece in Albus's mouth, motioning to myself, "Eyes." Then I darted back across just in time to see the man finally brush Ava off of him and turn around to search the floor for his wig.

"Where is it?" he grumbled, pushing Ava's hands away as she, struggling not to laugh, continued assaulting him with the handkerchief.

"Is that what you're looking for, Sir?" I asked, pointing across the room at Albus, the nasty fur hairpiece hanging from his mouth.

The man gasped, and as he stormed off toward Albus, he growled, "Damned mutt."

Ava and I both snickered, moving to the start of the stairs as the man stomped across the grand hall toward Albus. The moment he got close, I gave Albus the hand command to come. Albus dodged the man's grasp with the wig still in his teeth, and ran across the hall toward us. The man turned just in time to see Albus reach us, and Ava and I rubbed either side of Albus's head in praise, knowing that the man could see every bit of it. We glanced up right as he, red with fury, began to sprint across the hall.

We both snorted with laughter and took off up the stairs, with Albus following right behind us. As we rounded the hall at the top, we could hear the man's heavy footsteps sounding up the stairwell, and he wasn't far behind. We dashed down the corridor our room was in, throwing the door open and hurrying in. Once we reached the inside, Ava turned to put her back against the door while I put both my palms on it, and together we slammed it closed. Ava turned just enough to press an ear to it, and I leaned over her to do the same.

The man's thudding stride stopped at the top of the stairs. "Where are you!" he hollered.

We both threw a hand over our mouths to keep from bursting into loud laughter. Footsteps echoed down the opposite direction and away from our room, and when it was safe, we both laughed heartily and loudly. Especially when we noticed by the dim light of the fireplace that Albus had taken the hairpiece and lain down in a corner of the room, and was already tearing it to shreds.

"Gods have mercy," I said, struggling for breath and nearly collapsing forward through my laughter. Ava turned to lean back against the door once more. "You're bloody brilliant."

But I had both my palms against the door again, on either side of her head so she was fitted between the door and me. When we both realized it, realized how close we were, our laughter died down and ceased. There was so much tension so quickly in the new silence between us, and I knew what it meant, but I still couldn't bring myself to move. I wasn't touching her, I wasn't quite close enough to be, but it didn't prevent the thoughts that were flooding my mind.

I hadn't once stopped noticing how incredible Ava looked in her dress. Now she was breathing hard from the mixture of running and laughter, so that the exposed part of her chest was expanding deeply with each inhale. It called my attention to the delicate skin there, to the tempting bareness of her neck and shoulders. My palms were flat on the door, deliberately stuck to it so that I had the control not to touch her with them. But my lips... My head was bowed just inches from hers, and all it would take to explore that skin with my mouth was dropping my head a little lower.

Ava's hands had been stuck to the door too, but at the extended silence, she finally raised them. She cupped my face, and for a long moment she did nothing but caress my cheeks with her thumbs. Then she inched upward, and though I could gauge the trajectory of her lips, could see the intent in her eyes, I wasn't decided on stopping her. I let her shift closer. Let her get so close that I could feel the heat of her breath on my lips, and I wanted more than anything to let her kiss me. I wanted it so bad that I let her mouth graze mine. Wanted it so bad that I even parted my lips, preparing to return it the moment she finally did kiss me.

It seemed a surprise to us both when I jerked out of reach and whispered, "Don't."

Ava's hands and expression fell, and she plastered her head back against the door. "I can't do it anymore," she breathed, meeting my eyes with such a pained need that I felt the ache pierce straight through my heart. "I can't pretend like it isn't killing me not to have you."

I dropped my forehead against hers, still wanting to kiss her so badly that I was on the edge of surrender. "It'll hurt more to have you and let you go, than to never have you at all." One of my hands left the door to set against her jaw. Though, whether the action was apologetic or preliminary, I couldn't even be sure. "I'll be gone soon."

She shut her eyes and took in a deep breath, saying when she opened them again, "I'm leaving with you."

My hand fell from her face out of pure shock. She meant it, I could see that in her eyes, but she didn't know what she was saying. She didn't know the consequences. "My life's not comfortable, Ava. I have scarcely enough food. Some days I don't eat at all. My cottage is tiny. I may as well sleep on the ground." I couldn't let her leave with me and regret it. Couldn't let her abandon everything here only to resent me for it later. "Here, the king has accepted you. His wife and children have accepted you. You have a home now." Though I didn't take a step back, I straightened away from her. "Is it not what you wanted?"

"It's everything I've ever wanted." There were no tears in her eyes, but her bottom lip and voice were quivering with emotion. "It's *more* than I've ever wanted," she said brokenly. "I'm still leaving with you."

"You'd leave it all behind," I asked, "just like that?" She made no motion of agreement, didn't so much as nod, but I could see the decision reflected firmly in her gaze. "Why?"

As if the question spurred some deep pang, her eyes finally filled with tears. It was a stark contrast to the hint of a timid smile at one corner of her mouth, and she wiped the moisture away before answering. "Because," she said, "you feel more like home than any castle ever could." She let out a huff of resignation, smiling as her tender eyes met mine. "Because I love you deeply, and with *all* of my heart."

That hit me so hard that for an entire span of long seconds, I stopped breathing. I'd known it, but it was something else entirely for her to actually say it. For her to say it and show not a hint of uncertainty. And that lack of breath seemed to create a lack of thought, and for what felt like far too long, I simply stood there, staring at her. I couldn't move or think or speak over the incredible swelling in my chest. Then all at once I was *there*, pinning her back against the door and pressing myself against her and kissing her deeply like I'd *so desperately* been wanting to.

Unlike our first kiss, there wasn't a single part of me that was hesitating. There was nothing in me that was screaming to stop or to not push it too far. When her arms wrapped around my neck so she could pull herself up and closer to me, my own snaked tight around her waist. When the entire front of her body pressed flush against me, I pressed right back. I tightened my arms even more because I loved the curve of her breasts at my ribs. Loved the push of her hips against mine. And when her tongue slipped past my lips, it wasn't a reason for pause.

It was incentive. I loved the very taste of her, and wanted to know the taste of all of her. Wanted to sample with my eyes, hands, and lips every bit of her I could unveil. The feel of her tongue was incentive for my hands to leave her waist and reach for the ties that held her dress on. While my fingers worked the knot, my lips left hers for the flesh that had been teasing me all night. My mouth reached her neck, and I was so overcome with raw need that I had no capacity for being tame. I sucked hard at the smooth surface beside her throat, finding encouragement in the way one of her hands shot up to tangle in my hair, in the way her hips bucked at the abrupt intensity of it. I sucked harder still, and it drew a sharp hum from her lips and caused her to grind too far forward with her hips. So I used my hands at her torso to guide her back against the door again, holding her there firmly so I could continue working the complicated strings while my tongue nursed the forming bruise on her neck.

Half the laces were done as I loosened them from the waist up, and as I got higher, I could feel the push of her ribs against my hands. The heavy cadence of her breathing was so deep and fast that her chest strained against the restriction of her dress, and oh, how I longed to free her of it. My fingers worked quicker as the suction of my mouth moved from her neck to the muscle between it and her shoulder. And gods, I'd loved this dress all night, but now I *hated* it. By the time I finally got the laces undone, Ava was just as impatient to be rid of it as I was. She let go of me to reach for the front, pulling it open and shoving it as swiftly as she could down her body, until it pooled at her ankles, and she drew me back to her and into another kiss immediately.

But she still had the underdress. All those damn layers. And it was so hard with how much taller I was to pin her against the door at the same time I was trying to press myself against her *and* bend over to kiss her. I couldn't keep it up, so I held her by the waist and lifted her enough to get her feet out of the garment, and I backed her all the way to that dresser just inside the door. When the backs of her thighs hit it, I lifted her again, sitting her at the edge while I stood between her legs, finally able to kiss her without leaning so far.

I'd had so little patience to begin with. Now I stopped kissing her to reach for the ties of the stiff bodice around her torso, watching my fingers work so I could get it off that much faster. It was so easy to concentrate until Ava took the opportunity to kiss my neck. Every peck was light and gentle, but her lips were so open and wet, and each one left my head increasingly thick with the intoxication of her. She worked upward, from the lining of the shirt at my neck to my jaw, and her hand cupped the other side of my face so her lips could graze me more firmly.

It was distracting enough that I lost some of my focus on the ties of her bodice. One hand continued tugging lazily at the strings, but the other dropped to her hip, grasping tightly and pulling her nearer the edge. It brought her closer to me so I could press my own hips harder against her, fitting me snug between her legs, and her tongue skimmed upward along my jawline in a beat of desperation, not stopping until she'd reached my earlobe and taken it between her teeth.

I let out a sigh at the feeling, but despite the provocative drift of her mouth, my focus on removing her clothes halted as I was flooded with a sudden sentimentality. I remembered what I hadn't done yet. What I'd been so caught up in hearing that I hadn't said it back. "I do love you."

Ava's teeth released their grip, but she didn't move her lips away. "Say it again," she panted, so hot against my ear that it sent a desperate shudder down my spine.

My hand at her hip jerked upward when she released another scorching breath, digging into her back in a pathetic attempt to keep coherent. "I love you," I murmured.

Her lips trailed down my neck as she whispered pleadingly against my skin, "Once more," and then they opened against the side of it so her tongue could press deep into the muscle.

But the searing intensity of her endeavor left me completely incapable of saying anything. I *thought* it repeatedly as her lips and tongue left me weak, but I couldn't form the words. Not until she realized it, and left my neck to set her forehead against my own. Her lips grazed mine, every humid huff colliding with each of my own charged exhales, but instead of kissing me, she froze. Waiting.

I met her beautiful blue eyes, leaving the nearly undone tie of her bodice to cup her face, saying with every bit of sincerity, "I love you, Ava."

There wasn't the fragment of a missed second before her lips were back on mine with an earnestness like I'd never known, and I was right in it with her. Each kiss was open and deep and not nearly long enough because we were both panting for air. My hands returned to the ties, undoing the last of them so eagerly that I nearly ripped the thing off of her. And I was ready. So ready for it to be the shedding of everything keeping me from every inch of her flesh, but the stiff bodice was only one of the remaining two layers. It was a corset, and as I threw it to the floor and met the soft white underdress with my hands, I *groaned* my frustration into Ava's mouth.

I felt her lips thin against mine with a smile, but it only lasted a moment. I hadn't the patience to remove her final layer, but it was low cut enough that her chest, straight to the crown of her breasts, was exposed. My lips left hers to kiss down her neck to her collarbone, and when my hands and lips converged at the bare flesh of her chest at the same time, Ava sucked in a sharp breath. She arched into it as her legs wrapped around my hips, and her hands reached frenziedly for the belt around my waist. She undid it with ease, throwing it aside and grabbing the hem of my tunic, giving me no choice but to release her so she could pull it over my head.

Once it was gone, she didn't give me a chance to resume what I was doing. She took my lips with her own, fingers clutching at my upper body to remove my chest wraps while still trying to bring me as close as possible. But I wanted *more* of her. Though I couldn't get the dress off her without losing my mind with restlessness, I *could* get what I wanted. My hands reached behind me to find the bare flesh of her calves, and once they had, they started upward. My thumbs hooked over the skirt of Ava's dress, bringing it with them as my hands traced the lengths of her thighs, until I'd pushed the dress all the way up to her hips.

I hadn't been searching for it, but when it exposed Ava's core and I pushed my hips firmly between her legs, I felt her heartbeat. In my pores and in my blood and in my head. It was rushing and hard, and when my hands reached the top of her bare thighs, it stumbled out of rhythm. I had the same dazed reaction to it as I had the first time, but more than that, I could feel her pulled square against me, her heaving chest at mine and her core brushing the skin between my hips, exposed by the low waist of my trousers. My hands, too, had lingered at the apex of her thighs, so I could feel against them and against my stomach the strong heat radiating between her legs. And the next time her lips opened against mine, her hips throbbed into me, begging so thoroughly with their moist heat that it consumed my every desire.

My arms wrapped around her waist, and like she knew what I was doing, her legs tightened on my hips, so that when I pulled her completely off the dresser, I was holding her. Her lips didn't leave mine once as I carried her across the room to the bed. I set her down on it, climbing over her as she inched backward to lie at the center, and on my knees between her legs, I straightened up just to look at her. But she wasn't looking at my face. Her eyes had dropped to my stomach, to a damp spot low amid my hips, one *she'd* left by being so wet and so close to me. I didn't need to look down to know it was there, I could feel it. My gaze never left her face, and as she took in what the glimmering mark between my hips was, her cheeks darkened with a blush. One of her hands lifted, stroking across it with a delicate finger to wipe it away.

Right after she finished the action I caught her wrist and brought it upwards, pressing one gentle kiss to her knuckles before guiding that thieving finger past my lips. The moment my mouth shut around it, Ava took in a hard breath. My tongue swept over the pad of her finger, salvaging the taste of her, and I swear, for a moment as she let that breath out in a loud sigh, her erratic heartbeat stopped completely.

My eyes finally wandered away from hers to follow the shape of her chest, along the curve in her waist, to where her dress was hitched at her hips. By the time I met her gaze again, I could see the desperation in her eyes, the plea to delay no longer what we both yearned for. And I didn't delay. I didn't hesitate or tease or ease into it. There was no need to do anything but lower myself between her legs and bury my lips against her. Nothing to do but take what she had to offer, and give what I was *so* willing to.

The first stroke of my tongue through soaked flesh was met with her hands, shooting down and running through my hair as she let out a soft moan. The next time, her back arched. It pushed her hips down with her hands at the back of my head, pulling me deeper into her, and I *loved* it. Loved the way her fingers clutched without any hint of apology, because she wanted me too much to care. Loved every time she ground herself against my mouth and I could feel her heart skip out of rhythm. Loved every shaky exhale and each long, broken moan. And I didn't like sweet things, but I loved the taste of her.

Listening to the sounds she was making, to her breathing and her heartbeat, I knew I could've finished it like this. Finished *her* like this. But I wanted to know and feel all of her. So one of my hands slid beneath my chin, and I glanced up her torso to watch her reaction as I slipped one finger deep into her core. Ava threw her head back instantly, and her chest heaved with a stunted breath as her hands left me to grasp at the bed. She grabbed a fistful of blankets while I pushed into her again, gifting my ears with the sound of my own name, rolling clumsily off her tongue through a series of fragmented gasps.

I knew she was nearing the edge. Could sense it in the speed of her heart, see it in the tense locking of the arch in her spine, feel it in the tightening heat around my finger. In the end, all it took was a well-timed combination of a push with my tongue and finger, and Ava froze beneath me. For several long seconds, she took in a breath, and then all at once she was moaning and writhing, unable to decide whether to pull away from my tongue or press against it harder, so all she could do was rock herself against me. I wasn't even doing anything anymore. The movements of my tongue and hand had stopped and I just stayed there, letting her dictate each motion and thrust and enjoying the pulsing of her around me. And it lasted.

Even after she regained control and relaxed into the bed at her back, panting to recover breath, I could still feel her tightening around my finger. I was so reluctant to remove it. So tempted to start again and coax her to climax a second time. But more than that, I wanted to see her face and judge how satisfied she was. So I gently removed my hand, wiped my arm over my mouth and chin, and adjusted to sit over her hips. Though she had to have felt me move, her eyes were shut and she was still struggling for breath. It took a minute, but eventually she opened them to look at me, and her cheeks tinted once more.

I couldn't believe it, to be honest. Ava was so rarely shy. "Are you blushing, Little Will-o'?" I asked.

Her lips thinned with a smile, and she threw an embarrassed hand over her face. "You want the truth?" she asked. I hummed my affirmation. "I rather expected you to be a timid lover... and you're quite the opposite."

I laughed at that, saying, "The first time we ever even kissed, I had my hands *all* over you." I set my hands on her stomach to trace the shape of her through her dress. "And you thought I'd be timid?"

Ava giggled, pushing herself up to sit. "Well, when you say it like that..." Her face was at my chest, so as we both laughed about it, she pressed a joyful kiss between my breasts.

She didn't wait for our laughter to die before reaching for the lace down the front of my trousers, but when she did, I fell quiet to watch her. Her focus was locked on her hands until she undid it completely, and then her head tilted up to look at me. I wanted so badly to kiss her that it didn't cross my mind not to, and she didn't seem to care how I tasted when my mouth met hers. She parted her lips so my tongue could caress her own, and as I kissed her, I felt her hand meet the flesh at my stomach and slide down.

It slipped past the waist of my trousers, and I was so slick with lust that she didn't need to collect moisture before circling a finger around that sensitive point of nerves. My eyes were already closed, but they still rolled back at the pure ecstasy of it, and I hummed my approval into her mouth. In a matter of seconds, the motion made me so weak that I collapsed forward against her. She fell back on the bed, and I set my forearms next to either side of her head, holding myself up over her so I could continue to kiss her while her hand worked between my legs. And gods, it was incredible.

Like she'd done this a thousand times already, she settled so quickly into a pattern that had me breathless. I was struggling for air, panting into her lips as my hips rolled against her hand, following the stroke of her finger so earnestly it made it hard for her to be precise. She only let me do it for another minute before flipping us over, lowering the warmth of her mouth to my neck while her finger picked up pressure and speed. But I still couldn't stop. Gods, I couldn't stop pressing myself against her. She was giving me so overwhelmingly much, but somehow I wanted more.

And she knew it, and she dropped her hand to push two fingers into me, leaving the heel of her palm in the perfect place for me to keep moving against her. For me to grind down on her fingers while that glorious pressure rubbed higher up. It felt so unbelievably good that I moaned her name. I ran a hand back through her hair to encourage her lips against my neck, I dug my fingers into her back and I was completely lost to her. Lost to the heat of her body over mine. Lost to the way her name felt every time it was coaxed from my throat. Completely lost to how it felt having her inside me while I still had the taste of her on my lips.

I couldn't hold it back. I tried *so* hard because I didn't want this to end so fast, but I couldn't stop it. The building tension between my hips reached a peak, and one more thrust against her hand sent me spiraling over the edge. I pulled her down to me, holding tight so I could bury my face in her shoulder, using her heated flesh to muffle the euphoric shout that came bursting from my chest. My hips rocked hard and slow and I could feel her fingers pulsing inside me to keep stroking it out, to keep me riding on the climax for as long as she possibly could. I would've loved for it to last forever, but not long afterward I settled into the bed, gulping air and letting out an involuntary hum as Ava's fingers left me.

She dropped to the bed at my side, and said and did nothing for a long minute until I opened my eyes. She was just watching me, a pleased curve at one corner of her mouth and a thoughtful glimmer in her dark blue eyes.

I rolled onto my side to face her, and draped an arm over her waist to pull her into me. "What are you thinking?"

She wrapped her own arm around me to hold me even closer, and shut her eyes as she set her forehead against mine. "I've never seen you so without reserve," she answered. "It's…"

"Strange?" I supplied playfully.

She huffed with laughter, and pressed a slow kiss to my lips before saying, "Beautiful."

What I didn't expect was for her eyes to be full of tears when they opened again. It worried me instantly, and so much that my heart plummeted. "Is that sadness?"

"No, no," she said, planting a series of reassuring pecks all over my face. "I promise, no." And she did her best to sniffle the moisture away. "It's relief." Though my eyes narrowed with confusion, I pressed a comforting kiss to her forehead. "You'll never know how this choice plagued me, Kiena," she said. "We worked so hard to get here that I didn't want to make it for nothing. But I feared if I let you leave without me, I'd lose an important piece of myself." She hugged herself to me, burying her face against my chest. "But I know, I know beyond a doubt that I'm doing the right thing."

I nuzzled into the top of her head, taking in a deep breath of her scent. "You won't hear me complain," I said, and it was nothing but the sincerest truth. We lay like that for a minute in silence, simply enjoying the feel of each other, and then my hand wandered up her back, to the ties at the rear of her dress. I'd have never been able to get them undone... "I'm right bitter about all those layers you had on."

Ava snickered, and I could feel her shaking with laughter against me. "You worked so hard to get me out of them."

I leaned back away from her, motioning to her still covered body. "And look at the fruits of my labor!" I glared. "Useless."

"If I'd known where the night was taking us," she laughed, "I would've worn something simpler."

I chuckled and rolled my eyes, and not a moment later Ava pulled me back to her, returning her lips to mine. She didn't stop for a while either. Just kissed me long and slow, her smooth fingers running up and down my back, to the front of me to trace between my hips and up my ribs. There wasn't a single part of me that minded, not the kissing or the touching, and my own hands explored what they could of her. They traveled across her lower back, up to where the top part of her scar was exposed by the dip of her dress, around and down the front of her neck. Down her collarbone. Down her chest. Into the front of her dress...

The whole time, I could feel Ava's lips thinning against mine with a smile, and when I actually managed to get my hand in her dress to cup her breast, she laughed. "Ah," she said, "the ever-honorable Kiena is not so chivalrous as she'd have us all believe."

I flicked my thumb over her nipple, enjoying the way her eyelids fluttered with pleasure. "What was that?" I asked smugly.

"Something," she began, humming with half-hearted protest when I did it again, "about something."

I brought my lips in close to hers, pinching the hard skin gently between my fingers. "You don't recall, do you?"

"Bribery," she accused on a weak breath, trying to catch my mouth with a kiss. "Chivalry."

"Which was it?" I asked, and though my lips were curled with amusement, I was starting to feel a renewed itch of arousal deep in my stomach. "Would you like me to be chivalrous?" I slipped my hand out of her dress.

The action was met with a protesting whine, and to remedy it, I slid my hand down the front of her, until I'd reached the bottom of her dress and could slide it back up underneath, along the inside of her thigh. Ava's blue eyes were locked on mine as her legs parted, but I stopped halfway above her knee.

"Bribe me," she pleaded. I raised one eyebrow, inching my hand up a little higher as if to ask if that's what she wanted. "Kiena," Ava breathed, one corner of her mouth tugging into a smirk, "keep teasing me and I'll make you beg so hard you'll forget the very word dignity."

For a long second, I just blinked at her. That was the best kind of threat. The kind of threat that barreled straight to my core. The kind of threat I'd have loved to see her make good on, but that filled me so instantly with need that I couldn't hold out on giving her exactly what she wanted. I kissed her, and I bribed her. I bribed her so thoroughly well that afterward she couldn't keep her eyes open, and she fell asleep on my bare chest.

Chapter 13

I woke early the next morning with a shiver. It was cold, and the sun had yet to make a real appearance through the single window in our room, so it was a dark gray throughout. Ava was on her side next to me and, without opening my eyes, I rolled over and wrapped my arm around her waist. I scooted into her for warmth and nuzzled my face into her hair, taking in a deep and comforting breath of her scent, still tired enough that I was prepared to fall right back asleep. I nearly did, but in my half-woken state, I sensed something was off.

There was a soft clipping noise that I recognized as Albus's nails against the stone floor. After listening for a few moments, I could hear that he was pacing back and forth in front of the door. There was a commotion from the garden outside too – shouting, and the distant clanking of a dull bell. I inhaled again, finally recognizing the sharp, metallic smell that filled my nose. Blood.

My eyes shot wide at the same time as I understood the first distinct words from outside. "The king and queen are dead!"

While I sat up, Albus stopped his pacing, putting his nose to the door and letting out a low growl. But my eyes hit Ava, and my heart dropped. The pungent scent of blood was coming from her – her white underdress was covered in it. It stained her hands and was smeared up her arms.

"Ava!" I exclaimed, turning her onto her back.

She gasped deeply, and her eyes flew open as she hurled herself into a sitting position. She didn't so much as look at me. The only thing she did was hold her hands out before her, taking in the red that tinted them.

"Ava?" I said again, grabbing her hands in mine so I could move them out of the way, so I could examine her for the source of blood. There didn't appear to be a single injury. The blood wasn't hers. "Are you hurt?"

"No," she whispered, but she wasn't talking to me. Her eyes filled with tears, and she pressed her balled fists to her face and rocked forward, murmuring, "No, no, no, no, no."

Another distant shout of, "The king and queen have been murdered!"

My heart was hammering away in my chest, pounding wildly with a sudden shock of adrenaline. I was surprised and confused, and I couldn't make any sense of this, but I knew what it looked like. Knew what everyone would think if they came in here, if they saw Ava covered in blood that wasn't hers while people were yelling that the king and queen were killed. It wasn't my concern right now what *really* happened. All I could think was that this was bad, and I had to focus on keeping us alive, and that meant running.

"Ava, get up," I muttered, throwing myself off the bed to put my tunic on. "We have to leave."

She didn't move. Just kept rocking back and forth with her hands over her face. Sobbing. With my shirt on, I hurried to the window, pushing it open just a crack in order to see what was happening outside. Troops were gathering in the garden. There was shouting and organizing, and people looked frantic and angry. I shut the window again and hurried back to Ava.

"Look at me," I said, taking her face in my hands. I wanted more than anything to comfort her for the loss of her father, but there wasn't time, and the longer she sat there without so much as looking at me, the more I began to panic. "I need you to focus. I need you to be strong."

She wouldn't. She shook her head, eyes locked again on her blood-stained hands. I released her and rushed to the door, opening it enough for me to stick my head out. There were three exits from our room – the stairwell to the ballroom below us, and two different halls that veered off to separate wings of the castle. We could take any of these, but the chances of us being seen with so many people scurrying about the castle were great. I couldn't be sure which direction to go in order to guarantee safety. The risk to Ava was high, and with the way she was acting right now, I wasn't even sure I could get her in a clean dress before someone came to the room.

181

I shut the door and paced back to the bed. "Ava, please," I begged. "We cannot stay here."

She glanced down at the blood on her dress, taking in the stutter of a horrified breath as if finally recognizing that she was *completely* covered in it. Her hands shot to her back, prying at the strings to undo them so she could get out of the clothing, but her hands and fingers were shaking so badly that she didn't even manage to undo the tie before there was a soft knock on the door. My face paled at the sound.

"Kiena?" said a muffled voice.

It was too quiet to tell who it was, and Albus was sniffing at the crack under the door like he couldn't tell either. It took a swift moment of searching around to find my dagger. It was on the floor on Ava's side of the bed, just as covered in blood as she was. I picked it up and hurried to the door, ready to strike if someone was here for Ava. There was another knock, harder and more impatient.

I opened up just a crack to see who it was. The king's physician. "Sevedi?"

"You must come with me," she muttered. "Now!"

"Why?" I asked, suspicious of her motives.

Sevedi slammed her hand against the door to force it open, motioning to Ava. "A witness saw her in the halls last night." She reached into the neck of her shirt, pulling up a chained pendant that matched the one around my own neck. It matched the one Kingston had given me. "They're coming for her. We must go *now*."

Our options were so limited that trusting Sevedi was the best and only thing I could do, especially because Ava was nearly incapacitated with grief. I darted over to the bed while Sevedi waited at the door, and wrapped an arm around Ava's waist to pull her off. "Please, Ava, let's go," I begged, pausing for only a moment to make sure she'd stay on her feet.

There was no time to take anything else. No more clothes, no more weapons, and we certainly couldn't go and find Maddox. I grabbed Ava's hand to drag her through the door, but the moment we took a step out, Sevedi shoved us back in. I heard why, too. A handful of heavy footsteps were coming up the stairs, and I grabbed Ava by the torso, pulling her back through the doorway and plastering us beside the entrance.

"They've escaped toward the north wing," Sevedi told the group, pacing toward them with a convincing amount of urgency in her voice. "I believe they're going to find the children."

The moment Sevedi said 'children,' Ava took in a soft gasp of recognition, as if suddenly realizing that her siblings were probably more grief-stricken than she was. The gasp was shaky. The kind I knew would preface a louder sob, and probably one that would give us away. Though it killed me to do this to her, I slapped my hand over her mouth to muffle any noise she made.

"Shh," I whispered soothingly. My stifling of her emotion only seemed to make it worse, and as I could hear Sevedi leading the group away from us, Ava collapsed against me, shoulders shaking with muted sobs. "It's alright," I murmured, keeping my hand over her mouth and wrapping my other arm around her chest, supporting her weight to keep her on her feet. "They'll be alright."

Ava continued sobbing silently, and I noticed that there was no sound from the hall either. I couldn't hear any words, or footsteps, and I wasn't sure where Sevedi had gone. For a long minute we stood there, stuck against the wall in the tense silence, my arm burning with the effort of holding Ava up. I inched toward the door, intent on peering out to see if anyone was in the halls because we couldn't just stand here. Whatever had become of Sevedi, Ava and I had to escape. I was just about to crane my neck around the doorpost when Sevedi's face burst through the opening.

"Let's go," she commanded.

I released Ava to take her hand in my own, dragging her behind me while we followed Sevedi and Albus. She led us not to the stairs or toward a main hallway that would be our exit, but toward the back of the wing. Toward a dead end. Only, when we reached it, she swept aside a tall, decorative tapestry and pushed hard against the wall. The stones gave, moving back in the shape of small door, which she then worked sideways to reveal a long, narrow tunnel.

"Come," she motioned. I pulled Ava into the passageway, and Sevedi entered and sealed it behind us, creating a magical glow in her palm to light the path. "This way."

We started a swift pace along the tunnel and began to descend a flight of stairs. All around, echoing through the walls, I could hear hysterical shouts and the clanking of armor, of soldiers running to various positions. We made it down the stairs, a flight long enough that, when we reached the bottom, I knew we were underground, because it wasn't made of brick like the castle anymore, but dug out of crude stone and earth.

No matter how urgently I pulled on her hand, however, Ava hadn't been keeping up with Sevedi and me. After the passage leveled off and we picked up our pace, she yanked out of my grip and collapsed to the floor.

"Ava," I said, and Sevedi stopped to wait while I knelt in front of her. "We have to keep going." She didn't say anything, just kept sobbing as she buried her face in her hands. "Ava, *please*. I know you didn't do this."

Her hands lowered, and for the first time that morning, her eyes met mine. "I-" Her voice quivered, and she breathed the syllable a handful of times before finally managing to stutter, "I did." A fresh flow of tears cascaded from her eyes. "Kiena, I *did*." My brow furrowed in disbelief. "My scar," she said shakily. "Hazlitt. He was controlling me. I was glowing red, *everything was red*." She whimpered, arms wrapping around her torso as though her grief was excruciating. "I remember it all," she sobbed. "I killed them."

"Keep moving," Sevedi growled, pacing over and gripping Ava by the arm, jerking her to her feet. "If you didn't have those necklaces, I'd kill you both myself for what you've done to my kingdom."

I grabbed the collar of Sevedi's shirt, throwing her back against the wall of the tunnel and materializing a current of sparks in my hand. It didn't matter one bit if she was helping us, I wouldn't let her treat Ava like that, and especially not when Ava was on the verge of a complete breakdown. "Touch her like that again and you'll never get the chance." And Albus supported my threat with a rumbling growl of his own.

She glared at me, but said, "They'll kill us *all* if we don't *hurry*."

I let Sevedi go, rushing back to Ava and scooping her up in my arms, because if she couldn't run then I'd carry her myself. We hurried down the remaining length of passageway at the fastest pace possible. It led to a heavy gate that, once pushed open, I could see had brought us to the woods just outside the castle. I exited, squinting against the brightening light of morning. Sevedi had already prepared a single horse, and without being told, I helped Ava climb onto it.

"What about you?" I asked as I hopped up behind Ava.

"You murdered my rulers," Sevedi said, and at hearing it, Ava whimpered and curled further into herself. "My kingdom will need me."

"I'm sorry," I told her sincerely.

She didn't respond to that. "Don't stop riding until you reach Valens. If they catch you, you're dead."

I nodded my thanks and kicked back my heels. The horse took off at a gallop, as fast as it could go with both Ava and me on its back. I steered us in the direction of the road we'd arrived on, and so far it looked like the castle was still in such a state of confusion that the road hadn't been blocked. It was clear, leaving an opening for us to get away even quicker.

But I feared this was something we'd never escape. Even if we managed to get away from Ronan soldiers, Ava would live with this forever. She'd finally had a good, honest family. She'd finally had a place to call home, and found people to love and love her in return. It didn't matter that she was going to leave with me, because they were dead. She'd known her father and stepmother less than three days, and she'd killed them. If we managed to make it back to Valens before being caught, it would make little difference. This would haunt her. Then my goal would be to comfort her, but then, right that moment, my only goal was to make sure we were around later for that to happen.

We traveled as swiftly as we could. Past the city and the farmland. After that, the road became unfamiliar, because on our way here we'd journeyed through the woods. It wound through the forest, and we were moving so fast that the sharp bends in the road were a surprise every time. It took all of my focus to guide us through, and as much as I wanted to, I couldn't spare a moment to try and tend Ava. The only thing I *could* do was hold the reins in one hand and wrap the other arm around her. I pulled her into me, too focused to say anything but hoping my warmth did something for her spirit.

Though my heart was still pounding fiercely in my chest, it felt like we might actually make an escape. There was no indication that we were being followed, and I risked a brief glance back to check. We were turning another bend as I faced forward again, and it was so sharp that we nearly crashed into the blockade as it straightened out. A blockade of soldiers. I pulled back on the reins so abruptly the horse reared, throwing both Ava and me off and to the ground.

I bolted up, pulling my dagger and creating a ball of sparks, ready to fight back. But the moment I reached my feet, a crippling force shot through my body. It was magic, and it was agonizing, and paralyzing, and I fell to my knees as someone stepped forward from the thick line of soldiers blocking the road. And it wasn't someone Ronan.

It was Hazlitt, and at seeing him, I glanced side to side to finally look at the expanse of men that accompanied him. They didn't just obstruct the road. There were so many spanning out through the woods that they reached farther than I could see. Their numbers were so thick that they stretched back along the next bend, and all of them were clad in red and gold. Hazlitt had brought his *entire* army. He'd used Ava to kill the king so he could come in and conquer Ronan while it was in a state of panic.

"You bastard!" I shouted, vaulting forward with every intention of plunging my dagger straight through his armored chest.

He raised a hand and clenched his fist, strengthening his magic's crushing hold on me so that I dropped right to my face. Albus snarled at him, stalking forward a few strides to place himself between the king and me. That's when someone else stepped out of the line of men, raising a crossbow at Albus.

"Back off, Albus," the soldier warned.

"Silas," I pleaded from my paralyzed spot on the ground. "You're making a mistake." Albus snarled again, but Silas ignored me and just stood there, holding the aim of his crossbow steady. And I knew if Albus attacked Hazlitt, Silas would fire.

"Call him off," Silas warned.

I shook my head. *"What are you doing?"*

Hazlitt took a confident step toward me, ignoring Albus's growls. "He's helping his king win a war," he said. He strode all the way to Ava, who was too grief-stricken to have moved from where she fell off the horse. He grabbed a handful of hair at the back of her head, pulled her off the ground, and retreated with her to the line. "Silas," the king began as he motioned to another soldier, who came over to clasp a heavy set of chains over Ava's wrists, "is this the same girl we sent to retrieve Avarona?"

"Yes, Your Majesty," Silas answered.

Hazlitt peered at me, watching me for a long few seconds with an almost confused look in his eyes, like he didn't recognize me. Maybe it was my magic he didn't recognize. Then he turned to Ava, seized her by the chin and turned it to the side, scowling at the dark bruise in her neck. The one I'd put there last night. With an irritated huff, he let her go, raising his hand toward me and squeezing his fist again. But I was already incapacitated, and it hurt so bad that I cried out in agony.

"Stop!" Ava pleaded, but she was weak with emotion, and Hazlitt was so large that when she slammed her fists against his steel shoulder, it did nothing. He grabbed her by the back of the neck and tightened his hold on me. I curled into a ball, in too much pain now to make a sound, but Albus barked, taking another stride forward before setting his teeth in a ferocious snarl.

Hazlitt pointed an annoyed glare at Albus. "That racket is fucking tiresome." He motioned toward Silas. "Shoot the beast."

"Your Majesty," Silas protested. When Hazlitt turned a fierce look on him, he sighed, raising his elbows to take a more accurate aim.

"Silas, no!" I forced out through the crippling pain. "Albus, down!" Albus stopped snarling, though his upper lip was still curled menacingly. "There," I begged, tears flooding my eyes at the fear of losing more than I already had. I *couldn't* lose Albus. He was family. "I called him off. *Please.*"

Silas passed an almost equally pleading look at Hazlitt, but Hazlitt's eyes narrowed. "I gave you an order!" he roared.

Silas's brown eyes scanned the expanse of soldiers around us, and then met mine, full of remorse and apology.

"Silas, no!" I screamed, but he raised his weapon once more, and Ava began to fight in Hazlitt's grip out of protest of her own. "Silas!" Silas's eyebrows furrowed sadly. "Please, NO!" He was going to shoot. "Albus, *run!*"

It was no use. Silas pulled the trigger of his crossbow, and the bolt hit Albus so accurately in the heart that he only got out half a yelp before collapsing in the dirt. I screamed again, so incoherently and full of fury and pain that my throat was instantly raw. I tried to channel it. Tried to turn the tears streaming down my face into that uncontrollable magic I'd lost myself to the first time, but it wouldn't work. It wouldn't consume me, and all I got was a pitiful jump of current in Silas's direction. He skittered sideways so it missed him and then looked at me, his eyes wide with shock.

I wanted to create another spark. I wanted to kill Silas for what he'd just done, because he'd done it knowing *exactly* what Albus meant to me.

He'd done it knowing that I'd raised Albus since he was a week old, knowing that Albus had been my closest companion for *years and years.* Every day since he was a pup, Albus had spent at my side. *Every single day.* He'd been loyal and loving. He'd saved my life more than once, been my partner in caring for Mother and Nilson. Albus was *family*. And he was gone.

I couldn't do any more. Hazlitt's grip on me, and the emotional anguish in my stomach and head and heart... it was too much. I was useless with grief and had too little control over my power. I hadn't just failed Brande. I failed Albus, too. I'd never get to look in his big, gentle eyes again. Never get to brush his coarse fur, or hug him and feel how warm he was. Never again know how safe it felt to have him lay his head in my lap, and look at me with his soft brown eyes full of that godlike devotion so unique to dogs.

Hazlitt stomped to where I was lying and squatted down. "I believe it was *you* who wanted me to *find another way*," he said with a jarring amount of taunting in his voice.

I roared a miserable holler of nothing at him, feeling a current of sparks in my throat. He stood and took a hasty step back, eyes briefly wide, but the sparks never reached him. They died on my tongue as the shout was broken by a sob.

"You'll want to hear what I say next," Hazlitt growled. "Time is of the essence." I craned my neck to scowl upward at him, but he was blurred with the tears in my eyes, and Ava had fallen to her knees behind him, her gaze locked on Albus's limp body. "Your cottage outside Wicklin Moor," the king began, "your mother and brother live there." And my scowl faded as all the blood drained from my face. "I sent three of my riders just before you arrived. They've orders to kill them both." I let out a sad cry, and through the water in my eyes, I saw Silas's face fall too, like he had no idea. The king motioned to another man, who led a horse forward to give him the reins. "This is *my* horse. The strongest, fastest horse in the kingdom." With a flick of his wrist, the grip he had on me released. "Probably even the world."

I wanted to fight back, but I needed to hear what he'd say about my mother and brother, and as hard as it was through the emotion and fading pain, I struggled to my feet.

"You've been a pain in my ass, Kiena," Hazlitt said. "But you know what? Take the horse." He shrugged like it was nothing, but his voice was

188

bitter and taunting. "After all, you've already taken my gold. You've taken the lives of my men. God be damned, you even took my *daughter*. Why not take my best horse?" Hazlitt laughed dryly, stomping closer to get in my face, because at his derision and jeering, my gaze had dropped to my feet. "Perhaps you could reach your family on time." I sniffled, holding back more tears. "Tell you what," he continued. "I'll give you a choice. We can trade so it's finally even. Take the horse, and all you have to do is leave Avarona with me. Or you can stay. Join me, lend me your magic and help me win this war. I'll give you land, and a lordship. You can have Avarona too, if you want her."

I whimpered a tragic cry as that proposition pierced straight through my chest. The three people I loved most in this entire world. I didn't think I could live without a single one of them. I could never cause any of them pain, and Hazlitt was making me choose. He was going to make me hurt Ava, or he was going to make me hurt my mother and brother. I had no other choice. I wasn't strong enough to fight. I had nothing to negotiate. This was it.

This was him dangling everything I wanted right in front of me. With land and a lordship, I could have my surname back. I could have honor in the eyes of the law. With a lordship, I could be with Ava. I could *marry* her. I could have the comfortable life I'd always wanted, but I'd have it without my family. I'd have it knowing I'd supported a man who'd killed Brande, Albus, Mother, and Nilson, and thus stolen vital pieces of my very soul.

"You're wasting time," Hazlitt muttered.

My eyes met Ava's, and for a long minute as hot tears streamed down my face, we just stared at each other. It was quiet. Hazlitt and Silas were silent. The soldiers were silent. Ava and I were silent. That minute passed, and my eyebrows furrowed and the corners of my mouth tensed with a grievous frown. And Ava knew. Her bottom lip quivered and her eyes filled with fresh sorrow, because she knew what I had to do just as much as I did. And when it fully sank in, her face converged with a pain like I'd never seen. The tears broke and what was left of her heart broke, and she was already on her knees, but she collapsed forward with a gasping sob. Her forehead met the earth and her chained hands covered the back of her head. Her shoulders shook, and she wept.

My gaze fell as salt bit at my eyes, and I took in a deep, trembling breath, working up the nerve and the will to move my feet. I couldn't look at Ava, because her sobbing already threatened to rip my heart right out of my chest. Nor could I look at Silas, or Albus's body, as I paced forward and took the reins from Hazlitt. I mounted the horse, and for a moment, I just sat there. Staring at the leather in my hands as the bitter torment of what I was doing cut me to the core. I'd hate myself after this, and if Hazlitt didn't kill her, then surely Ava would hate me too. But I couldn't let my innocent mother and brother pay for what *we'd* done. It wasn't a choice. *They* were never a choice.

I bumped my heels back, refusing to take my eyes off of my hands as I steered the horse north. The soldiers blocking the road parted, creating an opening in the middle for me to ride through. I passed them slowly, part of me hoping Hazlitt would change his mind and put an arrow in my back so I wouldn't have to go through with this. So it wouldn't matter what choice I'd made and I wouldn't have to live with the consequences. But it didn't happen. I got past all the soldiers and couldn't bring myself to look back. I kicked hard, and the horse took off at a gallop, leaving Silas and Hazlitt and all the soldiers behind. Leaving Ava behind.

Hazlitt hadn't lied to me. The horse was fast. So fast that it didn't even feel like its hooves were touching the ground as we flew over miles and miles of land. It was strong too. The animal pushed on no matter how long I forced it to run, and the farther north we got, the colder it got, until the wind whipping by us had turned my flesh numb. Numb and cold like everything inside me.

I felt nothing. Had shut everything out because I couldn't allow myself to *feel* if I was going to make it, if I was going to rescue Mother and Nilson. Couldn't allow myself to think about what I'd left behind. Not Albus. Or Ava. Because if I let myself think about it, I'd let myself hesitate. I'd grow more conflicted and more tormented, and in my fragile state, a conflict like that would be enough to break me, and I'd stop, and I wouldn't make it to the cottage, and I wouldn't make it back to Ava.

So I shut everything out. Stared straight ahead with nothing in my mind but left, and right, and dodge a branch, listen to the hoof beats. I was so numb that even though the horse galloped miles and miles, all day and into the night, I wouldn't let it stop. It would kill the horse, pushing the beast so hard, but I didn't care. I needed it to keep going. Needed it to sacrifice because losing Mother and Nilson wasn't an option. I'd lost too much, and wouldn't survive losing any more.

It galloped well into the next day. Every time it tried to slow down just to breathe, I kicked it hard. Made running less painful than stopping. Two days, and on the close of the second, we finally burst out of the forest and were nearly there. The sun was setting, but on the horizon, over the few remaining miles I had to go, there was smoke. A thick, black pillar of it, rising high into the air and originating exactly where I knew my destination to be. NO.

My heels kicked as sharply as they could, trying to urge the horse faster, but it wouldn't move any quicker. "Go!" I hollered, kicking back again, and in my urgent fury, I felt a static start in my chest.

It was no use. I'd pushed the horse too hard. So hard that it stumbled, its front legs gave out and we were already going so fast that it skidded on its shoulder across the grassy dirt. I couldn't wait, and I knew the horse wouldn't have the strength to rise again. It was as good as dead. Before it had even stopped sliding, I hurled myself out of the saddle, and that static in my chest *finally* did something useful. Like that day with Ava, in a blink I'd traveled a distance without a step, but this time it was *so much greater*. One spark-fueled jump and I was halfway across the six miles to the cottage, hitting the ground again with such a powerful current like lightning that it burned the earth beneath me. I took in a deep breath, allowing the magic as much control as it needed to take me the remaining distance.

This time I landed right in front of the cottage, so close that I stumbled back a few steps at the singeing heat of the fire. The entire thing was in flames, and they were spreading to the dry grass around it.

"No," I whispered. I dashed forward, attempting to run past the fire to get inside, to see if they were trapped, but it was too hot. "Mother!" I hollered, sprinting to the back of our home. "Nilson!" They were nowhere in sight, and I squinted into the fading light of day to scan the distance. Searching for them or a group of soldiers or *anything*. There was nothing. "Please," I whimpered, feeling a heavy flow of tears flood my eyes.

The entire cottage was engulfed. Without a doubt, my mother and brother were dead. All I could hope was that they'd been killed before the fire had started. Defeat crept into the very core of my soul. Complete and utter defeat, and I fell to my knees as those tears streamed down my cheeks, because all I could do was watch my home burn. All I could do was sit there on the ground, sobbing as the fire devoured everything I had. I watched it burn all night, until it died and I was left with absolutely nothing.

Silas, Brande, Albus, Ava, my mother, and Nilson, I'd lost it all. I had nothing to my name but the clothes on my back, my dagger, and my two necklaces. No food. No home. And worst of all, I had no one. I'd lost *everyone* I loved. Soon, I probably wouldn't even have a kingdom. Who knows what Hazlitt would do with the power once he conquered Ronan and found the elixir he was after?

By the time morning came and the fire was out, I didn't even have any tears left. Those were gone, and there was nothing in me, either. No hope, no drive, no purpose. So I stayed there, on my knees and empty and unmoving for half the next day, undeterred by the cold or the suffocating smell of smoke. Eventually, I stood, if only because nothing was happening here, and I wandered toward the snow-covered Black Wood. I walked the miles to the forest, and I kept going.

I wandered, well into dusk and then into the night. Maybe these woods really were haunted, maybe with something that could put me out of my misery. If not, there were always the wolves, or the cold. Or bandits. I'd take whatever death would be swift, because that had to be better than this. Better than knowing that my best friend had killed Albus, and that my mother and brother were dead. Better than knowing I'd betrayed Ava and abandoned her to an unknown fate with a man that she hated. With a man who'd made her kill her own father.

There was so much more I should have done. So many things I could have tried to keep this from happening. I should have felt it when Ava left my side that night. Should've known when she rose from bed and left the room to kill the king and queen. If I had, I could've stopped her. Could've saved her from Hazlitt's control and from doing something that would torture her. That would haunt her for the rest of her life. I should have sought someone at the castle in those short days that could have taught me to control my magic. Maybe it wouldn't have been enough to defeat Hazlitt, but it would've been enough to save us – to save Albus, and Ava, and Mother, and Nilson. It would've been enough to keep me from losing *everything*.

I should have given my life. Begged Hazlitt to release Ava and my family and just kill me instead; it would keep me from causing him any more trouble. And what did he need Ava for? She'd already killed King Akhran.

She'd already given him his window to conquer Ronan. I should have begged him to free her. Then I wouldn't have to live with this. This guilt and this loss, and this feeling like my heart was gone and instead I'd been filled with burning lead. Because it *hurt*.

At points during my wandering, it hurt my chest so badly that I couldn't breathe. It was too heavy and too agonizing, and I collapsed into the snow just to sob. Just to choke on screams of misery, because screaming distracted from the burning in my chest by searing my throat instead. I choked because I couldn't breathe. I sobbed so hard I couldn't get air. So hard I got lightheaded and so hard that as I gulped air in rapid succession it made me sick. It turned my stomach and the raw burning in my throat was worsened, because I sobbed so hard I vomited.

I'd never kiss Ava again. Never touch her, hold her, or hear her laugh. And even worse, she'd hate me. I didn't just lose *her*. I lost her trust and her affection, because I'd told her I loved her. I'd *made* love to her and then I'd left her without even looking at her. She probably thought she was nothing to me. Probably thought my love had been a cruel lie, when truly she was *everything* to me. I deserved death for what I'd done to her. For how badly I'd hurt and betrayed her.

I deserved death for how badly I'd failed Brande, and Albus, and Mother, and Nilson. They were all dead because I was weak. No more motherly kisses on the forehead before I left for a hunt. No more hugs when I returned. No more childishly mirthful laughs from my brother when I tickled him. He'd never wrestle with Albus. Never fall asleep with his face buried in Albus's neck when we returned from a hunt, because he always missed Albus just as much as he'd missed me. I'd never get to tuck him in, press a kiss to his sandy hair and then sit at the table in our cottage, listening to my mother tell me about all the trouble he'd found while I was gone. I'd never feel their love, or Ava's love, or any love ever again. I'd never again feel anything but this crippling anguish.

I hardly noticed when the sun rose because I was dead inside, and cold, and I hadn't slept in days. But I couldn't go any farther. After how many times I'd fallen in a fit of despair and rose again, there was no strength in my head or my heart or my limbs. I fell in the snow beneath the nearest tree and leaned back against the trunk, and was so exhausted that I couldn't even keep my eyes open.

Some unknown hours later, with the setting sun beaming through the breaks in the branches, my eyes cracked open again. It was instinct that woke me, because I could feel a solitary heartbeat out there in the woods, and all I could think was that death had finally come for me. And I was grateful. I waited for whoever or whatever it was to attack. I waited and waited while the heartbeat circled, keeping a distance and always hidden amongst the trees. Sometimes, when behind me, it got closer, others it stopped circling for minutes at a time just to watch. It was infuriating, and I was losing my patience.

"Come out and face me!" I shouted hoarsely, my voice broken with fatigue and emotion.

The heartbeat picked up, and from some distance ahead there was the softest crunch of a stride in the snow – four legged, I could hear that much. I watched, squinting into the foliage. Then it appeared. A massive she-wolf, with paws larger than my hands and thick fur as gray as dawn. It was snarling at me, and I noticed a scar down its left eye as it neared. It was blind on that side, and I'm sure it could hear just fine, but its right ear was missing too. It was a survivor. A fighter. A creature worthy of ending my life.

"Come on, then," I pleaded. "Do it."

It stalked closer, its upper lip curled to bare its teeth, but it stopped ten feet away. And it watched me. No sound but its heartbeat, no movement but its hot breath fogging the frigid air.

"Do it," I murmured through my growing impatience. At the sound of my voice, it growled. "Come on!" I hollered. It snapped its jaws, teeth clashing loudly as it took a step forward. "Do it!" The wolf snarled, leaping through the air. For some reason, my heart skipped, and I shut my eyes out of instinct and threw my arms up defensively. "Don't!"

There was an unfamiliar tingle at the forefront of my mind, and the wolf never bit down, but I could feel its humid breaths on my skin. I opened my eyes, lowering my arms to find the wolf's long fangs just an inch from my flesh. It was still baring its teeth, still looked angry and hungry and ferocious. But I knew. I felt it in my gut that I'd done this. *I'd* made it stop.

"Back up," I commanded. Again, that ache tickled my brain, and the wolf took a few paces back. "Sit." Its haunches met the earth. "Am I controlling you?" I asked. "Are you letting me?"

194

During that moment of my curiosity, a breeze picked up, one I noticed only because it was cold enough that I felt it in my bones. And because branches high in the trees quivered, and the wolf's head cocked to the side of its good ear. It simply sat there for a long span of seconds, eye locked on me but ear turned up as though it were listening. Then all at once, the breeze was gone, and the wolf stood and began to stride toward me again.

"Stop," I ordered, but this time it didn't listen, and that tickle felt more like a painful pinch. It was like the beast was fighting my control, and I wasn't physically or mentally or emotionally strong enough to regain it. "Don't eat me," I whispered.

It paced all the way back to me, baring its teeth when it got close enough. The wolf snarled, snapping its fangs so near my face that I plastered my head back against the tree, trying to get out of reach. It didn't bite me, though. Those long canines skimmed the upper part of my chest, until its jaws had closed around the Vigilant necklace I was wearing. Then it pulled, breaking the chain from around my neck and prancing back out of reach, stealing the piece of jewelry.

"Hey!" That was one of the only things I had left in the world. I'd be damned if I was going to part with it. "Give that back!" The wolf growled, and I was so tired and so emotionally broken that I didn't have the will to fight. I simply dropped my head back and sniffled, feeling renewed tears sting my eyes. "You shouldn't have listened to me," I cried. "You should've just killed me." The wolf growled deeper. "Go away then," I spat, pulling my knees up to my chest to wrap my arms around them and bury my face. There was no response from the animal, but I could still sense its heartbeat, and that aggravated me. I picked up my head, only to grab a nearby rock poking out of the snow. I hurled the stone in the wolf's direction. "Go away!"

It came closer, and I watched it drop the necklace at my feet and then retreat into the woods. I don't know why, but it broke my heart all over again that the wolf left, and I was reduced to uncontrollable sobs. Everything left me. *Everyone* left me, and I couldn't keep anything around or alive and I was alone. *So alone.* I soaked my trousers with tears until the sun set, and I probably would've soaked myself until I froze if I weren't so tired. I fell asleep again.

195

When I woke the next morning, my eyes opened, immediately meeting the one good eye of that wolf. It was lying in the snow in front of me, staring. It was as much of a relief to see the animal as it was heartbreaking to have watched it walk away. My eyes flooded again, and I wiped the back of my hand over my cheeks when the warm drops spilled.

For the first time, I glanced around at where I was, because it was familiar. Though I'd given no thought to where I was going during my wandering, my feet had taken me in the direction of the Vigilant caves. I was close. I could feel it. I could see the mountain those caves were set in a short distance away.

It gave me a destination, even if I wasn't sure what I'd do once I got there, or how it would help. Maybe it would give me something to live for, something to throw myself into so I could deal with my grief. If anything, at least I wouldn't have to be alone. As weak as I was, I stood. I pushed myself to my feet and trudged past the wolf in the direction of the mountain. I walked, and the wolf walked, though I lost sight of it because it paced off ahead of me.

The mountain was farther than it looked, and my progress was slow because of how weak I was. It took me a better part of the day to reach it, and then I had to travel along the base of it in order to find the entrance to the caves. After a while, it felt like I'd never find it. I began to doubt myself and wonder if I was so tired that I was making the location up, if I was so desperate to find someone or something that I was imagining it.

I thought about giving in, but soon after I began to consider it, I saw the wolf in the distance, sitting on its haunches beside the mountain. I trudged to the animal, finally reaching the entrance – that wooden door set in the sheer rock. I slammed my fist against it once, not having the strength to knock any more than that, and the wolf ran back into the woods when I did. The single knock was all I needed. The door swung open, and Oren was the one who stood there.

"Kiena?" he said in shock. He motioned for me to come in, and then turned to the nearest man to shoo him away. "Go get them," he told the man, "go."

It was so warm in the caves compared to outside, and it was like being around other people for the first time in days reminded me of my nearing mortality. I'd hardly slept. I hadn't eaten. I was broken and defeated and weak. I could barely stand, and Oren caught me by the waist when my knees gave out, aiding me to a nearby wooden box to sit on.

"Are you injured?" he asked in concern.

I hardly knew Oren, but I was too upset to care. I buried my face against his shoulder out of weakness and because my eyes were blurring all over again.

"It's alright," he said, and patted my arm to get me to straighten up. "Look." I picked up my head to see what he wanted me to, and my heart sank.

"Kiena!" Nilson exclaimed, sprinting to me and throwing his arms around me. My mother was here too, and she left Kingston's side to hurry over.

I couldn't move. I was frozen in place as they hugged me, because all I could feel was the further shattering of my heart into a million abysmal pieces.

"Once you left," Kingston said with a smile, "I figured they'd be safer here."

It should've made me happy. It should've been a relief that they were alive and I should've been grateful for what Kingston had done. But I wasn't. I broke down with an earthshattering sob, collapsing off the box and to the floor. I curled into a tight ball as I was filled with so much despair that I felt like a dagger had been plunged into my heart and twisted, and it kept twisting and twisting. All it meant that they were here, and alive, and safe... the only thing it meant that my mother and Nilson were fine was that leaving Ava had been the biggest mistake of my life. I'd betrayed her trust. I'd betrayed her *love.* And for *nothing.*

Part 2

The Dragon

Chapter 14

 n my slumber, I was here again. In a world of black. There was nothing at first, not now or the last two nights I'd had these dreams. I simply hit the dark ground, unable to see or feel anything but what was under me. Then, like the last two nights, the only thing in this darkness was a voice, smooth and low and smoky. A whisper. *Go to her.* I sat up, searching the darkness for the source. And again, louder than last time, more urgent: *GO TO HER.* I began to push up, but it wasn't quick enough. *GO!* I struggled blindly to my feet, prepared for what would come because the same thing happened the previous two nights. The moment I stood, the ground gave out beneath me. I fell one story, and no matter how hard I tried to stay on my feet, I crashed down onto a stone floor on my back.

It knocked the breath out of me. I sat up gasping, and even though I expected it, just like the nights before, it was a painful shock to see *her*. Ava. We were in the room at King Akhran's castle, Ava seated at the edge of the dresser just inside the door. It seemed to startle her when I landed in the room, and we locked eyes as I sat up, and I stopped breathing. She stared, and I stared, with a growing agony in my chest that seemed to mirror in her as her blue eyes filled with tears.

But this dream was a nightmare, because this wasn't the Ava I knew. She wasn't full of life and joy. Her eyes were sunken with grief, as were her cheeks, and her collarbones. She was thin and pale, in a tattered dress, and she looked so weak that I feared she'd collapse. In this nightmare, everything seemed to scream at me that it was *my* fault she looked like this. My fault she was just a shell of what she used to be. Though she didn't say it, surely she thought so too, because just like the last two nights, after that brief shock wore off, she stopped looking at me.

It had been too painful the last couple of dreams for me to speak. This time, however, as she pushed herself off the dresser and went to open the door, I rushed to stand before she could walk out. "Ava," I pleaded. She froze, and this was so different from the last two nights that I didn't know what to do. Once she walked out that door and I tried to follow, I'd wake up, and even though this was excruciating, I didn't want the dream to end. I couldn't find peace in my waking hours, but if I kept having these dreams, maybe I'd find some here. "Please," I begged, my voice quivering, "please look at me."

Her head turned the slightest bit like she might meet my gaze, but her eyes never made it past the floor. "You're gone," she whispered. And she walked out the door.

"Ava!" I called, pacing for the exit and intent on following her.

My eyes bolted open as I woke, and I sat up with a shout. It startled the small group of Vigilant rebels around me, including Nira. It had been five months that she'd been here. After I recovered enough from the loss of Ava and Albus to be able to speak, I'd told Kingston that he needed to get Nira and Akamar out of Ronan. I owed it to them, and to King Akhran and Queen Gwinn. Most of all, I owed it to Ava. It had taken a month, but eventually Sevedi managed to escape Ronan with the royal children.

When Nira first saw me, she'd been furious. She didn't want to talk to me, hear of me, or even see me. All it had taken was a few weeks for her to calm down enough to understand and accept what had happened to her mother and father. Once she did, she'd come to me with a bow in her hand and two simple words: "teach me."

Now she looked at me in my startled, upright position, and then glanced around at the early gray of the morning. "This is supposed to be a surprise attack," she said, leaning back against the tree behind her and sticking her legs out to settle down again. "It won't be if you're shouting."

I folded my knees up to my chest, rubbing my hands over my face to try and work off the tiredness. We were with our usual group of rebels, twenty miles from the Vigilant caves, preparing to cut off a supply convoy to Hazlitt in the south. If there was one thing Valens did better than Ronan, it was making weapons. We hadn't the troops or the supplies to attack Hazlitt's army yet, but by robbing his supplies, we were building our inventory and weakening his.

Kingston had made me First Ward of the ranger company, which meant I oversaw all scouting and raiding parties. It was the rank I wore on the dark green tunic of my rebel uniform, on the opposite arm as the Vigilant symbol. A uniform that matched the one all my rangers were wearing under our hardened leather armor. I didn't necessarily need to go on raids like this – in fact, I think Mother would have preferred if I didn't – but it gave me something to do.

Because it kept me busy; which is why I suspected Kingston made me First Ward to begin with. Over the last six months, he'd graciously given me as many tasks as he could fill my time with – leading the rangers was an important one. Another of his favorites was sending me to swords practice, to be taught by a mysterious warrior that I only ever saw during my lessons, and who stressed its importance as heartily as Kingston did. Apparently Hazlitt was an excellent swordsman, and they thought I should have at least some training with the weapon before we went into battle. While I saw the importance of the skill, I *hated* it. I was horrible, and I had so little patience anymore to begin with, and on the worst days all it did was remind me of Ava. I avoided it as often as I could get away with.

Nira cocked her head, brown eyes taking me in with concern as she said, "You dreamt again." I nodded. "You should tell your mother, and Kingston."

"I'm not telling them," I whispered, glancing around to make sure nobody else had heard. "Nor will you." I'd been doing my best to keep up the appearance that I was healing, that I was sleeping at night and focused, and that the simple act of smiling wasn't an emotionally tolling struggle. No matter how hard I tried, I was never successful.

"They worry about you," she said, though the tone of her voice let me know that she was worried too. "The least you could do is take something to get a full night's rest."

It was a feat to keep from glaring at her with frustration. "We're not having this conversation again."

"Kiena," she sighed, "it's-"

"If you say it's been six months, Nira," I interrupted, "so help me." She took in a breath to continue her argument, but I growled, *"Not now,"* because this was the wrong time and place, and I was *tired* of hearing it.

I was tired of everyone telling me to make an effort to move on. Tired of everyone telling me that I had to forgive myself. Tired of everyone using time against me, and telling me it had been long enough now that I needed to give up for my own good. I knew exactly how long it had been. Six months. Twenty-five weeks. One hundred and seventy-three days. I knew better than they did. I knew every hour, minute, and second intimately because of the pain they caused, because I was never without the reminder that I was a traitor. I knew.

Before Nira could try and come up with anything else to hound me about, that one-eyed, one-eared she-wolf crept out of the woods. I could control her with my magic, as I'd learned to control any animal, but I didn't need to. She was wild and kept to the woods a majority of the time, but she followed me. Surely she'd decided I was her pack, and it helped that the magic allowed some communication – I couldn't understand her by any means, but she always seemed to understand me. Nor had I named her, not being ready yet to attach myself to another creature, but Nira had taken to calling her Haunt.

"You hear something coming?" I asked the wolf, and at the question, all the rebels around us quieted. I nodded toward the road, down the small hill of which we'd camped atop. "Go on and check, then. You know the signal."

The wolf padded off, keeping hidden from view of the winding road below us by creeping through the bushes. It wasn't long until I lost sight of her too, and we all waited tensely for the signal to alert us that the supply caravan was nearing. There was another group farther down the road, ready to flank the caravan at the same time we cut it off from the front. It got so still as we all waited, and each of us crept to the edge of the hill after a minute to peer over it and down to the road. Nira posted herself at my side, bow in hand and ready to attack.

I glanced sideways at her, whispering, "Make sure you keep your elbow up."

No matter how many times I told her, she always had the habit of relaxing her form. Still, my advice was met with a narrow scowl, which would have been followed by a snarky comment if the sounds of the caravan didn't come within range. There was the soft murmur of conversation, hoof beats against the dirt, and the rolling of carriage wheels. I pulled my dagger from the belt at my waist just as a deafening howl pierced the air.

Nira sprang to her feet at the signal, taking aim and firing her first shot as the others and I dashed down the hill. The lightly armored soldiers escorting the caravan pulled their weapons immediately, taking position to defend their supplies as we reached the road. I materialized a ball of sparks in my right hand and ran at the nearest soldier. He had a broadsword in his grip, and he swung hard as I neared him, but I had so much speed that I dropped to my knees, sliding across the dirt road toward him while the sword flew over my head. Before he even realized he'd missed, I'd struck him in an exposed leg with my spark hand. He fell to his knees in convulsions as I rose, eyes locked on my second target.

I dashed toward the next soldier, easily ducking the swing of his heavy weapon and pushing him into the momentum. It spun him around so he was facing the wolf, and she didn't even give him a chance to scream before snapping her jaws around his throat. The caravan was well guarded, and with enough men that two more were already coming at me. The first one to reach me was equipped with two light war axes, a set of weapons as hard to dodge as they would be to counter, but the man hesitated when I created a strong current in my hand.

In the split moment he hesitated, I heard the second one's light armor at my back, and there was no time to do anything but react. I twisted toward the second soldier, and because I knew I wouldn't be able to finish him by the time the first one attacked, I twirled my spark-wielding wrist. It sent the current wrapping around him, the static freezing him in place just as the first man wound up. He swung at me with both axes at once, arms arcing outward so that when I leapt back and he missed, it left his chest exposed.

There was no way I could plunge the dagger through his metal chest plate, and I'd learned from experience that the armor didn't sit close enough to their bodies for my sparks to penetrate. At best it would leave burns, but it wasn't fatal, and therefore not a good tactic. Leading with my shoulder, I threw myself forward and into him. He was already off balance from his swing, and his armor was heavy enough that when I bashed him, it knocked him backward. As he hit the ground, I shot a fatal orb of current toward his thigh, and turned back to the man I'd trapped. I could have easily finished him off like this, but I wouldn't. No matter how simple it was to kill a man that I'd frozen, it wasn't honorable. It wasn't right.

I released him from the static with another twirl of my wrist, and he stared at me for a moment, wide-eyed. It only took a second for him to recover. He came at me sword first, and in order to avoid the point of his weapon I moved myself on a shot of sparks, jumping directly behind him. He stopped charging, but knowing where I'd landed, he swung around with his sword. I leaned backward, barely managing to avoid being skimmed with the sharp edge, and my left arm pitched upward as the heavy swing turned him away from me, swiping my dagger across his forearm. It cut him so deep he dropped his weapon, and I rolled forward to get behind him before he could pick it up again, grabbing the back of his head at the same time I created a powerful current of sparks.

As the current carried through his skull, I noticed Nira sliding down the hill toward the road, and she knelt on one knee when she hit the ground, firing an urgent shot my direction. It soared right at me, nicking my arm just below the shoulder on its arc upward and then plunging point first into the neck of a soldier who'd been about to swing at me. I pushed the lifeless body of the man I'd shocked to the dirt as Nira rose to her feet.

The action around us was dying down, and I glanced at the wound she'd made as she strode over. It was bleeding, and painful even though not very deep. I'd live, but I still glared at her. "How many times have I got to tell you to keep your bloody elbow up?" She was a spectacular archer. She could be so accurate when she *really* tried.

She leaned in close to look at it, and then clapped her hand over the injury. "You're welcome."

I groaned at the shooting pain of her slap, muttering through clenched teeth, "Gods, woman, you're *trying* to kill me."

Nira simply gave me an exaggerated grin of apology, but it faded not a moment later as her gaze was pulled behind me. I turned to follow the look, only to find that there was still one enemy soldier remaining. The man was cowered behind a nearby bush as my troops surveyed the supplies we'd just taken ownership of. I twirled my wrist, guiding a static coil around him, and I yanked him out of cover with a flick of it, bringing him all the way to me. He was trembling with fear, even as I stood him in front of me and released him from the hold.

"P-p-please," he stuttered, head cowering and hands folded at his chest. "I have children. What will they do without me?"

For a long span of seconds, I just stared at him, taking in his fear and his words and his submission. We never took prisoners, and only sometimes took converts, but this man made no plea for either. Instead, when after a few moments I said nothing, he turned and started sprinting down the road. I was going to let him go – he clearly wasn't much of a soldier anyway – but Nira loaded an arrow into her bow.

"Trust me," she murmured in response to his unanswered question, and fired a shot that pierced through the back of his head. "They'll live." Then she looked at me, asking, "Was my elbow high enough, First Ward?" Instead of replying to her sarcasm with words, I touched a single finger to her neck, allowing a small spark to jump into her skin. It scared her more than it hurt, but she yelped with surprise. "Do that again and I'll offer Haunt a portion of all my meals to bite you in the ass."

I didn't have to touch her. This time I flicked a spark at her, and when she yelped a second time, the hint of a rare smile *almost* graced my lips. At least, until she retaliated by slapping the arrow wound in my arm, and then she hurried away before I could do anything to return the favor.

"Rangers!" I hollered so all the rebels could hear me, and shook out the stinging in my arm. "Gather the carts, let's move!"

I stood off to the side of the road, watching as some of my rangers drove the horse-drawn supply carts past and in the direction of the caves. I took up the rear, and waited patiently for the group to get a good distance ahead, putting space between them and me. Then I strode to the largest tree visible from the road, and did what I did every time we raided supplies and left bodies behind. I slapped my hand to the trunk in a surge of lightning, sending that power flowing like a river into the wood. It was deliberate in strength and placement and shape. It created the symbol of an owl, burning the mark of the Vigilant into the bark so that whoever happened to see this, whoever took the message to Hazlitt that they'd been robbed, would also take him the knowledge that it was me, and that I wasn't hiding from him. I was fighting back.

After leaving my message, I caught up with the rear of the caravan on a flash, where Nira and the she-wolf had positioned themselves, to travel at their sides. For a long few minutes, we walked behind the company in silence. It was almost enough time for me to start appreciating it, but it didn't last.

"Truly," Nira said, "is your arm alright?"

I adjusted my arm to take a look. It had nearly stopped seeping, and once we returned to the caves, Sevedi would be able to heal it quickly. "Aye."

There was a beat of tense silence, and I just knew that Nira was trying to find a way to bring up the dreams, or the fact that Kingston and my mother were worried, or that I hadn't been myself. Instead of going straight at it, she said, "Rhien fancies you."

I turned a hard eye on her, and growled in warning, "Nira."

She was talking about one of the kitchen ladies, a woman who Nira, Kingston, and my mother had all tried to get me to at least talk to. To say more to than 'please' and 'thank you.' Rhien was a fugitive who'd escaped from one of Ronan's magic sanctuaries when Hazlitt began purging the kingdom of the abled who wouldn't swear allegiance to him. She was kind, and if I actually tried to pay attention, attractive, but their requests only made me angry.

"Kiena," Nira sighed, "you're not the only one who lost something."

"You lost your father and mother," I said in irritation, "I didn't *lose* Ava. I left her. I betrayed her."

"And you think she wouldn't forgive you?" Nira argued. "She wouldn't want you to spend the rest of your life torturing yourself about it."

"And when we find her," I muttered, "I'll no longer have to."

"Kiena," she sighed again, and I knew what was coming.

"Don't," I spat.

"You look at me," she commanded. She reached over and grabbed the neck of my tunic, turning me toward her as she halted our pace. "You need to prepare yourself for what Kingston will say when we get back."

Over the last six months, Kingston had his spies searching every prison in Valens *and* Ronan for Ava. Every time we got word on a specific prison, it was that she wasn't being held there. Six months, and we were supposed to hear from a spy in the last place we hadn't searched. No one had said it to me, no one had yet had the courage to, but I knew they all believed she was dead.

"Kiena," Nira said, "you need to prepare yourself for hearing that she's not there, and you need to accept that she's gone." I knocked her hands away and took a step back, preparing to spark jump and put some distance between us. "Don't do the-"

I disappeared before she could finish, placing myself at the front of the caravan. I didn't want to hear what she had to say, nor did I want to hear it from Mother or Kingston. For six months, I'd lived with this guilt, with knowing how badly I'd betrayed Ava. The only thing that had kept me going was the belief that we'd find her, and that I could make it better. Even if she never forgave me, at least I could know she was safe. She could hate me for the rest of her life, she could be happy with someone else, as long as she *was* happy. That's all that mattered. I owed it to her, and I'd never stop searching, and I'd never give up on her.

Not once the entire, full day's trek back to the caves did Nira try and walk with me again. It was dark by the time we returned. The wolf made her escape into the woods, and it wasn't until we'd handed over the rations and weapons on the carts to the supply boys, stowed our armor and wandered into the food cavern, that Nira finally found me. She sat down at my side, but didn't say a thing as we were served leftovers from supper. Word of our return must have got around while we ate, because two young boys sprinted across the dining hall.

"Have you brought us anything?" Akamar asked Nira, skidding to a halt with Nilson at his side.

"Perhaps I have," Nira teased, "but you'll never know until I get a kiss hello." She leaned sideways in her seat so both the boys could plant a peck on her cheek. "And for Kiena, too."

I'd been raising my spoon to my lips for another slurp of stew, but paused to lean over so they could give me kisses as well. Once they'd both done as she asked, Nira reached into a pouch attached to her belt, and pulled out something wrapped in linen. She handed it over to the boys, who dashed around to the other side of the table and climbed onto the bench, opening the gift with wide eyes. It was a sweet roll, one I knew Nira had taken from the supply cart because this wasn't the first time she'd done it.

"Thieves," I accused, rolling my eyes. "The whole lot of you."

"Share," Nira told our brothers, reaching across the table to rip the roll in half and then looking at me. "You're a thief too, First Ward," she quipped. "Or have you forgotten we're rebels?"

"I've not forgotten," I said, taking another slurp of stew.

As all of us ate, I could feel Nilson's eyes falling on me every couple of seconds. The last six months had been good for him, and his presence had been a comfort to Akamar, but I could tell he regretted my behavior. I wasn't playful with him, didn't joke or tickle or laugh. After a few bites of his half of the sweet roll, he held it in his hand, skipped back around the table, and climbed up to sit beside me.

"Would you like a bite?" he asked me, holding out what was left of the roll and blinking his big hazel eyes.

He was doing it to try and cheer me up, and I couldn't possibly refuse him, even if we both knew that I didn't like sweets. I took a bite, offering a small smile and then kissing the side of his head. "Thank you."

Nira joked with and teased the boys until we were finished eating, and while they went off to play and Nira went to wash up, I went to look for Sevedi. She could usually be found in the infirmary, but we'd arrived late and she wasn't there. Reluctant to seek her out in her personal chamber, I figured my arm would be fine until morning, and sought out Kingston instead. I found him in the war room, down the same hall as the training grounds. He was discussing over a large map with Oren, but when I came in, Oren excused himself and closed the door behind him.

It was only Kingston and me, and he knew why I'd come to find him, but instead of saying anything right away, we both just stood there. Eventually he asked, "How was the raid?"

"A success," I answered, and though I was afraid to hear the answer, I prompted, "any word?"

He took in a deep breath, letting it out slowly as his eyes dropped to the table. "I'm sorry," he said. "She wasn't there."

Despite the overwhelming pang in my chest, I did my best to keep it off my face. "Keep searching."

Kingston strode around the table, coming over to set a hand on my shoulder. "There are no more prisons to search."

"*Keep searching*," I repeated, taking a step back out of reach. "Search Hazlitt's ranks. Search the castles of lords who support him. Search every damn town if we have to. She's out there."

"Kiena," he murmured, his voice full of sadness and condolence. I immediately turned to make an escape, because I didn't want to hear it, but when I reached for the door handle, Kingston forced his palm against the wood to stop me. "You cannot keep this up." He leaned a little to try and get my attention, but tears were flooding my eyes, and I refused to take them off the handle in my grip. "I know it hurts," he said, putting his other hand on my back, "but it will never stop hurting if you don't allow yourself to let go."

I pulled the door hard, and though he was strong enough to have kept it closed, he allowed me to open it and rush out. Blinking away the tears, I hurried back toward the main entrance of the cave and down another hall toward my personal room. I closed the door behind me when I got there, falling back against it and sliding to the floor as all the emotion I'd tried to contain struck me in the chest. Ava was *nowhere* to be found. She wasn't in any prison in either kingdom, and if she'd been moved somewhere else, wouldn't Kingston's spies have heard of it? Wouldn't there be something, even the smallest rumor, about where she'd been taken? There was nothing. No word, or rumor. But... wouldn't we know if she'd been killed? Wouldn't there be a rumor of that too? Wouldn't the spies know who to ask? Wouldn't people know about it?

The tears flowed over. I didn't know what to believe. Everyone wanted me to accept that Ava was dead so I would start moving on, but nobody knew for sure. Nobody knew anything even though they pressured me relentlessly, and I was stuck in the middle. Stuck because, on the one hand, I wished Ava was still alive, and if she *was* then I couldn't give up searching for her, couldn't condemn her to a life of captivity simply because I'd stopped looking. Stuck because, on the other hand, as much as I'd learned to accept how badly my own guilt tortured me, it hurt everyone I loved too. It hurt Mother and Kingston with their worry, it hurt Nilson because of how I neglected him, and it hurt Nira. She cared for me, she'd become my closest friend, and there was nothing she could do to help.

I sniffled, wiped my cheeks, and stood, forcing back everything I was feeling. I'd stay stuck because it was my only option. Because I couldn't betray Ava again by giving up and moving on, and I couldn't abandon everyone who loved me by devoting everything I had to finding her. I'd stay stuck, and tortured, and empty, until something swayed me.

Able to push the pain back to the very depths of me – where I could control it – I strode to a cabinet on the far side of my room, where I kept a small supply of medicines. I pulled out linen and my decanter of antiseptic, set them on the table right beside the cabinet, and then rolled up the sleeve of my tunic to clean the wound. After soaking the linen in antiseptic, I scrubbed at the injury, making sure it was clean so I could wrap it and forget about it until tomorrow. Truly, I probably didn't need to do any of this, because come morning Sevedi would heal it regardless of how little care I took tonight. But it gave me something to do, something mindless to focus on so I didn't have to think about anything else.

Once the wound was clean, I grabbed a fresh roll of linen to wrap it in, because it was bleeding again and I didn't want my clothes to get any bloodier than they already were. But the wound was in a hard spot. I tried to hold the end of the linen in place against my chest, but it kept slipping off before I could wrap the rest. I couldn't get the linen tight enough no matter how many times I tried, and blood was dripping down my arm and staining random spots of the wrapping, and I got frustrated. And I nearly had it when there was a knock on the door, unexpected enough that I flinched and lost the grip on the linen.

"What?" I snarled, because I was just... angry. So angry that, while whoever it was opened the door and came in, I threw the linen roll clear across the room and into the small fire.

As I set my palms flat on the table in frustration, I glanced briefly toward the door to see who had entered. Rhien.

She closed it behind her, brown eyes watching me cautiously as she said, "Nira said you were looking for me."

"She lied," I growled. One of Rhien's eyebrows rose with surprise, and she turned without saying anything and reached for the door handle to leave. In how little I knew of her, I knew she wasn't the type of person to stand being spoken to like that. She'd chastised Vigilant troops for lack of respect countless times in the dining hall. "I'm sorry," I said before she could pull the door open. I sighed, turning around to lean back against the table and rubbing my hands over my face, doing my best to calm down. "I'm sorry."

She just stood there for a minute, eyes going from me to the rolled up sleeve of my tunic and the blood, and then to the already charred linen roll in the fire. "You have more wrappings?" she asked as she strode over, and when my eyes wandered to the cabinet, she opened it and pulled out a new roll. "I take it you aren't as interested in seeing me as Nira made it seem." She pulled my elbow out so she could start coiling the linen around the wound.

I was still frustrated, especially because Nira had put me in this situation, but I couldn't take that out on Rhien. "It's not that I'm against conversation," I said, watching her hands circle my arm. "But I fear Nira may have misled your expectations."

Even though I didn't say it, she knew what I was implying. Knew that Nira had hoped a woman, and maybe even just sex, would be a distraction for me. But the very thought of it made me sick to my stomach – I'd betrayed Ava enough already.

Rhien hummed, and then said, "I fear she may have misled yours as well." I squinted at her curiously. "I'm not so daft as not to realize you've no interest in romance," she explained. "And I've no interest in investing in something which will yield no return." Hearing her say that was such a relief that I was instantly no longer angry with Nira, and such a relief that I sighed loudly. Only, Rhien mistook it for something other than relief. "Was that offensive?" she asked worriedly, and since she was done with wrapping my arm, she tore the linen from the rest of the roll and tied it off.

"Thank you," I said, pushing the sleeve of my tunic back down. "And no. On the contrary, it was... refreshing." Everyone was so eager for me to forget and move on, it was nice of someone to *actually* acknowledge and *know* that I wasn't ready for that to happen. "If you were aware of Nira's lie, why'd you come?"

"I see the way they look at you," she answered, turning to lean back against the table at my side. She smoothed the skirt of her dress, tucked a strand of her shoulder-length loose black curls behind her ear, and then folded her arms across her chest. "The pity and the concern. It's well intentioned, I'm sure you know." She shrugged, saying, "But sometimes the best support is being told that what you're feeling is perfectly fine."

I shut my eyes so she wouldn't see the fresh blur of tears in them, and took in a deep breath to stop the flood of emotion. It felt so good to have someone tell me that, so comforting. It did nothing to heal me, or to make me want to move on, but for once I felt no pressure to hide my torment, which was strange for me, considering I hardly knew Rhien.

"I've seen the way your expression falls when they stop looking at you. I've seen how hard it is for you to pick it up again when their eyes return." She unfolded her arms to set a hand on my back. "I can't imagine how exhausting it is."

Despite my efforts, a tear forced its way out and slid down my cheek. I opened my eyes, wiping the drop away with the back of my hand. "I *am* tired," I agreed. "Most nights I can't sleep, and lately, when I do fall asleep, I've been dreaming."

"What kind of dreams?" she asked, removing her hand from my back and folding both in her lap.

"You know what grieves me?" I asked, because I wasn't sure how much anyone really knew about my situation, though I was certain people talked. Rhien nodded. "I dream of her. I fall into a room, and she's there. It scares her. And she's thin and weak, but she won't talk to me. It was the same the first couple of nights. She walked out the door before I could say anything, and when I tried to follow, I woke up. Last night I said her name, and she stopped, told me I was gone, and left." I wiped away another tear, and for a few moments, there was no reply. When I glanced sideways at Rhien, she was staring at the ground. "What is it?" I asked.

"Do they feel real?" she asked, meeting my gaze. "The dreams."

"I'm not sure," I answered. "They're unlike any dream I've ever had. Why?"

"I came with the mages from Duskford Monastery," she said, "the mind masters, you know this?" I nodded. "I grew up there. We were taught history, heard stories, and learned of magic that could never be controlled because it was alive."

"What are you trying to say?" I prompted.

"There was a story of magic that sought out lovers, separated by betrayal." She pushed away from the table to pace in front of me, still watching the ground. "It would give them a chance to reconcile."

My eyes widened, watching Rhien with renewed and intense interest. "I'm dreaming to make amends? Does it mean she's alive?"

"If that's what this is," she answered, "then yes, and you can make amends if she'll let you. She, the betrayed, has total control when you meet." And all I could do was let out a stunted breath, full of so many powerful emotions that my eyes flooded once more. "Kiena, there is risk to you." I sniffled, trying to keep myself composed so she could speak, and nodded that I was listening. "There's always a door. If the betrayed closes that door, the betrayer will be stuck in the dream forever."

It was *so* much to take in. The dreams were real and Ava was alive. I had the confirmation I'd been so desperately searching for. In the morning I could tell Kingston, and he could tell his spies, and we could find her. Or maybe I could ask her, if I could get her to talk to me in the dream. Maybe she knew where she was being held. But, wait...

"Why is she in such poor health?" I asked. "In the dream."

Rhien's eyebrows converged with apology. "What you are in the dream is what you are in the world. If she's sick, you must find her."

The entire last six months, I'd dreaded the night. Lying down and trying to sleep had been agonizing, had been hours of reliving all the mistakes I'd made. Now, I *wanted* to sleep. I wanted to find Ava and rescue her.

"Thank you," I whispered, with so much overwhelming gratitude that I stood and gave Rhien a tight hug. "Thank you."

She returned it, nodding as I let her go. She must've known how desperate I was to figure this out, because she started toward the door of my room. "Kiena," she said when she reached it, pausing to look at me. "I hear the soldiers talk in the tavern. They admire you. You're an important part of this rebellion." She grabbed the handle to open the door, saying before she walked out, "Be careful."

Once she was gone, I dressed for sleep and smothered the fire, climbing into bed and shutting my eyes tight. I wanted to fall asleep instantly, because this was important and I had to figure out where Ava was. Had to let her know that we were getting closer to finding her, because she had to be aware that I was searching. However, I was so desperate for sleep that it was reluctant to come. I lay there for hours, getting more and more frustrated at the fact that I wouldn't drift off, which only made it more difficult. At one point, I considered going to the infirmary to find something to put me to sleep, but though it was illogical that I'd see someone there so late at night, I was reluctant to explain myself should I be caught.

I couldn't even say when I did manage to fall asleep, all I knew was that I'd hit that dark ground, and I was suddenly in the dream. This time had to be different, though. I had to make Ava talk to me. *Go to her.* I worked myself up to stand before that urging voice could gain importance, prepared for it when the blackness gave out beneath me. I plummeted, colliding with the stone floor in the castle room and immediately springing to my feet. Ava didn't even have time to wipe the surprise off her face.

215

"Ava," I said, my voice so full of relief because I could be sure that this *was* her. I was truly talking to Ava. The corners of her mouth pulled into an agonized frown while her eyes filled with tears. She shook her head as if the very sight of me was too much, and made a move for the door. "Wait," I pleaded, stepping forward and grabbing her hand.

She gasped at the contact, turning to face me with a mixture of shock and pain, and I knew why. I could feel it when I touched her, just how real this was. Her skin was cold, and her hand felt fragile, but she was *solid*.

She yanked out of my grip as the first tears cascaded down her cheeks. "Why?" she whispered to herself, blue eyes running over my face. "Why is this happening to me?"

I wasn't sure what she meant, wasn't sure what was causing her the most pain, but the look on her face put a sharp pang in my own chest. "Ava," I said, "this is real."

"It's not real," she murmured. Her bottom lip quivered with emotion, and I wanted so badly to convince her it *was* that I reached out to set my palm against her cheek. She closed her eyes and leaned into it for only a moment before pulling away. "You're not real," she whispered. "You're dead."

"I'm not." I reached for her again, with both hands this time, taking her face to get her to look at me. "Why do you think I'm dead?"

"Because," she whimpered, and a heavy flood of tears went streaming down her cheeks. "You haven't come for me."

And I'd thought my heart couldn't break any more than it already had, but that was *excruciating*. Even after I'd betrayed her, she'd had so much faith in me that the only reason she could think I hadn't rescued her yet was because I was dead. And *I* knew I'd been searching, but *she* didn't. It felt like I'd failed her again, betrayed her again, and my eyes blurred with tears.

"Ava," I said brokenly, "I'm trying to find you." I leaned to set my forehead against hers. "I swear to you, I'm trying. Where are you?"

"I don't know," she said, pulling away and shaking her head. "And it doesn't matter. You're a trick. You... this dream... you're a trick of instinct."

"What do you mean?" I asked, and a sinking feeling took root in my gut.

"No one's coming for me," she muttered to herself, refusing to look at me as though she truly believed I was a figment of her imagination. "I stopped eating. They force me to drink water, but they can't force me to eat." She wiped her fingers over her soaked cheeks. "I'll be dead soon and my mind is trying to stop it."

My heart dropped. That's why she looked so sickly. So thin. She'd given up on the thought of ever being rescued, and death was the next best option. "Ava, no, please," I begged, taking her face again, far more firmly and forcing her to look me in my tear-filled eyes. "I'm *real*. I'm coming for you. Please. *Please*, Ava, don't give up."

She inhaled a stuttering breath, one I knew would preface a sob, but she held it so she wouldn't break down. "That's exactly what I'd want you to say." But no matter how hard she tried, she couldn't stop it, and she slid her arms around my waist as she succumbed to sobs. "The mind is cruel," she cried, "and these dreams are torture." She released me and backed away, saying with difficulty, "I just want it to end."

"Ava," I whimpered, and I tried to go after her when she took a step toward the open door, but I couldn't move. She had complete control, and she didn't want me to follow. "Ava, stop, *please*." She kept going, and as she walked out of the room I hollered one last time, "Ava!"

But she was gone.

Chapter 15

I woke from the dream with a start, sitting up in bed and with tears already streaming down my face. It should've been a relief that I'd truly gotten to speak with Ava. Perhaps I should have felt some hope, because she *was alive*. All I felt was panic. She was alive, but just barely. I'd been trying to find her for six months, and it had been painful and stressful enough without being pressed for time. Now time was *everything*. I had to find her before she faded away.

Though I couldn't be sure what hour of the morning it was, or if it even *was* morning, I threw my blankets off and rushed to dress in the dark. In my haste, I was relying on thoughtless habit to get myself clothed and to the door, all the while pondering exactly how I'd tell Kingston. That thoughtlessness caused me to open the door and stand there for a long moment, simply holding it open. It's what I used to do so Albus could go out before me and I could close it behind us, but then I realized I'd done it purely out of old habit, and Albus was still gone.

It cut through my panic like a knife, and I stood there for a few moments more to regain my breath, to recover from the blow of the reminder as I wiped the renewed tears from my eyes. With the wiping of those tears, I felt the last of the panic fade, and it was replaced with determination. I'd lost Albus and Brande, and for six months I'd refused to accept that I'd completely lost Ava. Now I had the chance to get her back, and I wouldn't let anything stop me. The moment we found out where she was, I was going to get her. And I *would* get to her before she grew too weak. *That* was the only option.

I rushed out of my bedroom and down the hall toward Kingston's private chamber. It wasn't far, and my fist hammered at the door, but there was no answer. Considering there were people moving about the corridors, I could tell that it was early morning, and the only conclusion for Kingston not being in his room was that he'd already woken. The next likely place to find him was the dining hall. I hurried to it, stopping at the entrance to scan the tables. Eventually I found him, sitting across from my mother and Nilson as they all enjoyed their breakfast.

Reaching the table, I plopped down at my mother's side and directly across from Kingston. "Morning, Mother," I said on a breath, giving her an earnest kiss on the cheek, but I didn't leave her a chance to say anything. "Kingston," I greeted.

"Kiena," he returned, setting his spoon down with a curious look in his eyes.

I didn't know how else to get it out, so I blurted, "Ava's alive."

Kingston's gaze flashed a mixture of emotions – instinctive skepticism, surprise, and then interest. "You look like you know this to be true."

"It *is* true," I insisted. I glanced around the dining hall for a specific person, and when my eyes met Rhien's, I waved her over. Noting my sense of urgency, she hurried to me. "Tell him what you told me, about the dreams," I said, motioning toward Kingston and adding, "if you'd please." She explained it to him, and had hardly finished when I interjected, "She's alive, Kingston. I felt it. Felt her. It was *real* and she's out there."

He simply sat there for a while, glancing from me to Rhien, thinking heavily about what he'd just heard. Eventually, he nodded. "I'll send birds to all of my men. We'll make finding her a priority." That was *such* a relief. These last few months, after it began to seem like we'd never find her, I'd felt like everyone had put her rescue to the back of their minds. But now we knew she was alive, and Kingston making it a priority was such a comfort that I sighed. "For the next few days," he began to say.

"Days?" I interrupted. In my excitement, I'd completely ignored the fact that birds weren't instant communication, and at the realization, my heart sank. "Kingston, she's dying. We have to find her *now*."

"Kiena," he said, "what you ask is impossible. We will work as fast as we can, but we need reliable information for her rescue to be successful. We need to find her first."

I'd started to think we'd find her in time, and I knew Kingston would do everything he could, but that completely shattered my expectations. I was so immediately frustrated with myself for getting my hopes up that I slammed my fists down on the surface of the table. Kingston wasn't alarmed, but the heavy thump startled my mother, and I felt her flinch against me. I set my elbows on the table and buried my face in my hands, taking a long few seconds to let it fully sink in and to calm down. I couldn't keep doing this. Couldn't keep reacting with these outbursts that scared or offended the people I cared about.

It took a minute, but I managed to regain control of my emotions. Bottling them back up, I lowered my hands and nodded at Kingston. "Send the birds," I agreed. "Thank you."

It didn't even look like Kingston had finished his porridge, but he stood to go and do what he could. He disappeared out the entrance of the dining hall, and not knowing how else she could help, Rhien gave my shoulder a squeeze and walked away too. I let out a heavy sigh, folding my arms across the table and letting my head fall onto them. The only thing I wished was that there was more *I* could do, even were it helping to send the messages to Kingston's spies. But I couldn't even do that, because I couldn't write. All I could do was sit here, fretting over whether or not we'd get to Ava in time and worrying everyone around me. It was torture, and already there was a tense clump of anxiety in my chest.

A hand set on my back after a while, and I picked up my head to look at my mother. "Are you hungry?" she asked. I murmured a negative. "Come then, my sweet girl." She kissed my temple and then stood with Nilson. "The morning sun will do you good."

And there was nothing else I *could* do, so I followed her and Nilson to the meadow just outside the entrance of the caves. While Nilson ran off to play with the other children who were out here, my mother took me over to a rock, on which she'd hover to watch over Nilson. She sat down on it, and then motioned to the grass in front of her. I lowered myself where she'd pointed, and once I'd leaned back against her knees, she began to run her fingers through my hair to undo the braid.

It did nothing to take away the stress I was feeling about finding Ava, but it was soothing. The air was still chill, but I was facing the rising sun, and I had to close my eyes against the brightness of it as it warmed my skin. My mother's fingers pressed into my scalp and combed through my hair, and it was so relaxing that my head fell back into her lap. The children were playing and laughing and, with my eyes closed, it painted such a vivid picture of happiness that I *almost* forgot myself. It was the first time in six months I'd felt so cared for, and that wasn't my mother's fault. She'd tried to comfort me, many times. *So* many times, but I'd been too upset, or tense, or angry at the world to let anyone near me.

For a long span of minutes now, I just sat there, my mother's fingers massaging, working out tangles and beginning to braid again. Eventually, I relaxed so much that all the exhaustion from the last six months seemed to catch up with me, and I grew so tired with my head back in her lap that I could feel myself drifting off. No matter how much I worried about Ava, I was simply too tired to keep from melting under my mother's touch. Too physically exhausted from the lack of sleep, too emotionally drained from all the sadness and worry and guilt. So tired that I couldn't have resisted this act of kindness and love even if I'd wanted to.

And it was that love, a love I hadn't allowed myself to feel since I'd come to the caves, which caused my closed eyes to fill with tears. They weren't desolate or hopeless or frustrated like every other time I'd cried the last six months. They weren't happy, either, but I felt safe, and my mother's touch had lowered my guard. I'd been doing everything I could not to let them see how truly depressed I was. I hadn't wanted anyone to worry any more than they already were, but now the tiredness and comfort I felt made it impossible not to let some of those emotions I'd been bottling seep out. I didn't break down or sob, but for the first time, I was tired enough to let my mother see me cry.

A drop forced its way through and down my temple, and I felt her thumb wipe it away. From above me, I could hear her take in a soft breath, and it took a few moments before she finally spoke. "It was always my intention that you and Nilson never get near this rebellion." She finished braiding my hair and set to massaging her thumbs over my temples, whisking away the occasional tear. "For your father and me, it was nothing but separation. And then Kingston brought word of his death, and..." She paused, the backs of her fingers making a sympathetic stroke down my cheek. "Well, heartbreak doesn't quite come close, does it?"

All these months, I'd been so reluctant to feel anything that I'd forgotten my mother *knew* what this was like. At the realization, my eyebrows converged, and I sniffled with fresh tears as I reached for one of her hands, pulling it down so I could hug it to my chest.

"My baby girl," she said, "I see your strength." She traced the fingers of her other hand across my forehead. "You've always had enough to share."

Then that hand joined the one I was holding, and she pressed her palms to the top of my chest. "Take mine now." The weight and warmth of her hands amidst my emotions made me want to break down just as much as it made me want to steel myself. "Take what you need, and you'll get through this."

I picked my head up, the final few tears running down my cheeks. Sniffling, I wiped them away with the backs of my hands, and I don't know how she'd done it, but I *did* feel a renewed strength. It had been her touch, or her love, or her words. Maybe it had been a combination of all of these, but I blinked away the tears, and I felt ready to face the time it would take to find Ava. I felt ready to wait, and to put my faith in Kingston and that he would come through.

My mother's hands never left my collarbones as I leaned back into her knees again. After a minute, I rested my head to the side against her arm, and we sat there, watching Nilson and the other children, taking in the increasing warmth of morning. People came and went, in and out the entrance of the caves: troops leaving for scouts, hunters leaving for a hunt, loggers leaving to gather firewood. Eventually Rhien came out, and strode all the way to where we were sitting.

"Madam," she greeted my mother, who offered a friendly smile in return. Then she lowered herself in the grass next to me, saying, "I had a thought."

I sat forward and turned to face her, giving her my attention. "Alright."

"Well, I trained with the mind masters, right?" She shifted toward me with the sudden earnestness of her idea, and I nodded. "You've been closer to Ava *and* Hazlitt than anyone here." When she paused, I nodded once more, urging her to continue. "You've been understandably distracted the last handful of months, and perhaps there's something you've missed."

"What do you mean?"

"In your memories. A statement or a person in your encounters, something that would give us a clue about where Ava is." Rhien shrugged, offering with some timidity, "If you allow me access to your memories, maybe we can find something."

"With magic?" I clarified, and she nodded in confirmation.

To be honest, I wasn't entirely comfortable with sharing memories. Some were fine, others intimate, and the ones that she probably needed were excruciating. People had details about what happened with Ava, but letting Rhien into my mind, actually letting her see what happened that day, would be letting her see my guilt. It would be letting her see more of me than anyone here had. The very idea of it was terrifying, and she seemed to notice that fear on my face.

"You've every reason to decline," she said.

I shook my head. "I've an even better reason to accept." If there was even a slight chance that this could help find Ava, I *had* to accept. "Do it."

Rhien reached upward, pausing momentarily so her brown eyes could meet mine and so she could be sure of my acceptance. "Go wherever feels important," she told me. Her hands set on either side of my head when she was sure, and she closed her eyes and said, "Onlucan nin yngemina."

All at once my eyes slammed shut, and though I knew it was just a memory, I was there again. But not where I expected to be. I was in Hazlitt's throne room, being roared at by him that I had to find his daughter and bring her back. It wasn't a useful memory though; Kingston had already searched every corner of the castle at Guelder. As soon as that thought occurred to me, I was ripped forward to the day in the cave, when Ava finally told me why she'd run and about Hazlitt's treachery. Then Silas was there, shouting at me for trusting her, threatening to find us. It was as painful as the day it happened, but somewhere distant I could hear Rhien, her far off voice telling me to keep going.

Though I tried, I couldn't direct the memories, couldn't control *where* my mind went, only *when* it moved on. So I shifted forward, halting at the moment Ava told me she loved me. I couldn't stop a brief flash of what had happened afterward, but I took us ahead in time. To the next morning. To the blood, and the running, and being cut off by Hazlitt and his soldiers.

Every emotion I'd felt that day was back again, as fresh and alive as the moment it happened. The pain of Hazlitt's magic, and the extreme loss and betrayal when Silas killed Albus. Then the choice. Hazlitt's snide presentation of what was nothing other than a severe punishment for my transgressions against the crown. But what hurt more than anything was the look on Ava's face. It had been six months, and though I'd never stopped remembering, I'd lost the exact expression the moment she realized I was leaving. It was almost worse now, months later, because I *knew* what became of her. I knew that my mother and brother were fine, and that Hazlitt would lock Ava away, where I couldn't find her and she'd think I was dead. Where she'd give up on the thought of ever being rescued. Where she'd give up on life.

I ripped away from Rhien's hands so violently that I nearly fell backward. I caught myself with my palms, and after brushing the grass off them, I wiped at my tear-filled eyes. Though I could feel Rhien watching me, I couldn't bring myself to meet her gaze. After showing her all that, I felt ashamed. Felt like she'd judge me now that she'd seen what I'd done, seen how coldly I'd left Ava with Hazlitt. Instead of looking at Rhien or saying anything, I pulled my knees up, setting my elbows on them and putting my hands to my head.

"Kiena," she said, scooting forward to set a hand on my leg. "Are you alright?"

I wasn't, and she knew that, and if I looked at my mother, I'm sure it would've been clear to her too. "Did you see anything useful?" I asked without looking at them.

There was a lengthy silence before she answered, "I'm sorry, not what we were looking for." She cleared her throat, and her hand made a delicate pat against my leg as though she was apologizing for what she'd say next. "Kiena," she said again, "I know it hurts, but... will you take me back there?" Now I *did* look at her, because the request was unnerving, and the thought of doing it again was dreadful. "Please, just once."

For a long moment, I just stared at her, and I might've refused if she didn't look so earnest about it. There was clearly something in the memory that interested her, and if it would help in any way, I needed to do it. So I lowered my knees, crossing my legs beneath me. I didn't nod in response, but I didn't need to. Rhien stretched her hands forward again, setting them once more on the sides of my head and repeating that phrase, and we were back at the beginning of the most agonizing memory of my life. Ava and I fell from the horse. I went through the pain of the magic again, the pain of losing Albus again, and as Hazlitt stepped forward to begin his proposal, I heard Rhien's distant voice say 'here.'

Hazlitt knelt down, and I screamed at him with my throat full of sparks. His eyes widened, he rose and stepped back, and when those sparks died because I'd been too full of emotion, he came forward again to continue. He made his smug, cruel offer. The offer that took my joy, and my hope, and would rob me of sleep for the next six months of my life. I grabbed the reins from Hazlitt, but Rhien removed her hands before I could mount the horse, and I was back in the meadow.

I opened my eyes, my forehead creasing with confusion at the hint of a smile on her face. "What?" I asked, taking a deep breath to keep from losing myself to the pain of the memories.

"Have you not wondered why he didn't kill you that day?" she asked, and my lips pursed with concentration as my forehead creased even deeper. I hadn't wondered. It had never crossed my mind because for so long I'd wished he *had* killed me. It would have been so easy for him. "Kiena," Rhien said, and though it seemed like she was trying to contain her excitement, she huffed, "he's afraid of you."

"He's not afraid of me," I said instantly. Firmly. He'd taken everything I loved, and he'd done it looking smug. He'd done it while mocking me.

"Then why didn't he kill you?" she asked.

My mouth set with frustration, because for some reason I didn't like hearing this. If Hazlitt was afraid of me, there was a reason for it. And if there was a reason for it, then that might mean I could have prevented all of this. "Because it wasn't worth the effort," I muttered.

She dropped her chin to look at me sternly. "But it was worth it for him to give you his best horse?"

I'd almost forgotten my mother was still sitting with us, until she mused, "He wanted you out of the way."

Rhien snapped her fingers and pointed at my mother in agreement. "Think about his face," she urged. "How he stepped away from you in order to avoid your magic. The fear in his eyes." She reached forward and took my hands with growing excitement. "He didn't want you around. He couldn't threaten *your* life, couldn't back you into a corner where your only option was to fight because he didn't think he could win."

I sighed with reluctance and frustration, taking my hands from hers. "I couldn't even control my magic back then. He could have killed me, easy."

"Did *he* know that?" Rhien asked. "I sense your magic. Anyone with the gift can sense your magic, Kiena. It's unlike anything I've ever experienced." She glanced at the ground and thought to herself for a few moments. "He tried not to let it show," she chuckled in recollection. "He's a damn good liar, but oh, he was scared."

While I wanted nothing more than for it to not have been that simple, I could no longer disagree. Now that Rhien laid it out, I could recall the fear in Hazlitt's eyes. "People talk about the power of my magic," I said, reaching up to grasp the dragon pendant around my neck. "If it's so grand, why can I not do more with it?" I remembered what Kingston had told me about lessons, about how information surrounding my magic had died with my ancestors. Perhaps there truly *were* gifts that had been lost, but why could I not recover things on my own? Shouldn't it be in my blood?

At first, Rhien's only response was a shrug, but then her face lit up. "We should speak with the masters."

She meant the mind masters: the mage instructors she'd come with from the Duskford Monastery. These last months, I hadn't sought formal instruction in my magic. I'd been too broken. Isolated myself too much. Everything I'd learned to do with it, I'd learned on my own, through intense practice when I needed a distraction or couldn't sleep at night. Perhaps now was the time to do more.

I nodded my agreement, but before I could offer a better response, a familiar rebel on horseback came bursting from the trees. He nearly bypassed us for the entrance of the caves, but at seeing me, he made an abrupt stop.

"First Ward," he greeted, jumping off the horse. He wasn't one of my rangers, but I knew him.

"Miller," I returned, rising from my spot in the grass. "Is there a problem?"

"Found a Valenian soldier," he answered. "Man said he had information for you." My eyebrows furrowed at that, but Miller continued. "Nikon recommended I get Kingston as well."

"Aye," I agreed, gesturing toward the caves. I suspected this had something to do with Hazlitt and the fact that we'd been robbing his supplies. "Go and fetch him."

Miller nodded and hurried into the mountain, leaving his horse outside the entrance. He must have been a good distance ahead of the group who were following him with the prisoner, because before they'd even arrived, he'd found Kingston and brought him out. The fact that a rebel had arrived and brought Kingston didn't escape the attention of the older children playing around us, including Nilson. My brother trotted over, posting himself at my mother's side while he watched Kingston greet me.

The sound of hoof beats rose in the woods around us. It took half a minute, but then the rest of the group emerged. The rebel horsemen fanned out, their prisoner hidden behind them because he was tied to the back of one's saddle. The men dismounted, one of them striding behind the rest to retrieve the prisoner. He led the captive forward toward Kingston and me, but the moment I recognized who the man was, I felt all the blood in my veins ice over. Silas.

Hazlitt was the *true* enemy, I knew that. But each of Silas's betrayals had been more painful to me than any of Hazlitt's treachery. Silas had been like a brother, but *he'd* threatened to hunt Ava and me. *He'd* put the bolt through Albus's heart. *He'd* chosen not to defend me that day, and instead to support a king who was so clearly corrupt. The very sight of him felt like a slap in the face, and the second the shock of seeing him wore off, I felt a fury like I'd never known. The ice in my veins melted, and then it boiled, until I could feel the heat burning in my face.

I didn't wait for the man to bring Silas to us, and barely had the mind to turn Nilson toward my mother, so he wouldn't see as I spark jumped the distance between Silas and me. It didn't even matter to me that Silas's hands were bound in front of him. I reached him, and before he could react to the fact that I'd got there so quickly, I pulled my arm back. With all the strength I could get out of my torso and shoulder, I let my fist fly straight at his face. That first punch got him so hard it knocked him right off his feet, and he hit the ground on his back with a heavy thud. But all the fury in me... I wasn't done.

I pitched myself on top of him, kneeling over his hips and grabbing the collar of his uniform, yanking him up to meet my knuckles as I hit him a second time. There was already blood trickling from his nose, and a red split in his cheek, but I still hit him again. And again. I wanted him dead for everything he'd done, and I could've used my magic to make that happen, but more than I wanted him dead, I wanted him to hurt. If I couldn't make him feel all the agony I'd experienced the last six months, I'd make him feel something as damn close as I could, and even though his hands were bound, he didn't once try to raise them and stop me.

Every punch I threw was fueled by every bit of anger and strength I had in me. The next one I landed hit him in the mouth, and I was so lost in my madness that I barely noticed I split my knuckles on his teeth. I just kept hitting him, the blood from my fist mixing with the blood covering his face, until I couldn't tell what blood was his or mine. And nobody pulled me off. Nobody tried to stop me, though at one point through my rage, I heard Kingston mumble for someone to get Sevedi. They just let me beat him, until I was panting for breath and until the energy I'd expended left me tired enough to focus through the haze of animosity.

The first thing that registered was the tears in Silas's eyes. It didn't calm me, didn't make me feel bad. He didn't get to fucking cry. He hadn't earned it. He didn't deserve it.

I stopped hitting him and grabbed the other side of his tunic with my bloodied hand, pulling him even closer to me. "I should kill you," I growled.

He choked on the blood that had collected in his mouth, turning his head away so he could cough and spit it out. When he looked at me again, the tears had mixed with the red soaking his cheeks, and the whole right side of his face was already puffed up. His eye had swollen shut, but he looked at me with the one eye he could. "I know," he managed to croak.

Two pairs of hands finally grabbed me by the arms, hauling me off of Silas and back a couple steps. Silas was so weak that when I released his shirt, he fell back in the grass, and he just lay there. I was breathing heavily, panting from the exertion, and while I still felt furious, I wouldn't go back for more.

Everyone around was dead silent, watching to see what I'd do. For a moment, remembering that my mother was sitting there, that she'd seen what I'd just done, I felt repentant. Then Silas struggled to sit up, and as he worked himself to his feet, that feeling faded. I materialized a current of sparks, still undecided on whether or not I should kill him.

"You should," Silas murmured. He teetered on his feet, so unsteady and damaged that he couldn't stay standing, and he dropped to his knees. "Just let me say what I-"

"What could you possibly say that I have any interest in?" I spat.

He sniffled, and blood was pouring so steadily from the wounds in his face that the front of his shirt was already stained with it. He took a weak breath so he could answer, "I know where Ava is."

It was so unexpected that my heart skipped. "Tell me!" I commanded, and as the words left my mouth, I felt a splitting pain down the front of my skull. It was in the same exact place that tingled when I controlled animals, only now it was harrowing.

In response, Silas blurted, "There's a ship in Royal's Key Harbor. It's been moored in the shallows for six months. Flies a merchant's flag, but never once left to sea." He blinked rapidly after his answer, eyes fixing on me in confusion. "What did you just do to me?"

There was no time to absorb that I'd just controlled him. I needed to get to Ava. *Now.*

From behind me, Kingston said, "I'll gather horses."

There was no time for horses either. I paced past Silas to our rebel group's navigator. "Map," I ordered. He pulled one out, laying it flat on the grass. "Show me the harbor." He pointed to a place on the eastern coast of Ronan, over three hundred miles away and lying against the Balain Sea.

There was only one thing to do – a three hundred mile spark jump. I wasn't even sure if I *could* go that far. All I knew was that I *had* to, and if my magic was as powerful as people kept saying it was, then just maybe I could. I shut my eyes and took in a deep breath to prepare myself, to gather as much strength and energy as I could because failure was *not* an option.

"Kiena," Kingston warned, predicting what I was about to try. "It could be a trap."

It didn't matter. I was gone. Shot into the air and flickering on a bolt of lightning. Every time I jumped like this, it happened so fast that I didn't get to feel it. Now, it lasted *just* long enough for me to. I felt like static. I couldn't see anything but the blinding light that consumed me at each jump, but I could feel the charge around me. The hairs on my arms and neck rose to meet it. It tickled my flesh, vibrated through the blood in my veins. Though it was slow enough to feel, it was still at such a speed that not even five seconds passed before I landed again.

The moment my feet thudded against a wooden dock, I could smell it – the sharp salt in the air. I could hear the ocean, and the sea birds, and the shouts of the sailors I'd startled. I opened my eyes and glanced out over the bright water toward the harbor, searching for the ship Silas described. There were only three in the shallows. Two of those were flying merchant flags, but even from the docks, I could see that one of the ship's decks was populated with what looked like a working number of men, while the other had only a fraction of the crew.

I took in another breath to fuel my next jump, and catapulted myself to the more vacant ship. I touched down with a thunk against the wood, and the three men on deck were so confused at my arrival that, for a moment, they simply stared. It was a long enough moment for me to take in the king's crest on each of their chests, and for the hint of a smile to reach my lips. *This* was the ship.

"Oy!" one of the men hollered, pulling a rapier from his belt.

As he charged at me with his weapon, another one grabbed a bow and loaded an arrow. The archer took aim, but I didn't have time for playing fair. Just as he released the bowstring, I spark jumped behind him, wrapped him in static, and threw him overboard. The man with the sword rerouted, changing direction to charge at me once more. I let him, and I let him get close enough that the point of his sword nearly pierced through my chest, then I froze him with a current. He went stiff, dropping the sword from his hand. I jumped behind him and grabbed the back of his head with a lethal ball of sparks. As he collapsed, I turned on the third man, who let his own rapier fall to the deck when I met his gaze.

"Mercy," he said, dropping to his knees. "I surrender."

I flashed to him, scaring him so badly that he gasped, and I squatted down and grabbed the collar of his shirt. "Where is she?"

He didn't hesitate to tell me, "Captain's cabin," and reached for a ring of keys at his belt.

I took the keys, but once I released his shirt, I created a current in my free hand, shoving my palm against his chest and knocking him to his back in convulsions. I was at the door of the captain's cabin in the blink of an eye. It took three tries to find the right key, and when I finally got it unlocked, I threw it open. I expected Ava to be surprised when she saw me, but that wasn't what I got. There was no reaction, because Ava was lying on the only bed in the cabin, so weak that I wasn't even sure she knew the door had been opened.

"Ava?" I muttered, rushing to her side. Her eyes were closed and she didn't answer, so I reached out with my magic in the dim light of the room and searched for her heartbeat. For a long moment, I got nothing, and my own heart sank. But then I felt it. It was weak, and faint, but it was there. "I'll get you out of here."

I straightened up, smacking my hand to the wall of the cabin to create a deliberate shape of sparks. To form a current in the Vigilant symbol, and to burn that symbol into the wooden wall. Then I scooped Ava into my arms and carried her outside, trying not to think about how light she felt compared to six months ago.

I took in a deep breath, preparing for the jump. Never before had I tried to take someone else with me. There was no experience to tell me whether or not Ava would be able to go, or if she'd survive it. But if I left her here, she was dead anyway. She didn't have the time or the life left to wait for Kingston's horses to arrive. Just like my being able to jump all the way here *had* to work, taking her with me had to work too.

With that breath, I flashed on a bolt of lightning, and barely got to feel the true relief of Ava remaining in my arms before we touched down in the meadow. It had been such a short amount of time that nobody had really moved. Silas was still kneeling in the grass, though Sevedi was examining him, and Kingston was speaking to the horsemen, probably about to send them after me. But the moment I returned, a steady murmur sounded from those around me.

"Sevedi!" I called, laying Ava down in the grass.

Sevedi rushed over and knelt beside me, setting one hand on Ava's heart and the other on her head, but that healing orange glow didn't come. "Kiena... her heart's not beating."

"Fix it!"

"I can't," she murmured apologetically. "I can't bring people back from the dead."

This couldn't be it. It couldn't be over and there had to be something we could do. I threw my hands to my head in panic, my heart beating so fast it almost made me sick. And that's when it occurred to me.

My heart! I could feel people's heartbeats with my magic. How would that be possible if there wasn't something in the heart that spoke to my sparks? There had to be something I could do.

With that thought, I pushed Sevedi aside and set a hand to Ava's chest, letting out a short, determined breath. "Come on, Ava," I whispered. Focusing on my own heart, I shut my eyes and tried to calm down. Tried to slow its rhythm into something normal while I channeled its beat into my hand. I translated that beat into a soft pulse of current, feeling it throb through the flesh of my palm and disappear into her chest. "Ava, please," I begged with the next pulse, tears stinging my eyes when nothing happened. "Don't do this to me." It wasn't working, and in my desperation, I set my free hand beside the other on her chest, channeling the current through both so it was stronger. "Not now," I whimpered. The beat ebbed through my hands, a steady and consistent thump, and an overwhelmed tear forced its way out, leaving a hot streak down my cheek. "Not when we're so close, Ava, *please*."

With the next beat that pulsed through my fingers, Ava took in a soft breath. Her heart began to throb in rhythm with mine, and she was *alive*. It was such a relief, such an *unbelievable* relief that I let out a broken laugh as more tears spilled from my eyes.

I glanced over at Sevedi, ignoring the extreme awe in her expression to say, "Do it."

She jumped into action, placing one hand over mine, and the other to Ava's forehead. That orange glow started, and she nodded at me that it was safe to remove my hands. I pulled away, collapsing back into the grass with sudden exhaustion as two rebels came forward with a cot, and they moved Ava onto it, carrying her away with Sevedi to the infirmary.

For a minute, I lay there, feeling so many overwhelming emotions that I couldn't think. All I knew was that I had no idea what to do now, and this was such an astonishing triumph that a part of me was reluctant to believe it was real. There was another part of me that didn't want to celebrate yet, because Ava was still weak, and I wasn't even sure if she'd forgive me. So I stayed there, feeling *so* much that I felt nothing. Felt like nothing was different and all I had were steps to complete. Stand up. Maybe say something to someone. Go to my personal chamber and fix the deep gash in my knuckles from hitting Silas. Check on Ava.

Following the first of those steps, I rose to my feet, only to find that everyone around was staring at me, eyes wide. And they didn't stop staring, not until Kingston shooed them away and the only people left were my family, Rhien – who behind that look of awe was still cringing about what I'd done to Silas – Silas, and the rebels that had brought him.

Silas had been staring at me too, shock and wonder clear in the slack of his jaw and in the widening of the eye that wasn't swollen shut. "Kiena..." he murmured.

And in response to that, I fulfilled the second of my steps. "*Stay away from me*," I snarled.

I looked at nobody else before turning and hurrying for the entrance of the caves. Step three was to take care of my hand. I wouldn't go to the infirmary. Sevedi was busy making sure Ava survived, and so I'd take care of it on my own. I reached my room, closing the door behind me and pacing to the cabinet where I kept my medical supplies. There was so much blood on my hand that I couldn't even be sure where the wound started and ended anymore. Instead of soaking a linen with antiseptic, I simply opened the bottle and poured its contents over my hand. It washed all the blood from my flesh, spilling to the floor, but right now I didn't care about the mess. I was shaking. Both hands were trembling violently and I didn't know why.

As I set the bottle on the table beside me to try and compose myself, my door burst open. Nira rushed in, so excited that she hardly kicked it closed behind her. "You did it?" she asked as she paced over, a hint of disbelief in her voice. "You found her?"

I nodded in confirmation, and she reached me and threw herself upward, wrapping her arms around my neck and pulling me into a fierce hug. She was embracing me so tightly that her feet weren't even touching the ground, so I supported her weight, wrapping my own arms around her waist to return the hug.

"You did it," she repeated beside my ear. "You found her." For some unknown reason, those words caused a severe pang in my chest, and as I set Nira back down, she released me. "You're shaking," she observed, pulling back to look at me. "What's wrong?"

Her brown eyes were full of worry, and I tried to say something in order to assure her that I was fine, but the second I tried to speak, a sob escaped my throat instead. It startled her, and her eyebrows furrowed with a deepened concern, but I couldn't stop it now. I broke down into uncontrollable tears.

"Whoa," Nira murmured, directing me to sit at the edge of the table, where I was more level with her so she could step between my legs and pull me into a closer hug. "Kiena, it's alright," she assured me. "You found her." My shoulders shook with another sob, and my hands were trembling as I wrapped them around to her back. "It's all over," she said, tightening her hold on me.

And *that's* why I was crying, because it was all over. Six months of harrowing guilt, and the torture of not knowing whether we'd ever find Ava or not. Of living every day in a constant battle between the desolate emptiness I felt and trying not to let my family feel it too. Six months of nightmares, and sleeplessness, and unending exhaustion that plagued every minute until I got so tired I passed out. The worry, the hurt, and the complete and utter hopelessness – it was over. Whether Ava would forgive me or not, she was safe, and I didn't have to be stuck anymore. We could move forward. Move on. It was all over, and I was tired of being tired, and all I could do was tremble and cry because of my staggering fatigue and relief. So I did. Nira hugged me, and I cried. Cried until there wasn't a tear left to shed.

Chapter 16

evedi had spent a good portion of the day working over Ava and healing her. Ava was in poor health. She was weak, and emaciated, but Sevedi was strong enough that she could have Ava back to normal in a matter of days. Now that Ava was comfortable, and rescued, if she started eating again then Sevedi would keep healing her, and she'd recover. The only guarantees that Sevedi *couldn't* make were about Ava's heart and mind. I'd broken her heart and left her to isolation for six months. She hadn't thought the dream was real because she was convinced I was dead. For all we knew, she might think she was still in a dream. Might think I wasn't real even when she could truly see me and touch me.

After Sevedi had grown too tired with the energy she was expending to heal Ava, she'd needed a break. The sun had been setting anyway, so I'd relieved her and pulled up a seat at Ava's bedside in order to be there when she woke. She didn't wake all night, and eventually I'd fallen asleep too. Now my eyes fluttered open, because I'd always been so in tune to Ava's heartbeat, and even in my sleep, I could sense it racing.

Ava must have just woken as well, because when I looked at her, she appeared confused. She didn't know where she was, and just behind that confusion was fear. I could only imagine what it was like to be in the same small room for six months, and then to wake up somewhere else. She sat up and her eyes met mine, and everything about her froze. Her gaze locked onto me, her breathing stopped, and she just stared. The only thing that didn't stop or slow was her pulse. For a long minute, her gaping went uninterrupted, but during that minute her eyes filled with tears.

"Ava?" I said, entirely unsure of what to say or do because I couldn't tell what she was thinking. "It's me." And she took in a blubbering breath as the tears spilled over. "Alright," I murmured, leaving my seat for the edge of her cot and pulling her into a comforting hug. "You're safe now, it's alright." She didn't hug me back, but for the first few seconds, she just let me hold her while she cried. "We're at the caves."

Then I felt her hand against my stomach. She didn't shove me away, but her closed fist set with enough pressure that I recognized the request to let her go. Recognized that she didn't want me hugging her.

I released her immediately. "I'm sorry," I said, sitting back in my seat.

Even though I'd understood the possibility that she wouldn't forgive me, or at the very least wouldn't be ready to be close to me again, I'd be lying if I said it didn't hurt that she pushed me away. Because it *did*. It was painfully disappointing. So I sat there, waiting for her to do or say something. Only, she never did. She took a few deep breaths to calm herself down and pulled her knees halfway to her chest, staring at the cot beneath her as though she couldn't bring herself to look at me again.

"Ava?" I prompted once more, my voice a cautious whisper. Out of instinct, I began to reach out with my hand, aiming to set it on her arm to offer comfort, but she leaned away. My hand dropped as a pang hit my chest. "Do you..." Even though it killed me to expect the answer, I had to ask. "Would you like me to leave?"

Her eyes brimmed with fresh tears, and when she finally looked at me for a brief moment, a drop slid down her cheek. Her gaze returned to the cot while her hand wiped beneath her eye. She didn't respond at first, but then she folded forward to bury her face in her knees, and her shoulders shook with a cry as she nodded.

I felt salt sting my own eyes, but I'd known this could happen. Whatever she wanted, whatever she needed, I'd give and do. Even if that meant giving her space. I stood, taking in a breath so I could say something. Anything. Only, I had no idea what to say. "I, um," I began weakly, timidly, "I'm here if you need anything." But then I realized she might not want anything from *me*, and felt I should add, "Or you can ask anyone. It doesn't... doesn't have to be me."

I hurried out of the infirmary before the tears pooling in my eyes could pour over. Once outside, I leaned back against a cave wall, taking a moment and a deep breath to compose myself. Time. It had been six months, but it would still take *more* time. I just hoped that at some point Ava would speak to me. Forgive me.

After that, I went to the dining hall to get some breakfast, but as I ate, something bothered me. It wasn't Ava. It was the aching in my hand. The pain in the laceration on my knuckles, and the severe bruising in my bones. More than it was the physical pain, however, it was what that pain was attached to. It was Silas. That's what was bothering me. It didn't make sense why, after six months, he'd decided to come to me now. Why he'd decided to finally tell me where Ava was. I didn't want to look at him – the very thought of speaking with him put a disgusted bile in my throat – but I had to. Not knowing was worse.

Leaving my half-eaten breakfast, I paced out of the dining hall and toward the training grounds, veering to the left and down the stairs to the dungeon. I pushed open the door, noting how Silas's head picked up from the cot he was lying on to see who'd entered.

I motioned to the two guards standing inside the door. "Leave us."

They made small bows and left, closing the door behind them. Once they'd gone, I strode over to stand in front of Silas's cell. He sat up on his cot, kicking his legs over the side to set his feet on the floor. The entire right side of his face was still swollen, black and blue where it wasn't a deep red from various cuts. The wounds had been cleaned, but them even still being present came as a surprise. Sevedi had been occupied with Ava, but I thought she'd have come down here afterward to give the few minutes it would take to heal him.

"Why have you not been looked after?" I asked.

"Magic was offered," he answered, rising from his cot. "I refused." Standing, he strode to the bars of his cell, grabbing them in his hands and watching me for a few seconds while I absorbed his words. When I said nothing, he let out a sigh, saying with every bit of sincerity, "I deserve what you did, Kiena. I deserve this."

It appeared that he truly believed it, too, but *I* didn't want to believe it. Didn't want to think that he felt remorse for what he'd done, because I didn't think I could ever forgive him. Even if I did manage to forgive him, I would never fully trust him again. It would never be like it was.

When I still failed to say anything, he motioned toward my hand. "That's just like you, too," he said, and at first I thought he meant the fact that I'd beat him. "I remember that time you got head-butted by a ram. You took it home for supper, and wouldn't ice the bruise because you thought you'd earned it fair and square." I realized what he truly meant,

237

and he was right. Sevedi had offered to heal my hand when I'd come to stay with Ava, and I'd refused it just like Silas had refused it. I'd refused it because in some ways I *was* ashamed of what I'd done to him. That violence, that brutality, it wasn't me. I deserved the pain in my hand as much as he deserved the wounds in his face. "You don't need to keep that-"

"Why are you here, Silas?" I interrupted, growing irritated by his talking, by his knowledge of my emotions. I hadn't come to reminisce. Hadn't come so he could remind me of how close we'd been. *He'd* thrown all of that away. Not me.

I knew Silas well enough to catch the disappointment in the drop of his gaze, but he answered accordingly. "Have you spoken with Kingston today?" I shook my head. "I'll tell you what I told him. Hazlitt got what he was after in Ronan. He got the elixir and all its power."

"*Good*," I said with scathing sarcasm. "War's over, just like you wanted. Maybe now he'll restore the kingdom like you wanted."

Silas's head fell, because we both knew that would never happen. "War's not over," he said to the floor. He straightened again to look at me. "He's moving on Cornwall, and I doubt he'll stop there." Silas shook his head, as if he was in disbelief, or disappointed in himself. "I doubt he'll stop until he's taken Cornwall, and White Haven in the north, and Aelmon west of Ronan. God, Kiena, he might even cross the Balain Sea."

Wonderful. Here Silas was, telling me that Hazlitt wanted to conquer the world, and essentially admitting that he'd been wrong this whole time. Perfectly wonderful. All it did was frustrate me. I was *so* instantly frustrated that I turned and smashed my foot into the side of a bucket of water, sending it flying across the dungeon.

"I told you, Silas!" I shouted. "I bloody told you all he wanted was power, and all you had to do was trust me! Nineteen years! You were like a brother to me for *nineteen* godforsaken years, and you couldn't trust me!"

"I know," he murmured apologetically.

"You *don't* know!" I roared, and I hadn't come here to shout at him, but now I couldn't stop. "You have no idea what you put me through! You *betrayed* me! You killed Albus! *Albus*, Silas! Who I thought you loved as much as I did, and you put a fucking arrow in his heart!" I stomped forward, so heatedly that he took a step back. "And Ava," I growled. "She's everything to me. *Everything*! You look me in the eyes and tell me when

238

I've ever said that about a woman. Tell me when I've ever said that about someone who wasn't family." He looked at me, but he said nothing as his eyes filled with tears. "Never," I answered for him, and my throat was raw with shouting and my voice broke with emotion. "Not once in my entire life. But you stood there while Hazlitt made me choose. Now she's up there, and she can't even look at me because I broke her heart. And *you* broke *mine.*"

Silas's eyebrows converged with the severest kind of sadness. "I'm sorry," he whispered, sniffling as a tear slid down his cheek. "Kiena, I'm *so* sorry."

"Why'd you come here, Silas?" I asked again, blinking away the moisture in my own eyes. "You could've sent a message. Why come?"

"For you," he answered. "I saw it that day, exactly how much you loved her. I've spent the last six months agonizing about everything I did wrong, and I came to beg you for the chance to set this right."

The request was so painful that I took a wounded step back, but he rushed forward, reaching out and taking a hold of my hand in another form of begging. No matter how gentle the touch was, it startled me, and I ordered without thinking, "Let go." That splitting crack went down the front of my skull, and Silas's hand immediately released me.

That startled me too. Before yesterday, I hadn't even thought it would be possible for me to control a human, and now I'd done it twice. I didn't like it. Didn't like that I'd unintentionally controlled someone. Even if it was Silas, and even if I was furious with him. It was *his* mind, *his* body, and I had no right making it do things simply because I wanted. The very thought of committing this invasion against a person made me severely uncomfortable. Plus, it *hurt.*

Silas also looked shocked that I'd done it again, but he didn't say anything about it because he was too emotional. "I messed up, I know it," he said, letting the better side of his forehead rest against the bars of his cell. "I thought I was doing the right thing. I was blinded by my desire for victory, and I hurt the only person who's always been there for me." He took in a shaky breath, another tear slipping from the corner of his eye. "I'll fight for you. I'll join this rebellion. I'll do whatever I have to, and spend the rest of my life making it up to you. Please, Kiena, let me make this right."

I sniffled, completely unable to even consider what he was saying to me because of how much he'd hurt me. Not the wounds on his face, or the tears in his eyes, or his pleas for forgiveness could take that hurt away. "You got Ava back to me," I said, "and for that I'm grateful. But I set you free once, Silas, because of what you meant to me and against Ava's better judgment." I paused, and the corners of his mouth twitched with a desolate frown because he already knew what I'd decided. "I won't make that mistake again."

Though I knew they'd come, I didn't wait around to see the tears roll down his face. I rushed out of the dungeon, already feeling numb and nodding to the guards that they could return to their posts. When I reached the top of the stairs, however, I stopped. I froze at the corridor because now I wasn't sure what to do with myself. Ava was safe and I no longer had to fret about finding her or nag Kingston for updates, though I couldn't go and spend time with her either. Nor did I need something to keep my mind off the fact that we couldn't find her. It came as a complete shock, but for the first time in six months, I almost felt something akin to boredom. But there were always things to do, and I knew exactly what I needed.

I wandered back down the corridor and to the dining hall, searching for Rhien. After a few moments of seeking, I saw her delivering a mug of ale to a rebel. She happened to look up when I found her, meeting my gaze, and she set the mug down and started my direction.

"Morning," she greeted when she reached me.

I offered a small smile, but truly it had probably been the first time she'd *ever* seen me smile, and her lips curled with a grin in response. "Sleep well?" I asked.

"Indeed, thanks," she answered with a nod. "And yourself?" I shrugged to that, because falling asleep in a chair hadn't been entirely comfortable. "What have I done to earn a visit? If I'm honest, I thought you'd be inseparable from Ava for some time."

My gaze fell, but I answered with the truth. "She's not interested in my company quite yet." Rhien's mouth pursed with an apologetic smile. "I was hoping you might take me to the masters."

"Yes, I will!" she answered, but her smile instantly faded as her cheeks shaded a bit from her eagerness. "You did mean right now...?"

"Aye," I chuckled. I couldn't remember the last time I'd made a girl timid, and I was finally in a decent enough mood to at least feel flattered by it. "If you've got the time."

"I do," she agreed, and when she turned to leave the dining hall, I followed after her. "I spoke to them last night, after our conversation. They may be expecting you." She led me toward a deep part of the cave, where I knew a lot of the fugitives had been accommodated, and neither of us said anything for the first minute. Eventually she prompted, "Kiena?" I hummed. "Could I perhaps ask you for a favor?"

"Of course," I answered, "though I can't guarantee my ability to see it through."

She nodded understandingly, and I waited for her to voice her request. It took a bit, during which she occasionally glanced at me like she wasn't sure how to get it out. I'll admit that it started to make me nervous, and without realizing it, I'd held my breath. "I want to do something for this rebellion other than fetching food in the dining hall. Something more helpful."

I finally released that breath. I wasn't even sure what I thought she'd ask, but that wasn't nearly as complicated as I'd expected, given her hesitation. "Something like what?" I asked.

"Well, you know, the mind masters are amongst the most peaceful of Ronan's mage factions," she spoke rapidly, as though she believed if she didn't get it all out at once then I'd refuse, "I'm not a trained fighter, my magic is mostly limited to self-defense, but I like to work with my hands and I'm a fast learner. Kingston's a hard man to track down, he's so busy, and I wasn't sure who else to ask, or if you even have the authority-"

"Rhien," I interrupted with a laugh. "What interests you?"

"The blacksmith," she answered after a much-needed breath. "I want to apprentice with the blacksmith."

"Have you been wanting this for a while?" I asked, and her only response was an embarrassed nod. In these few short days I'd begun talking with her, she'd been kind to me, and understanding, and *so* very helpful. There was no way I could refuse. No way I could do anything less than my best in order to fulfill her wish. "I'll make it happen."

She must have wanted this change in assignment for longer than she'd let on, because to my surprise, she let out a soft squeal, turning to throw her arms around my neck. "Thank you!"

241

I returned the hug, laughing, "There's no need to thank me." She let me go, but as she took a step back to give me space, her brown eyes lingered on mine for a thoughtful span of seconds. "What is it?" I asked.

"It's good to see you improving already," she answered, "at her mere arrival," and I knew she meant Ava.

I shrugged, though there was the hint of a grateful smile on my lips. "I suppose I should thank you for being something of a distraction."

"Well, then," she said, motioning toward a nearby door, "shall we see what the masters have to say?"

At my nod, she turned and led the way through the door. It opened up to a large cavern with a multitude of cots inside. There wasn't room enough to give all the refugees individual spaces. There'd been so many, in fact, that we'd begun housing them with our own troops in nearby villages – something the residents were more than happy to allow for the sake of the rebellion and in exchange for food. At the very back of the cavern were the masters, sitting in a half circle, and who stood out from the rest of the refugees because of their light blue robes.

Rhien led me to this group, and when we reached them, she put her palms together in front of her. "Thought is life."

Each of them put their hands together like she did and murmured, "Life is thought."

She sat in front of them, folding her legs beneath her and then waving for me to sit too. I did, mirroring her position and entirely unsure of what to do with myself because I wasn't familiar with the mages' formalities.

"Savant Gadith," Rhien greeted the oldest of the masters. He was a dark, wrinkled man, who had to be over eighty years old. What was left of his white hair formed a bright crown around his head, and his eyes were a light, meditative gray. "This is Kiena."

He began to extend his hand, and thinking that he wanted to shake with me, I put my own out. But he stretched beyond that, until the very tips of his fingers grazed the dragon pendant around my neck. I reached up, removing my father's necklace and handing it over to him. The index finger of his other hand traced the shape of the dragon, circled the dark stone, and then hooked through the chain.

He hung the necklace on his finger before me, asking as he gave it back, "What is it you seek from the masters?" His voice was low and weighted by his eighty years, but it was also gentle, and I felt his wisdom in its tenor.

I slipped the chain back around my neck and glanced at Rhien for guidance, but all she did was offer an encouraging nod. "I'm not entirely sure," I admitted. "I've been told my ancestors may have had gifts that were lost over generations, as lessons about the magic were lost." I reached up to grasp the pendant. "If there's more I'm capable of... perhaps formal instruction. Or advice."

Savant Gadith made a thoughtful hum, his faded gray eyes taking me in. I couldn't tell what he was thinking. Nor was I sure what the mind masters were capable of, but I almost felt as if he were reading my thoughts. Before saying anything, he made a hand motion to the other masters. His middle finger ran up the outside length of the index on his other hand, and then that hand turned over, and he tapped his pinky twice. The others seemed to understand, because one at the end shifted onto her knees, and turned to dig through a small trunk behind them.

"Nothing is ever *truly* lost," Savant Gadith finally said. "The memories of our ancestors remain in our blood. Just as your memories would be in your children's, and their children's." As he spoke, the master who'd been digging through the trunk turned back around with a small bottle in her hand, and she began to pour its contents into a palm-sized bowl. "It's why a lone wolf howls, having no pack to call. Why we fear fire, having never been burned. Why you were drawn to a rebellion that you never knew existed."

My eyebrows furrowed at that, because that wasn't information people simply shared as gossip, and I didn't know how he was aware of it. Savant Gadith paid no attention to my surprise, and when he reached his hand out to the side, the female master gave him the bowl. He brought it into his lap, holding it there for a silent moment and contemplating again.

Then he motioned to the bowl. "We can reacquaint you with memories, but in those memories you are a captive to their will. You return to us only when your blood is ready."

"Is it dangerous?" I asked, thinking it could be something like my dreams with Ava, something where I had the potential to be trapped forever. But Savant Gadith gave the slightest shake of his head. "I've got time."

"Very well," he said, and motioned to the nearest cot.

243

I took the prompt and moved to the cot, stretching out on it to lie down. Each of the masters came to stand around me, while Rhien sat down on the closest cot to mine to observe.

"Do not fear," Savant Gadith said, setting one warm hand on my forehead. "The body knows what the blood wants it to know." I nodded, and he held the bowl in his other hand above my face. "Breathe," he instructed.

It made me nervous when he began to tilt the bowl, because I didn't want to breathe in all that liquid and choke. As the bowl sloped, however, its contents spilled, transforming halfway to my face into a heavy purple smoke. It was thick enough that it fell to my nose with the same weight as water, but when I breathed it in, it was smooth, and calming. The more of it I inhaled, the more my eyes drifted shut and the more I felt disconnected from my body, until my eyes closed completely and I felt and heard nothing.

It was almost like I blinked, and when I opened my eyes again, I wasn't in the caves. I was in a forest, crouching behind bushes as a nearby screaming pierced the air. It was an animal's screaming, but no animal I'd ever heard before. Its desperate cries were gravelly and low, like the deep wail of a forest cat, only from something so much larger. I tightened my grip on the weapon I was holding in my hand, and involuntarily glanced down at it as I turned it around, so I had the stone dagger in a reverse grip. And they weren't *my* hands. They were large, and rough, fingers thicker and palms heavier. They were male. I was in the body, or the memory, of one of my male ancestors.

There was the low crack of a stick from somewhere nearby, and I glanced toward the noise, locking eyes with another man. He nodded behind me, and I turned to find a woman. Both of them were armed like I was, creeping through the bush toward the animal. We tiptoed slowly, keeping our eyes peeled for threats as the screaming got louder, until eventually we came upon it. At first I couldn't tell what kind of animal this massive creature was. It was caught in a net made of thick, heavy rope, and its struggling was obscured in the leaves and pine needles that had also been caught. What I did know is that it was larger than a horse.

"Go," whispered one of my companions, Zoren, and when I looked at her, she nodded toward the animal. "Quickly."

I snuck out of cover, hurrying to the front of the animal so it could see me. The creature and I locked gazes. Its eyes were as big as my palm, a mix of soft golds and yellows, and its pupil a thin black slit down the center. *It was a dragon*, its scaled flesh a mixture of blacks and dark blues that made its eyes seem to glow, and with wings trapped at its sides. And when it recognized the knife in my hand, it roared at me in a shrill, intimidating howl, and it snapped its long jaws. I jumped back, but the dragon was too subdued to reach me, and I knew this creature wasn't developed enough yet to escape on its own. It was a young dragon, a baby, no doubt, even though it was already terrifying in size.

"Easy," I said in a deep voice, holding my hand out palm first, and I felt a pinch at the forefront of my mind. "Be still."

The dragon calmed down, its golden eyes watching me as I inched closer. It didn't roar at me or try to bite again. It let me get close enough to stick my large hand through the rope, and rest it on the wide space between the beast's eyes. I motioned that it was safe for my companions to come out, and as they hurried over to begin cutting the weights holding the net down, my fingers ran along the bridge of the dragon's nose.

It wasn't anything like I imagined it'd feel. I thought it would be rough. Thought I'd have to be gentle, and careful, lest the rigid scales prick and cut my fingers. But they weren't sharp at all, not here anyway. There were sharp spikes two inches long beneath its eyes, thick barbs down the ridge of its spine that had been sticking straight up when I arrived, but now that the dragon was calm were tucked in flat to its back. Then there were its teeth. Every single one of them was more honed than my knife, gleaming white and longer than my hand. The dragon was sharp, and dangerous to be sure, but when I ran my fingers down the length of its snout, its eyes shut contentedly. It nudged up against my touch like a dog does when it wants you to scratch its ears harder.

"How'd you get caught here?" my low voice asked the dragon. "You're not a yearling anymore, got to get smarter." I leaned sideways to see where my friends were at with the ropes. They had two of the eight weights cut away. "I should name you," I suggested. "You've got eyes like stars, flesh like the coming night. Like midnight."

From the side of the dragon, my friend, Hog, teased, "What kind of a name is Midnight for a dragon?" Though I still had my mind's hold on the creature, it turned its head, snapping its teeth toward Hog. It didn't reach him, but he still jumped back with a yelp. "Oy!" he laughed, "you want out of this net or not?"

I chuckled at that, giving Midnight an amused pat on the snout. "I like you."

My companions had just managed to cut away two more of the weights when there was a loud shout, and six large men burst out of the woods around us. "That's our dragon!" one of them yelled, jabbing his long spear toward us.

"It's nobody's dragon," muttered Zoren. In response to that, Hog shapeshifted into an enormous brown bear, rising to his hind legs and letting out a rumbling roar in support.

The six men took challenging steps forward. Three of them were equipped with spears, another with a bow, and two, I sensed, had dark magic. *Good*, I thought, *I can work with that.* And as that very thought occurred to me, one of the unarmed men circled his palms one above the other, creating a black sphere of magic that he then hurled at me. I caught it halfway, but instead of deflecting it, I latched on to the darkness in it. I couldn't create darkness or corruption all on my own, but to me they were like fuel for a fire. I could control dark magic, or even rust and rot, like I could control a mind; feed it, grow it, shape it. My hands motioned upward as I molded that dark magic into my own creation – a dragon that resembled the one caught in the net behind us. Once I'd forged that dragon with the magic the hunter had thrown at me, I set it loose on two of them.

Zoren turned her entire body into a cloud of smoke that could be as solid or indefinite as she wanted, and rushed forward at the man with the bow. Bear-shaped Hog did the same, and charged at a man with a spear. I could be certain the dragon hunters with magic wouldn't attempt using it against me anymore, so I gripped my dagger firmly in my hand, sprinting forward to meet them as they drew their own knives.

I dodged the fist of the first one, rolling past him and springing up at the feet of the second. Leading with my dagger, I swiped, slashing a shallow cut across his chest, but there wasn't time to finish the job. The first man dashed at me, leading with his knife, and I gripped him with my mind out of instinct, controlled him and made him freeze on the spot, mid-stab. He was fighting it though, and the sharp bite at the front of my skull was excruciating. I wouldn't be able to keep it up forever. So I threw myself at him, avoiding his knife and colliding into him with my shoulder to take him to the ground. I wrestled him onto his stomach and sat over his back, preparing to stab my dagger through him when I noticed the other was coming at me. I threw my weapon straight into his chest, and as he collapsed, I reached down to snap the neck of the man beneath me.

Hog, Zoren, and my magic dragon had finished off the other hunters. Now that there was no more need for that dragon, I transformed it back into the sphere and let it fly at the nearest tree. Midnight had been struggling out of the net while we'd been fighting, and managed to get halfway under it because of the reduced weight. The three of us hurried over, cutting off the rest of the anchors so the dragon could go free. The moment it was out of the net it spun in a joyful circle, stretched its long tail, and shook its head in a tremble that traveled down its body and to the tip of its tail.

"Hungry?" Zoren asked it, motioning to the dead men around us.

"Feast up," I said, striding forward to pet the dragon's nose one last time. "And try to avoid food that looks too easy in the future." It made a soft chittering noise, a rapid clicking through its nose, and somehow I knew that to be agreement.

Zoren, Hog, and I traveled back in the direction of our village, but we didn't go home right away. We joined other men and women at what our small village had designated as training grounds. Here, we practiced our magic and our fighting skills. Developed everything we could as deeply as we could. We stayed at the training grounds until nightfall, as we often did when we went, and then I traveled home, more beat up from training than from any fight I ever had with a hunter.

By the time I arrived at my cottage, all the blood from the wounds in my face had dried. They were small to begin with, and all it would take was a washing. I strode through my front door, set my stone dagger on the small table just inside it, and then walked left to the kitchen table. There was food already laid out, meat and vegetables, and I was too hungry to want to wash up before eating. I took a stealthy glance around, checking to make sure I wouldn't be scolded for not waiting, and then I reached for a piece of roast potato.

As I stuck the piece into my mouth, a pair of hands set on the back of my hips, slipping under my tunic and around to my stomach. The hands were small and a little rough, but they ran low across my abdomen as though well acquainted with this masculine body.

My lips twitched with a smirk. "That better be my wife," I said. "I pity the fool who has to meet Ceri's wrath."

The woman's body pressed against my back, and one of her hands slipped down the front of my trousers, her palm making a teasing stroke along the length of me. That unfamiliar part of me flooded at the touch, while the rest of me went slack.

"*That's* my wife," I chuckled. I pulled her hand away so I could turn around and look at her.

She was smiling mischievously, but at seeing the blood on my face, that smile turned stern. "Luc, you've not washed for supper."

"Couldn't wait to see you," I teased. I grabbed her by the hips and turned us around, lifting her easily to sit her at the edge of the table.

She rolled her eyes, extending a hand sideways and using her magic to draw a small amount of fresh water from the drinking bucket in the corner. "Hold your breath," she instructed.

I took in a deliberately deep breath and held it, and she used her magic to guide that water over every inch of my face, until she'd removed all the blood. Once I was clean, she flicked her wrist, sending the dirty water flying out an open window of our home.

"That's better," she said. "Now I can see your handsome face."

I leaned forward, catching her lips in a proper kiss, enjoying the way her hands came up to run over my flat chest. Her fingers traced the deep neckline of my tunic and then slid under to my stomach, and she froze trails of the lingering sweat along my abdomen as she caressed me, sending a delighted shiver down my spine. Even better was that, as I pulled away from the kiss for a breath, she used her other magic, her sparks, to send a jolt along my tongue.

A deep hum of approval left my throat as I set my forehead against hers. "I love when you do that."

"I know," she said with a smile, and she pecked me on the lips before slipping her arms around my neck. "I have news." My eyebrows rose in question. "Guess."

This time my hum was thoughtful. "Your mother made us one of her delicious bread loaves?" My wife shook her head. "Let's see… your father's decided to stop badgering us about grandchildren?"

She straightened up. "That was very good!"

"I was right?" I asked in shock, grinning triumphantly when she nodded. "About time," I teased. "What's convinced him?"

Her lips pursed like she was trying to hold back her smile, but it didn't work, and she said through a joyous laugh, "I'm pregnant."

I could feel my entire face light up instantly, and I was so happy and excited that I grabbed her by the waist, pulled her off the table and lifted her into the air, spinning her around. And I didn't know how to voice my delight, so all I could do was laugh and let out an incoherent and gleeful shout. After a couple of twirls, I set her back on her feet, pulling her into a tight hug.

"Pregnant," I said in disbelief. "*My* wife."

"Aye," she giggled. She reached up to run her fingers back through my neck-length hair, pushing it away from my forehead. "We'll be the first to mix gifted bloodlines." Her eyes dropped to the dragon pendant around my neck. "I wonder whose abilities our children will have."

"Maybe a little bit of both," I suggested with a shrug, and added optimistically, "maybe they'll have double the magic." Then I laughed to myself. "Just so long as they can't control fire like your niece. If I have to wake up in the middle of the night one more time to put their cottage out..." Ceri simply giggled, and I shook my head again in awe. "*Pregnant.*"

The next time I blinked, I opened my eyes and was back in the caves. Back on the cot and in my own, female body. It felt like it had been less than a minute that I was in the memory, but the masters were no longer standing over me. I pushed myself up, feeling weak, as though I'd just woken from a deep and unsatisfying sleep.

"You're back," Rhien said in surprise. She grabbed the mug of water on the floor next to her, carrying it over to me. "How are you feeling?"

I took the drink from her, kicking my legs over the side of the cot and scooting over to make room for her, so she could sit down next to me. "Fine," I answered. I was a little disoriented. Though it had only felt like less than a minute, I'd grown accustomed to the body in the memory. I knew it would fade, but right now I felt strange, foreign to myself. "How long was I gone?"

Rhien watched me lift the mug to my lips, taking it back after I'd drank so I could sink forward and rest my elbows on my knees. "Supper's about to be served," she answered, and I picked my head up to look at her in shock. All day, that's how long I'd been gone. I'd been gone for *hours*. "Did you get what you needed?"

"Possibly," I answered.

The water magic wasn't something I could do, I knew that because I'd tried. I'd tried to govern each of the elements during the last six months, and had never been able to manipulate anything but the sparks I could create. The corruptions, however, that was something I'd never considered. Something I never would've been able to come up with on my own, and might have never discovered. If I'd been drawn to that memory for a specific reason, that control of darkness and corruption had to be it. Part of me was eager to try it out, but the rest of me was too exhausted to do it right now.

"I'm starving," I mumbled.

Rhien chuckled, nodding her agreement. "You should be." She helped me to my feet, and before leaving, we both strode over to where the masters had resumed sitting in a half circle. She put her palms together like she had when we arrived, repeating the same sentiment. "Thought is life."

"Life is thought," they all returned.

Though I didn't repeat the phrase, I bowed in my own show of respect. "Thank you, masters."

They bowed to me, and I turned to follow Rhien out to the corridor so we could go and eat. I hadn't completely readjusted yet, and as we walked out the door, I paused, unable to shake a peculiar feeling. Rhien kept walking because she hadn't noticed me stop, and so I reached for the waist of my trousers. Pulling the front of them, I glanced down just to make sure. Yes, everything was as it should be, and with that confirmation I was able to shake that unfamiliar strangeness.

"What are you doing?" Rhien laughed.

I glanced up and released my waistline, letting it fall back at my hips as my cheeks colored. I opened my mouth, unable to answer at first and only managing to get out an embarrassed huff of laughter. "Nothing..."

I caught up with her and we continued walking, and though she looked thoroughly amused, she didn't say anything about it. For all I knew, she was familiar with all the possibilities of being in someone else's memories – she *had* been in mine.

When we reached the dining hall, I stopped at the entrance to see where my family was. I found Nilson and my mother, sitting with Kingston off to the right. The very next person I spotted was Ava. She was with Nira and Akamar at the far end of the hall, and as my eyes scanned their table, I locked gazes with Nira. She stood and started over, looking like she wanted to speak with me. Rhien recognized that too, because she said goodbye and parted ways with me.

"Where have you been all day?" Nira asked. "You're spending time with Rhien?" Her gaze dropped briefly and landed on my hand, and she grabbed it in surprise. "Why haven't you taken care of this yet?"

I pulled my hand out of her grip, because the more time that passed, the more ashamed of it I was. "Have any more questions you'd like to blurt?" I asked with feigned boredom. "So I can answer them all at once."

"Yes, actually," she said. "Were you born this cheeky?"

I couldn't help but smile, but my gaze wandered past Nira to the table she'd come from, and I realized Ava was watching. I met her blue eyes with mine for only a moment before she looked away. Nira noticed the fading of my smile, and glanced back over her shoulder.

"Have you talked to her?" she asked.

"I tried this morning," I answered, and just like that, my mood fell. I let out a deep sigh. "She doesn't want to be around me."

One corner of Nira's lips tugged into a sympathetic smile, and she wrapped her arms around my waist to pull me into a comforting hug. "Give her time," she said. "She'll get there."

I squeezed her back for a moment, and then let her go. "I take it she's speaking to you." It made sense, why else would they be sitting together?

"When I first saw her this afternoon, she broke down, crying and apologizing and begging for forgiveness." Nira shrugged. "Now she says a little here and there, but-" She stole a brief look at her sister. "She's just... broken, Kiena. And it's Hazlitt's fault. You shouldn't blame yourself."

"*She* does," I murmured.

"I don't think she does." Nira shook her head. "Not the way you expect her to."

I took another gander at the table, only to find that Ava was looking again. Once I caught her, though, she rapidly looked away. It did nothing to help me know what to think. I couldn't tell what *she* was thinking, or whether or not she really blamed me. Even though it was hard, I truly was going to have to do nothing other than wait. Wait for Ava to come to me, to either blame me or forgive me. To tell me she wanted me around or wanted nothing to do to me. It was torture, but there was nothing else to be done.

"Go and be with her," I told Nira. "She needs company."

Nira nodded in understanding, but for a few moments, she simply watched me. Then she gave me another hug, saying, "You'll be alright."

I smiled gratefully when she let me go, and as she went back to her family, I went to sit with mine. Supper passed normally, although, while I still wasn't back to completely being myself, I *was* happier now that Ava was here safe. My mother and brother seemed to recognize that, and even if I wasn't overjoyed in our interactions, they were happy enough for me.

After I'd finished eating, I excused myself to my personal chamber. Though usually I'd stay up later than this, I was exhausted from exploring my ancestor's memories. It had taken its toll on both my body and my mind, and I needed to rest. Plus, it was late enough that I didn't need an excuse for going to bed early. So I changed into my sleeping clothes, put out the fire, and slipped into bed. I was so tired that I fell asleep almost instantly, but I woke a short time later because of a sound like someone had knocked and opened a door, and a flood of light that reached my eyes.

Someone had opened *my* door, and the torchlight from the hall streamed into my room as they entered. I caught the person's silhouette just before they closed it from the inside.

"Ava?" I called in the dark, sitting up. I couldn't be dreaming. This was real.

There was no response, but soon I felt the bed beside me dip in, and her cold legs slipped under the blankets at my side. I wasn't quite sure what was happening. All I knew was that she'd just got into my bed and still hadn't said a word.

"Ava," I whispered, reaching out with a blind hand. It landed on her shoulder, low enough that I could tell she'd already lain down. I could've created a current of sparks to light the immediate area around us, to see what she was doing or judge by her expression what she expected, but I got the feeling that's not what she wanted. "Are you alright?" I asked, lowering myself back down at her side, facing her.

Though she'd let my hand set on her shoulder, I was afraid to do any more, afraid to touch her more firmly or anywhere else, because she hadn't wanted me to touch her at all this morning. But in the dark, there was a wet sniffle, and it broke my heart just to hear it. Just to know that she might cry.

"Whatever you need," I said. "Without expectation."

She sniffled again as one of her hands landed on my hip, and it lingered there for a long span of seconds in what I knew to be hesitation. But then she *sobbed*. She broke out into genuine, uncontainable cries, and her arm wrapped all the way around my waist as she pulled herself into me. Her face buried against my chest, and at first, I froze in her grip.

While she'd come to me, and she was close and holding me, I was still afraid to touch her. I was afraid of how much it had hurt when she pushed me away. But she was sobbing violently, and that overcame my fear of being hurt, because she was hurting far worse than it would hurt me to be rejected. So I risked draping an arm over her, lightly at first to test her reaction. She gave none. Not a strengthening of her own grip on me, nor a pulling away.

I set my hand more solidly against her back, holding her a little tighter. More than anything, I wanted to tell her that everything would be fine. I wanted to murmur comforting things, to tell her that I was here, and that I loved her. But like I'd known she didn't want the light, somehow I knew that she didn't want me to say anything else. So I just held her. I was unable to fall back asleep until she was finished crying, no matter how exhausted I was, because I didn't want her to think I wasn't devotedly and unconditionally here for her.

She cried all night and into the early hours of the morning. I knew because I could hear people begin to move about outside my door. And when there were no more tears, or she'd grown too fatigued with sobbing that she couldn't do it anymore, she fell asleep.

I didn't know what it meant. Didn't know if she'd speak to me after this, or if she'd just needed something familiar to get her through the night, but I was dead tired by morning, and content enough to drift off with her in my arms.

Chapter 17

 woke before Ava. It was the third night she'd come to my room, and last night she'd finally slept more than she cried. She cried less every night, but she still wouldn't speak to me. Not when she came here, and not during our waking hours. Nira had told me that Ava specifically asked where my room was, but when I asked why, she didn't know. She thought that maybe Ava simply needed to be somewhere she felt safe. Thought that even if Ava could hardly bring herself to look at me, it didn't change the fact that she still loved me. That I was the only person with who she felt she could safely break down. I wasn't entirely sure if I believed Ava still loved me, but if this helped her, so be it.

The first two times, she'd managed to slip out in the morning before I woke, but this time I'd been so eager to know when she left that I'd slept restlessly. I woke constantly, and now the morning was early enough that I couldn't get back to sleep. She was curled into me, but I didn't have an arm wrapped around her because she was hugging my hands to her chest. It was at an uncomfortable angle so her fingers could stay folded with mine, but I didn't care. I appreciated being close to her too much to care about the cramping in my wrists. My eyes were closed even though I was awake, and after lying there for a few minutes, I felt Ava's fingers move. She shifted slightly, and then began inching her hands out of mine, and I knew she was preparing to leave.

Despite that, I couldn't bring myself to open my eyes and let her know I was awake. She wouldn't speak to me, and she clearly didn't want me trying to talk with her about why she kept coming here at night. I felt... awkward. And afraid. I wanted her to do things on her own time, to forgive me or speak to me only if and when she felt like she could. But I also wanted her to know how sorry I was. Wanted her to know how much the last six months had tortured me, how much I'd worried about her, and how hard I'd been trying to find her.

Doing her best not to shift the bed, she slipped out from under the covers, and when I could hear her bare feet retreating toward the door, I finally opened my eyes. I watched her get halfway, and then I watched her stop. She just stood there in the middle of my room, as if hesitating about leaving or like maybe it wasn't easy for her to slip away without saying anything. I wanted her to be thinking that she should come back. That she should slip back into the covers and return to sleep, or that she should wake me to say something. The hesitation didn't last forever. After a short few seconds, she continued to the door.

"Ava..." I prompted as she reached for the handle, unable to mask the sadness in my voice. She froze, and though she didn't release her grip, she didn't leave. But she didn't turn to look at me either. "You don't have to say anything," I told her, sitting up so I could talk at her back. "Nor will I force you to listen to my apology." I don't know if it was the grief in my tone, but her chin fell as she dropped her forehead against the door. "But I *do* have one. You don't ever have to forgive me for what I did." And I meant it, but just the thought that she might never forgive me brought tears to my eyes. "All I ask is that, when you're ready, you let me say it... that you let me tell you how deeply sorry I am."

Even from here, I could see her shoulders rise and fall with a deep, heavy breath. Without turning around to look at me or say anything, she nodded, and then hurried out the door. This entire thing was painful, and confusing, but I could take that nod as nothing other than agreement to my request, and that was *something*.

I eased out of bed and put on my civilian trousers and tunic, and then went to get some breakfast. It was later in the morning than I'd thought, so I ate alone, got scraps of meat from the kitchen to take to the she-wolf, and then decided to head out to the meadow. That was where my mother and Nilson spent a majority of their mornings, as my mother watched over Nilson and the other children he played with. My mother was in her normal spot, sitting on the rock, and Nilson was running around with Oscar and Akamar and some other boys and girls.

What I didn't expect to see when I walked out of the caves was Ava. She wasn't sitting anywhere near my mother. Rather, she'd sat in the grass at the far side of the meadow to lean back against a tree. There was a leaflet of paper in her lap, and it appeared she had a piece of charcoal, but though she looked ready to draw, she wasn't. She was staring at the grass near where the children were playing, not watching any of them in particular because she was lost in her own mind. The only comfort to me was that she looked healthier. Sevedi was wonderful with her healing magic. Ava was nearly back to her normal weight, and in the bright morning sun, I could see clearly that the lively glow was returning to her tawny complexion.

I nodded at my mother in greeting, but continued past her to the edge of the woods with the meat scraps. When I got there, I let out a shrill whistle to call for the wolf. It took a minute, but eventually she stalked out of the foliage. Normally I'd have just tossed her the meat and let her go back to the forest, but this time, I knelt down.

"Come here," I said, motioning for her. I knew from experience that she wasn't fond of being touched – she was still wild – and the times she *did* withstand being touched, it was clear the affection made her tense. Now, however, I reached out with my hand, slowly and on the side of her good eye. "I know we're not the best of friends," I said, scratching behind her missing ear, "but I need to ask you a favor."

The wolf sniffed the air, so deliberately that I knew it to be a request for the meat she could smell. I dropped the scraps into the grass in front of her, running my hand through the fur at her shoulder and then letting it fall, because I knew better than to try and touch her while she ate.

"You see that woman over there?" I asked the wolf. "Sitting alone." She didn't stop chewing, but her head turned so she could glance with her good eye. "Will you keep close to the caves, and when she comes out here, will you watch over her?" Before I could garner any kind of response from the wolf, the leather ball the children were playing with landed nearby, and one of the children ran to retrieve it. The wolf's lip curled at the proximity, the hair on her neck rising in warning even though the child didn't seem to notice us. "Watch it," I warned her, "I don't control you because you behave yourself." The wolf huffed, ignoring the boy as he ran off and ducking her head to grab the last piece of meat. "Will you watch over Ava for me?" She swallowed down the food and stretched her nose forward in reply, nudging her snout against my palm. "Thank you," I said, running my hand once over her head.

She dodged back into the woods, and I rose to go and sit at my mother's side. I told her good morning and then stretched my hand out over the grass to practice my magic. I'd attempted to use that manipulation of corruption I'd seen in my ancestor's memory, and to my complete satisfaction, it worked. I could do it, and the last couple of days I'd come out here to practice it on the grass. I rotted blades that had been chewed by a bug, spread the rot to a whole patch, and then reversed it. I couldn't *heal* corruption, but I could return something to normal unless I'd completely destroyed it.

Before today, I hadn't been comfortable enough to test the magic on something other than grass, but now I felt ready to try. So I pulled out my dagger and focused on a pinpoint of rust in the blade. I set my finger on the spot and trailed it up the knife, spreading the rust until it had corroded through the metal. Then I reversed it, restoring my dagger to its original state. I went back and forth with the rust for a couple of minutes, but my eyes wandered across the meadow to Ava as I did, and eventually my work ceased as I lost myself in thought. Lost myself to wondering what she was thinking about, to wondering what was going on behind that empty stare. Was she thinking about all the things she'd been through the last six months? Or what she'd do with herself now that she was back? Was she thinking about me?

During my thoughtfulness, a gentle hand set on my shoulder and rubbed across my back to the other. I pulled my gaze away from Ava and glanced up at my mother, seeing the concern in her eyes even though she didn't voice it.

"She came to me again," I sighed. "I don't know what it means, and she still won't speak to me."

"That she comes to you at all tells me she wants to," my mother said. "Sometimes grief makes things hard to say, but give her time." Her hand made another soothing run across the backs of my shoulders. "She'll find the words she's searching for."

I nodded, unable to respond because Nilson ran up, throwing his arms around my neck for such an eager hug that it knocked me over. "Morning!" he greeted. I chuckled, returning the hug and pushing myself back up once he let me go. Though he'd been so excited to see me, he dropped to his knees at my side with a suddenly serious look on his face. "Kiena?" he asked, and I hummed curiously. "Is that the girl you were looking for all this time?"

I followed his gaze across the meadow to Ava. "Aye."

"Oh," he mumbled, and paused for a long moment to study her. "She looks sad."

"She is," I answered, stretching over to brush my fingers through his messy hair.

He reached up to smooth his hair on his own, turning more to face me. "Why aren't you trying to make her happy?"

It was an innocent question, and I tried to smile kindly at him, but it was difficult to smile at all while I tried to come up with a good answer. In the end, all I could say was, "It's complicated."

"Oh," he said again, sounding disappointed. A moment later, he asked more enthusiastically, "Could I try?"

"To make her happy?" I clarified, and he gave an eager nod.

At first, I wasn't entirely sure if that was a good idea. The last thing I wanted was for Ava to think I was trying to force her to cheer up, and that *I'd* sent Nilson. Nor did I want her to feel that she had to force herself to smile because she didn't want to hurt his feelings. On the other hand, however, maybe Nilson really could cheer her a bit. He had a unique way of making someone feel special, even if he couldn't completely get them to smile. Maybe it would help Ava just to know that he'd been thinking of her, and that *he* wanted to help.

"Alright," I agreed, and his face lit up. "Just don't bother her if she doesn't want to talk."

"I won't," he said, and got up to run across the meadow.

When he reached her, he sat down so earnestly that he practically slid into her side, and she'd been so focused on staring that it appeared to startle her. Nilson was all smiles, and even if I couldn't hear what he was saying, I knew he was introducing himself. He held out his hand, and though the hesitation was clear on Ava's face, she took it. Nilson pressed a kiss to her knuckles, something I knew he'd learned from me, and while Ava didn't laugh or smile at his exaggerated friendliness, her lips moved. She *spoke* to him. It was obvious she'd only just told him her name, but perhaps Nilson would do a better job of cheering her up than I thought.

Once she'd accepted his introduction, he leaned over to look at the paper in her lap. He said something to her, and she flipped to a different page in the leaflet and angled it so he could see. Then he *pointed at me*. Ava followed his finger and met my gaze, and my cheeks shaded darkly even though I had no idea why, and I was the first to look away this time. It took a few moments, but eventually I gathered the courage to look over at them again. She wasn't watching me anymore. Nilson was leaning so comfortably into her side it was as if he'd known her for years, talking with such animation that his arms were moving, and there was the faintest hint of a smile on her lips.

It was genuine, and it was the first time since she'd been back that I'd seen her look anything but desolate. She actually looked... content. It wasn't something I'd caused or was even remotely responsible for, but just the fact that she didn't look heartbroken was enough to make me grin. I don't know if she could sense the smile on my face, but Ava looked across the meadow at me once more, and she held my gaze. It wasn't a conciliatory stare, and it did nothing to brighten or darken her expression, but she was *looking* at me. Something she hadn't done like this since she'd got here.

Nilson's chattering eventually pulled her gaze from mine, and it looked like he was saying goodbye, because he pushed away from her side and stood up, and he kissed her on the cheek before leaving. One corner of Ava's lips curled with what looked like amusement, and my mother must have been watching too, because she chuckled.

I glanced up at her, mumbling, "The little shit."

My mother laughed harder. "Perhaps he could teach you a few things."

"*I* taught *him* everything he knows," I grumbled. Nilson ran back up to me, and I grabbed him and pulled him into my lap, attacking his ribs with my fingers. "You think you know how to talk to women?" I teased. He was squirming, laughing so loudly as he tried to get away from my hands that he couldn't answer.

I stopped tickling him, and he climbed out of my lap to sit cross-legged at my side. "She drew a portrait of you," he said. That came as such a shock that I just stared at him for a moment, wide-eyed. "She's very good."

"Aye, she is," I agreed, meeting those blue eyes across the meadow for half a second before she looked away.

"Oh," Nilson giggled with realization, shoving me in the shoulder. "You fancy her."

Before he could blink, I reached out and grabbed him, pulling him back into my lap and wrapping my arm around his neck like I'd choke him. "What was that?"

"Mum!" he shrieked through his laughter, tugging at my arm. "Mum, Kiena fancies that girl!" He snorted, cackling as he teased, "I kissed her."

"That's it," I chuckled, and he was light enough that I could stand with him in my arms, and I threw him over my shoulder. "Where's the wolf, I think she's hungry."

"Mum!" he giggled, kicking his arms and legs as he dangled. "Help!"

I'd hardly carried him a couple of feet when a group of rangers exited the caves. They were *my* rangers, and Nira and Kingston were among them. The group headed to the side of the entrance, where they'd go into a small inlet of the mountain to reach the stables. I set Nilson down and went over to where Nira and Kingston had stopped at the entrance of the caves to wait for me.

"What's happening?" I asked.

"A signal fire just went up at one of our villages," Kingston answered. His eyes wandered past me to make a deliberate glance at Ava. "I understand if you'd like to sit this one out."

A signal fire at a village meant an emergency, but since Ava had been back, Kingston hadn't been tasking me with things. I knew it was because he wanted me to have all the time I needed to make sure she was alright, and because I'd want to be here if she decided she was ready to talk to me. Now was no different. Even though a signal fire could mean danger, my rangers were well equipped to handle it.

"Which village?" I asked.

"Northpond," he said.

I hummed, considering my options while I could feel Nira's eyes scanning me intensely. Northpond was one of our smaller village allies, where we stored only a small bulk of food supplies and housed some of our troops with the civilians. It was protected well enough with the amount of rebels who stayed there, and surely the situation couldn't be too dire.

Nira, however, didn't wait for me to give a response before asking, "You're not coming?"

"I didn't say that," I said.

She looked instantly irritated. "You're thinking it."

And she was right. Nilson had gotten Ava to smile. That was more progress than had been made the last three days, and if she was ever going to seek me out, it might be today. I wanted to be around. I wanted to be nearby in case she decided to speak to me.

"You *have* to come," Nira protested. Kingston sidestepped away from us at the tone of her voice, looking like he didn't want to be involved, and when I nodded at him, he retreated back into the caves. "You're our *leader*. You're the strongest fighter."

"Hardly," I told her with an amused huff, trying to ease the tension.

All she did was narrow her eyes at me. There wasn't a single scouting or raiding mission that we hadn't been on together, but I couldn't understand why she was so irritated about this. The rangers were perfectly capable, and they didn't need me, but Nira was unexpectedly upset.

"What about our safety?" she asked. "Something's wrong at Northpond. What about *my* safety?"

"I'm only one person," I said. "My absence will hardly make a difference."

"You're still doing this?" she spat, and my forehead creased with confusion. "You're too damn humble, Kiena. We need you, and the wolf."

"I'll send the wolf," I told her, thinking that would be enough.

"It's not the same!" she hollered in exasperation, and she was so upset with me that she turned and started walking away.

"Wait, Nira," I protested, spark jumping in front of her.

"Don't do that," she scolded, gesturing angrily with her hands. "You can't just do that every time you want to talk to me or not." And she shoved past me toward the stables.

I grabbed her wrist to stop her. "Why are you so angry with me?" She yanked out of my grip and scowled. "I thought you'd understand," I pleaded.

"I *do* understand," she said. "But just because she's here now," she motioned toward Ava, and when I followed the movement, I noticed that Ava was watching us again even though she couldn't hear us, "it doesn't mean your fight is over. Doesn't mean you get to quit." I opened my mouth to protest that, because I wasn't quitting, but she didn't let me say anything. "What about the rest of us?" she asked, and while she was still undeniably upset, there was a hint of disappointment in her voice. "What about those of us who haven't yet got what we're fighting for?" She gave a sad shrug, anger fading as her eyes dewed with tears. "What about what *I'm* fighting for?"

My shoulders slumped. The whole reason Nira had wanted me to make her an archer in the first place was so she could help avenge her parents' deaths, but she wasn't just fighting for revenge. She was fighting for Akamar, and for the kingdom they'd left behind, and for anyone else whose family would be ripped apart because of Hazlitt. This was important to her, as important to her as Ava was to me.

At that, I glanced across the meadow once more to Ava, and she seemed so interested in my exchange with Nira that she didn't shy away from my gaze. I didn't want to leave. I was so anxious for her to say one word to me that the very thought of leaving was stressful. What if she decided she was ready while I was out fighting? But Nira was right. This rebellion was bigger than Ava and me. It was so much more than making amends, and I owed it to Nira to be as devoted as I'd always been.

Nira must not have thought I was going to agree, because while I'd been staring at Ava, she'd stomped off toward the inlet, where another rebel had already brought her a horse. She was just mounting when I noticed, with all the other rebels already in their saddles and prepared to ride off. Even though she didn't like it, I spark jumped to her.

"Wait for me," I told her.

She still appeared a little resentful that I'd even considered not going, but she couldn't keep her lips from curling with a pleased smile. That is, until I strode past her to grab my own horse, and touched my finger to her leg to shock her. She clicked her tongue in mock annoyance, leaning back in her saddle before I got too far away to slap me in the arm. I laughed, feeling better because I was as good as forgiven, and after I'd put on my armor and mounted my own horse, I led the way.

We galloped in the direction of Northpond, and I knew the she-wolf wouldn't follow because I'd asked her to look after Ava. The village was only about ten miles away from the caves, and it would take us less than an hour to get there, but it didn't take the full distance before I started to get the feeling like something was more wrong than I'd thought. The signal fire that had alerted Kingston to a problem was high up in a tower, and only large enough to see from the mountain. It certainly wasn't large enough to fill the woods with the smoke I could smell. It wasn't just smoke, either. As we neared the last mile to Northpond, there was something bitter in the air. Something that turned my stomach, and every one of us fall silent with tense anticipation as we slowed to a canter.

Where the trees ended and the outskirts of the village began, we reduced to a trot, dropping our pace out of pure shock. The edges were farmland, while houses and other edifices were gathered at the center, and the smoke in the village was thick. Huts and homes were in flames, but the largest fire seemed to be at the very middle of the village, from a source we couldn't see at this distance. Northpond had clearly been attacked, but there was nobody around the outskirts of the village to greet us, or to tell us what had happened. I thought perhaps everyone was at the core, working to put out the various fires that had been started. However, that bitter scent and the lack of commotion and people caused the turning in my stomach to sink.

The closer we got to the village center, the stronger that putrid smell became. It wasn't until we rode past dead soldiers bearing Hazlitt's crest, and burning homes, and finally reached the source, that I realized what it was. I didn't want to believe it at first, but I pulled my horse to a stop twenty feet from the flames, the rest of my rangers stopping beside me. I didn't want to think that the massive pile of burning bodies was *truly* what I was seeing.

Because it wasn't just bodies, and it wasn't just our rebel troops who'd been killed in the attack. It was villagers – civilians, men and women. Worst of all, there were children. All thrown into one cruel heap and set ablaze, and this wasn't a strategic attack on one of our barrack villages, or on one of our storage villages. It was a slaughter. The only bodies being burned were those of civilians and rebels, as the few bodies of Hazlitt's soldiers who'd been killed lay around us, untouched. This was a sacrilege. This was a *message*. And deep down in my gut, I *knew* the message was for me. It was retaliation for rescuing Ava.

It was more than the stench of burning flesh that caused my eyes to flood with tears. It was each innocent life being devoured by the greedy flames at our feet. It was the cruelty of our enemy. The fact that Hazlitt had sent his soldiers to murder an entire village. And for what? This village wasn't a large enough force for the Vigilant to determine whether we'd win this war. These people, these men and women and children, they were farmers. They were foresters, hunters, and gatherers. They weren't fighters.

I dismounted my horse, only to reach my feet and feel so stricken, so weakened by this sight that I had to squat down. Had to set my elbows on my knees and put my hands to my head to keep from feeling faint. Had to sniffle at the building moisture in my eyes and nose. Innocent people. Defenseless people. And Hazlitt had slaughtered them.

"Gods," I whispered, "shelter their spirits better than we have."

Nira squatted down at my side, her own head dropping with grief. "I never thought..."

From behind us, I could hear the rest of my rangers dismount and walk up, and while a few of them murmured their own prayers or sentiments, most of them said nothing. They stood in mournful silence, interrupted only by the crackling of the flames. But it was a *shifting* silence, the outrage at this injustice budding the longer we looked.

"Soldiers!" one of my rangers hollered.

Nira and I shot to our feet, watching a flood of Hazlitt's men come out from behind the buildings around us. They moved quickly, weapons drawn and circling until they'd trapped us all with our backs to the burning bodies. The rebels who'd been staying in this village had fought and managed to kill a good amount of the soldiers, but they still outnumbered us two to one. Only, they weren't attacking. They surrounded us and stopped as my allies raised their weapons.

"Hold!" I shouted, not wanting my rangers to attack yet because the soldiers were waiting for a reason.

A few mumbles of protest went up from my troops, but I ignored them as I locked eyes with one of Hazlitt's men. He was more heavily armored than the others, and with a helm adorned in a commander's symbol. What stuck out more than anything, however, was the burn scar in his neck. I recognized it because I'd seen it before. His was much smaller, but the branded shape of the crow was an exact replica of the massive scar on Ava's back, and of the emblem in Hazlitt's crown. I'd hardly finished taking in what that scar meant when it began to glow the same deep red as I'd seen Ava's do once. His eyes filled too, so that he was watching me with a burning stare the dark color of blood.

"Kiena," the man said in a singsong voice, and though his voice was his own, I knew the tone. Knew the jeering.

"Hazlitt," I growled.

264

The man smirked. "I was hoping you'd come. I've heard about the marks you've been leaving for me. The one you left when you took Ava back." He stepped forward and began to pace along the circle of soldiers in front of us. "The Vigilant," he said, and let out a huff of laughter as he motioned to the burning bodies behind us. "That's what I think of your rebellion."

My fist clenched at my side, and I wished more than anything it was actually Hazlitt standing in front of me right now. "We're coming for you," I threatened.

"I gave you a chance to escape all this!" he roared.

And that, his even implying that he'd done me some kind of a favor by killing Albus and taking Ava, it made me furious. I reached out, latching onto the dark magic that allowed Hazlitt to control this commander, and I squeezed the same way Hazlitt did when his magic had gripped me six months ago. I squeezed so hard that the commander grimaced and fell to his knees.

"You made a mistake letting me go," I said. As I spoke, I could feel Hazlitt trying to relinquish his control over the commander. I could feel that he was trying to leave the man's body, because he felt this pain as though it were his own. "You might have gotten stronger." I took in a focused breath, tightening my fist with every bit of concentration I could, and I held Hazlitt there. I locked him into the commander's body because I wasn't done. "But I have too."

"You can't kill me like this." The man let out a pained laugh. "You still have to go through an army to get to me. Two armies by the time I conquer Cornwall."

I glared right into those glowing hot eyes, and then closed my own. There was so much anger and frustration and hate in my chest that every muscle in my body was coiled tight. More than anything, I wanted Hazlitt dead, but he was too far away. Killing the commander wouldn't kill him, but I *could* make him fear me. With my eyes closed, I focused on the corruption and decay around us, on the death, and I picked out the soldiers. Using my newest magic, I singled out Hazlitt's fallen men and I manipulated that death. My hand steadily lifted, and with it rose those soldiers. I reanimated as many of his decaying troops as I had the strength to, lifted them to their feet, and turned that lack of life into a lack of rest. And before Hazlitt could give an order for his soldiers to fight, I instilled my will in the dead and set them loose.

There were nearly as many dead soldiers as there were of us rangers, and while I was only able to rouse twelve of them, that they were already dead made every strike of a living soldier's sword useless. There was no way for them to defend against something that couldn't be rekilled. My rangers were safe while Hazlitt's men clashed, as swords pierced through armor and flesh. Hazlitt was still trapped in the commander's body, and it forced him to watch as his soldiers were attacked. As they were slaughtered as easily as he'd slaughtered the men, women, and children in this village.

The fight didn't last long at all, and once the final living soldier had been killed, I released my hold on the dead and let them rest. Hazlitt was still trying to leave the commander's body, but I kept him there a little longer and strode over.

"An army," I mused, squatting down to meet the level of those glowing red eyes. And it was my turn to be smug, because I doubted he could see through my bluff. "Hazlitt," I chuckled, "not even two armies can save you." I materialized a current of sparks, holding it close to the commander's face. "You will answer for all you've done."

I let Hazlitt go and shot that current into the commander, dropping his lifeless body to the dirt. It was an accomplishment that we'd avoided a small battle, but for a long span of seconds, I just stayed there, taking in what Hazlitt had done, and what I'd just done. I'd used the dead. Disturbed them. Sure, they were the enemy, but somehow I still couldn't shake the feeling like it had been wrong. Nor had it been a fair fight, and the only small comfort to me was that those men hadn't given the villagers a fair fight either.

"Gods, forgive me," I muttered.

"Kiena," Nira laughed, pacing over while the rangers behind me erupted into murmurs. "Goddess, that was-" She pulled me to my feet. "A little bit terrifying, I admit. But incredible!" She slapped my shoulder. "I'll bet Hazlitt is cowering as we speak! He's no match for you!"

I was grateful that she was impressed, but certainly Hazlitt was more of a match for me than she thought, and this didn't feel like the time for celebrating. I turned to my rangers, telling them, "Search for survivors."

There were none. They searched the entire village, every hut and home that wasn't on fire. Not a single person was left alive, and Hazlitt's soldiers had burned all of the food and supplies we'd been storing here. The ride back to the caves was quiet, and though no one left at Northpond needed medical attention, we hurried. Once we returned, I shed my armor and went to find Kingston to deliver the news, locating him in the war room with Oren and a couple others, standing over the large table map. The moment the explanation of what happened at Northpond left my mouth, two of the four councilors bellowed their outrage.

"We've had villages attacked before," said one of Kingston's captains, Kiflin, her mouth pursed with fury. "But never civilians. Not deliberately."

"Hazlitt has resorted to killing his own people?" raged the other, Braug. Both Braug and Kiflin had been commanders in Hazlitt's army, and defected when they realized how suspicious it was that Hazlitt was far too devoted to the war. "We cannot afford to keep waiting in the shadows if it means our people suffer."

Kingston nodded his understanding while he thought about it, but Kiflin asked, "Have we the numbers to stand a chance?"

Oren shook his head. "We've the numbers to make a blemish."

"Say we even manage to reach Hazlitt, then what?" she asked. "That boy from the king's guard says he got power from Ronan. Not a one of us could kill him."

Oren made a noise of disagreement, and motioned around the table. "Not one of us four."

At that, all four of them looked at me, as if finally remembering that I was still standing there. There was an unspoken question in each of their eyes, a curiosity, and I couldn't quite tell just by looking at them whether they thought me capable or not.

Braug pointed at me. "I've heard talk of what you can do."

"You've not witnessed it," Oren said. "She traveled here," he pointed at the caves on the map, and then again at the harbor I'd rescued Ava from, "to here, on a bolt of lightning. Gone and back in little more than a minute."

Kiflin squinted at me. "Is it true you control minds?"

I opened my mouth to answer, but Braug interjected, "That's how she's got that wolf lurking in the woods." And he pointed to my father's pendant around my neck. "It's that dragon magic."

I nearly rolled my eyes at that, because the only people who'd known the story behind my magic were Kingston, Ava, and Nira. Surely it was Nira who'd been spreading the tale, a tale that had traveled through the ranks enough to reach Braug's ears.

"Yes, yes," Kiflin said, "but can she kill Hazlitt?"

They all looked at me again, that unspoken question in their eyes once more. In response to it, I nodded. "I can."

"Kiena," Kingston said, the concern clear on his face. "If you're not ready, we-"

"I'm ready," I interrupted.

He nodded in acknowledgement, but said, "But we aren't sure what he's capable of."

"You have to be sure," Kiflin added. "If we risk all our men on this battle and you fail, it's over. We have *one* chance."

"I'm ready," I said again, eagerly and confidently.

Kingston was right, we didn't know exactly what Hazlitt was capable of, but I didn't care because Braug was right too. We couldn't keep rebuilding in the shadows if it gave Hazlitt chances to kill innocent people. We had to take the fight to him, whether we were completely ready or not, whether we had as many troops as we needed or not. All we needed was to find a way in.

"Get me to him," I said, "let me face him, and I'll defeat him." I wouldn't fail. I wouldn't let Hazlitt keep terrorizing innocent civilians and threatening everything I loved.

For the first time, Kiflin appeared satisfied, and her nod mirrored ones that went up around the table.

"Oren," Kingston said, "send birds to all our captains. Tell everyone it's time. We leave in three days for Cornwall to rally in a fortnight." He glanced at the other two. "Braug, Kiflin, gather our local rebels and prepare the armory." As they all nodded again, there was a soft knock from the other side of the door. "Enter," Kingston called, while Braug and Kiflin began discussing over locations on the map.

To my surprise, Ava opened the door, and she was so clearly distraught that all four of the councilors immediately set to staring at her in confusion. Her arms were folded across her chest, head down so we couldn't see her face, and her shoulders were shaking with cries. What concerned me the most was the racing of her heart.

268

"Ava?" I said, pacing over to her. And because *she'd* sought *me* out, I put my hands on her shoulders. "What's happened?"

She said nothing, and her cries and her pulse worried me so much that I took her face in my hands to try and get her to look at me, because even if she wouldn't speak to me, maybe I could find out what was wrong. I set my palms on either side of her jaw, angling her face toward mine. Kingston shouted my name at the same time as Ava looked up, her eyes that dark, blood red. But it was too late. Before I could react, a sharp pain pierced through my ribs, upwards beneath my breast and deep into my chest.

A commotion erupted in the war room. I stumbled backward away from Ava, robbed of breath and in such shock and agony that I almost lost my footing. My hands searched my ribs for the source of pain, clasping around the hilt of the dagger buried deep in my torso. Through the pain and breathlessness, I managed to think that Hazlitt might keep trying. Might try to make sure I was truly dead. So I ignored the torment just long enough to latch on to the dark magic and make a motion with one hand, banishing Hazlitt from Ava so he wouldn't come at me again.

The very moment the red faded because Hazlitt lost his control, Ava's deep blue gaze met mine. She took in the excruciating pain on my face, and her eyes flooded with tears as she let out a shaky breath, like she'd just been hit so hard that all the air was knocked out of her. It was like the trauma of that day in the castle all over again. Her mouth hung open as she reached out with a trembling hand. It caused her to glance at the blood on it, and there was a world of apology and concern and pure, overwhelming guilt in her eyes as tears went spilling down her cheeks.

It looked like she wanted to come to me, but I yanked the dagger from my flesh while she took a weak step forward to try, and her focus dropped to it. She looked away from the severe shaking of her bloody fingers to the wound in my ribs, and she froze. A flood of red spilled down my side and stained my tunic, and though it was my veins being emptied, her face paled so severely it was like every drop of blood had been stolen from her. I wanted to tell her it was alright, that it wasn't her fault because I could see on her face that she blamed herself.

In those brief seconds, Braug and Kiflin had vaulted themselves across the room to grab Ava, but she collapsed with the crushing anxiety of what she'd just done. They caught her before she hit the floor, and I let the dagger slip from my hand because I already felt too weak to hold it.

"Get Sevedi!" Kingston hollered, and Oren sprinted out the open door.

I could feel blood pouring from the wound, the heat of it running down my stomach to my hip. If I'd had the strength or the breath, I'd have pushed my hand to it to try and slow the bleeding, but even if I did, it wouldn't have helped. Though the dagger was gone, it still felt as though the blade was tearing through my flesh. My chest felt like it would burst if I took too deep a breath, but I needed air because my head was getting light. White spots were blurring my vision, and I was so disoriented by pain and weakness that I dropped to my knees.

Kingston didn't wait another second. He scooped me into his arms and rushed out the door to take me to Sevedi. I tried to protest, because I wasn't sure what Braug and Kiflin would do with Ava, and I didn't want them to hurt her. I didn't want her to be punished for this. Especially not when I'd seen by the look in her eyes that she was already punishing herself. But I hadn't the strength to say anything, and I could just see Sevedi dashing down the hall in front of Oren when everything went dark.

Chapter 18

ome unknown time after passing out, I woke up on the ground in my personal chamber, coughing and choking on blood. Most of it was swimming in my pierced lung, but what I managed to cough up I spit into the rag my mother held to my mouth. Sevedi never took her hand away from the wound in my ribs, no matter how violently I shook and heaved with the strain of feeling like I was drowning. But I couldn't breathe, and the pain was unbearable, and after a minute of agony I gladly fell back to blackness. I woke like that four times before finally managing to free my chest of the weight, and I took one gasp of precious, welcome air before giving in to the exhaustion.

Eventually, my eyes cracked open again. I was in my bed now, and the blanket was pulled up over my bare torso, all the way to my shoulders. I took in a deep breath to help wake myself up, but that air burned in my lungs like fire. I shot into a sitting position as a cough tore through my chest, trying to get enough air to stop it, but the more I breathed, the more I coughed.

"Easy," Sevedi said from the foot of the bed, while my mother came to my side with a cup of water. "I healed you, but that was no arrow wound to the shoulder."

Struggling not to choke, I sipped down as much water as I could, eventually managing to cease the burning. It didn't calm me though, because the moment I could breathe enough to think, my mind immediately went to Ava. And I panicked.

"Where is she?" I demanded, pushing the blanket off and kicking out of bed. "How long has it been? Is she hurt?"

"Kiena," my mother scolded, *"you're* hurt."

"You need to rest," Sevedi agreed.

I got to my feet and stretched, wincing at the ache in my chest. There was a new scar across my ribs, and though the wound had been healed, I was *so sore*. I staggered to my dresser and grabbed a fresh tunic, pulling it over my head. *"Where is she?"*

"The infirmary," Sevedi answered in defeat. "But please," I was already pacing to the door, and she called after me, "go slowly!"

I made it to the hall and started off in the direction of the infirmary. Word must have spread about what happened, because I got curious and concerned looks from everyone I passed, but I ignored them. I would've run if I had the strength, because I had no idea if Ava knew I was still alive, and I could only imagine what this event was doing to her. I'd been so unsure about whether or not she even still cared for me, but after this, I knew. Whether she ever wanted to be with me again or not, she'd never stopped caring. My chest had been *exploding* with pain, but the sheer anguish I could see on her face had looked far more excruciating than the hot pulse of injury that had been ripping through my flesh. She cared.

When I reached the infirmary, I threw the door open, prepared to console her and assure her that I was alright. She was sitting on the single cot, and her focus snapped to me when I burst in. A wave of relief washed over her face as her eyes filled with tears, but I wasn't glad for it, because her hands were cuffed in heavy shackles. It angered me. She was as much a victim in this as I was, and she certainly didn't deserve to be in chains.

"They shackled you?" I asked, hurrying to her and reaching for the metal around her wrists.

She yanked her hands away so I couldn't take them off, and she finally spoke to me for the first time in six months. "I should be in the dungeon," she said, a guilty tear cascading down her cheek.

"No," I muttered. The very idea of it was unthinkable. "I can't leave you in a cell... not after-"

"Not after what?" she interrupted, an unexpected sharpness to her tone. "Not after I was locked up for six months? Or have you forgotten?" She sat forward on the cot, eyebrows converging with frustration. *"Six months*, Kiena. I'll survive another if it means you're safe from me."

The fact that she'd do that, that she'd sacrifice her own freedom after just getting it back, it hurt so much that I felt the pang of it over the soreness in my chest. "Ava," I protested, "I-"

"I almost killed you!" she shouted, and the reminder of it caused her voice to crack. "I almost..." A heavy stream of tears fell from her eyes. "Please," she begged, "I'm a danger. Don't give me the chance to do it again. I won't survive it." She took in a stuttering breath and buried her face in her hands. "If I kill you too... I won't... *Please*."

"I won't lock you up," I said, lowering myself onto the cot next to her. I understood what she meant, but I couldn't do it. Not wouldn't. *Couldn't*. My conscience couldn't bear the idea of her being locked up after she'd spent six months in solitude. Just seeing her in chains was enough to make me sick.

The moment I sat down, she pulled her hands away from her face in panic. "Get away from me!" She scrambled to the far edge of the cot. "Don't touch me. Don't come close. Just go!"

"Ava, please," I whispered, my eyes dewing with hurt tears because she'd never yelled at me before.

"Leave!" she hollered. "If you won't lock me up, then go! Get out!" As much as I wanted her to feel better, it hurt too much to hear her say this, and I stood. "Go away!"

I turned and hurried to the door, unable to keep the tears from slipping down my cheeks and reluctant for her to see it. But when I reached for the handle, I froze. I stood there with my back to her, listening to her sniffling and her frantic heartbeat as the hurt in my chest changed to determination.

"What if I could fix it?" I asked, turning back around to look at her. That magic that allowed Hazlitt to control her was dark magic. I'd been able to manipulate it with the commander. Maybe I could do the same with Ava. "What if I could sever the link to Hazlitt and give you control?"

Her soggy eyes filled with a mild hope. "Could you do that?"

I shrugged, entirely unsure of what my limits were because this power was so new. "I don't know," I answered. "But, if you're willing, I could try."

She watched me for a silent minute in thought, and then glanced down to stare at her hands. "Only if you promise me one thing," she said. I gave a curious tilt of my head. "Be on your guard." I nodded my immediate consent. "Please, Kiena," she begged, "don't let me hurt you again."

"I promise." Cautiously, in case she'd try to stop me, I inched back over to her and lowered myself onto the cot. She didn't say anything about it, and so I motioned toward the chains on her wrists. "Will you let me remove those? If not for you, then for me. Please."

She held them out to me with lingering reluctance. I searched for the pointiest tool I could find in the infirmary, and used it to undo the lock that held the shackles closed. They were easy enough to get off, and while I put them and the tool down on the nearest table, Ava set to rubbing out the already sore indents on her skin.

"Ava," I asked, "they didn't hurt you, did they?"

She shook her head, and though it wasn't entirely convincing, she didn't appear to have any injuries. If anything, they'd only been a little rough, and if there was one thing I knew about Ava, it was that she wasn't fragile. I scooted forward on the cot to examine the situation and figure out how I wanted to go about her scar, and she watched me curiously, waiting for instruction. It had been so long since I'd seen the mark on her back, and in order to make sure I did this correctly, I wanted to make myself intimately familiar with it. I wanted to examine it with my new magic, and learn everything I could about what I was manipulating.

"Would you, perhaps," I began, hesitating because she'd hardly wanted me near her since she'd returned, and I wasn't sure if this was asking too much. "Can I look at your back?"

Instead of answering, she turned away from me, grabbing the bottom of her tunic and pulling it upward until she'd removed the entire thing and her whole upper body was bare. I set to studying the branded shape of the crow, but I was struggling to locate the magic while it lay dormant. I could sense it, but I couldn't feel enough of it to know what to do.

Unable to come up with anything, I extended one hand toward Ava's back, asking, "May I?"

She glanced over her shoulder at me to see what I was asking, and gods, just the way she looked at me... she was still the most beautiful woman I'd ever seen. My face flushed, and to make it even worse, she huffed amusedly and said in a light enough tone that it was *almost* like old times, "Is this an excuse for you to get your hands on me?"

And just like old times, my cheeks shaded darker. I blushed *so* deeply, and even if she'd only said it to ease the tension, it was such a relief to have her actually tease me that I chuckled, dropping my head with embarrassment. "What a surprise," I said, "you're cruel as ever." She gave a small smile but didn't say anything else, so I motioned to her back again. "So…?"

She nodded, and I set one hand to her back to run it down the scar. It was smooth to the touch, and I felt more of the magic than I had before as I traced the outline of the crow, but it still wasn't enough for me to be able to manipulate it. The corruption was buried deep in her blood, too deep for me to control. I sighed and dropped my hand with defeat.

"It's not working," I complained, reaching up to grab the dragon pendant around my neck. "I could only control it when it was active." Ava turned and pursed her lips with a smile, as if to tell me it was alright even though her eyes were full of disappointment, and she began to put her tunic back on. "Wait," I blurted, reaching out to stop her with an idea. "Do you remember when I first got this necklace? You touched it, and saw Hazlitt."

She hummed a confirmation, glancing back at me while it sank in what I was suggesting. That she touch my necklace, which was warded against dark magic, in order to activate her scar. "Kiena, *no*."

"You won't hurt me," I said, but she didn't look like she believed it. "I promise, Ava, I can control it when it's active. I know I can." I pulled the necklace over my head and held it out. "Neither of us will be in danger."

For a long minute while I held it out to her, she simply glanced back and forth between it and me. There was a severe amount of reluctance on her face, but I must have appeared confident enough for her to trust me, because she let out a heavy sigh, turning back around and holding her hand out in front of her.

I leaned close to her to extend my arm over her shoulder, lining the necklace up with her hand. It put my face just beside hers, and the only time I'd been this near to her the last few days was when she came to me at night. "I won't hurt you either."

She turned her head enough to look at me, and she was *so* close. I wanted things to be like they used to. Wanted to feel comfortable being this near, wanted to know that I could set my forehead against hers or kiss her. But she was finally speaking to me, and for now, I had to be satisfied with that.

Her blue eyes met mine as she said, "It's not me I'm concerned for."

There was no reason for her to worry about me, so I glanced toward her hand. "Ready?" I asked. She nodded. "Try and hold on to it."

When she nodded again, I dropped the pendant into her open palm. Like the first time this happened, a spark shot into her flesh, and despite the painful gasp as her eyes and scar illuminated red, she closed her fingers around the necklace. And *now* I could feel it, just as well as I'd been able to in Northpond. I could sense all the magic in her blood as powerfully as if I could see it with my eyes. I could latch on to it as simply, control it as easily. Unlike Northpond, however, now I didn't just have to control Hazlitt with the power. I had to change it, transform it, and that was something I hadn't yet done with my new magic.

Closing my eyes, I focused while I reached out with both hands, setting my palms against the glowing scar. The moment I touched it, I was ripped into Ava's vision. I could see what she was seeing – Hazlitt – and we saw what he did. He was in his military tent, probably outside Cornwall, staring wide-eyed into a tall looking glass. And more satisfying than being able to force myself into their link was that I could see the fear on his face when he realized it. When he felt my presence and realized that I wasn't dead. I wish I could've spoken to him. Wish I could've told him that he'd only made me more determined than ever, but the link didn't work like that, and I didn't want to waste any time or give him a chance to thwart me.

Though I kept my eyes closed, I forced myself out of the vision in order to devote all my focus to the magic itself. It was more powerful than the link with the commander had been. I don't know why, but Hazlitt had needed *more* magic, stronger magic in order to create his connection of control over Ava – perhaps that's why her scar was so much larger – and I could feel the depth of it swirling in my head. There was no knowledge or experience to tell me what I should do. It wasn't possible for me to cure corruption and darkness, I could only change it, and thus, I couldn't cure Ava of the magic. The only thing that made any sense was taking control from Hazlitt and giving it to her.

Though I'd left the vision, I knew Ava was still there, and I could feel her pulse in the silence of the room around us. Her heart was racing, and I could only imagine it was because of Hazlitt. He'd been cruel to her for her whole life, controlled her to make her kill her true father, locked her away for six months, and then tried using her to kill me. I wasn't sure whether it was rage, or terror, or anxiety, or even a combination of the three, but her heartbeat was out of control. She wanted out of the vision, out of the magic. Even if she was determined not to let go of my necklace, in my hold on the power, I could feel her desperately pulling away.

In order to separate her from it as fast as I could, I put all my concentration on Hazlitt, and on what he felt like in the connection. Like I had with the commander, I locked in on Hazlitt's power and gripped it, but this time I didn't hold him there. Once I had it, I directed all my will on forcing him out for good, on severing his end of the connection so all that'd be left was Ava. I wasn't sure whether Hazlitt was fighting it, but breaking his tie permanently was so much harder than simply forcing him out like I'd done when he stabbed me.

It was a true test of my abilities, and the strain of the effort I was putting into fighting his power and ignoring the stress of Ava's heartbeat... it was exhausting. A sheen of sweat began to cool my forehead. Behind that, a dull ache settled in at the center of my skull, and there was no work being done in my chest, but the soreness in it was intensifying almost more than I could stand. But I nearly had it, and so I panted for air and pushed on, putting every mental effort toward transforming Hazlitt's end.

Then all at once it was gone. Hazlitt was gone. I couldn't feel him, and when I tapped into Ava's vision, I couldn't see him. At the same moment I sensed his power explode from her with a violent burst of energy, Ava let out a sharp cry of pain. It wasn't in her blood anymore, or in the scar. I could feel the physical thickness of the aura that had escaped into the room, like a chaotic fog against my skin. I opened my eyes to check on Ava, and even though she'd dropped the necklace from her hand, she was still glowing. The scar on her back was still a bright red despite that the connection had been severed and Hazlitt wasn't around anymore.

I was panicking. Her heart was racing faster than ever, and at such a pace that I knew it to be nothing other than pain and terror. She'd trusted me to do this, and something was wrong. Snapping my eyes shut, I did my best to block out my growing hysteria and focus on the unbound energy in the infirmary. I expanded my grasp to seize it all, and then I compressed it. I reeled it in to begin willing it all back into Ava, hoping more than anything that it would do what I wanted and give her control.

But she was fighting it. She was terrified, and she was battling this new feeling so ardently that I finally realized she *already* had control. She had more control than Hazlitt ever did, and it was combatting my authority and my efforts so that my task was impossibly difficult. I exerted so much energy trying to gather the unchecked magic, the magic she was simultaneously trying to keep at large, that I was gasping for air.

I thought to tell her to calm down, to try and relax because I couldn't do this if she was fighting it, but I was so focused that the words never left my tongue. In a matter of intensely concentrated moments, I felt the collection of energy implode as violently as it had been released. Before I could even open my eyes, there was a crash of glass bottles on a table across the room. Then I looked, and my heart dropped.

Ava wasn't sitting in front of me anymore, but there was a massive black crow with dark red eyes, off balance and in such a struggle to gain its footing that it was making a mess of the infirmary. It flapped its wings, taking flight for less than a second before smashing into another table of medical supplies. The bird beat its wings to try and stand again, but was so distressed and unsure of itself that it thrashed right off the table and plummeted to the floor.

I threw my hands to my head, immediately panicked enough that I was sick to my stomach. "What have I done?" I whispered.

The bird was Ava – there was no other explanation. She'd trusted me to help her and *I'd turned her into a crow*. I'd turned her into the very symbol of her captivity. But *I* hadn't done this. Her control had rivaled mine, and *she'd* done this. All I'd unwittingly done was give her a choice. Was give her the power to make that magic whatever she wanted, and *she'd* turned that darkness's purpose and ability into something entirely different. It was clear by how frenzied she was that she hadn't meant to do it, but if she didn't stop flailing she'd hurt herself.

"Ava!" I hollered, wincing as she crashed headfirst into an already strewn table of medicines. She didn't seem to hear me, and glass was shattered all over the floor and I couldn't let her keep doing this or she'd be injured. As much as I hated it, I had to use my abilities. "Ava, stop!" That splitting crack went down the front of my skull, and she stopped flailing and simply laid there, chest heaving with breaths. "*You* can fix this."

I didn't know if that was true, but the crow lay there for a long minute as if taking in my words. She calmed down during that minute, her heartbeat slowed and her breaths became steady, and then I could see the focus in her crimson eyes. As I watched, wings became arms, and feathers became flesh. It happened so fast I would've missed it had I so much as blinked, but the crow grew and twisted and changed, and then it was

278

gone, and Ava was lying in its place. I let out a heavy sigh of relief as Ava pushed herself up, sitting at the edge of the table with a confused but comforted look on her face.

And we just stared at each other for a while, both of us seeming unsure of what to say until she gave a soft smile. "That's not exactly what I expected," she said. She huffed with dry amusement. Or maybe it was disbelief. "Honestly, I'm not sure what I expected."

"Are you..." I hesitated, unsure if I should even ask because maybe it was a stupid question given the circumstances. "Are you alright?"

I could tell by the way her eyes lingered on mine, by the way she contemplated my words deeply and for a long minute, that she knew I didn't just mean physically. "I think so," she answered with some reserve, adding, "I will be."

At least she wasn't angry about the outcome, and it was such a consolation that I nearly sighed a second time. "You're like that story now," I said in an attempt to stay optimistic, and I was finally calm enough to realize that she wasn't fully dressed. I grabbed her tunic off the cot and handed it to her. "About the skin walker in the mountains of the Amalgam Plains."

She smiled gratefully, and took the shirt from me as she slipped off the table. She clearly wasn't shy about being exposed, but I turned my face away regardless and on account of how unpredictable she'd been lately. "Apparently I've got to learn to fly."

I let out a soft laugh. "You hate heights."

"That's just my luck, isn't it?" she quipped.

I'd thought she was done dressing, but she was twisting to pull the shirt on as I looked again, and I couldn't help but notice that, while her eyes had returned to their deep blue, the scar on her back hadn't gone to normal. It wasn't glowing anymore, but it had stayed that shadowed shade of crimson. I took a step forward to stop her so I could examine the mark, but as I took that step, I found that my legs were wobbly. All the energy I'd exerted on helping Ava was energy I didn't have in the first place, and I had very little left to even stand. I nearly collapsed, but managed to catch myself on a table and fall clumsily onto the cot.

"Kiena?" Ava finished pulling on her shirt as she rushed to my side.

I motioned to her back to finish my thought. "It's still red," I told her. "I'm sorry I couldn't fix it."

Part 2: The Dragon

"Kiena," Ava repeated, this time with a reprimanding tone behind her concern. "Are *you* alright?"

I wasn't, not entirely. My head hurt, my limbs were heavy, and I had so little strength that I wasn't even sure I'd be able to get off the cot on my own. Worse than all of it was the burning soreness in my chest that made even breathing painful. Despite that, I nodded. "I think I just need to rest."

"Come," she said, lifting my arm behind her neck and helping me stand. "Let me take you back to your room."

With my arm over her shoulders and her own clasped tight around my waist, she walked me all the way back to my private chamber. I wanted to speak to her, because she was actually talking to me and I wanted more than anything to hear more of her voice. I never wanted her to stop talking, but I barely had the energy to lift my feet to walk, let alone to form words. Once we reached my room, she closed the door behind us and guided me to the bed. She threw back the covers so I could get in and then pulled them up to my chin, and it felt so good to lie down that I hardly got out a mumbled 'thank you' before I passed out.

Chapter 19

n the dim light of my fire lit room, I took a wakening breath and opened my eyes. I was curled up under the thick blankets, lying on my side and facing away from the rest of the chamber. It felt as though I'd been sleeping for days, but I was still so tired that I was prepared to go right back to sleep. I rolled over to adjust my position, but at seeing a figure hunched over the small table in my room, my eyes widened with surprise. It was Ava, and though she was facing me, she was so wrapped up in drawing on her leaflet of paper that she hadn't noticed I was awake.

"You stayed," I said, easing myself up to sit and dangling my legs over the side of the waist high bed. "All this time?" I stretched my torso by raising my arms above me, pleased to find that the previously aggravating soreness was now no more than a tight feeling in my ribs.

Ava glanced up from the paper she was drawing on, lips curling with a small smile. "I stayed." After setting the paper aside, she stood and began to walk over, asking as she sat down next to me, "How are you feeling?"

"Better," I answered. "Was I asleep long?"

"A few hours," she said. "You've missed supper, I hope you're not hungry."

I shook my head, but worried that she'd stayed here instead of going for food, asked, "Have you eaten?"

"Your mother came by," she answered with a nod. "She looked rightly concerned that I was here, but offered to bring me something." She looked over at me, making a telling glance down at where the dagger had pierced through my ribs. "She was very kind to me... Too kind."

I wanted to tell her that it wasn't her fault. That she didn't deserve any punishment or scorn for what happened. But with her so close, and finally looking me in the eyes and speaking to me normally, I could do nothing but stare at her. What I wanted more than anything was for her to just look at me and talk about anything and everything, and I wanted to bask in it.

After a few moments of me staring at her, her eyebrows furrowed curiously. "What?" She brushed her hands together and then ran the back of one across her cheek. "Have I got charcoal on my face?"

I couldn't help it. I got so emotional that my eyes filled with tears. "There was a time I thought I'd never see you again," I admitted. "I was beginning to think you'd never speak to me." Though she hadn't told me that she was ready to hear my apology, it felt like she was. Felt like I could finally say it without her breaking down. Only, I couldn't say it without breaking down myself. "I'm so sorry, Ava," I said, and my voice cracked with emotion as all the guilt I'd been harboring for the last six months rushed to the surface, finally ready to be released. "We looked for you. Gods, I *swear* to you, we looked. Not a second went by that I didn't hate myself for what I did, and not a moment passed that I didn't think of you and worry."

I reached up to wipe at the moisture on my cheeks. "You don't have to forgive me," I told her. "You can go back to avoiding me, please just know that I regretted my betrayal every day. I never forgot you, and I never stopped looking." My head dropped with remorse, and there were too many tears streaming down my face to wipe them away. They ran along my chin and fell into my lap. "I never should have left you. I betrayed your trust, and you have every right to be angry with me. I never should have left, I just..." I took in a stunted breath, trying my best to keep from sobbing. "I'm sorry. I'm *so* sorry."

Ava didn't say anything at first, but slid off the edge of the bed and moved to stand in front of me. For a few long moments, I could feel her simply watching me, but then she wrapped her arms around my neck, and she hugged me tight for half a minute before pulling away and reaching for my face. "Kiena," she said, thumbing away my tears, "look at me." It took a few seconds, but eventually I managed to collect myself and meet her gaze. "You made the choice that we *both* knew you'd make all along if it came to it. It's the choice I'd have you make again." She let go with one hand to stroke the backs of her fingers down my cheek, brushing away another tear. "Your mother is a wonderful woman, and Nilson is so full of love. I'd do it all again if it meant their safety, and yours."

I took a hard and broken breath in order to say, "But they were safe all along. I left you for nothing."

Ava shook her head, making another comforting caress against my cheek. "You couldn't have known." Letting go of my face, she dropped her hands to mine to hold them. "I'm not angry with you." Her lips pursed at that, and while her cheeks tinted with embarrassment, she admitted, "Well... I *was*... sometimes. I know it's not your fault, but it took you *so* long to find me, and on the worst days I couldn't help doubting every-thing, especially your feelings for me. I *was* angry with you, but more than anything, I've been so furious with myself." I met her eyes curiously when she paused, and she gave a sad smile. "I held on for so long, thinking you'd come. I *knew* you would, but it took so long that I surrendered. I gave up on hope and life, and I wanted to die, Kiena." Her eyes filled with tears, and now it was my turn to reach up and wipe them away. "That's not me. I've never surrendered to anything in my twenty-one years, but... I *did*. I thought you were dead, too, and I couldn't do it anymore."

With my hands on her face, she reached up to set her palms against the backs of them. "I'm sorry I've not spoken to you," she said. "Being back has been overwhelming. I've needed time to take in that I *was* rescued, and how much everything has changed. I've had to sort through my emo-tions, and I've not known what to say or how to begin. I've been angry and ashamed, and it's been hard for me to forgive myself for losing faith." She nuzzled her cheek into my palm, saying, "But speaking to you now, taking comfort in you these last days, I finally feel like I'm home again. After eve-rything... After all this time... You still feel as much like home as you al-ways have."

My gaze dropped from her eyes to her mouth as I took in exactly what that meant to her, and what she was telling me. I could feel her watching me, but when her tongue slipped out to wet her bottom lip, it felt like all the permission I needed. I eased forward and kissed her. It was soft, and slow, and though her heart skipped and my own felt like it would burst with joy, I didn't kiss her long. She stopped it, but was so reluctant to completely pull away that she set her forehead against mine.

Her eyes scanned my face as she asked, "What about Nira?"

"Nira?" All she did was nod, and it took a long moment for me to realize what she was asking. What she was implying was going on between Nira and me. "What? *No*," I said, in such shock that I didn't even know how to react. "Ava, she's your *sister*."

"And the closest thing to me," she explained. "You said yourself once that we're very much alike."

"Aye, but..." I was so thrown by the concept that I was still struggling for words. "But she's *not* you." I let go of Ava's face and leaned back a little to see her better. "Where did you get this idea?"

"It seems like there's a lot of tension between you on account of my return." She shrugged, a faint blush coloring her cheeks. "And it appears as though you bicker like a couple." All I could do was stare at her and blink, and her eyebrows converged with worry as she asked, "Have I offended you?"

"No, you haven't." I chuckled. "I'm a bit stunned is all. We've tension because Nira is stubborn, and we don't always agree." Now that I'd got over the shock, I couldn't help but laugh more wholly at the complete absurdity of it. "It's never even crossed my mind, and I'm fairly certain she hasn't much interest in women." I was still chuckling, but narrowed my eyes at Ava. "You'd kiss me if I were courting your sister?"

"*You* kissed *me*!" she laughed.

"You've been flirting," I accused, and I leaned forward once more, saying amusedly against her lips, "and you made no attempt at stopping me." I was about to kiss her again, and she parted her lips in preparation for it, but I couldn't help it that I snorted with laughter, which pulled me away again. "*Nira*," I snickered. "Gods have mercy. I love your sister, but I don't *love* your sister."

"You've quite made your point," Ava giggled, rolling her eyes.

"Alright," I said, tapering off my laughter because there was still an embarrassed tint in her cheeks. "You and I never bickered," I mused, shifting the subject away from Nira.

Ava put her hands on my knees, saying with a somber shrug, "We also never got to be a proper couple." There was a lengthy pause, during which she watched her hands and appeared to be in such deep thought that I didn't want to say anything. So I set my hands on top of hers, and she responded by slipping her fingers through mine and meeting my gaze.

"Kiena," she prompted, and I hummed that I was listening. "I wanted to say thank you... For liberating me."

"I would never have left you on that ship," I said.

She shook her head. "I mean from Hazlitt's control." Holding my hand, she directed it under the hem of her tunic and around to her back, setting it against her scar. "From this." And with my palm at her back, she used the opportunity to step further between my legs, putting herself closer to me and effectively making my stomach flip. "While you were sleeping, I was sitting there, and I was thinking about how I feel more free now than I ever have in my life." She wrapped her arms around my neck and touched her forehead to mine. "I've been out of sorts for so long, but now I feel as though I can finally start being myself again, and I have you to thank for that."

"I'd do anything for you," I said. Closing my eyes, I took a moment to marvel in the sensations of being so near to her. How it felt to be in her arms. What it was like to be surrounded by her scent. She was being so affectionate and open, and it seemed quite clear how she felt about me, but after so many months, I was almost terrified to tell her, "I still love you, Ava." And in the stillness between us, I felt her heart stutter at hearing that. "More than life."

Ava leaned back just enough to look at me, and when I opened my eyes and saw the grin on her face, I couldn't keep my own lips from pulling into a smile. "I still love you too," she said, and there was nothing else I wanted to do but kiss her.

So I did. I tightened my hold on her back to bring her nearer to me, I met her lips with my own, and I kissed her like it was the last thing I'd ever do. And it wasn't just deep in the openness of it, or the way her tongue kept gifting my lips with its taste. It was in the way we were both so content not to rush this that it was slow and delicate, allowing me to notice all the things I'd miss if I lost myself completely. Like the way it felt to have my arms circled so perfectly around her waist, or her hips against the insides of my thighs. How it felt to have her heartbeat pulsing in my ears and in my blood, and to feel the heat of her body against the front of me, matching the already exhilarated heat in my cheeks. How it felt to have her fingers stroking the back of my neck and toying with the short hairs at the base of my skull.

It had only been my intention to kiss her for a minute... or two... but now I couldn't stop. Didn't *ever* want to stop, and she seemed just as willing for this to last as long as possible. After a while, she climbed onto the bed, a knee on either side of my hips so she could sit back in my lap. A while after that, I maneuvered us onto the center and lay beneath her, and nothing changed but the amount of unadulterated contentment that was building in my chest.

Though my hands slipped under her tunic, it wasn't to satiate a lust. It was because there was a time I thought I'd never kiss her even once more, or get to remember what her skin felt like against my fingertips. I'd never allow that to happen again, and so I kissed her for what seemed like hours while my hands drank her in. They ran up and down her back so many times I lost track. Traced the shape of her waist while my thumbs counted her ribs or followed the lines of her hips. Caressed her cheeks and her jaw and her neck. I couldn't get enough of her.

We kissed so long I felt hypnotized by it, until Ava's lips curled against mine with a smile. It felt like the kind of smile to preface a laugh, and it pulled me out of my daze and I finally realized *just* how long we'd been doing this.

Ava stopped kissing me, lifting herself up enough so she could look me in the eyes. "Have you missed me all this time?" she teased.

My cheeks tinted, but now that her mouth was gone, it felt like something was missing. It was such an abrupt end, and I lifted my head to peck her once more. "Perhaps," I answered. "Is it obvious?"

"A bit," she said, dropping to kiss me again in return, "not that I'm opposed." She rolled off of me to lie at my side, and I turned to face her, scooting as close as I could while draping an arm over her waist. For a long few minutes, we just lay there looking at each other, my hand drawing lines on her back and her fingers tracing my jaw. Eventually, she said, "I heard about how you saved me."

"What did you hear?" I asked.

"That you turned into lightning," she said with a proud smile, "and traveled three hundred miles and back in hardly three seconds."

I chuckled, which only made Ava laugh because she'd seen me spark jump, and though it may have looked like I turned into lightning, that wasn't exactly what happened. And it certainly hadn't happened that fast. "It appears they like to exaggerate my accomplishments."

"Apparently," she agreed. "So you didn't bring me back from the dead?"

I shrugged self-consciously and said, "...Your heart stopped." Ava's eyebrows rose with shock, and she pushed up onto an elbow to see me more clearly. "I started it again."

"*You brought me back from the dead*," she emphasized in complete awe, staring at the bed as if she could hardly process it.

"I wasn't ready to lose you again," I said. That look of awe didn't leave Ava's eyes as she met my gaze, and she looked so deeply impressed that I felt a bashful heat rise in my cheeks. "I've learned to use my magic. It's making me capable of the greatness you always saw in me."

She cupped my face, leaning in to kiss me once before settling back into the bed. "It's not the magic that makes you capable." I smiled gratefully at that. "Did you use magic to find me?"

"Nobody told you?" I asked. She shook her head, watching me with interest. "Silas... he finally realized he was on the wrong side."

"Silas?" she repeated, a hard to read emptiness glazing her eyes, and I hummed a confirmation. It took a minute, but when she recovered from that surprised emotion, she looked at me with concern. "How did you take it when he returned?"

"I hit him," I admitted as my gaze dropped. "Until I couldn't hit him anymore."

"Your hand," she mused, recalling the gash in my knuckles from hitting Silas's teeth.

"You noticed." I sighed deeply when she nodded. "I might've killed him if he didn't know where you were."

Ava scanned my expression, and pursed her lips with a sympathetic smile. "You *didn't* kill him," she said. "Don't haunt yourself with possibilities."

I nodded, and we both fell silent to watch each other for another span of minutes. It felt so good just to look her in the eyes, and have her looking back at me. To be near her and comfortable and... safe. That wouldn't last forever. The world outside my door was still moving, and that safe feeling wouldn't be permanent until this war was over, but for now this was everything I wanted. And Ava seemed to understand exactly what I was thinking, and to feel exactly how I felt, because her deep blue eyes never left mine, and her face was set with contentment.

I reached up with one hand to cup her cheek, caressing beneath her bottom lip with my thumb. "I did miss you, Ava. More than I could ever express."

She tilted her head just enough to catch the pad of my thumb with her lips, pressing a kiss to it. "I know," she said, with a deep understanding that told me she truly did know. She'd felt it too, and though she wouldn't say it, I knew it had been worse for her. Far worse. I could see it in the sudden distance that darkened her gaze, as if the very reminder had pulled her back.

"Do you want to talk about it?" I asked.

She watched me silently for a few moments, contemplating the question. "Yes," she answered eventually, "but not yet. I'm not ready."

"Alright," I agreed, running my thumb over her cheek. But she still looked haunted, and I was well aware that she wouldn't completely heal overnight. It might even take months or years, but I wanted her to know that I was here for her. "We'll make this right," I assured her. "We'll get our kingdom back, our home. We'll get your mother too."

Only, though I'd meant to put her at ease, for some reason her eyes filled with tears. She blinked rapidly and sniffled, but despite her efforts, a drop escaped out the side of her eye and slid over the bridge of her nose. I whisked away the moisture, waiting patiently for her to say something because I didn't want to ask questions and make her talk about it if she didn't want to. I'd let her cry without explanation, and hold her for no other reason than to give her a shoulder if that's what she needed.

After a few moments of making sure she could maintain composure, Ava whispered, "Hazlitt killed her."

My brow furrowed with sympathy, but I asked, "Are you sure?" I wouldn't put it past Hazlitt simply to taunt her with it, to tell her that her mother was dead even if she truly wasn't. But, despite Ava's efforts to keep her emotions under control, her face contorted with a deep pain that I understood immediately. "He made you watch," I realized.

Ava reached up as droplets spilled from her eyes, wiping them away herself. "He wanted the location of the Vigilant," she whimpered, "and I wouldn't give it to him." She inhaled a quivering breath, briefly squeezing her eyes shut. "I had no way of knowing about Nira or Akamar, and everyone else was dead... I thought you were too, I just..." She couldn't finish. She still felt too angry with herself for giving up, and I could see in the damaged and devastated tears in her eyes that she harbored more guilt than even *I* could imagine.

"It's alright, Ava," I said, pulling her into a tight hug. She buried her face in my neck, sniffling through her tears. "I understand." I ran my hand up and down her back soothingly, holding her to offer as much comfort as I possibly could. "It's not your fault. None of it is your fault."

She cried against me as I murmured that reassurance over and over again, and took in a deep breath after a long while, letting it out in an emotional sigh as she collected herself and stopped the tears. She leaned back, swallowing down her misery as she set her forehead against mine. "Do you think we'll ever be as happy as we were?"

"Were we happy?" I teased, because our relationship had always been one primarily of restraint and torment.

"You know what I mean," she said through a soggy huff of laughter.

I pressed a kiss to her lips and answered seriously, "If we make it through this, we'll be happier than we were."

She nodded her agreement while I brought one of her hands to my lips, and for the next few minutes, I planted delicate kisses to her fingers. A kiss for every month we'd spent apart, for every tear, and for every day of pain. I kissed her hand until the affection banished the moisture from her eyes, until it tickled her flesh and her mouth curled with a smile.

"I'm not a princess anymore," she mused, reaching up to touch my face. "I never had a birth claim to the Valenian throne, and Nira and Akamar have more of a claim to the Ronan throne." She met my gaze, finally able to move past the desolation and look hopeful. "We can be together, *truly* together. For real and forever... and officially, if you wanted."

My eyebrows furrowed with instinctive curiosity as I contemplated what she'd just said, while my mind made the connection between her not being a princess and us being together. "Did you just-" I faltered in shock, pushing myself up onto an elbow to look at her. "Did you just ask me to marry you?" And I couldn't help it that the mixture of surprise and amusement made my cheeks tint as I chuckled. "Did you just go from not speaking to me to asking my hand in the matter of a day?"

"I suppose I did," Ava agreed through a laugh. "I've been thinking cottage life might suit me better than-" I cut her off with a kiss, which wasn't more than simply bumping my mouth against hers because I was grinning too much to really kiss her. "Does that mean yes?" she asked when I pulled away.

"Aye," I said. "I'd marry you this very instant if I could." At that, Ava's eyebrows rose, and I could quite clearly read the thoughts behind her expression. "We're not getting married this very instant," I said with scolding sarcasm, which made her laugh. "When this is over, we'll do it proper."

"You're no fun," she grumbled.

I gave her another joyful kiss on the lips. The thought of marrying her was almost enough to make me even more eager to finish this war. All I had to do was defeat Hazlitt, and then we could all be free and Ava and I could be together without a worry. I knew it wouldn't be that simple, and that's *if* I even made it out alive, but I didn't want to think about that right now.

So I glanced back toward the table. "What have you been drawing?"

She followed my gaze. "Would you like to see?"

When I nodded, she got off the bed to retrieve her leaflet of paper, and I sat up to lean back against the headboard. Ava got the paper and climbed back onto the bed, sitting at my side and placing the leaflet in my lap. I flipped open to the first page while she leaned her head on my shoulder – she'd drawn a landscape of the meadow outside the caves. There was another landscape on the next, and I had to admit that I was surprised she'd actually been drawing. Every time I'd looked at her, she'd appeared distant, and it hadn't seemed she'd been doing much drawing at all.

The next page was a portrait of Akamar, and when Ava saw it, she said, "He begged me to draw him." I chuckled. "Your mother's been caring for him?"

I nodded, turning to the next page. "He and Nilson have grown attached," I explained, "and he and Nira... they've become very much like family."

Ava didn't say anything, but I could feel her gratefulness in the kiss she pressed to my shoulder. I moved on to the next sheet, and though it was a portrait of me, I wasn't entirely surprised – Nilson had said she'd drawn me. However, when I turned the page once more, I froze at an intense mixture of shock and excitement. Ava had sketched me, and though the perspective was hers, I recognized it as our first night together in the Ronan castle. I was on my knees before her in nothing but trousers, and my cheeks flared with such a deep blush when I saw it that I was sure Ava could feel the heat.

She could also sense my bashful tension, because she laughed, "I've a perfectly good explanation for that."

"Have you?" I asked, clearing my throat because I hadn't been prepared for seeing it, and the fact that she'd drawn something like that had caused a very physical reaction in me.

Ava hummed the affirmative. "I thought remembering good things from before would help me heal faster, and be ready to speak to you sooner." She shrugged, and then said, "I never felt so good as that night."

I silently thumbed the bottom corner of the paper. I'd never felt better than that night either, but in my mind, it felt tainted. It was attached to the memory of the next morning, of losing everything, and I wanted nothing more than to make new memories that weren't darkened by Hazlitt. I wanted to be free of all this. Free of worrying about the safety of everyone I loved.

"Can you defeat him?" Ava asked, intuitively catching the turn of my thoughts.

My shoulders slumped as I let out a soft sigh. "I don't know," I answered, only comfortable enough to admit that to Ava. I could kill him, of that I was almost certain, but I didn't know if I could do it and survive. "It'll be hard even getting to him."

Ava mirrored my sigh, and we were both quiet for a somber minute. "If only dragons were still alive," she mused. "I bet you could use your magic to get one of them to help."

"Dragons?" I repeated, to which she nodded.

Though her speculation had been purely wishful thinking, something about it excited me. How could we ever know for sure if the dragons were truly gone? How could we know if we didn't see for ourselves? I could vaguely recall some details from the few of Kingston's war meetings I'd caught moments of. The castle at Cornwall was set against a mountain, and the only way for us to storm in was to battle our way in from the front. But was that *truly* the only way to get there?

What if we could get in from above? What if we could bypass the battlefields outside the castle and get straight to Hazlitt beyond the walls? I couldn't spark jump over the castle walls because I'd be going in alone, and against an unknown number of Hazlitt's men. I *could* take someone with me, but Ava's heart had stopped when I'd brought her back from the coast, and though it may have been on account of her condition, I wouldn't risk it again. Ava, however, was more right than she might think. It was a desperate play, and likely one that would be a huge waste of our time, but if we left early and by some miracle of the gods managed to recruit a dragon, our chances of reaching Hazlitt – and of winning this war – would improve tenfold.

"Will you come with me in the morning?" I asked. "To talk to Kingston about something."

Ava nodded, but she must have been stuck on the idea of how I'd get a dragon, because she said, "I hear you've learned to control minds. Is that what I got a taste of in the infirmary?"

She didn't seem at all upset about it, but my own discomfort with the ability caused me to wince. "I'm sorry."

She looked suddenly excited. "So you can?" she asked, and she moved the leaflet off my lap to throw a leg over and straddle me. "Show me."

"Show you?" I repeated. She nodded, but there was no way I was going to control her for no reason. "I can't."

"Why?"

"Because I can't do that to you again," I said. "It's wrong."

Her eyebrows furrowed with disagreement. "You saved me from hurting myself the first time, and this time I'm giving you permission." And she took in an excited breath as she slid her arms around my neck. "Can you do it without speaking?"

"Ava," I protested, "I don't want to know. How's this power any different from what Hazlitt's done to you?"

She blinked at me for a long moment while her arms fell from my neck, as though she truly didn't know what to think or how to respond. Then she said, "It's different because I trust you. Because I love you and I know you'd never try and hurt me." She gave a small smile as if it would help ease my discomfort. "There's not a vile bone in your body."

It didn't work, and my eyes dropped to the wound across my knuckles. "Isn't there?"

There was a lengthy pause, and then her fingers set beneath my chin, drawing my gaze back to hers. "You lashed out because of how badly he hurt you," she said. "Because of your own pain. Not because of malice harbored in your heart."

I took in a deep breath, admitting on a sigh, "I'm not so sure." I'd beat Silas because I wanted him to hurt like I had, because I was angry with him. Was that not vengeance? Was that not malice? I'd first discovered that I could also control people because of my fury with him. A part of me didn't want to believe that ability was born of benevolent intent.

"I am," Ava said.

But I shook my head. "You weren't there."

When my gaze nearly fell away with shame, she moved to catch it, saying firmly, "I'm sure." And there was such a devoted look of confidence on her face that I almost had no choice but to believe it, if only because of how deeply *she* believed in me. "Now come on," she added, returning her arms around my neck. "How's it work?"

"I don't know," I answered. "And it's painful."

"Oh," she murmured, dropping her arms again. Though, she wasn't entirely deterred. "Does it hurt even if someone's letting it happen?" All I did was shrug. "Shouldn't you know for certain? For when we face Hazlitt?"

"*We?*"

Her expression fell flat as she asked, "You didn't honestly think I'd let you find him alone?" Before I could even protest that, she said, "Let's go, test it out on me. You need to know your limits. I won't fight it, I promise."

I sighed in defeat, trying to take comfort in the fact that this is what she wanted. "Raise your hand," I commanded. That familiar feeling went down the front of my skull, and though it was far from being pleasant, it didn't hurt nearly as bad as it did when I'd controlled Silas.

Ava's hand shot in the air, and she snorted with laughter. "That's incredible!" she exclaimed. "Did it hurt?"

"Not as much," I answered, studying the amusement in her expression. "You really don't mind that I was in your head?"

"I'm safe with you," she said without a hitch. "Try again without speaking."

And since she seemed so genuinely comfortable with this, I was able to grow slightly curious of my own abilities. So I tried it. I thought *snap* as forcefully as I could, and at the vibrating in my head, Ava snapped her fingers. She laughed loudly, a bright excitement lighting her face. I couldn't keep a slightly pleased smile off my own face, because I hadn't known I could do it without giving a verbal command.

"You're impressed with yourself," Ava observed. "Can we try one more thing?" When I raised one curious eyebrow, she said, "See how well you can multitask while controlling me."

"Um," I breathed, "alright... How?"

She shrugged. "Perhaps try counting to ten."

I chuckled because that sounded terribly easy, but I'd try it anyway. This time, I made Ava wave her hand, and I kept her doing it so that the heavy tingling never left my head. And I discovered that counting wasn't quite so simple when I had to focus on controlling another person. It was hard enough to put the numbers in order in my mind, and though my mouth hung open in preparation for saying them out loud, I couldn't form the sounds in my throat. After a good half minute of trying, I laughed and gave up.

"It appears I can't multitask," I admitted.

Ava gave an exaggerated grin. "Aren't you glad you know now instead of finding out when we get to Hazlitt?"

I nodded. "What does it feel like for you?"

Her mouth pursed thoughtfully for a moment before she answered, "It doesn't feel like anything. I just know my hand is moving and I hadn't told it to."

I hummed my acknowledgment, glad that it at least wasn't painful for her, though I couldn't say I'd have minded if it hurt Hazlitt. For a few moments now, we sat in silence. My hands had set on Ava's thighs, and I could feel her studying me as we held each other's stare. Part of me thought she might be coming up with some new way to test my abilities, but a long minute passed without her saying anything.

It made me want to kiss her, being so close to her while looking into her eyes like this. I might've even closed the distance if she didn't appear to be in such deep thought, and eventually I asked, "What is it?"

She reached up, brushing her fingers back through my hair. "Are you afraid?"

My head tilted in consideration while her hand fell to my neck. I wasn't afraid of Hazlitt. He was powerful, but so was I, and after everything he'd put us through, I was too furious to be afraid of him. Nor was I afraid of pain, because it couldn't be worse than all I'd experienced the last six months. But I *was* afraid. "Yes," I answered, reaching for Ava's hand and bringing the back of it to my lips. "I'm afraid of missing out on a lifetime of this."

"Me too," she agreed, but behind that admission of fear was the fortitude so characteristic of the Ava I'd always known. "But we've got tonight," she said, and a comforted smile curled her lips as she grabbed my hands, moving them to her hips. "And you should meet no resistance in getting me out of *these* clothes."

I felt a smile of my own tug at my mouth, and after six months, I was more than eager to test the truth of that statement for myself. So I grabbed the bottom of her tunic, and her arms lifted readily for me to slide it up and over her head. The result left me breathless. Though my hands fell back to her hips after I'd tossed the article to the floor, they didn't stay there. They traced up the curves of her naked waist as I tried desperately hard not to let my mouth hang open.

"Have I ever told you how beautiful you are?" I asked, tearing my focus away from her upper body so I could meet her gaze.

"You've never needed to," she answered, leaning forward to say against my lips, "I've always seen it in your eyes."

And her mouth met mine so openly that whatever breath I had left was gone. We *did* have tonight. We had *all* night, and there was so much of her that my lips and hands had yet to explore. I wasn't going to be impatient like I had our first time together. I was going to take it slow. I was going to learn every sight, sound, and taste of her, because I didn't plan on sleeping. We could sleep when this was over.

$\mathscr{C}$hapter 20

n the stillness of the cold morning, I relished the heat of the bare body next to mine, and the weight of the warm blankets we were buried under. Not only had Ava remained in bed with me *all* night, but she was curled into me, her face hidden against my chest and her limbs tangled up with mine. I nuzzled into the top of her head as I blinked my eyes open, pressing a kiss to it.

Whether the action had woken her or she'd already been awake, she let out a huff of laughter, running her hand up my back. "*This* is how I imagined ending up naked with you."

I hummed my agreement as she tilted her head back to look at me, saying, "We've finally got it right."

"Let's get it right again," she whispered, pressing an open peck to the underside of my jaw. "And again." Another kiss. "And again."

The next time she tried to kiss me, I dropped my chin, catching her lips with my own. I kissed her slow and deep, so immediately consumed by her that I broke only long enough to say, "You could make me forget we've a war to fight."

"Forget," she urged, rolling onto her back when I moved to lie above her. "If only for another hour."

There was nothing I wanted more than to give in to her request. I fitted myself between her legs, one hand reaching behind her knee, guiding it to cradle the curve of my hip while my lips fell to her neck. She was already pressing up into me, her chin angling outward to encourage my mouth while her hands roamed my back, and gods, it was so easy to get lost in her. After such a long absence, I could lose myself in her for days.

I very well *would* have, but Nira's familiar voice called, "Kiena," followed by a knock on the door. "May I come in?"

My cheeks tinted as I pulled away and met Ava's gaze – we were on our way to being quite in the middle of something... "No," I called back. "I'll be up soon."

That didn't seem like the answer Nira had been expecting, because there was a short pause before her muffled voice said, "...Oh, alright..." Another pause, long enough that I thought she'd left to wait for me somewhere else, and had begun to lower myself again to Ava's neck. "Are you up yet?" Nira asked.

Ava snorted with laughter, throwing a hand over her mouth to remain quiet, and it was difficult for me to keep the amusement out of my own voice while I answered, "Not yet."

"Are you feeling well?" Nira questioned, and I answered an affirmative while Ava's giggling shook her beneath me. "There'll be festivities all day," she continued, "so that fighters can spend time with their families before we march to Cornwall." She paused once more, as if waiting to see if that would get me out of bed. "If you're ever to make amends with Ava, it's today."

"I assure you, Nira," I called, playfully shoving my palm to Ava's face because her laughter was making it difficult for me to respond, "you needn't worry about it."

"Needn't worry?" Nira repeated, sounding appalled. It was enough to get her to throw the door open and stomp toward the bed, muttering to herself, "I swear to the goddess you've lost y-" She stopped short when she caught sight of Ava and me, of the position we were in under the covers, and froze halfway on her journey to get me up. "Oh!" she exclaimed, an entertaining mix of shock and joy on her face. "Oh, never mind!" And she turned to make a swift exit. "Please continue, so sorry, forget I was here, we'll speak later, farewell."

The door slammed shut behind her, leaving Ava and me alone once more. We looked from each other to where Nira had disappeared, and then back again while Ava's grin widened, and we both burst into laughter.

"Well," Ava chortled, "that's one way for her to discover we've worked things out."

I rolled off of her, chuckling, "She'll never let me hear the end of this." Ava turned just enough to peck me on the cheek, and then slipped out of bed to collect her clothes off the floor. "Are we rising?" I asked.

She gave an eager nod and pulled her trousers up to her hips. "I've spent the last six months a captive, you know. I could use a good day of festivities."

I sat up, stretching off the side of the bed toward the floor to grab my tunic, asking as I put it on, "Who am I to keep a princess from a party?"

Finished dressing, Ava climbed onto the bed with a smirk, setting herself over my lap. "Not a princess," she said, and pressed a lingering kiss to my lips. "Come the end of this war, I'll be a Thaon." I leaned back to look at her in shock, but my heart skipped powerfully, and I could feel the awe in my expression. "I'm not a Gaveston," she said with a shrug, "nor have I ever felt like an Ironwood, but I'd be proud to take your surname."

I didn't know what to say, or what else to do to express exactly how much that meant to me, so I cupped her face and gave her one long, deep kiss.

She pulled away slowly and with a content hum. "You could make me forget we've festivities to attend."

"Alright," I smiled, nodding for her to get off me. "Let's get some breakfast then. You've worked me up a fierce appetite."

She bounced off, and waited for me to finish dressing and putting on my boots before hauling me out the door. We traversed the mountain halls to the dining cavern, where I could see Nira sitting with my mother and our brothers. Both Ava and I made our way through the busy cave, and sat down across from Nira and the boys.

"Morning," I greeted the group, pecking my mother on the cheek as I lowered myself beside her. "Mother."

She smiled at me, and then passed one across at Ava before looking at me again. Her lips widened to a grin, and she grabbed my face in both her hands, giving it a joyful shake as if to say that she was glad for my obvious reconciliation with Ava. It made me terribly self-conscious, and it was no better when I glanced across the table at Nira. She was beaming at me, and she set her elbow on the surface and propped her chin in her hand when I met her gaze, baring her teeth in the most obnoxious way possible.

"No need to be so smug about it," I scolded, feeling my cheeks warm with a blush.

"I put up with your brooding for five months," she teased. "I'll be as smug as I'd like."

298

Nilson's head picked up from his bowl of porridge, and he looked from Nira to me. "Why's Nira being smug?"

Nira's smile grew, and she leaned closer to Nilson like she was going to tell him a secret, but answered loud enough for us to hear, "I caught Kiena and Ava kissing." My face shaded darker, and both Nilson and Akamar snorted with laughter.

"Kissing!?" Nilson exclaimed. "Mum, I told you Kiena fancied her!"

"Indeed," my mother chuckled, "you did."

Akamar was giggling with his hand over his mouth, but he lowered it to point at us, snickering, "They were kissing."

"See what you've started?" I asked Nira with a mock glare, and then looked at Ava, "I told you she'd never let me hear the end of it." All both of them did was smile wider.

"Come on, boys," my mother laughed, rising from the table as someone brought food to Ava and me. "Let the girls eat in peace."

Nilson and Akamar stood, but before Nilson walked away, he came around the table to me, blinking his hazel eyes hopefully. "Will you come and play after?"

I had no doubt he'd noticed how my mood had improved these last few days, and he deserved my time and attention as much as Ava did, especially because we'd be leaving soon. "Of course," I answered, reaching over to comb my fingers back through his hair. Then I nudged Akamar's chin, because he'd come to stand by Nilson, "But no more talk of kissing, you hear? Or I'll get my revenge when either of you have got a girl."

Akamar's eyes widened, and he pointed an accusing finger at Nira. "It's *her* fault!" Nilson's head bobbed in agreement.

Nira gasped in feigned offense. "Squealers!" she exclaimed, trying to hold back a smirk as she shot out of her seat. "The both of you!" They screamed and took off running toward the exit of the cavern, my mother rushing to catch up with them. Nira sat back down, laughing and muttering to herself, "Caught you two doing more than kissing."

Even Ava was giggling beside me, and I turned sideways in my seat to squint my eyes at her. "Think it's funny, do you?"

She tried unsuccessfully to wipe the smile off her face, and reached up to pinch my still colored cheeks. "I can't help it, you get so red."

"Right, then," I teased, "should I tell Nira what you thought about us?" Ava's eyes widened, and she shook her head.

"What did she think?" Nira asked me.

I took a breath to answer, but Ava threw an arm around my neck to cover my mouth with both her hands. "She thought," I chuckled, trying to pull sideways to speak. Ava followed, and I had to wrestle her hands away through my amusement in order to say, "She thought you and I were something of a couple."

Nira snorted, bursting into loud laughter. "A couple?" she repeated on a breath. "*Me*? Court *this* cheeky shit?" She was still laughing so hard that she smacked her hand against her knee. "Not in this lifetime!"

Ava groaned, her dark cheeks flushing a rare shade of pink as she dropped her forehead onto the table. "It's not *that* funny."

"It *is*," Nira cackled, taking deep breaths to try and calm herself down. "Oh, dear sister," she sighed, still entertained enough that she was grinning. "As if anyone could get Kiena to cast a mere glance in another woman's direction." She spooned a bite of porridge to her mouth, shaking her head. "That was a good laugh."

Ava picked her head up and rolled her eyes, giving me a sporty nudge with her shoulder. We both pulled our bowls of food closer to begin eating, and Nira gave us a few minutes of silence while she finished her own breakfast. The dining cavern was busy today, likely because of all the supposed festivities that would be going on – eating and celebrating, giving the warriors time to spend with their families before going off to fight at Cornwall. It was something I was glad for as well, because it had been too long since I'd spent happy hours with my mother and brother. If I never made it back from this battle, I wanted this joyful day to be what they remembered, to be the *me* that they remembered. Not the me that I'd been the last six months.

"There's an archery contest at midday," Nira said, pushing aside her empty bowl. "The winner gets a brand new bow made specially for the occasion."

"Oh?" I asked. "Are you going to participate?"

She nodded and said, "You are too," with her lips curling into a smile. "I've got to win the bow fair and square."

"If you want to win the bow at all," I told her, "you shouldn't want me to compete." I shrugged easily to add to my teasing. "Besides, I like *my* bow."

Nira scowled at me, clearly trying to come up with some witty retort, but Ava laughed and asked before she could, "Will there be other contests? With swords?"

"Yes," Nira answered, brown eyes lighting with interest. "In a couple of hours. Are you experienced with a sword?"

I gave an earnest nod in reply, and Ava passed me a proud and grateful smile before admitting, "It's been quite some time. Competition should be an exciting way to revive my senses."

"Well, let's go then!" Nira said. "You can warm up before competition, and I'd love to see what you can do."

Ava glanced down at her nearly finished food, pushed the bowl away, and then looked at me, as if to ask if I was coming.

"I need to speak with Kingston first," I told her, and she nodded in remembrance.

"What about?" Nira asked.

I opened my mouth to reply, but Ava answered, "About going to find a dragon." I glanced at her in shock, because I hadn't thought she'd so thoroughly deciphered my thoughts last night, and she passed me a beaming grin.

"A dragon?" Nira repeated, eyes growing wide. "Say you could even find a dragon, what are you going to do with it besides get eaten?"

"Make a friend of it, I hope," I said.

"With her magic," Ava added.

At that, Nira seemed a bit less skeptical. Her eyes went from me to Ava, and then back to me with deep consideration. She stared at me for a long minute before her chin dropped with a sharp nod. "Splendid! When do we leave?"

I sighed, knowing there was no possible way I could convince Nira not to come if she'd made up her mind about it. It wouldn't matter to her that it was dangerous. If anything, it was encouraging. "First thing in the morning," I answered, "if Kingston agrees."

Nira set to scanning the dining hall, no doubt searching for Kingston amongst the crowds. "There he is!" She pointed. "He's just sat down, come on."

I managed to shovel down one more bite of food before they both dragged me from my seat. Upon reaching Kingston, Ava and Nira plopped me down on the bench between them, both of them grinning.

"Morning, Commander," Nira greeted.

Kingston looked up from his bowl of porridge, eyes going back and forth between the three of us. Though I felt rather calm, he could clearly read the excitement on Ava and Nira's faces, and he already looked exasperated about the request we hadn't yet made – it was nowhere near the first time these last five months that Nira and I, mostly Nira, had requisitioned him for something outrageous. He held up his index finger to make us wait while he swallowed down a couple bites of food.

"Good morning," he said finally, and looked at me. "How are you feeling?"

"Good as new," I answered.

His eyes wandered to Ava. "Kiena's mother explained your situation with Haztlitt's magic. Are you doing well?"

"Very," Ava answered, and I wasn't sure when my mother had even been told about Ava's situation, but it must have been when she brought Ava food last night. "It's a great peace of mind, my will invariably being my own."

"I imagine so," Kingston agreed. When Nira opened her mouth with an excited breath, he held up his index finger again, slowly taking a few more bites. Part of me imagined he was doing it just to mess with us, and I couldn't help but smirk as Nira's heel began to tap. After another minute, he lowered his finger and set his spoon aside, giving us his full attention. "What have you sought me for?"

At the exact same moment, both Ava and Nira answered, "We want to find a dragon."

Though several people close enough to have heard turned around with interest, it didn't look like Kingston knew how to react. Part of him appeared to be in disbelief, and another part seemed so appalled he wanted to laugh. "Pardon?"

There was a lengthy pause as Ava and Nira waited for me to explain. "Cornwall is set against a mountain," I began, and he nodded. "I can't jump beyond the walls alone, but if I could control a dragon with my magic, it could take a few of us straight to the door, or to a tower where we could infiltrate the castle and find Hazlitt before our troops fight through." I glanced around at the various people who'd leaned in to listen, suddenly worried that I'd get their hopes up on something I couldn't deliver. "What if we could end the battle early, without losing more lives than we need to?"

Kingston shook his head, saying, "You'd be facing Hazlitt without our army. You'd be alone."

"Not alone," Nira protested, and out of the corner of my eye, I could see Ava's chin drop with agreement.

It was no comfort, however, and both Kingston and I knew it. There seemed to be very little Ava or Nira could do against Hazlitt's magic. "I always was going to face Hazlitt alone," I said, pursing my lips with a reassuring smile. "You know that."

"Kiena," Kingston sighed, "I've not heard of anyone who's even seen a dragon in *hundreds* of years. Where do you intend to search?"

"Deep in the mountains of the Amalgam Plains," I answered, and I could see his face fall with reluctance and recognition. "You told me the legend yourself."

"A *legend*," he agreed. "One so old and perhaps altered that you can't even be sure if there's any truth to it."

"What if I told you I'd seen it?" I asked, suddenly eager to make him believe as I did. "In a memory evoked by the mind masters. What if I told you that I'd seen proof of my magic's origins? That I'd been eye to eye with a dragon, and touched it with my own hands?"

Kingston didn't respond right away. It appeared he didn't know what to say at all, and he just sat there, pressing his palms together to put his fingertips against his mouth and stare at me. "If you fail to find one?" he asked eventually, letting his hands fall.

"Then all that's lost is a few days," I told him. "We'll be at Cornwall to rally with the rest of you."

"And if you do find one," he suggested, "and you can't control it. It could kill you."

"Is it not worth the risk?" I asked. "We don't know that we can succeed at fighting our way into the castle in the first place, or that Hazlitt won't have hundreds more of his soldiers waiting beyond the walls to protect him." I leaned forward with the sheer importance and weight of this mission, an importance I felt more deeply the more I talked about it. "I don't know if his troops will lay down arms the very moment they see that we've a dragon on our side, but if I could get one to fight for us, Kingston, so many more of our rebels will get to see their families again."

303

Kingston let out a heavy breath, and thought on everything I'd said for a long minute more. "You two," he pointed at Ava and Nira, "you'll be accompanying her?" They both nodded. "Give me your word," he requested, returning his focus to me, "that no matter the outcome, you'll be at Cornwall." His brow furrowed imploringly. "We *need* you there, Kiena."

"You have my word," I said. "I swear it."

"Very well," he agreed, and I heard murmurs go up amongst the people who'd been eavesdropping. He added in an endearingly stern tone, "The three of you spend the day with your family, be sure to enjoy yourselves."

"Yes, Commander," I said. "You be sure to attend the festivities as well."

"Yes, First Ward," he replied with a teasing smile. "Go on."

All three of us left him to eat his breakfast in peace. I knew Nira was eager to be active in the competitions, but they didn't begin for a while, and I'd promised Nilson I'd spend time with him and Akamar. So we strode out of the caves to the meadow outside, where plenty of the mountain's inhabitants had already set up an abundance of games. It took a bit of wandering to locate our brothers and my mother, but eventually we found them. They were playing at a game of horseshoes against two grown rebels, and despite our brothers being so much younger and so much smaller, the scores were actually quite close.

Seeing as they'd be preoccupied for the next handful of minutes, I told Ava that I'd be right back, and left her and Nira with my mother while I headed toward the edge of the meadow. Because there were so many people around, I paced well into the woods, a good distance from the noise so the she-wolf wouldn't be intimidated by it. Once I felt I was in a safe place, I let out a shrill whistle, and waited a minute for her to find me.

She padded toward me, already sniffing the air for food. "I'm sorry," I apologized, squatting down and holding out my empty hands, "I haven't brought you anything today." Whether she cared or not, she stopped in front of me, sitting back on her haunches and watching me with her good eye. "We're going to war," I told her, "I leave tomorrow," and her head cocked just slightly. "You haven't got to come," I added, saying under my breath, "don't know why you've even stayed this long." I extended my hand, grateful that she let me scratch her neck. "What have I done to earn your loyalty all these months, huh?" My fingers lifted to trace her missing ear. "What's a wild thing like you doing following me around?"

In response to my wondering aloud, the wolf stretched forward, touching the tip of her nose to the dragon pendant behind my tunic. At first I thought maybe the magic was why she stuck around, but I never controlled her. She'd always seemed more than content to follow my instructions despite refusing to be tamed.

"If I didn't know any better," I said with an amused huff, "I'd think the gods sent you to save me that day in the woods."

And at that, for the first time since I'd known her, she did something to show attachment. She bowed her head, leaning forward to press the top of it to my chest, and it lingered, and it was gentle. It was the kind of affection a dog would give when it knew you needed it most, and it had been so long since I'd felt this kind of fondness and devotion from an animal that I couldn't help it. My eyes filled with tears. I set my hand against the back of her head, stroking down the back of her neck to return the gesture.

"You stop that," I said after a moment of affection, sniffling away the moisture and grabbing her head in my hands. "Or I might think you're starting to like me." She let out a low growl as her upper lip curled, and she pulled away from my hands. "That's more like it," I laughed, and ventured to pet her again despite the growl. "We leave first thing in the morning." She huffed an acknowledgement, pressing against my hand for only a moment before she turned to start making her retreat into the forest. "See you tomorrow, Haunt."

Once she'd disappeared into the foliage, I strolled back to where I'd left my family. Ava and Nira were in conversation with my mother when I returned, and all three of them were laughing about something. It left me immediately skeptical, especially because, as I reached them, Ava threw her arms around my neck in an endearing hug.

"Do I want to know what you're all laughing for?" I asked.

Ava released me, saying as she pulled away, "Your mother was just telling us about the day she realized you fancied women."

My face burned with embarrassment as I looked at my mother. "I was hardly gone for five minutes," I complained, "and you had to go and tell them *that* story?"

"Seven years old," Nira laughed, "and holding the hands of random women in town. Shame on you."

"What did you say to her?" Ava prompted, cheeks bulging with a smile. "The first one."

"You mean she didn't tell you?" I asked with a scowl, motioning to my mother.

"I was just about to," my mother answered. "Go on, tell them what you said."

"*Mum*," I whined, but all three of them simply blinked at me with expectation. So I sighed and mumbled in hopes they wouldn't hear, "I'd like my cottage better with someone as beautiful as you around."

Ava snickered while Nira asked, "And what did *she* say?"

My shoulders slumped. "She laughed and said to come and find her when I was old enough."

They passed curious looks to my mother, who guffawed, "She was a working girl at the local tavern!" Ava and Nira burst into laughter, and because of my grumbling about them being relentless, my mother cupped my face, giving it a playful pat. "You had good taste even if you couldn't afford her company," she chuckled. "She was pretty."

Having finished their game with the rebels, Nilson and Akamar ran over. "Nilson," I prompted, still blushing while I knelt down and motioned for him to climb onto my back. "Tell the women what happens when they tease me."

Nilson looked from me to them as I stood, and pointed in rebuke, "She'll feed you to the wolf!"

"Aw," Nira drawled in feigned remorse.

"We're sorry," Ava agreed.

I narrowed my eyes, humming in disbelief while I considered their apology, even though I couldn't keep from smirking. "Fine," I conceded, looking at Ava while I tapped my finger to my cheek, "right here, and all's forgiven."

She planted a kiss to my cheek, and Nilson immediately leaned over my shoulder and tapped the same spot on his own face, saying with a smile in his voice, "Right here."

"Haunt!" I yelled before he could get his own peck, pulling him around into my arms. "Where's the wolf?"

"No!" he shrieked through a giggle. "Mum!"

"Sorry, lamb," my mother laughed, "you've earned that one."

Before Nilson could squirm his way out of my grip, another lighter weight grabbed around one of my legs. "I'll rescue you, Nilson!" Akamar hollered, whipping side to side to try and throw me off balance.

He was too small to make much of a difference, so I took a large step, struggling to hold Nilson in my arms while I dragged Akamar along with my leg. I made grunting noises with every step just to play along and make Akamar feel that he was helping, but it truly *was* taking the breath out of me to fight Nilson's squirming and drag Akamar along while I was laughing like I was.

I managed to take a handful of steps before Nilson shouted, "You'll never take me alive!" and knifed his fingers into my ribs.

I don't know whether it hurt or tickled more, but I jerked sideways in reaction at the same time as one of Akamar's feet stuck between both of my own. It tripped me, and I let out a yelp as I stumbled sideways and toppled to the ground. I hit the dirt on my back and with all of Nilson's extra weight on top of me, but neither he nor Akamar relented. Akamar shot to his feet and grabbed my arm, pulling it out sideways while Nilson sat atop my torso, continuing to poke at my ribs.

"Alright!" I gasped, rolling as much as I could to try and knock Nilson off of me. "Alright! You got me!"

"Who's getting fed to the wolf?" Nilson asked, posing his fingers in threat over my side.

"Not Nilson," I surrendered.

"Or?" he asked expectantly.

I glanced sideways at Akamar. "Or Akamar."

Akamar let go of my arm to put his fists to his hips and ask, "*Or?*"

I chuckled, answering, "Or Mother, or Nira, or Ava."

"Well..." Nilson considered.

Akamar finished for him, "She could have Nira."

They both set to giggling when they caught the scowl on Nira's face. That is, until she said, "No more stolen sweet rolls for you two." Then they threw themselves to her feet to beg dramatically.

I laughed as I pushed myself up and brushed the dirt off. "Shall we go and see the competitions?"

"Who's competing?" Nilson asked, turning me around to pat my back and indicate that he wanted a ride.

I squatted down enough for him to jump up, and answered as all of us started for the caves, "Ava and Nira."

Nilson glanced over at Ava, who'd fallen into step at my side. "Are you an archer too?"

Ava shook her head. "I'll be participating in the sword tournaments."

Nilson took in a breath, his eyes going wide. "You are? Are you skilled? How long have you been practicing? Can you teach me?"

Ava's lips curled, and she answered in as swift a manner as Nilson had asked, "I'm not bad, I've been practicing for years, and I'd love to teach you when leisure permits."

He'd always wanted Silas to teach him how to use a sword, but Silas had never had the time because of his duty as a knight. I'd have taught him myself if I was any good, but I wasn't, and he was too young to join the soldiers' training just yet. Now he was so overjoyed about the fact that Ava would finally teach him that he bounced and wiggled on my back all the way to the training grounds. There were already people warming up when we got there, practicing with swords and bows and other weapons. After a while, everyone was cleared from the heart of the massive cavern so that the sword tournaments could start.

There were several circles created on the ground with rope, in which the competitors would fight with practice weapons. Ava was one of the first, and winning that round meant that she moved on to the next. We spent the better part of the day watching Ava move through the competition, and then watching Nira do the same in archery when the tournaments would alternate. Though our brothers, my mother, and I were only spectating, we were still having a great time watching and cheering along, making competition of our own out of predicting victors when it wasn't Ava or Nira's turn. In the end, while Ava had won third place amongst the swordsmen, Nira went on to win top archer, and got that bow she was after.

It was well into the evening by the time all of that was finished, and supper was being served in spite of the fact that all the tables in the dining cavern had been shoved to one side. It cleared the other side, and lively music already filled the cave, echoing off the walls in such a way that you could feel it in your soul. Plenty who'd finished eating were already dancing, and others were drinking and laughing, celebrating and enjoying their time with loved ones before going off to war. It was the first time in six months that I felt truly at ease, at least when I didn't think about the days ahead of us. I jested with my family while we ate, and drank enough ale to feel the warmth in my veins. I even ate so much food that, when we finished and Nilson wanted to dance, I needed a few minutes to get over the sluggishness of a full belly.

I sat there while he and Akamar dragged Nira and my mother into the crowd of dancers, with Ava leaned comfortably against my side. We watched them for a few minutes before a familiar face blocked our view.

"Kiena," Rhien greeted with a brief smile, immediately turning her gaze on Ava. "You're Ava," she said, grabbing the skirt of her dress to bend in a curtsy – an awkward sort of movement for her, it appeared, probably because of Ronan's lack of physical signs of respect. "It's a pleasure to finally meet you."

Ava stood, and though she wasn't wearing a dress, she went through the movement to mirror the formal gesture. "And you..." she agreed, her voice trailing off to leave room for introduction.

"Rhien," Rhien supplied.

"Well met," Ava said with a friendly grin, one inviting enough to rid Rhien's stiffness, and she motioned beside her as she sat back down. "Will you join us?"

"For a minute, thank you," Rhien agreed, dropping down next to her. "I watched some of the tournaments today, you were splendid."

"You're very kind," Ava said, and added with a chuckle, "although I'm afraid it was me and not the sword that was rusty."

Rhien laughed, her lips pulling into the genuine kind of smile that Ava's friendliness so easily brought about. "I'd not have noticed," she complimented, "I envy your skill."

"Are you a warrior?" Ava asked.

"No," Rhien answered, turning on her seat more to look at me. "To be honest, that's why I've come. I have a request..." I studied the expression on her face, how she looked more reluctant to make her request now than she did when she told me she wanted to apprentice with the blacksmith. When I stayed silent to let her speak, she said, "I've heard rumors of you going to seek a dragon."

I straightened out of my relaxed position. She wasn't truly about to ask what I thought she was... "Rhien," I protested.

She didn't let it prevent her from saying, "I want to help."

But she wasn't a fighter. She'd spent the better part of her life with a faction of peaceful mages, never learning to battle or wield a weapon. "Your magic is limited to-"

"Self-defense, I know," she interrupted readily, "but that doesn't mean I can't be useful. Look how much I've helped you already."

It was how much she'd helped already, how kind and how good of a friend she'd been to me that made me so reluctant. This was dangerous, especially for someone who wasn't trained in battle, and that made me afraid for her. "That was the masters," I replied without thinking, because they'd been the ones to reacquaint me with my magic, but I regretted it the very moment her eyes narrowed with offense. She appeared so hurt by that disregard for her support that she didn't even know what to say, so she just sat there, wavering between her determination to help and the obvious desire to walk away. "I'm sorry," I said immediately, sighing as I bent forward to set my elbows on my knees.

There were a few moments of silence before Rhien murmured, "That was unfair."

"I know." I sat up again, turning on my seat so she could see the apology on my face. "I'm sorry. You *have* been an incredible help, and a better friend than I've deserved. But that's the root of my fear, Rhien. I'm not worried about your usefulness to me. I'm worried about your safety."

"As I worry about yours," she replied, "and Ava's, and Nira's." Her brow furrowed with desperation. "As I worry about every person going to fight at Cornwall, or every person here whose lives have been ruined by this war. Every person who's been thrust from their home or lost someone they loved. I never got to apprentice with the blacksmith. I've done nothing for this rebellion, but I *need* to. While I still have the chance. Please, let me give back."

All I could do was watch her indecisively. It was enough stress already that Ava and Nira were coming. Just because I'd readily let them accompany me didn't mean I wasn't worried about them, but at least they could protect themselves, and attack if they needed to. They could fight. If something happened to Rhien... I couldn't lose even one more person that I cared about to this war. I just couldn't.

Before I could make up my mind, Ava's hand landed on my thigh. She met my gaze, offered a small smile, and said, "Perhaps she's not so delicate as you seem to think she is."

I felt my face soften with recognition as those words sank in. I'd learned so quickly not to underestimate Ava, and had been taught the same lesson when Nira asked me to make her an archer. Was it possible I was making the same mistake with Rhien? After all, did she not know best what she was capable of? What she could protect herself from, or what she could contribute? As much as I wanted for her to be safe – especially now that we were so near the end of this war – this wasn't *my* choice to make.

"Will you promise me that this isn't a whim?" I asked Rhien. "That you know the dangers of what we're doing?"

"You have my word," she said. "I can handle it. My magic may be limited to self-defense, but it's enough."

I nodded my consent, slightly comforted by her confidence. "We leave at first light."

"Thank you!" She nearly vibrated with excitement, but I could see by the hopeful light in her eyes that it was about more than adventure. She was glad to be doing something for the people at this mountain who were like her. "Thank you."

"Now's the time for celebration," Ava said. "Are you going to dance?"

"I am," Rhien answered, her chin tilting down bashfully. "In fact, that nice warrior is saving one for me."

She threw too brief a gesture behind her for it to be specific, but I could tell who the rebel was. It was a modestly attractive woman with short hair and battle developed brawn, and when she saw Ava and me lean to look, she passed an easy salute our direction. I shifted my grin on Rhien, and she returned the knowing smile with a blush coloring her cheeks.

"Go," I chuckled. "Get yourself more than one dance. Don't let us keep you any longer."

Rhien stood and grabbed one of each of our hands, giving them both a joyful and grateful squeeze. "I'll see you in the morning."

When she was gone, I turned my cheerfulness on Ava. "Are you ready to dance too, Little Will-o'?"

"Are you eagerly volunteering?" she teased. "I never thought I'd see the day."

"I'll have you know," I began with mock offense, standing and offering my hand, "that I quite enjoy ones I'm familiar with, and without the pressures of impressing nobles."

She took my hand and rose from her seat, lips pulling into an amused grin. "Well then, on account of never being taught folk dances at the castle, you'll have to show me the steps."

I gave an assenting nod, glad that she didn't seem nearly as self-conscious about being unfamiliar as I'd been in Ronan. She followed me out into the crowd, to where our family were still enjoying themselves. With the combination of the ale I'd drunk and my elation at being with Ava and seeing my family so happy, I felt a deep seated contentment that I hadn't experienced in a long time, and it only grew. Every time Ava messed up one of the lively and fast-paced steps and laughed at herself. Every time our brothers pulled us apart from each other in order to get some attention of their own. When Nira partnered off with Ava to adapt a Ronan dance to the music, and some of the Ronan refugees joined in. Even when Nilson dragged me to him so that we could perform the steps we'd created to entertain ourselves one slow winter so many years ago.

There was energy and mirth and fun, things that had been a rare commodity these last months for everyone here. Things that had been rare for me, and most certainly for Ava, and I didn't know how much I'd needed this until I danced and laughed so much that I worked myself into a thirst. I snuck away to grab a mug of water and leaned against a wall while I replenished myself, taking the opportunity to watch. Only, watching how happy my family was offered such a different and satisfying view that, even after I'd finished drinking, I couldn't bring myself to rejoin them.

Nilson and my mother looked healthier than I'd ever seen them, Ava looked happier, and Nira and Akamar appeared more content than they'd been these last five months. I wanted nights like these more often. Wanted there to be days they all smiled so endlessly and danced so tirelessly. Wanted this war to end so we could stop worrying about safety or food or hiding, so we could go home and be a comfortable family again, and so Ava could be a part of that. But we had to end this war first, and I had to ensure that every one of us would be around when we did. Despite the warmth and contentment in my veins, I felt that concern at the very depths of my soul, with a severity that rooted itself more every second I watched.

After a few more minutes of standing there, my mother wandered over, panting from dancing and reaching for my mug to drink what was left in it. "I know that look," she said, the excitement fading from her face as it filled with worry. "It's the look of a young girl who's not managed to catch supper, and who always thought it was her fault when we hadn't food to eat."

I took in a deep, sobering breath, and let it out in a heavy sigh as I thought about how to articulate the concern of my thoughts. "We're leaving tomorrow. Nearly every fighter in the mountain and the surrounding villages will be leaving to fight at Cornwall." I paused, and my mother hummed in acknowledgment. "Hazlitt is a cruel and vengeful man, and I don't trust that he wouldn't send soldiers to strike out at the mountain while it was unguarded just to hurt Ava or me." Ava had said that she'd never told Hazlitt where the caves were, but that didn't mean he was incapable of knowing or finding out. "If he did, I've no doubt that you, and Nilson, and Akamar would be the only targets, and all the fighters staying back are ones too unprepared for the heart of battle. There may as well be no fighters at all here to protect you." I glanced back at my brother and Akamar, and though I was so unwilling to risk my family, I was still unsure that what I was thinking was right. Whether it was the best thing to do, or whether it would truly bring me comfort. "None but one."

I could feel it the moment realization dawned on her, but there was none of the fear or reluctance I expected to see on her face. "Silas."

"Is it foolish?" I asked. "I don't even know if I trust him, but he'll be the best fighter left, the only one capable of taking you from here and keeping you safe until this is truly over." I looked at her, my brow furrowing from my own reluctance and unease with the idea. "Tell me you're uncomfortable with it. Tell me you don't trust him, and I'll put it from my mind." I shook my head in disbelief, and then sighed as I squeezed my eyes shut and leaned my head back against the wall, murmuring, "Gods, what am I thinking?"

My mother set a comforting hand on my shoulder. "You're thinking you've so little faith in Hazlitt, that us staying in the comfort of these caves is a greater risk than leaving here with Silas."

"But *is* it?" I asked on a stressed breath. "Or am I being paranoid?"

"You've never been one to take chances," my mother said. "Especially where Nilson and I were concerned."

"And what do you think?" I asked.

"I think," she said, pausing for a long moment to consider it. "I think that Silas failed you last winter, and that he hurt you in ways you may never forget. But I also think there's a part of you that remembers a time before he failed, and that knows he's always done what he could to help you care for Nilson and me."

That's what was so hard about this. I'd said I wouldn't let Silas free again, and I wasn't even close to being ready to forgive him for everything he'd done – just the very thought of him caused a severe pain in my chest. Nor did I want him mistaking what little faith I had for forgiveness. But I *did* have some faith. If in nothing else, I had faith in his abilities to protect them, and in his guilt being severe enough that he'd do everything he could not to fail at this. Perhaps that was enough.

"You'd go with him?" I asked. "If he agreed."

She nodded. "I would."

That was it then. "Thank you," I said, leaning enough to kiss her cheek. I gave the best smile I could and told her, "Keep enjoying yourself. I do love to see you all so happy."

She wrapped her arms around me, giving me a long, tight hug. "It's been a weight off my heart to see you happy too."

"I'll return shortly," I said when she let me go, and at her nod of consent, I started for the exit of the dining cavern. I only got a short distance before a familiar hand grabbed mine, and I turned to meet Ava's gaze. "I'm going to see Silas," I explained. "You haven't got to come."

Her eyes fell as she considered where I was going, and whether or not she wanted to accompany me. "I do have to."

Chapter 21

va and I headed away from the festivities and out to the halls, through the caves and down the stairs to the dungeon. I dismissed the two guards just inside the door, and closed it behind us after we entered. Silas rose from his cot at the noise to see who was visiting him, but the very moment he saw Ava, he came forward and dropped to one knee.

"Princess," he said, bowing his head.

In the days since our first encounter, having got some space from him, my rage had cooled, but the very fact of his acknowledging Ava and speaking to her made me painfully tense. She'd been hurt so greatly as a result of his actions that it was a wonder to me why she even wanted to come. However, she *had* wanted to, and it wasn't my place to forbid their interaction.

"Rise," Ava said, but her voice was hollow and quiet and her heartbeat had sped up, and a part of me wondered if she was regretting this. "I'm not a princess anymore."

"I'm sorry," he offered as he rose to his feet. "I had thought you'd take the throne as Hazlitt's successor should the rebels win this war." He'd been given civilian clothes to wear instead of his soldier's garb, and his face looked better than it had the last time I'd seen him. It was no longer swollen and the bruises were fading, though he still hadn't accepted magic to heal the deep cuts.

Ava looked sideways at me, motioning briefly toward the cell as she asked, "May I?" Though I knew Silas posed no threat to her, and knew he had no remaining desire to harm her regardless of whether or not he could, I couldn't help it that my jaw clenched. Still, I gave a stiff nod. "All

I've *ever* wanted, Silas," Ava said, taking a few hesitant steps toward him, "was to be free of Hazlitt."

She didn't say how that day six months ago had made it impossible for her to be free of him, or what she'd lost because of it. She didn't say that Hazlitt wasn't her true father, or how he'd filled her life with torment. It seemed, however, that Silas realized some of the pain that she'd been through, because his eyes dropped guiltily.

"I apologize, Avarona," he said, lifting his repentant gaze to hers, "with my deepest sincerity, for the part I've played in any of your suffering."

"You've never been so great a force in my circumstances," she replied, with some hint of uncalculated warmth in the hollow of her voice.

"Merely a bystander with imprudent allegiance," Silas muttered. "I became a knight to fight for my kingdom, and all I succeeded in doing was failing my kingdom's people. I failed my princess, and my queen."

At mention of the queen, I could sense a falter in Ava's heart, and there was a visible slump in her shoulders. "Do you know why I came?" she asked in an emotional whisper, seeming reluctant to linger on it. Silas shook his head. "While you've played a far more active role in Kiena's suffering, and though I felt Albus's loss dearly, you're part of the reason I'm standing here." Ava paused, and Silas's eyes shot to me, as though expecting me to show some reaction at the mention of my suffering, or of Albus. Though I felt the agony in my chest, I kept it off my face.

"I'd resigned myself to death," she continued, "and had you not come here when you did, Kiena wouldn't have reached me on time. I'd have died in my prison, and I'd *never* have been free of Hazlitt. I'd have remained his captive even in death." She paused to take in a deep breath, gathering the composure to finish. "I came for closure, Silas. To tell you that whatever obligations you may have felt toward me are cleared, and any lingering resentment I have for you is on account of feeling Kiena's pain as my own."

It didn't seem like Silas knew what to say to that, or that he expected Ava to be so forgiving – it was a shock even to me – but his eyes filled with tears. He tried to blink them away, and when that didn't work, he sniffled, nodding for a moment for lack of a better response. It took a minute for him to collect himself, and during that time, Ava turned and trudged back to me. She offered the smallest of smiles, looking somewhat unsure of herself, as though perhaps she wasn't certain I'd be satisfied with how charitable she'd been.

However, while I *was* shocked, it shouldn't have been unexpected. Ava had always been kind, and forgiving, and far more reasonable than anyone deserved. To assure her that the compassion she gave was her own to offer, even if I couldn't offer mine, I returned that small smile in spite of the somberness of my mood.

Silence hovered for a while before Silas's gaze returned to me. "And you, Kiena?" he asked, eyes dewing with fresh tears. "You've not remained in my presence without purpose."

Thus far, I'd been so able to remain disconnected and cold to keep from growing angry like I had the first time I came here. But the look in his eyes, the pure guilt which I could see so clearly now that I wasn't motivated by rage, it broke my heart all over again. I couldn't have been angry if I tried. I wished I could be as kind and forgiving as Ava, because I wanted to be free of this pain, but forgiving him wouldn't bring Albus back, and it wouldn't change the last six months. So I swallowed down the searing emotion creeping through my chest before it could form a lump in my throat, and steeled myself in order to get through this.

"I have a job for you," I said, unmoving from my stiff position. "If you want it."

"Anything," he replied. "Whatever you need."

It came as no surprise, but I wasn't ready to trust him with the task just yet, no matter how true I believed his guilt to be. "Six months ago," I started, swallowing hard again at the pang of the reminder, "when Hazlitt sent riders to the cottage for Mother and Nilson, did you know?"

Silas's eyes widened in horror, and the brim of tears in them deepened. "*No.*" He shook his head, not bothering to whisk away the single drop that slid down his cheek. "I *swear* to you, I had no idea. I never would've... Please, Kiena, you must know I'd never put them in harm's way, they had nothing to do with this. I was afraid that day. There were soldiers and Hazlitt; fighting would've been death, and I was afraid, but I started doubting everything then. When he told you he sent riders, I-"

I held up my hand to silence him, because I didn't want any more apology or explanation. I couldn't take it. Couldn't bear thinking that he'd been as scared of Hazlitt killing him as Ava or me. All I wanted were facts.

317

"If not you," I asked as emotionlessly as I possibly could, "then who? Who knew and told him where our cottage was?"

Silas's gaze fell with concentration, and his mouth hung open in preparation for giving an answer. It took him a minute, but then he glanced up at me. "The soldiers," he said. "The day I came to take you to the castle. There were plenty of us at your cottage then, it had to have been one of them." He paused for another moment in thought. "Oh, I know the one," he said, his upper lip curling with disgust. "That bastard. He scaled the ranks far too quickly, leading raids on innocent villages. Hazlitt saw-" He stopped short at the disinterested look in my eyes, bowing his head in apology and saying, "I betrayed you, Kiena. I hurt you. I know that, and I'll live with it, but not them. I'd have never involved Bibbette or Nilson, you have my word."

Whether or not it was the soldier that Silas suspected, I believed he was telling the truth. "Have you any scars?" I asked.

"Scars?" Silas repeated. "I've plenty of scars..."

"Branding scars," I said. "In the shape of a crow, given you by Hazlitt with or without your knowledge."

His eyebrows furrowed with further dismay, and before I could explain any more, Ava turned her back to him. She grabbed the bottom of her tunic and lifted it up to her shoulder blades, exposing most of the blood red mark. It seemed more respectful instinct than timidity that caused Silas to turn his head so he couldn't see, but it only took a moment for him to realize that Ava *wanted* him to see. He looked, and then he stared, his mouth steadily dropping open.

"H-Hazlitt did that to you?" he stuttered, a conflicted look of alarm and sympathy in his eyes, as if he was finally realizing that he had no true grasp of Hazlitt's treachery toward Ava.

She let the garment fall back to her hips and turned around, nodding in reply.

"Do you have one?" I asked. "It may not be so large." Silas blinked away his shock, only managing to meet my gaze and shake his head. But I was reluctant to be entirely convinced. "Show me."

In full compliance, he pulled his tunic up and over his head, gripping it in his hand while he held his arms out. He turned slowly, allowing me to scan his arms, neck, chest, and back for a scar similar to Ava's. There was none, and while some part of me was relieved that his will belonged to none but him, another part was stung by it. He finished his turn, and at seeing the mild satisfaction on my face, he put his tunic back on.

"We're leaving tomorrow morning for Cornwall," I told him, finally convinced enough to make my request. "You remember the old meadow?" I hesitated with the severe emotion the memory brought, of our lazy days hiding from his squire duties and my chores, and fought to bite it back. "Where we used to sneak away and-"

"I remember," he interrupted, his lips pursing with an understanding smile, and in spite of myself, I was grateful that he wouldn't make me explain. Wouldn't make me linger on the pain of how close we'd been.

"I want you to take my mother and Nilson, and Akamar, the young prince of Ronan," I paused only momentarily to see if he'd give a reaction at the inclusion of Akamar. There was none. "Take them to the meadow and keep them safe until this war is over." And because there was no guarantee I'd even make it back, I added in a forced whisper, "As long as it takes."

There was a long moment of hesitation, and I could read the surprise on his face. "You'd trust me with them?"

"My trust is in your abilities and your desire for absolution," I answered. "Let me be clear, Silas," I added, so he'd know that this wasn't something to be taken lightly. Regardless of how much I believed in his skill, and his guilt-guided loyalty, I wasn't doing this for *him*. And I truly wouldn't have the strength to control my grief if he let something happen to my family. Thinking I'd lost them once was more than I could bear, and this was a warning, not a threat: "Do *not* accept this task unless you'd give your life protecting them, because if you fail, I *will* kill you myself."

"They're safe with me," he said, without a hitch and with an earnestness that I could take comfort in. "For as long as it takes."

I gave a shallow nod. "You leave at daybreak." I waited a few short moments to see if he'd voice any questions, but he didn't, and so I turned to leave. Ava and I retreated out the door of the dungeon, but before the guards could return to their posts and shut themselves in behind us, I stopped one of them. "Would you go and fetch the prisoner a meal from the festivities?" I asked him. Despite the fact that I couldn't yet forgive Silas, or give him the chance he wanted to revive our friendship, he was giving me some grand peace of mind in accepting this task. Though I couldn't express my gratitude in person, or in words, I hoped he would accept this much. "Choice portions and a mug of ale, if you'd please."

"Yes, First Ward," the man answered, heading up the steps into the high caves while the other closed the door of the dungeon, leaving Ava and me alone outside of it.

"You know," Ava said, nodding toward where the guard had disappeared up the stairs, "that's not the kind of thing a vile person would do."

One corner of my mouth twitched with a brief half-smile at the reassurance, but I couldn't help letting out a sigh that carried with it all the weight of speaking with Silas. "Where have you learned to be so full of forgiveness?" I asked, meeting her deep blue eyes with a mixture of pain and adoration.

"Where I've come from," she answered, her voice low with emotion, "where I've been... it's the only way I've learned to keep my heart together."

She believed her forgiveness was survival rather than the desire or graciousness I saw it as, but I could believe nothing other than that she was far too pure for these circumstances. For the life she'd been bound to. She deserved a life far from here, one where she'd never need to forgive anyone ever again. One where she got the love and the peace that the gods so gravely owed her.

"I wish you would go with them," I whispered.

It took her a moment to realize that I meant with our family and Silas, so she'd be safe until this was over, but then her brow furrowed, and I watched a range of emotions play across her face: confusion, anger, sympathy, sadness. "When I ran from the castle at Guelder," she said, "I left with the belief that I'd be doing this alone." She reached for my hands, and held them between both of hers. "Your companionship, your *love*, it's been the most precious thing in the world to me, and I'm certain every success would not have been so without you." Her eyes filled with tears, and she closed them tight as if to rid the moisture. "But I see it, Kiena... how you've taken this responsibility as your own... and it haunts me." She opened her eyes again, releasing the flood of tears that had built behind them. "Please, don't ask me to let you do this alone. I won't."

I took my hands out from between hers so I could cup her face, running my thumbs over her cheeks to wipe away the tears. "You'll not be asked," I assured her, pressing a kiss to her forehead. "We'll do this together." And to try and get her into a better mood again, I added with a smile, "As neither of us intended."

Ava let out a teary laugh, pulling away from my hands so she could dry her eyes. "We shouldn't be doing this now," she said. "This lamenting. We should be celebrating."

"Yes," I agreed, having no desire to do anything but spend our remaining hours together, and with our family. "We should."

And we did. We spent long hours in the dining hall, enjoying each other's company until it was so late in the night that Nilson and Akamar could barely keep their eyes open. We retired at the same time as they did because we had to be up just as early. By morning, however, I'd hardly slept a minute of those short hours left of night. It wouldn't have mattered how late we'd retired from the festivities, because once I'd slipped into bed, I could only think of the days to come.

I lay there contemplating what war would be like – as certainly our raids against supply caravans were but a glimpse – and wondering if there were even any dragons left alive, and hoping my family would be safe with Silas, and that Ava, Nira, Rhien, and I would make it back home. I thought on our strategies, our strengths and weaknesses, our preparedness. I ran over every detail I could in order to convince myself that we were truly ready for this – that *I* was ready for this.

Before long, there was a knock on the door – my signal that it was time. I woke Ava. We dressed. We had a small breakfast in silence. And we wandered to the outside of the caves. The sun hadn't yet risen, but its light was beginning to creep on the horizon, and the gray morning was just bright enough for us to see. I greeted Rhien, and then Nira, and Akamar, whose eyes were barely open, and then my mother and Nilson. I don't know if everyone else had slept as little as I had, but nobody said much of anything as horses were led over, two for my mother's group and four for ours, along with saddlebags filled with supplies to sustain our journeys.

Just as another few rebels carried out our armor and weapons, Silas exited the cave, being led by Kingston and two others. They stopped a distance away from us – too great a distance to hear what Kingston was saying – but after making brief eye contact with Silas, I didn't so much as look at him. Not while I fitted into my thick leather armor – the harness with leather flanks that fell just past my hips, the stiff rounded shoulder guards that almost reached my elbows, and the bracers – and not while my companions did the same. Whatever Kingston had been saying, however, he finished, and Silas nodded at him and came over.

He dipped his head with respect at my mother, and said more timidly than he ever had, "Morning, Bib."

She barely muttered, "Silas," loud enough to hear, and then brushed past him with Nilson and Akamar to check on the horses.

He clearly didn't know how to react to that, and it must have made him feel awkward, because for a long minute he just stood there. Surely Rhien was the most at ease, having little history with Silas, but Ava appeared just as unsure as he did, and while my attitude was one of avoidance, Nira seemed bordering on contempt. In the thick tension amongst our small company, his eyes kept darting from me, to Ava, to Nira and Rhien, and then lingered on the ground before making rounds again. After that minute, his gaze fixed on me, and I could feel him staring as I tightened the straps and buckles on my armor. I was about to tell him to stop when he finally spoke.

"Kiena…" he prompted.

"What?"

He passed another deliberate glance around again at Ava, Nira, and Rhien, before looking back at me. "You can't go to battle in that."

My jaw clenched, because he was in no position to be telling me what to do. He didn't know what I was capable of because he hadn't been around, and the doubt behind his expression only reminded me of how he'd doubted me all those months ago. "I can," I murmured without looking at him. "And I will."

"It'll hardly be enough for war," he argued. "Your safety is at-"

"My safety," I interrupted, turning my stern gaze on him as I pulled the final strap, "is none of your concern. You don't always know best."

The only safety he should be concerned about was that of my mother, brother, and Akamar. But it wasn't just that I didn't want his advice, or his acting like he cared about my safety. I'd been told before that I should be more heavily armored than with this hardened leather. Even my companions were more protected. Nira and Ava had been fitted with leather like mine, but theirs was plated with thin steel, and though Rhien decided only last night that she was coming, she'd been given a shirt of chainmail.

However, no matter how hard I'd tried to adjust to armor like that, I couldn't. It was heavy, and bulky, and I'd probably have been uncomfortable in even this leather if I wasn't so accustomed to my winter furs. More than that, I couldn't wear steel and still use my sparks. I'd tried it once, but that much metal surrounding me interfered with my magic, and it'd nearly set me on fire. It didn't matter anyway; my magic was a greater defense than armor.

Silas didn't say anything in response, but I could feel that my words had stung him. I'd been harsh when all he'd done was voice a well-intentioned concern, but I didn't know how else to react to it. Acknowledging it would only hurt, because that would mean accepting that he still cared. It would be like I *wanted* him to care, but I didn't want him to care *now*. I'd wanted him to care six months ago. Only, he *did* care now, and in the lingering stillness of what could be our final parting, some bit of me felt bad for it. He was doing his penance, and whether or not I was ready to forgive him, I knew he felt guilty enough without me taking stabs at his mistakes. I'd gotten my retribution when I beat him half to death, and any further retaliation was petty.

Before the tension could get any worse, a rebel dropped off a sword by the horses that my mother and the boys were waiting near. Knowing it was for him, Silas wandered away without another word to put it on.

"You're sure he can be trusted?" Nira asked after a minute, watching him with pursed lips as he strapped the sword to his hip.

But even as she asked, Silas finished putting on the sword, and the first thing he did afterward was kneel on one knee in front of Akamar. We couldn't hear what he was saying, but it was clear he was introducing himself, and his gestures were gentle enough that Akamar seemed at ease.

"It's in his best interest not to fail," I answered.

I strapped my own sword around my waist – the one it was insisted I needed if I was going to be facing Hazlitt – while Silas made his way back over. He didn't come to me, but went straight to Nira. "You're the princess of Ronan?" he asked.

Nira's gaze darted over to me, and there was a mixture of confusion and distrust in her eyes. "Yes..."

Silas looked at me too, though it appeared more that he was trying to determine whether or not he was crossing a line. I made no move to keep him from speaking to her, and so he bowed deeply. "I wanted to assure you myself, Princess," he said, straightening again, "that your brother is safe with me. No harm will come to him, I swear it." Nira simply stared at him for a long few seconds not knowing what to say, until, eventually, she managed to nod. Silas was satisfied enough with that, and said to me, "It's time."

Both Nira and I followed him to the horses so we could say goodbye, and my mother pulled me into a hug tighter than she'd ever given me in my life. "You'll be alright," I said, returning the embrace.

"I know *we* will," she replied, and when she pulled away, her eyes were full of tears. "It's good we're leaving first," she whispered, wiping a hand across her cheek as the tears spilled over. "I'm not sure I could've watched you ride away like he did countless times, not knowing if…"

It was clear that she was trying so hard not to cry, but when she said that, I understood why she was. My father had gone off to war and never came back, and she didn't seem convinced that I'd be coming back either. "I'll see you again before you know it," I told her, bringing her in for another hug.

"You know better than to make promises," she sniffled. I nodded, planted one last kiss to her cheek, and then turned to Nilson. He must've sensed the graveness of this parting, because he looked on the verge of tears too.

"When will you be back?" he asked, his eyebrows meeting in the middle.

"I don't know," I answered, squatting down to meet him eye to eye. His bottom lip quivered with the struggle to hold back tears. "Come here." I wrapped my arms around him, and truly not knowing whether I'd ever see him again or not made my own eyes blur. It took a minute, but I blinked away the moisture before letting him go – that way he wouldn't see it – and set my hands on his shoulders. "You take care of Mum and Akamar till I get back, alright?" He sniffled, reaching up to wipe the back of his hand under his nose while he nodded. "Maybe Silas will teach you how to swing a sword, so you've had some practice by the time Ava can give you lessons."

That seemed to cheer him up a little, at least enough that his lips twitched with a smile. "Up you go," I said, turning him around to grab under his arms, lifting him high enough that he could climb onto the horse. "I bet Mother will even let you take the reins."

Once he was on, I held my hand out to help my mother climb into the saddle. Silas had been standing near while we'd been speaking, waiting for Nira to finish saying goodbye to Akamar. I met his eyes after my mother was on the horse, and it looked like he wanted to talk to me, but was unsure enough because of how I'd spoken to him earlier that he didn't request it. After a moment, he turned away, seeming prepared to leave without ever getting it out.

"Say what you need to, Silas," I told him, and though I didn't voice it, I knew by the way his gaze lingered on mine that he could read the other half of that sentence. That this might be his last and only chance. I don't know if it was for him or for me that I was prepared to listen, but either way, some part of me couldn't leave without saying goodbye.

He strode a bit closer, watching the hand he set on the horse's neck because he couldn't quite bring himself to look me in the eyes. "I just wanted to say again that I'm sorry... for everything."

"I know," I said.

"I realize now," he continued, "after last night, after seeing more of what Avarona's been through, and having these last days to really think about what I put *you* through..." He paused, forcing himself to meet my gaze. "I had no right to beg your forgiveness. I wanted you to know that I knew that, in case-" He stopped, casting a weary glance toward my mother and brother, but he didn't need to finish. I knew what he meant. "I wanted you to be at peace," he nodded toward my family, "and know that I've got them. No matter what, and for as long as it takes."

I felt those words at the very core of my heart, and though it didn't suddenly make me ready to forgive him, my eyes flooded with tears. *This was the Silas I'd grown up with.* The Silas who'd always done what he could to care for me, and for my family, and whatever doubts I might've had left about him taking them were gone. "Thank you," I whispered.

There was a short pause, during which he took in a breath and hesitated. "May you be one with the earth," he began to recite, and I felt the corners of my mouth tense with sadness. "May the gods protect you and guide your hand. And may they teach you humility in the face of sacrifice."

Silas had always bowed to the Caelen god of Valens, and he'd never understood my adoption of my father's ancient religion, but that was a prayer to the earth gods. One he'd heard me say only once or twice over the years before going out on a hunt. I wasn't going on a hunt now, but

325

somehow it felt strangely appropriate, and it was the only prayer he knew and he was saying it solely for me, and I couldn't keep a tear from slipping down my cheek.

I didn't know how to respond, or that I even could without letting more tears fall. After a few moments, Silas gave a small smile and turned to walk to his horse. "Silas," I blurted, and he stopped to face me again, but I hadn't thought of what to say. I couldn't forgive him, not yet, but I couldn't let him leave without knowing that I wanted to try – not with our futures so uncertain. But someday... if I got the chance, and the time. "Be safe."

He ducked his head in a shallow bow. "Goodbye, Kiena."

He hopped up into the saddle behind Akamar, and Nira and I watched them ride off with my mother and Nilson at their side. Once they were out of sight, we trudged to where Ava and Rhien had taken to waiting near our horses.

"We should be going too," I announced, and at hearing it, Kingston found his way over. "We'll meet you at Cornwall," I told him, climbing into my saddle while my companions did the same.

"Good luck," he said to all of us.

"Don't start the fight without us, Commander," Nira teased from her horse.

"That's a reprimand I wouldn't dream of," Kingston chuckled, and patted his hand against my horse's flank. "Safe travels."

I nodded, and since there was nothing left to say, I kicked my heels back. We started at a trot toward the woods, and even though we didn't know what was ahead of us, whether we'd find a dragon or I'd even be able to control one before it killed us, I didn't want our journey to the mountains to be one of tension and wondering and silence. "Rhien," I called, passing a glance over my shoulder so she could see the playfulness on my face, "I saw you retiring last night, with company, down a hall that wasn't yours."

Even though I heard Rhien laugh, Ava clicked her tongue and scolded, "You said you wouldn't tease her about it."

"Not teasing," I chuckled, "simply making an observation."

"I know what you're thinking," Rhien accused, "and if you truly *must* know, Celeste sleeps in the barracks."

"Shame," Nira said from the back of our line, and I nodded my agreement because there was no privacy in the barracks, and I supposed Rhien hadn't gotten a long goodbye from her dance partner after all.

"Indeed," Rhien said, but there was something of a smile in her voice even though she'd tried to sound disappointed, and after a long pause, she laughed, "we made good use of the empty infirmary though."

I snorted as Ava burst into laughter behind me, and from Nira at the rear there was a series of proud claps. I had no idea what to say now – Rhien had shut me right up – and so, still laughing, I kicked my heels back to pick up our pace. I let out a shrill whistle as we quickened to a canter, knowing that if Haunt weren't already sulking along in the foliage then she'd catch up. And we were off to try and find ourselves a dragon.

Chapter 22

va spun around, swinging her longsword with the movement, and I managed to lift mine just in time to meet the metal with metal. "Left," she called, immediately taking it hard around the other way. I countered the leftward blow. "Point," she said, bringing her elbows into her side and stabbing straight ahead. Instead of countering, I spark jumped backward to avoid it, but we both knew it wasn't a calculated defensive move. It was instinct and fear. Fighting with a sword wasn't comfortable for me, and I resorted to dodging at every first sign of danger. Regardless, Ava didn't correct me about it. "You did well, let's go again."

Nira and Rhien were sitting nearby, talking and rationing out our breakfast, while Haunt lay a short distance away from them, sleeping in a beam of morning sun that had broken through the tree cover. We'd been traveling for over a week now, and though we were deep in the mountains of the Amalgam Plains – so deep that we hadn't seen any signs of civilization for at least four days – we'd yet to see anything indicating we were at all near to finding a dragon. No swift shadows in the sky. No large footprints on the earth. Nothing burned, or broken, or bitten.

"Ava," I sighed, motioning with my sword, "I'm not suited for this." The last few days that she'd brought up further preparing me for war, she'd been so patient with me, no matter how much I lacked the skill. In turn, her patience had made me a more patient study, but I still felt a twinge of frustration every time I did something wrong. I tried, I truly did, but... "None of this feels natural."

"Hazlitt won't care whether you're suited for it or not," Ava replied, with a building concern in her eyes that made an appearance every time she could feel I wanted to quit a lesson. "Say you face him alone, and your manipulation magic counters all of his, what'll he do?"

Knowing what she wanted to hear, I murmured, "Draw his sword."

"He may even draw it straight away, and use it as a distraction to throw you off," she added. "To give him openings to use his magic. You need this." She beckoned with her hand. "Swing at me as hard as you can." I hesitated for a moment before charging at her, lifting my sword and bringing it down at her diagonally. She made a smooth motion with her own weapon, using my momentum to knock my swing off course, so the point of my sword hit the ground instead. "You need to deflect, like that. Hazlitt is too large and strong for you to counter all his blows, and constantly dodging will only tire you. Deflect and you'll tire *him*, and eventually you'll have the opening for an attack."

It felt hopeless, but it was clear that this was important to her, so I nodded to try again. She started slowly, easing me through the motions of each swing and giving me time to run through the unfamiliarity of deflecting. I still slipped. *Often*. I cut left or right or jumped backward to dodge, and blocked instead of using her momentum to redirect. However, she knew that *I* knew what I was supposed to be doing, so she never corrected me or became frustrated, even though I could see the urgency in her eyes every time I did something wrong. She was worried. And I was still unprepared.

We practiced long enough that eventually I risked growing impatient or short-tempered should I suffer failing any longer. The next time she swung at me, I spark jumped behind her, wrapping my arms around her shoulders. "Got you."

And I could tell that she knew I was done. "That's cheating," she accused with a smile in her voice.

"There won't be any rules when I'm fighting Hazlitt." I leaned over her from behind to kiss her on the cheek. "Fair is fair."

"Oh?" she asked, turning around when I let her go. "Going to kiss him to death, are you?"

I squinted, cocking my head in consideration. "Think that would work?"

I was glad when that earned a genuine laugh. "We'll practice more tomorrow?" she asked, sheathing her longsword, and we started for where Nira and Rhien were sitting. Though I nodded, we both knew it wouldn't do much good. "Rhien," Ava prompted as I sat down, and she nodded toward where we'd been practicing, "would you like to try?"

"If it were allowed, I would like that very much," Rhien answered as she handed me a plate of food, and then she extended one to Ava too. "But my faction forbids me from wielding a weapon against a person."

Ava sat down beside me to eat her breakfast, and I asked, "Would you have been allowed to apprentice with the blacksmith?"

"Making a weapon is not the same as using one," Rhien said, tugging her mouth to one side and adding, "though I'm sure at least one of the masters would've felt differently."

"What was it like?" Ava asked, leaning forward with interest while she swallowed down a bite of food. "Living at a monastery?"

"Simple," Rhien answered, her lips curling with a reminiscent smile. "Peaceful, and quiet. My favorite place to study was in the eastern garden – the sun warmed the grass and it overlooked the countryside. Everything glowed in the morning." The smile faded, and she glanced down at the food in her lap, tracing the edge of the tin plate with her finger for a moment before saying, "Quite a shock, I'm sure you can imagine, to look out one morning and see soldiers from another kingdom on the hill."

"I don't need to imagine," Nira agreed with a sympathetic smile. Ava and I shared a look, one full of guilt, and though my gaze dropped, it wasn't before I saw the hint of tears collecting in Ava's eyes. "Don't start that, you two," Nira scolded, catching the exchange. "If either of us blamed either of you," she gestured toward Rhien, "then we wouldn't be here now, would we?" And Rhien nodded her agreement. "None of *us* started this war, but we're damn well going to end it." Rhien nodded again, and I was glad to see that Ava's eyes were dry as she mirrored the action.

But that sparked a curiosity of my own. "How did the masters feel about you coming to fight with us?"

Rhien's cheeks shaded as she admitted, "I didn't tell them..." She glanced around at the looks of surprise on all of our faces. "They wouldn't have understood. Nor believed that I could help without breaking my vows and taking life."

"Because you *can't* go to war without taking life," Nira said.

"I'm not so sure," Rhien disagreed. "Magic of the mind provides non-violent ways of dealing with threats. I fled an invasion without killing."

"You're not running this time," Nira pointed out, motioning between her, Ava, and me, "not a one of us has clean hands."

In the short pause, I could feel Ava's heart stutter, and I recognized the intake of breath that sought to swallow emotion. "Nira," I murmured, and she followed my gaze to Ava, reading the thoughts behind my warning. All the blood on Ava's hands was there through no fault of her own, and it was *all* from people she'd loved. Her mother. Her father. Her stepmother. Me...

"Sorry," Nira said, adding carefully, "I just... I think it's unrealistic."

In spite of the sadness on Ava's face, she offered a smile, telling Rhien, "I think it's admirable," and Rhien dipped her head gratefully. "So much destruction and loss result from unnecessary violence. Soldiers don't decide war, rulers do. But when we can't find other ways besides bloodshed, it's the soldiers and their families who pay for it."

"You're a kinder soldier than I am," Nira admitted, giving Ava an almost apologetic smile.

We sat there for a few minutes, finishing the remainder of our meal in silence. It wasn't until we rose to pack up our small camp that Rhien asked, "Do you think we're getting close to where the dragons might be?"

I glanced up from where I'd squatted to roll my sleeping fur. "I'm not sure," I answered honestly. "I've been trying to take us to where the mountain is thickest, but I thought we'd at least have some sign by now that the dragons were even still around..."

"You can spark jump three hundred miles," Nira said as she threw her own fur onto her horse's back, and nodded toward the sky. "Can't you jump up there and see if there's anything?"

"It's jumping," I said, "not flying."

But at the word 'flying,' I couldn't help but glance at Ava, because *she* could fly if she used her new magic... Nira and Rhien followed the look, and when Ava realized we were all watching her, she stopped shoving her tin plate into a saddlebag to look back. Her eyes went around to each of us as she took in what the looks were requesting, and then stared upward through the trees at the empty sky.

"It's awfully high," she mused, but I knew what she *wasn't* saying. That she hadn't tried flying since she'd turned into a crow in the infirmary, and going that far up without any practice was her worst nightmare.

"You haven't got to," I told her.

She looked at me, and then again at Nira and Rhien, taking a long minute to consider it. She stared at the sky, and then at the ground, and kicked her toe into the dirt. Then she inhaled deeply, letting it out in a heavy sigh. "I'll do it." She strode away from her horse so she'd have space, and glanced at Rhien. "Don't suppose you have some mind magic to remove fear?"

Rhien winced. "Would you like me to pretend I do?"

Ava stared upward again, and then blew a loud breath through her lips and looked at me. "You've been good to me... Love you."

"You'll be alright," I chuckled, and added encouragingly, "we'll catch you if you're falling."

"Just stay a crow then, yeah?" Nira said. "Can't catch an entire woman falling out of the sky."

"That's very comforting, sister," Ava rolled her eyes, "thank you."

"Ava," I prompted, waiting until she looked at me and then saying seriously, "I'll catch you if you're falling."

"With magic?" she asked, and I hummed my confirmation. "Right, then..."

She inhaled another breath, shut her eyes to focus, and in the next moment, she was changing. Just like she had in the infirmary, and just as quickly. Flesh became feathers, her arms became wings, and she shrank and twisted until a crow was in her place. She blinked her red eyes and gave a testing flap of her wings. It took another few moments for her to build up courage, but then she was off.

Ava flew through the trees, gaining speed and getting the hang of it, and then she swooped upward. She disappeared in the branches, and when I caught a glimpse of her in the sky above our heads, I thought she made it look easy. We squinted while she circled, watching her go higher and higher to search the mountains around us. After a minute, she flew off in some direction that I lost sight of her because of the forest, and I hoped that meant she'd spotted something of interest. A minute passed. And then another.

And another.

"You think she's alright?" Rhien asked, shielding her eyes with her hand as she peered up to search the sky.

"I hope so." I squinted for a good thirty seconds before catching a glimpse. "There she is," I said, pointing.

332

"What if she doesn't find anything?" Nira asked.

I watched Ava soar for another minute before replying. We'd been searching for about a week and a half, but I'd promised Kingston that we'd be at Cornwall when the rest of them got there, so we wouldn't delay the battle or miss any of it. This left only five remaining days to get there, which was almost less time than it would take us to travel the distance. Though Nira hadn't said anything about it, I could feel her growing more impatient by the day.

"We'll search a bit longer," I answered eventually.

She hesitated to say, "Kiena, we've already been out here longer than we should've."

I couldn't argue with her – she was right. I don't know if it was my true belief that we needed a dragon to win this war, or an unconscious desire to see firsthand where my magic had come from, or to satisfy some deep need to discover if there were any of my kind left before I potentially sacrificed myself to this war, but there was something in my gut that wouldn't let me abandon this without pushing a bit further. There *had* to be dragons here. In my ancestor's memory, his people had been devoted to protecting them, and I'd seen for myself what our power was capable of. I couldn't let myself believe that all of it had been for nothing. That they'd failed at keeping the dragons from going extinct.

Despite the instinct that told me we had to be close, there was the nag of reason at the back of my mind. We had a responsibility to be at Cornwall with or without a dragon. "We'll start for Cornwall tomorrow," I told Nira. "No matter what. I promise."

While Nira nodded, I noticed up above that Ava had started a decent, circling lower and lower until she couldn't circle any more because of the trees. It seemed that all she knew was to dive downward, but I could tell that she was heading toward the ground with far too much speed. She didn't know how to land, and I'd promised to catch her if she was falling. As she neared, I sent out a stream of static, wrapping it around her and freezing her just a foot before she collided with the earth. The very moment after I set her down gently, she shifted back, letting out something of a relieved breath.

"Thank you," she said to me.

"How was it?" I asked, noting how her heart was racing.

333

"Terrifying," she admitted with a laugh. "But everything looks so different up there, it's actually somewhat... exhilarating." She took in a deep breath to calm herself down. "I think," she began, her forehead creasing with thought. "I think there's a village."

"A village?" Nira repeated. "Which way?"

"The way we've been heading," Ava answered. "Can't be more than four miles."

"We're nearly there," Nira said with a grin. "I'll bet you they-"

I held up my hand to quiet her, and she stopped short. Something wasn't right... "Ava," I whispered, suddenly tense, "did you see anything else while you were up there?" Even Haunt knew it, because she finally rose from where she'd been sleeping, and sauntered over to us with her head down and her one ear shifting with caution. "Something big?"

There was a heartbeat out there in the woods. I could feel it, and it was huge.

"Dragon big?" Rhien asked, eyes wide as she scanned the empty forest.

I shook my head, because it wasn't quite *that* big, and focused on the direction of the pulse while I grabbed the dagger from my waist. Nira took the hint and untied her bow from her saddle, while Ava did the same and drew her sword. Haunt let out a rumbling growl as the beating got closer, and the horses shifted with fright, but there was no sound in the woods – not the crunch of a footstep that there should be from something so large, not a warning sound from a bird. In fact, it had grown so eerily silent that I could hear all six heartbeats. Four were thudding with fear, one was familiar and deep, and one was slow and steady and powerful. Whatever was out there, it was too large to risk fighting.

"Mount up," I breathed.

No sooner had we reached for our saddles than there was a deafening roar, and the biggest bear I'd ever seen came crashing out of the foliage, stopping thirty feet away to rise onto its hind legs and roar again. It was no shorter than ten feet, with teeth the size of my longest finger and claws twice that, and our horses took off faster than I could blink.

"Stop!" I shouted at the animal, but though that splitting crack went down the front of my skull, the bear let out such a furious rumble that it shook the ground beneath my feet. I couldn't control it, and my face paled.

"RUN!" Nira screamed, fitting an arrow into her bow and letting it fly, immediately turning to sprint.

Ava and Rhien ran after her as the arrow pierced the bear's shoulder, but it was so large that all that seemed to do was make it angrier. I wasn't waiting around to get mauled. I knew it was stupid, I knew we could never outrun a bear, but I turned and sprinted as fast as my legs would carry me, hearing the crashing of paws behind me. Haunt was at my side, and though she could've passed me easily if she'd wanted to, she matched me pace for pace.

But the bear was right on our heels, and getting closer. A split moment later, Haunt pivoted around to meet the beast face to face, with such momentum that she slid backward through the dirt before getting the leverage to spring. She launched forward, just missing the swipe of a massive paw and sinking her teeth into the side of the bear's neck. I skidded to a halt. I couldn't leave her.

"Kiena!" Ava shouted from up ahead.

Before she could even stop, I commanded, "Keep running!" And though I could see the reluctance on her face, she obeyed.

The bear was whipping side to side to try and fling Haunt off of it, and the next swing of its upper body threw her into the nearest tree. I spark jumped before the bear could turn on her, landing directly on top of it. It felt the weight of me and reared, and I managed to slam my spark-filled hand down onto its back before I plummeted off and to the ground. The beast wheeled on me, twitching as the sparks shot through it, but it was far too large for the amount to have been fatal. It raised one massive paw, preparing to strike me when Haunt leapt through the air.

She clamped down on the bear's arm, and it snarled as it raised its paw high into the air, bringing it down with as much force as it could. As it slammed Haunt into the earth, I spark jumped again, landing behind the beast and grabbing its leg with both hands. I sent out as much lightning as I possibly could, and though the bear roared and trembled with convulsions that should've killed it, it stayed standing. It turned on me with a heavy swipe that caught the back of my armored shoulder, throwing me six feet sideways so that I hit the ground hard.

Just before it could charge at me again, Haunt recovered. As she landed on the bear's back and began tearing into it with her teeth, I stood, and I sprinted after where my companions had disappeared. There was a yelp from behind me, but I could no longer stop to check on Haunt. If my magic couldn't kill this beast, then I didn't know what could. I flew over the dirt, hearing the thunder of the bear's paws pick up after me, but I couldn't see Ava and Nira and Rhien. I didn't know where they'd gone.

I was about to call out for them, to beg for help or tell them to get as far away as they could, when Rhien popped out from behind a tree. She grabbed me by the neck of my armor and whipped me sideways, throwing me back to pin me against the trunk. "Gidreshnap," she muttered with an intense look of focus, and then she pressed her finger to her mouth, telling me to be silent. It was nearly impossible with the crashing that got closer and closer, and I almost screamed when the bear slid to a stop right at our side. The last place it had seen us.

I could see Nira and Ava on the other side of it, backs to a tree just like I was, but the bear couldn't see them. Or us. It was huffing and panting, each breath carrying the low rumble of a growl. It was only two feet away, close enough to reach out and touch, but whatever Rhien had done, she'd made us invisible to it. I couldn't resist waving one hand to test it out, but she caught my hand in mid air and froze, making us both so still that she barely managed to shake her head at me in warning.

The bear's head turned toward us, as if I'd almost alerted it to our presence. It sniffed the air, leaning forward and getting so near that I could feel the warmth of its breath, and the breeze of it tickled my hair against my neck. It stood back on its hind legs, letting out another deafening roar that made me close my eyes with a terrified wince.

"Lost them?" called a male voice.

I opened my eyes to see a man running toward the bear, but no sooner had he spoken than the bear began to shrink. It changed just as Ava had only minutes before, until a large man with dark brown hair and piercing green eyes was standing in its place. He was a shapeshifter, and they both appeared to be about our age.

As the second man, with light brown hair and brown eyes, reached him, he grabbed at the arrow Nira had put in his shoulder, grunting as he ripped it out. "They shot me," he growled. There were other tears in his tunic, and wounds where Haunt had bitten him.

"I'd have shot you too," laughed the other one. "Come bursting out of the woods like you did. No tact."

"They've got magic," said the bear man, pulling off his shirt to examine the rips and holes. "We should head back and grab some of the others."

But now that he'd taken his shirt off, I couldn't keep from staring at his chest. At the dragon pendant dangling there from the chain around his neck. It was made of the same dark metal as the one I was wearing, but the stone was a shiny black that reflected different colors every time the sun hit it. I looked at the other man, finally noticing that his pendant was hanging outside his shirt. The same dragon, but with a red gemstone curled in its tail.

As they turned to leave, I reached up and pulled my own necklace over my head, holding it out even though Rhien tried to stop me. "Wait!" I shouted. It broke the spell, and the men turned, one lighting a flame in his hand while the other looked ready to turn back into a bear. Haunt recovered and reached us at the same time, and bounded in front of me, baring her teeth. "Wait," I pleaded, gesturing at them with the hand I was holding my necklace in. "Haunt, stop."

The bear man squinted his green eyes in shock, while the other's mouth pulled into a grin. "You're Dragonkin!" he exclaimed, flicking his wrist and putting out the fire in his hand. He glanced side to side as my companions came out from behind their trees, Ava taking place at my side. "Hello!"

"You're the one who shot me," the other said, eyes landing on Nira.

Though he looked rather unsure of us, he didn't appear to be as angry or menacing as he had been as a bear. Nira shrugged, saying with a friendly smile to try and put him at ease, "You did come bursting out of the woods."

He pursed his lips to hold back a smile, and his eyes looked her up and down with something of an impressed glimmer. "It was a good shot, and I suppose I've had worse." The very next moment, his wounds began to heal, and he winced only slightly with pain as the cuts sealed themselves, disappearing in a matter of seconds. It was the second of his abilities.

"Playing it off now," Nira teased, but her eyes were wide with intrigue, and she was leaning slightly forward as if to get a better look. "Tactful, I see."

"He's not the one who needs tact," Ava muttered under her breath, and I couldn't help but laugh as I returned the chain around my neck.

337

Neither could the other man, who chuckled as he extended his hand to me. "I'm Skif."

"Kiena," I replied, shaking with him and then reaching out for the other's hand as Skif moved on to my companions.

"Denig," said the bear man, asking with a friendly smile, "what was that you hit me with? Lightning? Gods, that was painful."

"I was trying to kill you," I pointed out.

"Try all you like," Skif said, grinning at the glare Denig gave him. "Can't kill other Dragonkin with our own magic."

"Come here, Haunt," I said and knelt down, checking her for injuries while I nodded toward Denig. "He seemed right ready to kill me."

"Couldn't have done more than bruise you with my best magical effort," Denig said.

"I didn't know if there'd be any of you left out here," I mused. Haunt was fine, if only a little battered, and she sulked off into the woods once I let her go.

"Where did *you* come from?" asked Skif.

"Valens," I answered, standing again. "Outside the capital, Guelder."

"No Dragonkin have left the mountain for over five decades," Skif mused. "And I've never heard of any coming back. What line are you?" I cocked my head, unsure of what he meant. "May I see it?" he asked, motioning to my necklace. I took it off and gave it to him, and he turned it over in his hand. "Never seen this one."

He showed it to Denig, who said, "Nor I."

"Lightning, though," Skif said, handing the necklace back, "that's an element. Could be related, you and I."

"Could we?" I asked in surprise, slipping the pendant over my head. I'd never met another blood relative other than my mother, and the idea that I might actually have one was exciting.

"Elder Numa might know for sure," Skif answered, nodding. "We could go and-"

Denig cleared his throat, cutting off whatever invitation Skif might've been about to offer. "Forgive my suspicion," Denig said, "but why are you out here? You wouldn't be looking for Dragonkin if you didn't think there were any of us left."

I glanced side to side at my companions, unsure of whether or not I should tell the truth. If Skif and Denig were anything like my ancestors,

338

then they were here to protect dragons if there were any left, and for all I knew, they wouldn't even want us searching for one. But I didn't want to lie either, because Denig seemed too perceptive to fall for it, and just maybe they *would* help. "We're searching for a dragon."

Denig got visibly tense, and Skif did a double take. "Dragonkin don't hunt dragons," Skif said, and though it was subtle, he began to rub at his palm with the fingers of the same hand, and I picked up the faint smell of smoke. "To hurt one would cost your entire bloodline its magic."

"Not hunting," I said earnestly. "We've no intention of doing any harm." They both just watched me, waiting for an explanation. "We're at war, I was hoping to get help."

"War?" Denig repeated.

I nodded. "The king of Valens invaded Ronan, in the south. He'll take Cornwall too if we don't stop him." They looked at each other, and Skif shrugged at Denig.

"*You don't know that we're at war?*" Nira asked in shock, and I was just as surprised. Surely they had someone who occasionally left the mountain to gather news from the outside world. "It's been going on for sixty years."

"Our only concern this deep in the mountains," Skif answered, "is keeping the dragons safe."

My eyes lit up, and I could no longer be surprised about them not knowing of the war. They *still* kept the dragons safe, after all these years. That had to mean... "Does that mean they're still alive?" I asked, unable to keep an excited smile off my face. Our journey might not have been for nothing. We might not have wasted this last week and a half, and we'd make it back to Cornwall and *maybe* with a dragon that would help us win the war. My hoping wasn't done in vain. "The dragons still live on the mountain?"

"They are," Denig said, wary eyes scanning my expression. "They do."

At Denig's confirmation that the dragons still lived, every one of us grinned, but though my heart was nearly soaring with excitement, I didn't want to get ahead of myself. "Could we meet them?" I asked. "Could we converse with one to get help?"

Skif's eyebrows furrowed, and he let out a huff of laughter as though he thought I was joking. "You don't converse with them," he said. "You get close enough to their home and they'll defend it."

"But I'm Dragonkin," I murmured. "Surely they'll recognize that?"

"They do," Skif agreed. "That's why they don't hunt us, but that doesn't mean we go marching into the mountain caves after them."

"That's not why they don't hunt us," Denig said, passing Skif a look that made him roll his eyes.

Skif motioned at him. "He thinks the dragons are docile because one saved him as a boy."

"They *are* docile," Denig argued, in the annoyed kind of tone that said this wasn't a new discussion. "*You're* the one speculating."

"Tell that to Old Ovata," Skif said, glancing at each of us to catch us up on the story. "Who got dropped from the sky into the village at night by a dragon only after he'd been poisoned to death by its breath."

Denig clicked his tongue. "Ovata was a greedy fool with foul intentions, and the dragons knew it."

"They're docile," I cut in before Skif could come up with a retort. "Enough to understand us."

"What?" Skif asked in shock.

"How do you know?" Denig prompted.

"I've seen it," I answered, eager to convince them that showing us where the dragons lived was the best decision. "I've come face to face with one in a memory, and I've seen that they can be controlled with magic."

"Not adult dragons," Denig replied.

"I'll go anyway," I said. We'd come too far to turn back now.

Skif shrugged. "It's your funeral, I suppose."

I looked at Denig, asking, "So you'll take us?"

"I didn't say that," he answered. I opened my mouth to protest, but he said, "Just because you might survive meeting one doesn't mean that it's what is best for the dragons, and that's what we're here to ensure."

"We're at war," I pleaded. "Do you know how many lives we could save if we got help?"

"At risk to the *dragon's* life," Denig argued, "the very thing that we were born to protect."

"That *you* were born to protect," I corrected. "I'm not saying we'll be careless, but this is far too importa-"

"You took the magic," Denig interrupted. "That's like taking an oath, you understand? Whether you like it or not, your duty is-"

"Don't speak to me of oaths and duty," I said. "I've made no oath, and my entire life has been a service. You've no idea the sacrifices we've made to get here, and we're not leaving until I make my request to a creature that we both know is capable of deciding for itself."

"You've got responsibilities," he said. "I understand, I do, but I cannot abandon mine, no matter how honorable your intentions."

"Unbelievable," Nira muttered, stepping forward with irritation and seeming to have lost her patience. "You'd refuse to let us even try all for the sake of some selfish nobility?"

"*Selfish nobility?*" Denig repeated with offense, meeting her advance.

"You heard me," Nira spat, squaring herself in front of him even though he towered over her. "You Dragonkin are so wrapped up in protecting them that you didn't even know we've been at war for generations. Forget the world you live in, kingdoms and humankind be damned so long as the dragons are cozy."

"There are only *six* dragons left in this mountain," Denig growled, "and as far as we know, they're the last six in the *world*. You'd take one to war, risk its life and perhaps drive them nearer to extinction, and you call *my* aim selfish?"

"At the very least, it's shortsighted and stupid," Nira quipped, and Denig's lips pursed angrily. "You think you're immune to it? You think war can't reach you way up here? Well just you wait."

Denig glared. "Is that a thr-"

"*That's enough*," Ava snapped, and though she didn't raise her voice, it was so stern that each one of us looked at her in surprise. "Nira, step back." Nira obeyed, but not before passing a final glare at Denig. "Denig," Ava prompted more kindly, "if I may?" And he nodded his consent. "What my sister means is that the man fueling this war and moving on Cornwall is a glutton for power. He won't stop until he's unstoppable, and he's had glimpses of what Dragonkin are capable of. If we don't do everything we can to stop him, it seems only a matter of time before he also comes to seek the source of *your* power," she motioned toward the pendant around my neck, avoiding touching it so she wouldn't get shocked. "And how many dragons do you think he'll kill in his search for it?"

"Right," Nira agreed.

Ava glanced over just long enough to cast her a scolding look, and then returned her focus to Denig and Skif. "If you truly care about the dragons having a future," she urged, "then you'll help us secure present circumstances."

Denig's face softened with understanding. Ava had gotten through to him, and I nearly sighed my relief as he stood there for a silent minute to consider what she'd said. His eyes wandered from her to Nira, and then to me and Rhien, finally landing on Skif. All Skif did was nod.

"We'll take you to Elder Numa," Denig said finally. "They decide whether or not we show you the way."

"Thank you," I said, making sure my expression portrayed my sincere gratitude. It was better than flat-out refusal. "We need to find our horses."

"We'll help," Skif volunteered.

As we split off to search for the horses – Ava and me, Nira and Rhien, and Denig and Skif – I wrapped my arm around Ava's shoulders and pulled her into me for a hug. "You saved us back there," I told her.

"Perhaps my aim was the most selfish of all," she admitted, taking in the curious look I gave her. "If a dragon would help ensure that we make it through this, that you and I get a life together afterward, I'd do whatever I could to enlist one."

"Let's just hope it doesn't kill us before I can try to reason with it," I said.

Truly, I had no idea what to expect. Denig seemed to think the dragons were highly intelligent and friendly, which I believed because I'd seen it in my ancestor's memory. Skif, however, seemed convinced that whether or not a dragon could be reasoned with, they would feel so threatened by us entering their home that we'd never get the chance to try. I couldn't be sure which opinion was the more accurate one, but I was here on the belief that a full grown dragon was a fearsome thing to behold, and not knowing what to expect in temperament, or ability, or even size, made me more anxious about finding one than I'd been yet.

Chapter 23

fter we'd managed to find our horses in the woods, Denig and Skif led us to their village a couple of miles away. The village was almost exactly as it had been in my memory – though few of the homes were in the same places, the cottages were built the same. They were the same sizes and the same shapes, made of the same materials with the same small gardens and goat pens in their yards. And every single person around stopped to stare at us as we arrived. Some of them whispered, some of them looked confused, and some noticed the dragon pendant around my neck and grew excited. Others nodded or extended greetings to Denig and Skif, and were polite enough to acknowledge us. Quite a few, though not all, had pendants of their own.

Despite the commotion we were causing, our guides were undeterred, and didn't stop until they'd led us to a small cottage at the very heart of the village. Denig stopped at the closed entrance, which was only a long sheet of leather hanging in the empty doorway, stepping between it and us. "Elder Numa is easily overwhelmed by company," he said.

"Should I meet them alone?" I asked, glancing around him at the entrance.

"Not alone," he answered.

"I'll wait with you," Skif said, with a friendly smile to cut through Denig's renewed guardedness, and he brushed aside the flap in the doorway. "You lot can take the horses for a drink."

Nira and Rhien leaned to try and get a curious glimpse into the cottage, but Ava met my gaze, her head tilted in question. I nodded at her that everything was fine, smiled at them, and then followed Skif into the cottage. It took my eyes a moment to adjust once he let the flap fall closed behind us. It was dark in here, with only a couple of candles on a table at the left side casting shadows across the single room. That table was the only piece of furniture in the small cottage, but the floor was littered inches thick with furs.

"You can sit, if you'd like," Skif offered, motioning to the cushioned floor. I moved to the center of the room and sat, folding my legs beneath me. "Forgive Denig," he continued, using his fire magic to light the hearth on the opposite side of the cottage as the table. "He's protective enough over the dragons even when I talk about them." He laughed to himself, passing me to grab the only jar on the table, which was full of blue sand. "Don't know how he's remained even this collected since you've told him you were searching for one."

I watched Skif pace past me again toward the hearth, carrying that jar. "Is it all because one rescued him?"

"Not entirely." Skif paused by the fire to turn and look at me. "Old Ovata was from his immediate bloodline, and there hasn't been a dragon hunter on the mountain since we were children."

"Everyone thinks they're gone," I told him.

Skif hummed in acknowledgment. "Fewer of us Dragonkin are born with magic these days," he continued. "And not everyone can endure that kind of power." I glanced away guiltily at that, thinking about how I'd acted when I'd first gotten the magic. "But they don't need protecting like they used to. Denig's the only one of his line with the ability, and he takes it seriously."

I nodded, feeling more forgiving toward Denig's stubbornness now that I knew its source. When it came down to it, he and I weren't so different. Duty. That was his motivation just as well as it was mine, and I understood, and I respected it. The issue had been that our senses of duty opposed the other. But now, thanks to Ava, we might have acquired a common responsibility.

Skif turned back to the hearth, opened the jar of blue sand, and scooped a handful out into his palm. "This is my favorite part," he said over his shoulder at me, and then tossed the sand into the fire. The flames changed color in a matter of moments, burning blue and steadily getting greener, until they were a dark emerald. "It's a mystery how Elder Numa knows they're being summoned," Skif mused, and he returned the jar to the table and then came over to sit by me, "but they'll be here shortly."

It took a long minute for me to be able to tear my eyes away from the beautiful fire, but eventually I looked at Skif. "Do you see the dragons often?"

"No one does," he answered. "Never seen one in my lifetime. Word is they're hibernating."

My eyebrows furrowed in disbelief. "How do you know how many there are?"

"Elder Numa knows." He pulled his knees up to his chest, resting his forearms over them. "They're one of the first Dragonkin." At the look of surprise on my face, he nodded. "Part of their magic is immunity to age. They've been around since the beginning, and they're the only one I've ever heard of that can talk to the gods directly."

"They talk to the gods?" I asked in wonder, suddenly more nervous about meeting them. He smiled as he nodded once more, and I glanced again at the fire. "What other magic do you have?"

He didn't answer straight away even though he smiled again at the question, but then something pushed through the leather flap covering a window at the far end of the cottage. It was a branch from the tree just outside, and it grew and stretched all the way across the room until it reached me, and then it dropped a pinecone in my lap and shrank until it retreated. I laughed, holding up the full, healthy cone.

"Controlling plants requires a bit of creativity in a fight though," Skif chuckled.

He reached out to take the pinecone, and once he held it in his hand, he raised the index finger of his other. A small flame emerged from the tip of that finger, and he used it to light the topmost spike of the cone like a candle. We watched it burn for a few moments before he tossed it in the air and flared his other hand open, and with the gesture, the flame shot down the center length of the pinecone. It burst, sending sparks flying and scaring me so badly that I flinched backward to scramble away. But he caught the flaming seeds before they got too far, holding them in midair so that the embers decorated the space between us like stars.

"That's..." I could barely speak through my awe. "That's incredible."

"Thanks." Skif grinned, using his magic to toss the remnants of the pinecone sideways into the hearth. "More useful," he said, and reached into his boot, from which he pulled a knife, "is my immunity to injury." He flipped the knife so he was holding the blade, and extended the handle to me. "Go ahead," he said when I took it from him, and tapped a spot on the inside of his forearm.

"*Cut you?*" I asked, glancing from the weapon to his arm with extreme reluctance.

"Give it your best," he challenged.

I set the blade against his skin, but was too afraid to apply much pressure, and he laughed at my hesitation, nodding with encouragement. So I pressed harder, somewhat worried that his skin gave to the knife, but I decided to trust him and try it. I swiped, and though his skin moved like flesh under the pressure, the blade slid over it like water over a stone, leaving no trace of injury. No cut, no blood. No damage to the weapon. I couldn't help but grin.

"Can you heal like Denig?" I asked, giving him the knife back.

He shook his head. "And I have to be thinking about it in order to keep from being hurt. If I'm caught off guard and wounded, I've got to wait for it to heal like everyone else." He added with a laugh, "Everyone except Denig."

"What's his third ability?"

"He hasn't got one," Skif answered. "How about you? Other than the lightning?"

"I can manipulate corruptions," I answered. "Like dark magic, or rot in a tree."

"Oh!" he exclaimed. "Let me guess your third, then. It's not an element, is it?"

"How'd you know?" I asked.

"Lucky guess," he chuckled. "But if you've three abilities, two of them tend to be a similar type, see? Elements," he gestured to himself, and then at me, "manipulations. Had Denig a third, he likely would've been able to heal others as well. Or change his human appearance or his state of being – that's the shapeshifting." I nodded in understanding. "You, in this case, either manipulate the will or the senses." That sparked my curiosity, but I waited to see if he'd guess correctly. "The senses?" I shook my head, and he laughed, "I tried."

"How does that work?"

"The senses?" he clarified, to which I nodded again. "You can change what people see, hear, smell, taste, and, to an extent, feel. It's a fun magic if you're fond of mischief."

"I could imagine," I agreed with a laugh.

Before either of us could say anything else, there was movement at the entrance of the cottage, but it wasn't a person who entered. A thick cloud of dark gray smoke billowed through the cracks between the leather and the doorway, filtering in but not spreading through the air like a normal cloud of smoke. It was concentrated, rolling with purpose low across the floor. It collected just in front of Skif and me, and flowed upward and gained in thickness, until it had become a very solid person.

They weren't at all what I expected. Elder Numa was dressed in robes the same dark gray as that smoke had been, and their hair was braided at the back of their head, and it and their eyes were a color impossible to distinguish in the low light of the cottage. One second I was sure both were black, but then they turned and caught the light of the fire, and eyes and hair appeared almost the same color as their robes. Nor could I distinguish whether Elder Numa was male or female. Not by their face, nor their body, which was hidden beneath their clothing.

"Hello, Kiena," Elder Numa said, in a voice that did nothing to enlighten me but felt entirely too familiar – the kind of familiar to numb the brain. It was neutral, and smooth. Soft. And their lips curled as if they could read my confusion. "Lean forward," they said, holding out their hand, and in the palm of it shone a bright light. It wasn't like Skif's fire, or my lightning, or even the small energy I'd seen Sevedi use in Ronan. It was very much like Elder Numa held the sun in their hand, and it illuminated the entire room. "It's my turn for a close look at you."

Though I was wildly unsure of myself, or what that meant, Elder Numa's presence was easy and comforting. I did as they asked and leaned forward, squinting my eyes from the light. They leaned in too, and moved the glow from one side of my face to the other, studying me for a long minute before letting out a soft laugh and leaning back again. They dropped the light, and it had been so brilliant that my eyes set to readjusting to the darkness.

"Skif wants to know if you're related," Elder Numa said, with that hint of laughter still in their voice.

I glanced at Skif, chuckling at the embarrassment on his face. "I wouldn't mind knowing either."

"Your father, Nilan," Elder Numa said, their voice so low I wasn't sure how I could even hear them. "Born to Niemi and Agnes. Niemi's mother, Ceana, and her mother and father, Una and Tero."

"Hah!" Skif exclaimed, grinning ear to ear. "My great, great grandparents!"

Elder Numa tilted their head in acknowledgment, saying, "Third cousins." I couldn't help but grin myself, because I had *blood relatives* – diluted family, and not immediate, but family all the same. "You are the first since Una to stray from the elements," they told me, passing that friendly look at Skif. "They run strong in your bloodline."

Elder Numa paused, and even in the dim lighting of the cabin, I knew they were studying me again. Staring at me. For a long minute, they said nothing, and Skif and I sat there in complete silence. I thought to mention why I was here, and what I needed, but some part of me felt that Elder Numa already knew. Just like they'd known my name, or that Skif was wondering about our relation.

"Kiena," Elder Numa said eventually, "if you're prepared for the challenge, Skif and Denig will show you and your company to the dragons."

My eyes widened. "You don't want to hear my intentions?"

"The gods know your intentions," they answered. "And they're satisfied." All I could do was sit there, stunned. I hadn't needed to make a single statement or promise. Nothing on our behalf to assure that we had no aim to harm a dragon. "Farewell."

"Elder Numa," I prompted hastily, before they could leave or turn to smoke again and disappear. "May I ask... will you... thank the gods for me?" Though Elder Numa didn't look surprised, or confused, their head gave an almost curious tilt as those mysterious eyes set to studying me again. "I pray to them," I explained, "but if I could make sure they heard me..."

Their lips curled in their gentle smile. "They hear you," Elder Numa assured me. "May memory serve you well." And again they were smoke, a thick cloud of it that moved toward the door until it was gone.

"Well," Skif said, and he cleared his throat as he rose to his feet. "I suppose we're taking you to the dragons."

He was clearly concerned, or afraid. It was he, and not Denig, who believed the dragons weren't docile, and surely he thought this was a dangerous task. I couldn't deny that I was slightly worried myself. "You could simply tell us where to go," I said. "If you hadn't wanted to meet one face to face."

He gave a considerate hum as he started toward the entrance. "As frightened as I am," he said, holding the flap open for me to leave first, "my curiosity is greater. I would like to see one." We stopped outside the cottage, searching our surroundings for a glimpse of our companions. "Just don't expect me to stick around should you get eaten," he teased.

"Right," I laughed.

Skif led the way to a cottage nearby, where our group was letting the horses get a drink from a trough just outside of it. I expected Denig to feel reluctant when he heard the news that we were to be taken to the dragons, but he wasn't. Whether he'd changed his mind in my absence, or his faith in Elder Numa was unwavering, he accepted the task without a complaint.

"We'll leave the horses," he said, and Skif nodded his agreement.

It wasn't just because a dragon would terrify the horses that we didn't take them – the way to where the dragons lived was a more difficult trek than this last week in its entirety. The village resided at the base of the mountain's highest peak, and from it we ascended so steeply that I was even glad Haunt had stayed behind. We traversed beyond the woods, to where the trees thinned until we crossed nothing but stone. Until we traveled between and up boulders the size of a cottage, lost our footing uphill as we slipped on loose gravel, and even climbed steep ledges with footholds worn into the rock.

At each of these climbs, I could see the reluctance on Ava's face for fear of falling. "You know," she panted, reaching for my hand so I could pull her up the remaining foot of ledge, "if I knew what to expect at the top of this mountain, I might be tempted to fly up and meet you all there."

I helped her to her feet. "Perhaps I'll spark jump. We can race to the top."

"I do believe you have an unfair advantage," she laughed.

The last one to climb, Denig was large enough that he took a running start, leaping to grab the very top of the ledge and pulling himself up. He, too, was panting hard from the hike while he stood, but he managed a breathy laugh. "We're nearly there." He pointed upwards, to where our trail wound around the mountain below its peak. "They live in a cave just on the other side."

"Thank the goddess," Nira mumbled, wiping the back of her hand across her damp forehead.

We picked up walking, struggling up the steep switchbacks for a few minutes in silence before Denig fell into step at my side. "It's not just the danger to whichever dragon may help you," he told me, breathing heavily. "I expect we'll start getting hunters on the mountain again once people know the dragons are still around."

"I *do* care about their fate," I told him.

He nodded. "If you didn't, I don't believe Elder Numa would have let you come."

"What happened to you as a boy?" I asked. "To make you so protective?"

"I was out exploring on my own," he answered, "something I thought safe because we so rarely get hunters on the mountain anymore." He paused to take a few huffing breaths. "I set off a trap. It was only a snare set to catch their dinner, but it took me straight up into the air. I was dangling upside down by a foot when they came around and recognized me as Dragonkin." He took another few gulps of air. "They decided they were going to kill me and make one less obstacle on their hunt for a dragon. They stabbed me once, but I healed, and twice more before one shouted to take off my head."

"You wouldn't have survived it," Nira guessed, having dropped back from the head of the group to listen.

"There are some wounds that are simply too grave," he confirmed. "Once the cold steel set against the back of my neck, I thought I was dead for sure. But the man raised his sword, and a spike this large," he held his hands more than a foot apart, "went straight through his chest." Both Rhien and Ava took awed breaths, crowding in so intently that it was hard to keep our pace steady. "A huge dragon slithered through the trees, surprising them all and saving my life. Never since have I seen a creature like it. It was beautiful."

"Will you describe it?" Rhien asked.

"It was a deep, dark green," Skif answered for him, reciting it over his shoulder at us like he'd heard it a thousand times. "An old, healthy emerald, like the evergreen trees that sing of hope in the harshest of winters, with warm tones of brown along its stomach and tail, and eyes the comforting shade of mahogany."

350

Denig gave a good-natured shrug. "He tells it just as well."

"Is it still alive?" Ava asked.

"It is," Denig said with a smile. "Dragons live for hundreds of years, and it was young when we met."

"Did you name it?" Nira questioned.

"Pine Shadow," Denig answered.

Her eyebrows furrowed. "You named the dragon Pine Shadow?"

He chuckled, nodding. "It appeared as smooth as a phantom from the trees, killed all four men without making a sound, and then disappeared again."

"What about the others?" Rhien prompted, glancing back and forth between Denig and Skif. "Have you named them?"

"We've not seen them," Skif answered. "But we have names passed down through generations." He counted on his fingers. "There's Pine Shadow. Ember..."

"A fire breather?" I guessed.

Denig hummed excitedly. "Whose flesh is said to mimic the dancing of flames."

"Monarch," Skif added, counting a third finger. "The one with poison breath, and scales the black and brilliant yellow of a monarch butterfly."

"Scorpion," Denig added.

"Oh," Skif drawled in wonder. "I've seen a drawing of that one. Can't see it amongst the rocks because it's pebbled like stone, and the end of its tail is sharp and poisoned."

"Perhaps we should turn back now," Nira pointed out, "while we still can."

"You know the way down," Denig teased, and Nira passed him a smirking glare.

"Which others?" Skif prompted, holding up four fingers, and his face lit up as he counted another and recalled, "White Water."

"Said to favor the river that flows down the mountain," Denig explained, "its glassy black flesh is swirled with white like the rapids."

"And Night Phoenix," Skif finished. "The oldest of them. A dark dragon that dissolves into pile of stardust upon its death, and in that stardust can be found an egg, for the dragon to be reborn."

"That sounds beautiful," Ava mused, and Rhien nodded her eager agreement.

As we rounded the final switchback to the top of the mountain, I asked, "Which do you think is more likely to help us?"

Denig shrugged, bringing us to a halt below the peak. "Your guess is as good as mine."

Our trail had ended at the start of a cave, the opening of which was larger than castle gates – three stories high at the topmost part of the arch, and just as wide. The inside was so dark that we couldn't see very deep into it, but there was an eerie sort of stillness that washed over us that told me this was the right place. None of us made a sound as we stared at the massive opening, peering into the darkness as though expecting to be greeted by a dragon.

"What now?" Skif whispered.

Denig took in a breath to answer, but I waved my hand to keep him quiet. I could sense a heartbeat, one so large and deep and steady that it would've been impossible to miss. The only reason I hadn't recognized it the moment we stopped was because it was slow. Unnaturally slow. Each beat came five seconds apart so that it hardly sounded like a pulse at all, but there was no mistaking the uneven throb of a heart.

Almost as if the dragon knew I'd become aware of it, there was movement. The rocks at the topmost part of the opening shifted just slightly, and the creature was so perfectly blended to the grays of the mountain stone that its shape was indistinguishable amongst them. It looked as though entire boulders were moving, as though they slipped down from where they'd been resting at the top lip of the entrance, and disappeared in a scurry into the darkness.

There was no doubt in my mind that each and every one of us had seen it, but nobody said a word. Nobody so much as moved, and we stood there for almost a minute, barely even breathing.

Then Nira's hand set on my back, and she pushed me a step forward. "Go after it," she urged, sidestepping closer to Denig and shoving him out next to me. "You're the ones who think they're docile."

Denig and I looked at each other, and despite his insisting earlier that the dragons *were* docile, he seemed rather reluctant to go into the cave after them. "Any stories?" I asked, also glancing behind us at Skif. "About people who've done this before?" They both shook their heads.

I looked at Ava, for advice or encouragement or maybe just comfort, but she gave an unsure shake of her head. "If you're not confident..."

And though I hadn't asked, Rhien said, "I agree... maybe you shouldn't risk it."

I *wasn't* confident, but though I didn't want to leave without trying, I didn't know what to do. Call out to them? Wander into the cave? We didn't even know how deep it went, or if the rest of the dragons were *truly* in there. So I stood there for a long minute, simply looking and growing more nervous by the second, until my heart was pounding behind my ribs.

"You going sometime this month, maybe?" Nira asked impatiently.

"Give me a minute," I murmured, taking in a deep breath to work up the courage.

But Nira seemed done waiting. "It's been a minute," she said, reaching down to pick up a fist-sized stone. "I've a better idea." And she cocked her arm back.

Ava gasped. "Nira, no-"

It was too late. Nira had thrown the rock as hard as she could into the entrance of the cave, and it disappeared into the darkness. The inside must have sloped downward, because the stone didn't hit the ground for a few moments, and then it bounced repeatedly. The heavy clicks of it striking the floor of the cave echoed back out to us, getting farther and farther, until it rolled so far we couldn't hear it.

Two more seconds passed, and then something else rang out – a booming roar. A terrifying sound so loud and powerful that it shook the ground beneath our feet, rocked a handful of pebbles straight over the opening of the cave to the ground below, and sent a flock of birds over a mile away scattering from their tree. It was so powerful a sound that it knocked Denig a step back, and my heart jumped into my throat.

It froze every one of us to where we were standing, but we wouldn't have had the chance to run even if we tried. There was a flash of movement in the darkness, and then a dragon came swooping out and upward, stretching its body out of the cave and landing with such an enormous thud that my balance wavered. And it faced us and straightened.

Its thick, canine shaped body was a brilliant swirl of black and dark blue, with quills straight down its neck and back. Sharp spikes as big as my forearm lined its cheekbones, and its head alone was the size of a four-person carriage – large enough to swallow two of us whole if it didn't decide to cut us in half with the teeth that lined its jaws. Its eyes, which were each larger than my midsection, were a pale golden yellow that sparkled in the sunlight. It had wings between its front shoulders, each as long as its body, which it fanned out as it straightened and that were so big they left us all in shadow. *This* was Night Phoenix.

It would've been a sight to marvel at for hours and hours, but Night Phoenix's jaws stretched wide, and it craned its long neck our direction so we could see all *three* rows of its massive teeth. And it let out another shrill roar. That sound was *paralyzing* this close up. My heart stopped, and my lungs stopped. My brain locked up. I stood there wide-eyed, staring into the rows of teeth until the sound ended and left my ears ringing.

Night Phoenix marched forward, taking earth-shaking steps until its enormous head was hanging only feet in front of me. In my frozen, terrified state, I forgot that Denig said our magic didn't work on adult dragons. "Stop!" I ordered in panic, but it didn't just *not* work. The pain that was usually a dull ache when I controlled animals flared, cracking through my skull so powerfully that the agony was blinding. I buckled over, throwing my hands to my head as Night Phoenix let out a furious rumble.

Something crashed into my ribs, and as I hit the ground with Denig on top of me, the dragon's open jaws slammed into the earth where I'd been standing. It turned on us, preparing to strike again, but Nira grabbed another stone and hurled it at the dragon's head.

"Over here!" she yelled as it hit Night Phoenix in the cheek.

Skif had already taken five paces backward in retreat, but Ava and Rhien were still standing at Nira's side. The dragon huffed in annoyance, giving a single flick of its long tail that hit all three of them square in the chest. They went flying, crashing to the ground in a messy heap while Night Phoenix snarled at Denig and me. It seemed ready to take another snap with its jaws, and neither of us would be able to reach our feet and run in time. So I spark jumped off to the side, unable to land on my feet so that I hit the ground on my back, and the dragon wheeled around to face me.

There seemed nothing to be done. I couldn't control it, and I couldn't hurt it, and I couldn't run. But at that very moment, as Night Phoenix bared its fangs over my face, staring down at me to show me just what kind of death I'd meet, my brain started working again. I recognized the nighttime swirls of color in its scales. Felt the familiarity of those soft yellow eyes. Memory served me well.

Just as the dragon's head started crashing down toward me, I threw up my arms to cover my face, screaming, "Midnight!"

The pain of being crushed in a dragon's jaws never came, and after a tense, silent pause, I found the courage to lower my arms. Night Phoenix's head was hovering only inches above me, so large that it blotted out the sun. It inhaled deeply to get my scent, and then let out a warm puff of air as it backed off, turning its head to get a better look at me with one of its huge eyes.

In the corner of my vision, I could see Denig, Ava, Nira, and Rhien struggling to their feet. Night Phoenix caught the movement too, and though it didn't turn on any of them, one of its gleaming eyes locked onto them, a warning rumble sounding from its chest.

"It's alright," I whispered, not daring to raise my voice any louder as I slowly sat up. "Midnight," I repeated. The dragon's gaze fixed on me again, and I could see the confusion in its focus. "You don't know me," I said, steadily working to my feet. "But I know you."

I stood, holding my breath as Night Phoenix turned its head to the side, getting so close to me that I could see my own reflection in the golden eye it was studying me with. It had been so long since my ancestor's memory, surely hundreds of years longer than a dragon's lifespan, and I doubted this was the exact Night Phoenix I'd met in the memory. Whether it had been reborn once or twice, or more times than that, this *wasn't* Midnight, not truly. I couldn't even be sure it remembered exactly where it had heard that name, or if its memories were reborn with it. But the mind masters had told me that memories lived on in blood, and in some way, in some instinct, Night Phoenix remembered that name.

"Gods, you've grown." I stretched out a cautious hand, gradually bringing it closer and closer, until the dragon let me touch the side of its long snout. The moment my palm set on its smooth scales, it turned to face me straight on, the spikes along its neck and back rested flat against its body, and its eyes drifted shut as it pressed up against my hand. "There you go," I said with a laugh, stroking between the tip of its pointed nose and the middle of its eyes. "We're here as friends." Night Phoenix made a soft chittering noise, a familiar rapid clicking sound that left its nose, and one I knew to be friendly.

I glanced over at my companions, taking in the shock on each of their faces. Nira and Rhien were staring in awe, Denig was grinning triumphantly, and Skif's mouth had fallen open. Ava, however, appeared uncertain of how to feel. She was in awe, clearly, but behind that fascination was a deep sense of concern. I smiled at her, motioning her to me with my free hand. It took a while for her to work up the courage, but eventually she tiptoed over, standing behind me to peer around my shoulder at Night Phoenix.

"Are you hurt?" I asked, quiet enough not to disturb the dragon, even though it had opened one eye to watch Ava – something she was so nervous about that she barely shook her head. "Would you like to touch it?" She hesitated for a long span of seconds before nodding, but she still wasn't confident enough to do it on her own. "Give me your hand," I encouraged.

She held out her hand, and I took it in my own while I moved behind her, guiding it out and onto the same place I'd been petting only moments before. She took in an amazed breath the second her palm touched down, and it was all she needed to begin stroking the dragon's snout of her own accord. "Night Phoenix," she whispered. The dragon's eyes shifted upward, and even from behind her, I could tell that they were looking right at each other. "You're extraordinary." The dragon's head dropped with a thud, so that its chin was set flat on the ground, and its eyes narrowed to slits as it let out a heavy, content sigh.

"I think it likes you," Denig chuckled.

"Look!" Nira exclaimed, and we all looked at her only to see that she was pointing toward the entrance of the caves.

There was another dragon there, with only its head sticking out and the rest of it hidden in darkness, but I recognized it from its description. Rich brown eyes, scales the deep green of the forest. It was Pine Shadow, and when he saw it, Denig took a few joyful steps forward.

"Hello, old friend," he said, and the dragon recognized him.

It slithered out of the cave in a fashion vastly different from the way Night Phoenix had, and it was far more beautiful than I could have imagined. Its emerald flesh wasn't as glossy as Night Phoenix's, but it looked just as smooth, and in the light of the sun, its large brown eyes appeared immensely deep. It was winged, but rather than having two powerful wings between its front shoulders, Pine Shadow's extended down the sides of its body. They stretched out in width at the middle of its back, but swooped inward and hugged close along its ribs, and then fanned out again halfway down its tail, like a swallow. At the end of its tail was another sort of fan, spreading out horizontally. The bone structure and vein systems in each of these wings were the same brown as its eyes and belly, while the translucent flesh was as green as the rest of it.

Where Night Phoenix's chest was broad and deep, and its long neck ended at its boxy head, the shape of Pine Shadow's body was far more lizard-like. Its entire belly hovered only a foot off the ground, and it moved forward on its four short limbs, reaching Denig and wrapping its great body around where he was standing. Its wings tucked into its sides, and the bark-colored horns on the back of each side of its head were laid flat as it stretched up toward Denig's hand. It had another horn above the tip of its tail, a sort of barb, which must have been the spike Denig said the dragon had defended him with.

"I remember you too," Denig laughed, and passed that grin to me. "We knew they were docile."

"At my initial greeting," I said with a smile, "I'm inclined to call it luck."

He laughed again, glancing behind him at our companions. "Skif, would you like a feel?"

"I'm quite alright," Skif called, having yet to move from where he'd retreated. "I'm satisfied with a look..."

"Nira?" Denig prompted. "Rhien?"

They both jumped at the chance, hurrying over to admire Pine Shadow. While they did, I felt a steady breeze pick up. It was cold enough this high on the mountain that it chilled me to the core, and the wind was so swift that it sang in the air. Night Phoenix seemed particularly interested. It left the gentleness of Ava's hand to raise its head high. Its eyes closed, and for a long minute, it simply listened. The dragon's focus and the breeze itself felt oddly familiar to me, but I couldn't quite place why.

Not much time passed before the breeze died down, and Night Phoenix looked back down at us. Then it dropped. It fell as flat to the earth as it could, extending one wing while its tail reached around, all the way to the back of Ava and me, pulling us toward it. It was almost as though it wanted us to climb onto its back, and I realized that Pine Shadow had done the same when I glanced over at the others.

"Do you know why we've come?" I asked Night Phoenix. "Does this mean you'll help?"

It made that chittering noise through its nose, giving us another nudge with its tail. I saw nothing else to do but what it wanted, and I couldn't deny that the idea of riding a dragon was thrilling in its own right. I used its outstretched wing to climb onto its back, sitting at the base of its neck, and then helped Ava climb up too. Nira came over to get on behind Ava, while Rhien stayed with Pine Shadow and Denig. It took some pleading and lots of encouragement for them to convince Skif to get on as well, but before long every one of us was seated. Night Phoenix gave one beat of its wings, but it was so powerful that it lifted us off the ground.

"Oh, no," Ava muttered as another beat took us higher from the earth. "No, no, no." Her arms wrapped tight around my waist, and I felt her face bury into the back of my shoulder.

Nira, on the other hand, was hooting with excitement, which more closely mirrored what I was feeling myself. In mere seconds, we were soaring down the mountain, over the tops of trees and at such a speed that the wind was stealing tears from my eyes. Everything below us looked small, and I could see the village in the distance, and this is what Ava must have been talking about. This is what she'd seen as a crow, and it *was* exhilarating.

The ride hardly lasted minutes, and then we were swooping toward the earth, outside the village enough that our location was hidden amongst the trees. Night Phoenix thudded down on the ground, and the three of us climbed off as the others did the same. Skif retreated a safe distance from the dragons once he was down, but the rest of us were comfortable enough by now to linger.

"Looks like we've got what we needed," I told Denig and Skif, reaching out to touch Night Phoenix's snout.

"We'll fetch your horses," Skif volunteered, seeming all too eager to get away.

But Night Phoenix's tail came around again, drawing me nearer to it. "I suppose we've got a different means of travel now," I laughed.

"Do come back," Skif told me, and were he not so afraid still of the dragons, I was certain he'd have come over to shake my hand or hug me. "I'm sure there's so much we could teach you."

"Thank you for everything," I said, and my companions nodded their agreement.

Skif glanced over at Denig expectantly, waiting for him to say his goodbyes too, but he didn't. He looked from Skif to me, around the group, and then at the dragons. He thought quietly to himself with an intense focus in his green eyes, and eventually told Skif, "I'm going with them."

Skif choked on air, coughing through his shock. "What?" And that shock was reflected on each of our faces as well.

"You heard what Ava said," Denig replied. "If they lose this fight, the king will likely come for the dragons. It's our duty to protect them in whatever ways necessary." As he spoke, Pine Shadow slid up beneath his hand, and he set it on the dragon's head. "Right now, that way is by going to war." He met my gaze as though seeking permission, and I nodded my eager consent.

"But Denig, *war?*" Skif whined. "We've never been to war." Denig made no reply. While it seemed as though he and Skif were nearly inseparable friends, Denig appeared determined to do this no matter what. Skif had to know that, because he glanced back and forth between us, weighing his options. He took in a breath as if to make another protest. Whimpered his reluctance. Glanced between the dragons and grabbed the pendant around his neck. He whimpered again and threw his hands up. "*Fine.*"

I couldn't keep a massive grin off my face, and when I met Ava's eyes, they were full of a similar relief. Three Dragonkin were most certainly better than one, just as two dragons were better than one. And I suddenly felt a lot more confident about the outcome of this war.

Chapter 24

n Night Phoenix's back, we were soaring through the low, overcast clouds. It had taken us long enough to find the dragons that, had we traveled to Cornwall on horseback, we'd have arrived later than I'd promised Kingston. It was fortunate, then, that the dragons were more than willing to carry us the distance. Our speed was *so* much greater than it would have been with the horses. We'd stayed the night in the mountain village and only been traveling since this morning, but we were already nearly at the castle in Cornwall.

Even Ava trusted the dragons more, and had grown comfortable enough by now that she was no longer hiding her face in my shoulder. She and Nira were reaching out behind me, making a game of trying to catch the clouds. In fact, the only one who didn't seem thrilled with our means of travel, aside from Skif, was Haunt. She was strewn sideways over Night Phoenix's neck just in front of my lap, and in the rare moments that her one eye wasn't lidded with sickness, it was casting me indignant glares.

It had been an amazing journey, going over the Amalgam Plains instead of around them. The oranges and reds of the desert were a brilliant mix of colors I'd never seen but in a sunset. The marshes were dark and mysterious even under the light of the sun. The stony mountains were jagged and tall, spotted with trees and rivers and great waterfalls. It was the kind of place I could see the danger in trying to cross, but beautiful enough from above that I could also see why people risked it.

Luckily for Haunt, before long and nearing midafternoon, we were descending. We dropped beneath the clouds and came into view of everything below, casting a swift shadow on the ground as we traveled. We passed over the final range to the mountain-surrounded land that was

Cornwall. The castle was so large that if I squinted I could see it in the distance, carved into an encasing mountain. And as we got closer, I could see that what looked from far away like scattered lines of boulders and trees weren't boulders and trees at all. They were people. Armies.

Two armies were visible as we neared Cornwall's capital. The first was just outside the castle walls. It was vast and broad, and littered with such a mix of Valens's red and gold and Cornwall's blue and gray that it made my stomach drop. They weren't fighting, which could only mean that our rebel army had arrived too late. Whether Hazlitt had conquered Cornwall or the soldiers had simply surrendered, a majority of them were now fighting for Hazlitt.

The sight of the second army, however, was enough to lift my spirits. It was our army camped over a mile away from the castle walls. It was the Vigilant, and our numbers were so much greater than I ever could have imagined. I'd heard talk of how large our army had grown – though some still doubted it being big enough – but it was something else entirely to see the thickness of it. To see the wide expanse of our fighters, which almost rivaled the size of Hazlitt's combined army, ready and waiting.

As we got closer to the Vigilant camps, I spotted the largest tent flying the commander's flag, and shouted to Night Phoenix to drop down near it. The soldiers in the immediate area cleared spots big enough for the dragons to land, all looking a mixture of confused and terrified and defensive. Some of them ran as we touched down. The rest crowded around in a massive circle, some of them too stunned and curious to have run, while others pulled their weapons.

"Hold your fire!" I hollered to the archers, and they lowered their bows when they recognized me as murmurs went up around the camp.

Haunt slid off of Night Phoenix's back first, retching with nausea as I reached the ground after her, and she made sure to glare at me at least once more. While Ava and Nira got off, Kingston rushed out of the tent to see what all the commotion was about. His eyes locked on the dragons, widening with shock and awe as a smile reached the corner of his open mouth. When his eyes finally met mine, I hurried over, so overcome at the unexpected size of our army and the pride in his expression that I didn't know what else to do. I hugged him, feeling his arms wrap around me while his hand slapped my back with uncontainable excitement.

361

"I can't believe it," he muttered, letting me go. "You did it." He stared at the dragons again. "You *really* did it." His eyes filled with amazed tears and he grabbed my shoulders, looking like he wanted to give me another hug. "Your father would be so proud of you."

"Of *us*," I told him, making a deliberate glance at the vastness of our army camp.

He smiled a wide, beaming grin, and cleared his throat to rid the emotion from his voice. "Well, we've not won yet." His hands fell from my shoulders, and he glanced around at my gathered companions, finally noticing Denig and Skif. "Hello?"

"They're still there, Kingston," I told him, motioning for Denig and Skif to step forward. "The people in the village you told me about. They still protect the dragons after all this time." I motioned to our new friends. "This is Denig, and Skif. They've come to fight with us." As they stuck out their hands to shake with him, I told them, "This is our commander, Kingston."

"Come," Kingston instructed the moment he finished the introductions. "Now that you're here, we have no time to waste."

Before we all started for the tent, I turned to Night Phoenix, giving the dragon a grateful pat on the snout. "You can wait in the mountains outside camp if you'd like." And it nudged up against my hand and took off into the air with Pine Shadow.

"Are we the last to arrive?" Nira asked while Kingston led us all into his tent. He nodded, motioning us around the war table set up at the center, with a large replica of the castle on top, and we all spread out around it.

"And Hazlitt's already infiltrated the castle," I predicted.

"Yes," Kingston confirmed. "An inside source reported that it happened two days ago. That was yesterday." His chin dropped with the sign of loss. "We've not heard from him since."

"And Cornwall's rulers?" Nira asked.

"We've no word," Kingston said. "No idea whether they live or not."

"There may be hope," Ava told him, pausing until he motioned for her to continue. "Hazlitt's ultimate goal is to establish himself as High King." We all nodded. "He's cruel, and ruthless, but he's not stupid. I believe he would try to negotiate or force their allegiance before killing them – sway a ruler's loyalty, and their subjects follow more easily."

"If such were the case," Kingston agreed, "and given that Valens and Cornwall appear allied outside the castle walls, we must assume that Hazlitt got his allegiance." He glanced around at each of us. "This is no longer a rescue, but a conquering of our own."

"The plan, then?" I prompted.

"Our army goes head to head with Hazlitt's," Kingston answered, pointing along the outside of the castle walls on the model. "We keep them occupied while those of you who are willing infiltrate the castle." At that, he looked questioningly at Denig, Skif, and Rhien, because he already knew where Ava, Nira, and I stood.

"We're going," Denig said, and Skif nodded his agreement.

"I am too," Rhien said.

Nira set her hands on the edge of the table, leaning in with interest. "How do we do it?"

"There are three main entrances to the castle," Kingston began, showing us on the replica. Because it was carved into the mountain, the castle was longer and higher than it was deep. Its length was curved to follow the shape of the range, and there were massive entrances in the middle and on either side. The long bowed stretch between the two side entrances was only one floor, but there was a tower on each end that rose stories upward. "The throne room is here," he said, pointing to a place near the center of the castle, situated within the mountain. "You should enter at the heart of the castle and fight your way to the throne room. If luck is on our side, Hazlitt will be there."

"If not?" I asked.

"Then I'm not sure where he'll be," Kingston admitted. "He could be anywhere in the castle, and our insider is missing."

I glanced over at Ava, hoping she would know some bit of information, be it Hazlitt's habit or a better layout of the castle. When she recognized my searching gaze, she shook her head. "I'm sorry, I've never been to Cornwall."

"Nor I," Nira said when my eyes transferred to her.

"We will do everything we can to fight our way in and to you," Kingston continued. "But you'll be largely on your own, and Hazlitt will have troops beyond the walls and in the castle. Not to mention his magic, which we still have no idea about."

"We'll find a way," I assured him.

He nodded, pausing for a moment to look over the war table and think. "I have no doubt that they saw the dragons. It's a sight more intimidating than I thought it'd be." He reached over to a stack of parchment at the corner, pulling one to him and grabbing the quill from the inkwell beside it. "I'll send a messenger. We'll give them one hour to agree to our terms of surrender." We all watched while he scribbled out the message, and then whistled to call for a soldier, who came in to take the parchment. "Rhien," Kingston prompted when the soldier left, and she looked surprised at the fact that he was addressing her directly. "I received an earful from one of the masters for *sending* you to war."

Her eyes widened. "I am *so* sorry, Sir," she blurted, her face turning redder than even mine did when I was embarrassed. "My vows are *my* responsibility, they should not have brought that on you."

"Vows," Kingston repeated. "I do recall that being a theme of my reproach." But he was smiling as he reached down under the table, pulling up a small wooden chest the size of a bread loaf, which he set on the edge of the table with a thump. "And I believe it's why they sent this with me."

Rhien inhaled a shocked breath, reaching out to take the chest from him. "Bless them," she whispered, lifting the lid of the box. "I hadn't time..." She ran her hand over whatever was inside as she looked up, catching our curious expressions. "Potions," she explained, picking up a fist-sized, round glass vial, with a cloudy maroon mist inside and sealed with a cork. "Non-violent means of fighting, to help me keep my vows." She put it back only to grab another. "There are only a few, but it's better than none."

"Good," Kingston said, glancing around our group. "If I might speak with Kiena for a minute." They began to filter out, but as they passed through the exit, he seemed to have changed his mind. "Ava," he called, and she stopped and turned, making her way back to us. He didn't say anything right away once the others were gone, and instead simply stood there, staring directly between Ava and me like he couldn't quite bring himself to speak.

"Are you alright?" I asked.

He nodded, took a few more moments to collect his thoughts, and then met my gaze. "Kiena," he said, "your father died fighting for a better life, for *you*, and for your mother." He paused and swallowed hard. "But now you're here, defending what he couldn't." He glanced at Ava, gave her a small smile, and then returned his gaze to me. "You have both suffered. You should owe nothing more to your kingdom, or to this rebellion, but you're here, risking all that you've got left. I want you to know that I recognize it, and I'm at a loss to express the depth of my gratitude."

Both Ava and I nodded, and he looked over at her again. "Ava," he began, his voice low and gentle, "a casualty as grave as the queen's is not something which could escape my knowledge." Her chin dropped, and as if to assure her that he knew of her pain, and to offer comfort, he reached out and set a hand on her shoulder. "I can't imagine your grief, but not once during your imprisonment was our life in the caves threatened." She glanced up, meeting his eyes with shock that he knew exactly what she'd gone through. What she'd given. "You've displayed a strength of heart and will that I admire greatly." He paused, saying almost cautiously, "It's the kind of strength that could guide Valens to prosper..."

Ava's eyebrows furrowed as it sank in what Kingston was suggesting, and though her gaze fell and she didn't look at me, she reached out blindly and took my hand. "Thank you, Kingston," she said, meeting his eyes once more, "for your sympathy, your acknowledgment, and your faith. But if Kiena and I truly owe nothing more to our kingdom, then that's a sacrifice I should hope never to make. I have no desire to be queen, and the people of Valens deserve a ruler who is motivated to guide them." She smiled at him, saying with utmost confidence and sincerity, "They deserve a ruler who started fighting for them long before I was born. A ruler who has experience leading, and who's more than proved his devotion to their wellbeing."

When he realized what she was saying, Kingston did a double take. He looked from her to me, and then back again, blinking away his surprise. He took in a breath and his mouth fell open as if to say something, but he couldn't get anything out. It was as if the idea had never crossed his mind, as if he'd never pictured *himself* as king, nor thought it was a possibility, and surely all it did was prove that Ava's decision was well informed. It proved that all these years he hadn't been fighting for himself, but for our people, and that he'd continue to do so should he take the crown.

"Well..." Kingston managed eventually, but he was still in such shock that it didn't seem like he knew what else to say. "I'll give you two some time alone. Excuse me." And he paced out the exit of the tent.

"I think you flattered him," I chuckled.

"He deserves it," Ava laughed, glancing toward where he'd disappeared. "We're here because of him. This entire army is here because of him. He'd make a great ruler."

"You would have too," I assured her, "if it's what you'd wanted." I let go of her hand to turn toward her, and set my hands on her hips.

"Perhaps." She shrugged, stretching upward and slipping her arms around my neck. "But if I'm to be a ruler, the only thing I have any desire to rule over is a household."

"Is that right?" I laughed. "Do you foresee child subjects in this household?"

"Indeed," she answered, her lips curling with a smirk. "Twelve of them."

"Twelve!" I exclaimed, falling dramatically sideways against the war table. "Gods help me."

Ava giggled at that, and when I straightened up and leaned back against the table, she leaned herself forward against me. "I'm only joking," she said with a smile, wrapping her arms around my waist. "I should be satisfied with a couple."

"Alright," I agreed, taking her face in my hands. "A couple it is, then." I leaned down to give her a slow kiss, and couldn't help murmuring against her mouth, "But could I have you all to myself for a while first?"

Her lips thinned against mine with a smile, but she didn't stop kissing me long enough to answer, and simply released a soft hum of agreement. The kiss only lasted another short minute though, and then she pulled away to set her forehead against mine. In the sudden stillness of the war tent, I could feel the new stutter of fear in her heartbeat. I didn't know if it was because of everything she'd been through, or because we were about to face Hazlitt, or because she was afraid that one of us wouldn't make it through this, but my thumbs made soothing strokes over her cheeks while she did what she could with that fear. While I tried not to let my own fear of what we were about to face show.

"Is there a prayer to the earth gods?" she asked eventually. "For war?"

"Yes," I answered, leaning back enough to look her in the eyes. "But I don't believe it's the comfort you're searching for."

"Say it anyway," she requested.

I nodded, kissed her, and took in a breath. "Should I prosper in this battle," I began to recite, and her hands came up to set against the backs of mine, "gods, I ask of you: please forgive the lives I've taken, and let their spirits be at peace. May those they've loved not curse my soul, and their deaths not be in vain. But gods, if I should perish, I beg you much the same: forgive the one who shed my blood, and watch over those who've stayed. Please bring them joy someday without me, and may my death be worth their pain." I thumbed away the single tear that slid down her cheek. "To war."

She took a few moments to sniffle away the moisture in her eyes, and then whispered, "Are you certain?" She dropped her hands from mine to wrap her arms around my waist again. "Are you certain that we'll get our future together?"

I knew better than to promise, and I knew that she couldn't promise me either. "When you first met me, Ava, I was afraid to want things. I was terrified of wanting you. But you've shown me that life isn't worth living without it." I pressed the most comforting kiss I could to her forehead. "There's nothing I want more than a life with you, and what I'm certain of is that I'll fight with everything I have to make sure I get it."

She nodded, but her fingers were clutching tight at the small part of my lower back that was exposed by my armor. "We'll do this together," she reminded me almost pleadingly.

"Not as either of us intended," I agreed with a small smile, adding, "but as we always have."

Ava smiled, managing to kiss me one more time before someone outside shouted, "We've received a reply!" We hurried out of the tent, standing next to our friends, Haunt, and Kingston, while soldiers crowded around to hear the response. The messenger who was holding the parchment in his hands unfolded it, held it before him, and cleared his throat. "To the rebels!" he read in a yell. "To the force that declares themselves the Vigilant! We hereby reject your terms of surrender, and offer one of our own! Lay down your arms and swear fealty to the High King, His Royal Highness Hazlitt Gaveston, and not a one will be harmed! Refusal of these terms will be punishable by death!"

First a murmur went up around the camp as soldiers passed the message further back, and then there was uproar. But it wasn't because our rebels were afraid of Hazlitt's threat. They were outraged.

"Quiet!" Kingston shouted, raising one hand to signal for silence. It took a few moments for the outcry to die down. "Vigilant!" He yelled at the top of his voice so as many troops as possible could hear him. "This is what we've trained for! The moment we've waited so patiently for! Some of us all our lives! While we built our army in the shadows, Hazlitt spat in our faces! He attacked our homes! His own people! And he wants to punish us with death?" There was a rumble of spiteful laughter from the troops. "We! Know! Death!" Kingston roared, and a shout of agreement went up from the soldiers. "I think it's nigh time we brought that death to our High King's doorstep!"

A deafening pandemonium of shouts sounded throughout the camp, but even as it traveled so far that I was sure our enemy soldiers could hear it, it was overpowered by another deafening sound. Night Phoenix's roar. The dragon screeched its deep, earth-shaking cry while it and Pine Shadow swooped down. They landed in the space that soldiers cleared out behind us, and while Pine Shadow slithered up beneath Denig's hand, Night Phoenix's head hung mere feet above mine. And the dragon added to the continuous thunder of our rallied troops, so that it echoed off the enclosing mountains around us. So that I was certain if the enemy soldiers didn't already regret refusing to surrender, then they would soon.

As we stood there preparing to march, I felt Ava's fingers slip through mine, and beneath the clamor of battle cries, she recited two words as she squeezed my hand. "To war."

Chapter 25

he soldiers began to march, chanting and yelling. The battle cries that echoed all around us were enough to make *me* nervous, and these warriors were my allies. I couldn't imagine that our rivals weren't getting anxious. We stood there and watched for a minute as our entire camp stirred to life, letting some of them clear before we'd take off on the dragons. During that minute, Kingston had retrieved his horse, and he walked over with it to say his final goodbyes.

"Be careful," he said, glancing at each and every one of us. He shoved his helmet down over his head and mounted his horse. "We'll meet again when this is done."

He kicked his heels back and began to trot off, and I hurried to kneel down to Haunt. "That's our future king," I told the wolf. "I want you to go after him. Keep him alive, no matter what." I reached out to scratch behind her ear. "Keep yourself alive too." Haunt pressed affectionately against my hand for half a second, and then she was off after Kingston.

I stood again, and I didn't need to say anything to my companions for them to know that it was time. We all turned, climbing onto Night Phoenix's and Pine Shadow's backs, and we were soaring toward the castle within seconds. We flew over our troops, over the sea of enemy soldiers advancing to meet them, and then straight over the cobbled castle walls, where we passed over all the other stone buildings beyond them until we reached the castle. As we descended, I leaned farther over Night Phoenix's shoulder to get a better look at the ground below, nearly meeting the head of an arrow.

The arrow flew right by my face, and another passed by my knee, glancing off the dragon's sturdy scales. The large yard beyond the walls was littered with soldiers, at least sixty, and the few archers I could see were already firing relentlessly. Our fight had begun.

"Nira!" I yelled over my shoulder as Night Phoenix brought us closer to the ground, "we've got the archers!"

I heard her shout an affirmative as the dragons landed at the heart of the yard. Night Phoenix immediately snapped a soldier up in its jaws, and one of Nira's arrows hit the first archer up on a tower. I pulled my dagger and spark jumped off the dragon's back to the next nearest archer, grabbing his neck with a current while I searched for my second target.

Skif was hurling fire at enemy troops and covering Denig, who'd turned into a bear and was swiping and charging through multiple men at once. Ava and Rhien – who'd transferred her vials of potions to a small bag over her shoulder – had taken defensive positions on either side of Nira, blocking her from close range attacks while she helped take out the archers. It was the best decision we'd ever made, going to find the dragons. Not only were they devouring men faster than I could blink, but they were drawing most of the archers' fire as well.

I spark jumped onto a tower, burying my dagger in the heart of a bowman and then immediately vaulting back to the ground. I landed in front of an archer who'd been about to fire at Denig, knocking her aim off and then shooting her with current. Just as I turned to move on, Skif reached where I was standing, and curled himself around me to block the arrow of the last archer. The arrow bounced off his impenetrable flesh, and before the archer could wind up again, Denig had reached him.

Now that all the archers were taken care of, I swiveled around to check on Ava, and what I saw made me freeze in awe for an entire handful of seconds. I'd watched her fight only twice – the first day I found out she could wield a sword, while she was practicing with a rebel, and again on occasion of the competitions at the caves – but it was something else to actually *see* her in the midst of battle. Her skill lay not in her strength or her speed. The soldiers who came at her were larger and stronger, and she didn't beat them by matching their aggressions.

The brilliance of her defensive technique was in her intelligence and her perception. She could read body language and movement perfectly, and in the split moment it took her to predict the soldier's next blow, she'd already decided how to deflect it. Ava knocked the sword's swing off course, leaving the soldier's upper body unguarded. And she brought her

370

sword hand around through the swing, smashing the hilt of it against the man's temple and instantly knocking him unconscious. The next soldier that came at her, she deflected much the same way, only this time she didn't get the same opening to knock the woman out. Ava pushed her toward Rhien instead, and Rhien sidestepped the soldier's sword and grabbed the woman's head, putting her right to sleep and then passing a beaming grin at Ava.

It was spectacular, and I'd have stood there all day admiring and thinking that maybe they *could* get through this battle without bloodshed, but I caught movement heading my direction. I spark jumped backward to avoid the point of the poleax a soldier had charged me with, and then I flicked my wrist, wrapped a static coil around him, and threw him upward. It hadn't been my intention when Night Phoenix caught the man in its jaws in midair, but it worked just as well...

"Retreat!" came a holler near the entrance of the castle, and one of the enemy soldiers was waving frantically. "Inside! Beyond the dragons' rea-" One of Pine Shadow's long spikes got him before he could finish, and Night Phoenix whipped his impressive tail, knocking back the first few soldiers who tried to run for the door.

The enemy troops on the outskirts started sprinting for the entrances on either far side of the long yard, but the ones nearer to us couldn't run in time. We finished off the last handful of them, and then I paused long enough to take in the state of my companions. Denig and Skif hadn't a scratch between the two of them; Rhien was pulling up her chainmail and tunic to look at the forming bruise across her side, where the chainmail she was wearing had saved her from being cut; Nira was taking stock of her dwindling supply of arrows; and Ava was poking with the toe of her boot at the soldier Rhien had put to sleep, perhaps to see if the woman would wake.

Without any more enemies out here for the dragons to fight, I turned to Night Phoenix, stretching out my hand to touch its snout. "Would you go and fight with our troops beyond the walls?" Night Phoenix made that friendly clicking noise. "Thank you." The dragons soared into the air and disappeared over the wall. "Everyone alright?" I asked. Each of them nodded, and we headed for the open doors.

"Off to a good start," Skif observed as we strode through.

"Let's keep it that way," Nira agreed.

We stopped inside the massive entrance hall of the castle, glancing up and down the halls to check for soldiers. There were none, and so I motioned for the others to follow as we headed off in the direction of the throne room. We paced through the corridors until we reached another section where the ceilings were high, and at the back of the circular foyer were the throne room doors. The area was deserted, but only for a few moments longer. There was the sound of heavy footsteps echoing from either direction.

"The soldiers?" Rhien guessed, and I nodded, because surely the enemies who'd retreated from the courtyard would try to cut us off.

"We're in a bad spot here," Nira said, glancing around the hall we were standing in. There were the doors behind us that led to the throne room, but we couldn't retreat through them in case Hazlitt was there. If I had a choice, I wouldn't face him with the distraction of other soldiers around.

I looked around at where we were, and then down each of the curved halls where the thudding of footsteps were getting closer. "Get to the edges of the hall," I ordered, and as we scattered, added, "Rhien, I trust you know what to do."

She looked confused for all of a moment before her eyes widened with recognition, and she gave a sharp nod. "Nobody move," she said once we'd each plastered ourselves against the walls, "I've got this, and remember to hold your breath." She searched the sack over her shoulder for a specific round vial, and pulled it out as her lips moved with the same phrase she'd said in the mountains of the Amalgam Plains – the one that had made us invisible to Denig and Skif – and then she held the vial up to her mouth. She murmured something to it, and the red mist inside turned black.

The footsteps reached us, and from both halls in either direction came a flood of the remaining soldiers from the courtyard. They filtered in ready to attack, but as each one came into the hall and found it seemingly empty, they slowed, searching around in surprise.

"They're not here!" one of them shouted, while the rest collected at the center of the hall. He paced down the opposite side he'd come, peering down it as if to see if the other soldiers had somehow passed us by, and then turned around to survey the gathered troops.

My eyes dashed across the hall to Rhien. She was poised with the vial over her head, prepared to throw it toward the group, but it looked like

372

she was waiting for that last man to return. For him to get closer so she could be sure this would work. Only, he didn't. He glared over his shoulder at the empty corridor, then again at the soldiers.

"Get upstairs," he commanded, finally stomping back to the middle, "search the corridors and warn the others."

Before the soldiers could leave position, Rhien lobbed the vial toward the center of the crowd. I held my breath as the glass shattered loudly, and in an instant the entire hall was filled with that black mist. The soldiers erupted in panic, choking on their shouts as they dropped unconscious one by one. It took long enough that my lungs started to burn, but I refrained from inhaling until the last one had fallen.

Then Rhien stepped forward, called, "Tuslypa," and clapped her hands together and brushed them outward. The mist turned red and began to clear, but just before it did, Skif had fallen right to his face.

"Looks like he forgot to hold his breath," Nira chuckled, and bear-Denig gave an amused snort.

"Can you wake him?" I asked Rhien while Ava and I met them on the opposite side of the hall.

Rhien nodded and squatted down near Skif's head. "Awresi," she whispered, snapping her fingers.

Skif's eyes shot open, and then squeezed shut again as he realized what happened and groaned, "Ow."

"She did warn you," I laughed, watching him push off the ground.

Once he reached his feet, he bent over to put his hands on his knees, his head lolling tiredly. "Gods that's heavy," he mumbled. He shook the grogginess out and straightened once more, rubbing at the spot of his face he'd fallen on. "I've never been affected by magic before. Can't say I'm keen on it."

"We'll move on when you're ready," I told him.

He waved it off with the hand that wasn't rubbing his face. "I'm ready."

At that, we turned toward the doors at the rear of the hall. Nira was the first to reach them, and she grabbed the handle and gave it a hard tug. It didn't budge. She pulled harder, so forcefully that the door shook in its frame, but it wouldn't come open. "Locked," she complained, and in case Hazlitt was hiding on the other side, she kicked it. "Coward!" She sighed and turned to us. "Now what?"

"I could burn it down," Skif suggested, rapping his knuckles against the thick wood.

"It would fill the castle with smoke," Ava said, shaking her head, "alerting anyone upstairs who doesn't know we're here yet of our presence."

Nira looked at me. "Could you use those gripping sparks of yours to twist it open?"

"The lock?" I asked. "Not a chance. If anything, I'd break it and we'd never get in." But something else occurred to me. "Let me see," I said.

I stepped up to the doors, setting my palm flat against the brass frame of the keyhole. In the stillness that followed as my companions watched silently, I closed my eyes and reached out with my magic, searching for something I couldn't see, but may be able to feel. It took a minute, but then I *did* feel it – the corruption. There was corrosion deep in the inner workings of the lock. With that hold of my magic, I spread it through the metal, decaying it far beyond use and eating it through every piece of metal it touched, until even the brass frame had turned a sickly green and I could feel that it was falling apart. I gave the handle a wrench and the door broke free.

"Here we go," I whispered, taking in a quick breath to maintain my nerve, because if Hazlitt was just beyond, then it was finally time. I pulled it open.

No sooner than I had, an arrow came flying out of the throne room, and it hit bear-Denig straight in the upper part of his chest. We all fell to the sides of the entrance to avoid being shot, but Denig let out a fury-filled roar and went blasting through. I peered around the corner of the doorframe to watch as he charged the single archer inside, taking one more arrow to the shoulder before crushing the man in his massive jaws. The rest of us rushed in, casting suspicious looks around as we paced to the far end where Denig was.

It was empty, and Rhien pointed at the man and asked, "What was he doing in here alone?"

"Hiding," Nira said, turning a full circle to search the throne room.

There was nothing in here but the massive thrones and the decorations. There was nowhere to hide that we couldn't see. Hazlitt wasn't here. "He could be anywhere," I muttered, my lips pursing angrily.

"What do you propose we do?" Skif asked, pulling the first arrow out of bear-Denig's chest so he could heal. He reached for the second arrow while I considered our options, and Denig rumbled with pain when it was yanked free.

"There are two sides of this castle," I thought out loud, "and there's no telling which end he's on." They all nodded in understanding. "The faster we end this, the faster we end the war. I doubt Cornwall's soldiers will keep fighting once Hazlitt's dead. His own troops may surrender as well."

There was a silent pause, and then Ava realized what I was thinking. "You want us to split up…"

"If we go three and three," I explained, "we'll find him faster. Denig and Skif may be just as well-equipped to handle him as I am."

"I'm for it," Skif said, and Denig huffed his agreement.

"I'll go with them," Nira volunteered, passing us a smile, "a gold coin says we find him first."

"Joke's on you," I chuckled. "Can't say I've *ever* had a gold coin."

She laughed, and then paced forward and startled Ava with a fierce hug. "Be safe," she said, moving on to embrace me, "all of you." She hugged Rhien last and turned for the door, calling at Denig and Skif, "Come on, mountain boys, let's hunt us a High King."

They left and veered to the rightward corridor, and Ava, Rhien, and I headed into the opposite one without a word. As we traveled down the long lower hall of the castle, it was clear that Hazlitt hadn't been a welcome guest upon his arrival. There were scattered bodies of Cornwall soldiers who'd fought his infiltration, as well as the occasional staff member that we saw hiding through an open door. One woman in the massive kitchen was crouching toward the rear of a brick oven, and all she did when she noticed that we'd seen her was sink farther behind it.

We journeyed to the very end, reaching the stairs without meeting a single live enemy. There wasn't a soul on our way up either, and not until we reached the end of the steps did we finally see someone. I peered around at the top, at the hall that wrapped around the corner that the stairs opened upon, and caught a glimpse of two soldiers heading straight for us. I drew back, motioning Ava and Rhien down until we were hidden from view. The soldiers' footsteps drew nearer, eventually echoing past the stairwell to continue around the corner to the left side, and I crept back up to get a good look at the corridors.

375

Those two that were patrolling weren't the only soldiers on the floor. There were two more halfway down the right side that were standing in front of a door, two more across from them, and I could hear a handful of voices and a loud ruckus coming from an open door on the left. I crept back a bit until we were out of sight once more.

"There are two soldiers patrolling the halls," I whispered to Ava and Rhien. "A number in one of the rooms, and four guarding a door."

"Guarding?" Rhien repeated.

"Hazlitt could be in there," Ava said.

"Perhaps," I agreed. "But we can't go out without being seen. There's nowhere to hide and I don't know how many are in that open room. Or even how many could be in the guarded room to protect Hazlitt." I'd have tried to reach out with my magic and feel heartbeats to take a count, but the stone was too thick for me to get a read. I paused and held up my hand so nobody would speak, because I could hear the footsteps of the patrolling soldiers heading our way again. It took a few moments for them to pass by our location.

"I've got a potion that might be able to help," Rhien said once the troops had passed us. "It'll give us an opening to reach the door."

"Without alerting the others?" Ava asked.

Rhien gave a side-to-side nod. "If we can get in the room quick enough, it'll give us enough time to secure ourselves in it."

"When the patrollers pass," I instructed, and hearing their footsteps already returning, I motioned toward Rhien's bag. "Quickly."

She reached in and pulled out another round vial, raised it near her lips and whispered, "Heftes nauwran."

There had been a white mist inside of it, but at the words, the mist collected, turning into what looked like vibrating purple sand. Instead of throwing the vial like she'd done last time, Rhien uncorked it and poured the sand into her palm, clutching it tight so none of it would escape. She inched past Ava and me to get at the head. The patrolling soldiers got closer, walked right past our hiding place, and continued on. The moment they'd gone, Rhien leaned out of the stairwell just enough to get a clear view down the right corridor. She opened her hand toward the soldiers at the door, and blew the sand from her grip.

It hit the floor, and wafted down the hall on some invisible wind toward the men until it reached their boots. It crawled upward beneath their trousers, and the moment that I imagined it hit skin, every one of them went stiff. Their arms stuck straight to their sides, their eyes went wide, and their lips pursed together. It was as though an invisible force had bound them, and every one of them tried to fight it. They wriggled in the magic's grip, but were so stiff from it that they couldn't balance, and one by one each of the four toppled to the ground.

Rhien tossed a brief look down the left hall, and seeing that the patrollers were still moving away from us, she rushed out. Ava and I were right behind her as she raced toward the squirming soldiers on the ground. I tried the door they were guarding and found it locked, and we immediately set to searching the soldiers' pockets for the keys. In our haste, it took less than a couple of seconds for Ava to find them, and she unlocked the door and threw it open. There was a shout from the inside as the single occupant came charging at us with a sword, so I spark jumped behind him and reached out.

"Wait, don't!" Ava hissed in panic, and I don't know if she was talking to the man or to me, but both of us froze. Even more, the man instantly lowered his weapon and straightened out of his attack pose.

Rhien cleared her throat loudly as she tried to drag a soldier's body through the door, and seeing as the man had ceased his assault, I rushed past him to help her before the patrollers could come back around. I flicked my wrist and wrapped each of the stiff soldiers in static, dragged them into the room, and left Rhien to close and lock the door. I returned to Ava's side to finally look at the man. He was young – I couldn't imagine more than a couple of years older than myself – tall, and very handsome. He had light brown hair and gentle gray eyes, and the kind of sharp jawline on his clean-shaven face to make any man envious.

"Avarona?" he asked, thick eyebrows meeting with complete and utter confusion.

"Destrian..." Ava breathed, sounding just as surprised as he did.

But he recovered from his shock, immediately raising his sword again. "Why are you here?" he demanded. "Are you with your father?"

"We're *not* with Hazlitt," Ava answered. "We're here to stop him."

He gave a dry laugh, shaking his sword toward her. "You tricked me once," he accused. "Exploited my affections so we'd turn a blind eye to your father's vile ambition." He glared, gripping his weapon a little tighter. Even without his accusation, it was clear who he was – the prince of

Cornwall. The man Ava had been prepared to marry if it would get her away from Guelder, and he clearly wasn't happy about having been used. "What now?" he asked. "I suppose you've come to persuade me of what he couldn't, to play to your charms." He shook his head, passing a direct and disdainful look up the length of her body. "It won't work. No matter what he's convinced you to offer."

I took an angry step forward, prepared to put him in his place for making suggestions like that, or for implying that Ava would help Hazlitt win this war when we were here to stop him, but Ava reached out and grabbed my hand. "Don't," she told me in a murmur, gently pulling me back to her. "I deserved that."

The prince's gaze wandered from Ava to our hands, and I could see the consideration in his eyes as he looked at me.

"Destrian," Ava prompted, letting me go and stepping toward him, "I am sorry for my deceit last summer. It was wrong, and you never deserved it, but I swear to you that my intention wasn't malicious. I had no knowledge of Hazlitt's design." She took another step forward, carefully brushing aside the point of his sword. "You can stay bitter toward me, but now is not the time to let personal grievances interfere with our common goal." She turned enough to point at the soldiers I'd dragged in. "We fought our way in here," she said, as if that would prove we weren't with Hazlitt, and then offered her hand in reparation. "Help us fight our way to Hazlitt."

He stared at her for almost a minute while he considered her apology, and then he glanced past her at Rhien and me. After a few more tense seconds, the prince nodded, and he'd just grabbed Ava's hand to shake with her when there was a shout from the hall.

"They know we're here," Rhien said, and as if in response, there was a heavy thud against the door, followed by more shouting. "The door won't hold forever."

"What was Hazlitt trying to persuade you of?" I asked the prince urgently, and I pulled my dagger to prepare for a fight.

"Loyalty," Destrian answered. "Said he'd make me king and spare my mother if I swore allegiance to him."

"But he'd kill your father?" Ava asked, turning away from the prince to face the door, and there was another heavy thud and more yelling from the other side.

Destrian nodded. "But it wasn't just my word he wanted. He wanted a blood oath, given with some sort of magic. It'd kill me if I ever betrayed him. That's why I refused." Another crack against the door, and the wood strained as it began to break. "He's taken my parents to the dungeon below the castle, but if I know them at all, they won't give him what he wants either." This time, the thud against the door was enough to put a hole near the handle, and the prince gripped his sword in both hands. "I doubt it'll be long before he kills them both and declares a ruler of his choosing."

"We'll go straight there if you lead the way," I said.

The next thud broke the door from its frame. It swung open, and nine soldiers burst in with their weapons drawn. The first one through the door passed by close to Rhien, and she touched her hand to the man's head and he dropped unconscious. The rest of them spread out, two of them coming right for me. It was too close in this room to spark jump, so I drew my sword instead, and had it out just in time to counter the first soldier's swing. I deflected the blow, having to block right away again as he left no chance for a counter.

The very moment my sword met the man's, the second one got behind me and slashed. I turned just in time to twist away from the sharp edge of the sword, but it still cut across my armor, slicing a gash halfway through the thick leather. I flicked my wrist, wrapping him in static and pulling him forward as I sidestepped out of the way. It impaled him on his ally's weapon, and as the first soldier struggled to pull his sword free, I grabbed his arm with a current of sparks.

The fight around me was nearly over too, and as Ava and Rhien helped each other to subdue the last soldier, I met the prince's gaze. His gray eyes were wide, and there was a smile at one corner of his mouth. "Nicely done!" he praised, casting an amused glance at the man I'd shocked.

I looked down at the slash across my chest. "Not nice enough..."

He turned that interested look on Ava. "Do you have magic too? Like your father?"

"He's *not-*" Ava began to say, but stopped and let out an almost irritated sigh. "I don't." That wasn't entirely true since she could turn into a crow, but it didn't look like she wanted to explain. "Take us to the dungeon."

The prince led the way out the door. We backtracked down the stairs, but instead of heading along the corridor to the main entrance hall that we'd come from in the first place, we exited the castle out the side entrance.

"The door's just there," Destrian said, pointing at a wooden door halfway between where we'd exited and the main entrance.

"Cut them off!" came a shout from the buildings around the yard, and a group of soldiers came sprinting out from between them. There was no way we could beat them there, and I counted as they headed to block our path to the dungeon. Twenty-five. "Go warn the king!" the leader yelled at one of them, who picked up speed.

I glanced from the sprinting soldier to the door of the dungeon with indecision. If he got there before us and told Hazlitt we were coming, anything could happen. Hazlitt may kill the king and queen of Cornwall if he hadn't already. He may escape before we could reach him. He may come out to fight, and I wasn't sure we could handle him while battling other troops too because I didn't yet know what his magic was like.

"Go!" Ava said, catching my hesitation and probably thinking the same things I was.

I looked from her to the door. "Are you sure?"

"We've got this," Rhien agreed. I glanced at the prince, who peered down at his unarmored body and grumbled a reluctant concurrence.

Before I could leave, Ava grabbed the neck of my armor, pulling me down so she could press an urgent kiss to my lips. "*Please* be careful," she begged, letting me go. "We're right behind you."

I nodded and sheathed my sword, immediately spark jumping beyond the collecting blockade of soldiers and landing behind the man who'd just reached the door. I grabbed him with a current and didn't wait for him to collapse, or for any of the other troops to turn and catch me. I squeezed through the door and closed it behind me.

Once inside, I stood at the top of the descending stairs for a long moment to let my eyes adjust to the darkness. There were torches on the wall every twenty feet or so, but it wasn't nearly enough to see everything in the stony passageway. At least there was no sign of any enemy soldiers yet, and I took my first step down. I walked as silently as possible, not wanting my presence to be known and trying to convince myself that I wasn't afraid.

But my pulse was picking up with every step I took farther underground. I could feel my mouth going dry with nervousness as an icy clump formed at the pit of my stomach. My palms were itching with static, a defensive current coursing just beneath the surface of my skin. Every time the flicker of a torch cast a long shadow on the wall, my heart skipped, but I wouldn't stop. I could hear voices, and was almost close enough now to make them out. I could see the bottom of the stairs.

A few more steps and I was there, and I hesitated for a moment before descending the rest of the way. The dungeon was a large, open space, lined along the outside with cells. There was a heavy metal gate ten feet in front of the bottom of the stairs, which spanned from one side of the dungeon to the other, and might have been impenetrable if the barred door at the center of it wasn't wide open. There were two armored soldiers just inside this door, standing on either side of it, but they weren't facing me. They were facing the rest of the dungeon. Facing Hazlitt.

"Sign it!" Hazlitt yelled at one of the two people he'd chained to the far wall. Even from here, I knew it was the king and queen, and even though they were both vulnerable – wrists shackled to the wall above their heads – the king stared defiantly at Hazlitt. "If you care at all about your citizens, you'll sign this contract," Hazlitt growled. "You follow, and the rest of your regions will follow. Sign it!"

I crept forward silently as Cornwall's king narrowed his eyes. "My regions' armies will be here by nightfall to take back this castle. They'll never follow you."

"Perhaps I'll fetch your son," Hazlitt threatened. "How much torture could he stand before one of you gives in?" At that, the king made a frightened but considering glance at the parchment Hazlitt was holding.

I'd reached the gate, and I stepped through the door at the same time as I grabbed each of the guards' exposed necks. The sparks shot through their bodies, and their armor made a loud clamor as they both collapsed to the stone floor. Hazlitt wheeled around, eyes fixing on me with surprise. In the moment it took me to see what he was equipped with – a sword and dagger at his waist – he collected himself, his surprise fading into the smug grin he always wore. Instead of saying anything to me, he simply pulled his sword and turned back to the king to continue his threats.

"HAZLITT!" I roared, my voice echoing off the cold walls of the dungeon.

Hazlitt froze, standing with his back to me for a long few seconds. I wasn't sure what he was going to do, and I wasn't sure I could get there in time if he attacked the royals. But just when I thought he was going to ignore me again, he spun around, throwing one arm toward me as he did. The motion sent a massive dark orb shooting across the length of the dungeon. It reached me almost faster than I could react, but I managed to throw my hands up, catching the dark magic with my own and deflecting it sideways into the wall.

"Impressive," Hazlitt mused, taking a step forward. I drew my sword, and he stopped his progress as his lips curled. "Tell me how you got this magic. I *know* you didn't have it when we first met."

"You know nothing," I snarled.

He hummed in consideration, staring at me for a long moment before musing, "Dragonkin." My eyes widened, and he smiled even bigger. "You're even more foolish than I thought if you believe I've never heard of Dragonkin. I didn't recognize it at first. Not until I realized who you really were, who your father was. Not until I came to you in Ava's body and buried that dagger in your chest, and saw Nilan Thaon's dragon hanging around your neck." Hazlitt's eyes dropped from my neck to my chest, as though searching for the pendant that was beneath my armor. "That's the source, isn't it?" He met my gaze again, his lips thinning with frustration. "I knew when I met your father that there had to be a source. Magic like that... magic that great isn't born. It's *made*. Your abilities are proof." I simply scowled at him, waiting for the moment he tried to catch me off guard and hurl more magic at me. "Tell me where you got it!"

"If you don't know where I got it," I said, refusing to look away from his intense stare, "then you don't know as much about Dragonkin as you think you do."

He inhaled a raging breath as he took another stomp forward, but he stopped himself, rotating the handle of the sword in his grip. "Give me the necklace!"

"It doesn't matter if you have the necklace," I told him, huffing amusedly at his petty attempts. "It won't give you my magic."

"You insolent girl!" he shouted. "You stupid, arrogant child! I'll cut it out of you!" He took another irate step. "You think you can kill me? You can't! Just like your father couldn't because he was weak, like you're weak!"

I'd been afraid on my way down the dungeon steps, and I'd been nervous, but not now. Not since I'd caught my first glimpse of Hazlitt's face and been reminded of everything he put me through. Everything he put *Ava* through. I wasn't afraid of him. He was power hungry, and greedy, and desperate. He was pathetic.

"I could say the same for you," I told him. "Why didn't you kill me outside of Ronan?" I paused, waiting a few moments for him to answer while his jaw worked back and forth with fury. "You were afraid. You're still afraid because you overreached, because you're trapped here and there's nowhere to go. I told you that you'd answer for all you've done. Your treachery ends today."

Hazlitt's upper lip curled as he transferred the grip of his sword to both hands. "I'm going to make your death slow, and agonizing, and gruesome." He smirked again through his sneer, so that his face was darker and more terrifying than I'd ever seen it. "And I think I'll make Ava watch."

My teeth clenched. If he'd been trying to get a reaction out of me, he got it. I spark jumped across the entire dungeon, landing behind him with my sword already raised high above my head. But as I brought it down, Hazlitt turned, blocking the blow with the length of his own weapon.

"If you think I haven't heard of what you can do," he said, bringing his massive sword around to heave it down at me, "then you are gravely mistaken."

I met his swing, but he was so much larger, and there was so much force behind it that it sent me back a step. He followed, bringing his sword around the other way. I countered again, feeling his strength in the clash of metal on metal that sang through my bones, not getting a single moment to balance myself before he was slicing his sword center. I spark jumped out of the way, landing on the opposite side of which he'd swung. Experience told me that shooting current into an armored opponent wouldn't shock them to death, but it would hurt them, and I'd take every edge I could get against Hazlitt. I grabbed his steel shoulder and let the current flow through me, but the sparks met steel and turned back on me, biting at my fingers so painfully that I yelped.

I'd have stumbled back, but Hazlitt grabbed me by the arm, turning on me with a cold grin. "Warded against lightning, thanks to a Ronan mage."

His other fist met my cheek, an agonizing mix of steel and bone, and I forgot all about the stinging sparks in my hand as he let me go. I ignored the pain in my face too as I fell, spark jumping away from him so I landed on my back on the opposite side of the dungeon. Right when I hit the ground, Hazlitt hurled another dark sphere of energy at me, and this time I was too disoriented to dodge it. It collided with my chest as I sat up, and everything went dark for a brief moment as a long and wheezing breath was forced from my lungs, bringing with it the copper taste of blood.

Then I realized that everything was dark because there was a shadow in front of my eyes. It was coming *from* me, being drawn out of me with the breath and blood it took. And it took shape. It got deeper and darker as it gained human form at my feet, until it was familiar. It was a silhouette of *me*, with a shadowed sword and gleaming red eyes. Those eyes fixed on me, and I didn't even get a chance to process what was happening before that sword was being thrust at me.

I dodged sideways just quick enough not to be stuck with it, but it caught the side of my arm, slashing through my flesh even though nothing about this figure was solid. The shadow raised its weapon, bringing it crashing down as I somersaulted backward, so that it hit the floor with so much force that it cracked the stone. I scrambled to my feet, raising my sword defensively while I glanced across the dungeon to see where Hazlitt was. He hadn't moved. He was watching as though entertained.

The figure advanced, grabbing its sword in both hands and preparing to strike, but my mind was working now. This was evil magic. All of Hazlitt's magic was, and so I reached out with a hand at the shadow of myself, and I manipulated the magic to change its target. The figure shifted course, turning around and picking up pace to start sprinting toward Hazlitt. He didn't look alarmed. He waved his hand and the figure disappeared, and it hit me then that he wasn't yet taking this seriously.

"Your lightning is ineffective," Hazlitt called across the dungeon, striding slowly forward. "Your sword skill is clumsy at best." He stayed quiet until he'd crossed the dungeon and stood only feet in front of me, and though he had his sword held carelessly at his side, I wouldn't make the mistake of trying to strike. He was clearly waiting for it. "I must admit, I thought you were going to make this difficult for me."

Hazlitt struck first. He slashed diagonally with his sword, and it didn't matter that he was only holding it with one hand, he was so strong that it sent me staggering sideways when I blocked. *Deflect*, I told myself as I raised my sword to meet his next blow. But Hazlitt was faster and more tenacious than I'd ever trained for. Deflecting wasn't engrained in the memory of my muscles like it was for my sword instructor in the caves, or for Ava. I needed time to think, time to prepare, but I wasn't getting time. Hazlitt was raining blow after blow on me, beating me back so that all I *could* do was meet each swing to keep it from cutting me in half.

He drove me all the way to the wall of the cave, and when my back hit it I spark jumped away, landing at the center while the crash of his sword against the wall echoed throughout the dungeon. He turned to glare at me, but he wasn't angry.

"Getting tired?" he asked, because I was panting for air, and my muscles were burning and fatigued already from protecting myself against his weapon. "You're in over your head."

"Am I?" I breathed, gulping as much air as I could. I *was* tired, and my cheek was swollen and my arm was bleeding, but I wasn't done fighting. Not nearly. "Where's all this magic you worked so hard to find?"

He sneered and gestured at me with his hand. I prepared myself to catch and manipulate whatever he threw at me, but he *hadn't* thrown anything at me. There was a dull ringing in my head, which grew steadily louder for a few moments before...

"Kiena," came a childish sob. My focus shot to the source, to Nilson. He was chained to the wall beside the king and queen, higher than he was tall so that he was dangling by his wrists. He was beaten and bloody, taking rapid, stunted breaths through his sobs like he was in immense pain.

It's not real. I swallowed hard as tears filled my eyes. *It's* not *real.* But it *looked* real, it sounded real, and instantly my heart was in agony and my stomach queasy.

"Kiena," pleaded another familiar voice. A weak whisper. I didn't want to look, I tried so hard not to, but I couldn't help it. My eyes followed the sound into one of the many cages, to my mother. Lying on the dirty dungeon floor, pale arm stretched toward me, her other hand clutching at the bars of the cell as if clutching for dear life.

I knew it wasn't real, but it was so striking and agonizing that I couldn't think of what to do. Couldn't focus on manipulating the darkness that fueled these visions because all I could feel was the instinct to protect. To rescue.

"This is their fate," Hazlitt snarled, "should you fail to kill me today." I turned my furious gaze on him while he paced to the king and unlocked the man's chains. "Let's see if you want me bad enough to kill an innocent man." The king fell to the floor with weakness. "That magic I found means I no longer need the blood ritual for possession."

Hazlitt's palm filled with a swirling red haze, and he directed it away from his hand and into the king. It flowed through the king's head, into his chest until all of it had been absorbed. The king straightened to his feet, strong and sturdy, his eyes a familiar red as he began to advance toward me.

It was nothing, and he'd let the visions of my mother and brother fade in his effort to possess the king. "You didn't learn the first time," I scolded, reaching out to grip that possessing magic. It was more powerful than it used to be, it wasn't as easy to control as it had been when I'd manipulated the commander Hazlitt possessed, but I could still do it. I shifted the intent, and though it was beyond my ability to destroy the magic and free the king of it, I changed it to something different. I put the king to sleep, and as he fell unconscious, Hazlitt stared at me with a mix of awe and rage.

"What is that magic!?" he demanded, pacing forward with his face twisted in resentment. "You *will* give it to me!"

"How does it feel?" I asked, my mouth pursing with disgust. "Knowing you wasted your life searching for that elixir, and it's useless." His face burned red, but it didn't deter me. "How does it feel having everything you wanted, only to find that not even the power could make you worth a damn thing?"

Hazlitt roared, lifting his weapon and charging across the dungeon. I spark jumped behind him right when he reached me, but he used his momentum to spin around. I countered the hit, angling my own weapon just enough to deflect it. Like every time before, I didn't get a chance to retaliate. Hazlitt was fast and fueled by his anger. He swung again, and again, and again. And every time that I couldn't meet the blow, I spark jumped behind him, only to have him pivot and strike another time.

I was waiting for my opening, waiting for his rage to make him clumsy and for him to mess up. But it wasn't coming soon enough, and it wasn't just blocking each of his heavy hits that was wearing on my energy. It was all the magic I was using. I'd felt the pull of the drain every time I used magic, but I'd never used it so much, and so rapidly. Every jump cost me precious stamina, stamina that I was already losing at drastic rates because of our clashing weapons. My lungs were burning with each gasp for air. My forehead and neck were dripping with sweat.

I was getting weak, and all it took was one blunder, because Hazlitt was waiting for it just as much as I was. I sparked myself behind him, catching my heel on an unleveled stone of the floor. It put me off balance so that with Hazlitt's next swing, I lost my footing, and it sent me crashing down on my back. Hazlitt didn't waste the opportunity. He lifted his sword, pointed the tip of it straight at me, and began to drive it down with all his might. I didn't have any other options, and I thought *STOP!* with every bit of energy I had left.

That splitting crack went down the front of my head, and Hazlitt froze with the point of his sword mere inches above my armor. His eyes went wide with shock, but it didn't stop him from trying. Though I kept my mind's hold on him, freezing him to keep him from plunging his thick sword through my chest, he was fighting it. He was fighting it as hard as he possibly could, trying with his weight and his strength to force his sword those last few inches. I'd never experienced someone resisting, and I'd never felt pain like it in my entire life.

It was beyond harrowing. As I stared Hazlitt in the eyes, both of us straining against each other's will, it felt like my skull was being beat open. The pain ripped through the front of my mind, searing the insides of it and the back of my eyes. It was *blinding*, and it took so much focus to maintain my control and force myself through the pain that I couldn't even think to take a breath. All I could see were the white hot flashes of my pulse in my eyes, and just beyond it, the sharp point of a sword and the exertion on Hazlitt's face, both trembling with his effort.

But I was losing this fight. The pain was so bad that I could feel a trickle of blood slipping from my nose, and my vision was blurring with nearing unconsciousness, and every second that passed, Hazlitt's sword got that much closer to my chest. I couldn't keep it up, and I had to do something but I couldn't multitask with this control. I didn't know if I could spark jump effectively, and I couldn't risk striking out with my own weapon while his sword was so near to me. But I *had* to do something.

The very moment I let go of my control, I spark jumped, but the pain was so great and my focus so limited that I didn't get as far as I wanted. I only shifted a few feet upward, so that when Hazlitt finally managed to slam the point of his sword down to the dungeon floor, it pierced through my shin and calf instead. I cried out in agony, but Hazlitt didn't give me a moment to recover. He withdrew the weapon from my flesh, only to heave it upward and start slashing it back down. I was done. I hadn't the strength or the focus to spark jump in time or to block it with my own sword.

Just when I expected to feel the sharp edge cutting through me, another sword appeared, knocking Hazlitt's swing off course. "No!" Ava shouted, advancing another step and fighting Hazlitt away from me. "You will *not* take her too!" Ava wasn't alone. A handful of footsteps were clattering down the stairs after her, but it was a group of enemy soldiers that ran into the dungeon. "Kiena?" she called behind her, her voice shaking with worry as she squared off against Hazlitt, keeping him from advancing again.

She'd saved my life, but it wasn't over. Doing everything I could to ignore the excruciating wound in my leg and the fading pain in my head, I scrambled to my feet, wiping the blood from under my nose with the back of my hand. I could barely stand, but I had to. I had to keep fighting. I backed up as the soldiers spread out in front of me, knowing Ava was right behind me facing Hazlitt.

"Are you alright?" she asked. She was breathing heavily and her heart was racing, but I couldn't tell if it was from physical exertion or panic.

"Fine," I answered, keeping my sword out to counter if any of the soldiers attacked. "Rhien and the prince?"

"Finding the others," Ava answered.

Hazlitt roared angrily at that, shouting over Ava and me at the soldiers, "Kill her!"

The soldiers charged, and I mustered all the strength I had left. Ava was more adept than I was with a sword, and surely she could handle herself against Hazlitt. All I had to do was keep an eye out, and make sure he didn't use magic against her while I was preoccupied.

It was a struggle. My primary concern was with Ava, and I couldn't put much weight on or trust in my leg, so I countered and spark jumped to avoid as many of the soldiers' blows as I could. Someone had warned them about my sparks, because every time I tried to reach out they leaned or jumped away. It seemed pure luck when I finally managed to deflect a swing, leaving an opening for me to kill the man with my own sword. I spark jumped again to avoid another buffet, glancing once more at Hazlitt and Ava.

Hazlitt was fighting with her much the same way he had with me. He was on the attack, raining hit after hit down on her, but she was deflecting them all with ease. And even after just that short minute, I could tell it was doing exactly what she wanted it to. Hazlitt's strikes were coming slower. He was getting tired. That's when he finally decided to use his magic, but I was watching. The very moment he tried to hurl something at her, I reached out, knocking it off course so it hit the wall, and just in time for me to dodge one of my own enemies.

Hazlitt howled with rage at my interference. "You spoiled, ungrateful brat!" he shouted at Ava, and the clashing of their swords sounded off the walls. "I raised you!"

I was losing the energy to spark jump, so this time I ducked under a high swing, collapsing onto one knee because of the weakness in my other leg. It put me at the perfect level to reach out and grab the soldier's thigh with a current of sparks. Only three more to go.

"I gave you a roof!" Hazlitt continued breathily, blocking a daring swing from Ava. "I gave you every luxury you could have ever wanted! And this is how you repay me! How you repay your father!"

"*YOU ARE NOT MY FATHER!*" Ava screamed, at such volume and so full of fury that it nearly froze every one of us on the spot. Hazlitt stared at her in shock for all of a moment before she charged at him, and she was so angry that she went on a powerful offensive. "My father was a good man!" she hollered, striking at him with a strength and a fierceness I'd never seen in her before. "An honest!" she smashed out strike after brutal strike, "gentle!" beating Hazlitt back toward the side of the dungeon, "loving man!" But when her voice cracked, it wasn't with exhaustion. It was overwhelming emotion. "And you killed him!"

I spark jumped again, getting behind one of the final three soldiers and shoving my sword through his back.

"You destroy everything I love!" Ava yelled, her voice breaking with tears as Hazlitt's back hit the wall. "And I *hate* you!"

It happened too fast to think. Ava swung at Hazlitt a final time, but he countered it with a mighty strike of his own. It was so forceful that it knocked the sword out of Ava's hands, and he instantly reached out, grabbed her, and switched their positions. Her back slammed against the wall, and Hazlitt's sword would have been through her stomach the very next second if I hadn't reached out with my mind. I stopped him, put all my focus on keeping him from killing her, and it gave her the opening she needed. Ava's hand didn't hesitate to shoot out faster than I could blink. She grabbed the dagger from Hazlitt's belt and sent it flying upward, burying the point of it through his chin and into his skull.

But that opening, that lull in my focus, it was just enough for one of my enemy soldiers to land a strike of their own. The man rushed, and right as Ava killed Hazlitt, his sword went clean through my heart. I didn't even feel it. Just knew that everything had stopped and I couldn't breathe or hear or speak, and my gaze met Ava's just long enough to take in the horror on her face before everything was dark.

It felt like only a moment before I opened my eyes again, but nothing was the same. *I* wasn't the same, and wasn't even in the same place. I was standing elsewhere, but I watched the man who'd killed me withdraw his sword from my chest. My lifeless body collapsed to the dungeon floor at the same time Hazlitt's did, and Ava raced away from him. She sprinted over, her face pale and panic-stricken as she dropped to her knees where I'd fallen without even acknowledging the two remaining enemies. They looked surprised about it as she grabbed me, tears already streaming down her face as she pulled me up to hug me to her. One of the men decided to kill her, but just as he raised his sword, an arrow shot through his skull. The other had hardly turned toward the dungeon exit before meeting the same fate, and Nira and the others came bounding down the stairs.

But Ava. Ava was crushed. More devastated than I'd ever seen her. More than that day in castle. Even more than when I'd left her with Hazlitt. And me? I was... "What have I done?" I whispered, throwing my hands to my head as tears filled my eyes. I was dead, but my heart wasn't breaking because I hadn't wanted to die. It was because I was all Ava wanted. The only thing she'd cared about and so desperately wanted was getting her life with me after this was over, and I'd sacrificed it all on a whim. After everything she'd been through, all I ever wanted was for her to be happy, and I'd stolen the last glimmer of hope she had left. I couldn't watch this. Couldn't watch Ava sobbing over me, because a sob broke in my own throat as I whimpered, "Gods, *what have I done?*"

"Kiena," murmured a familiar voice from behind me.

I wheeled around to meet it, facing three looming figures, and at first I thought I couldn't be seeing right. I swiped at my eyes to rid them of moisture, hoping that freeing them of the blur would help me see more clearly, but I wasn't mistaken. I was seeing exactly what I thought I was, and met the gaze of the person on the left.

"Elder Numa?" I said in shock, and glanced at the figure in the middle. "The witch from the Black Wood..." And the one on the right. "...My sword instructor..." I took in a shaky, emotional breath to try and ask a question, but I didn't know what to say. I wiped at my cheek as another tear fell, but I couldn't look behind me. It hurt too much. "You're not dead," I said. That was all I thought I knew for sure. They couldn't be.

"Never dead," the witch answered.

"Never living," said my mysterious sword instructor.

"Always both," added Elder Numa in their soft voice.

"I don't understand," I stammered, sniffling and choking on another sob.

"You've long been a favorite of ours, Kiena," Elder Numa said, and I finally remembered why their voice had sounded so familiar to me when I'd met them in the mountains. My dreams. When Ava and I were separated, Elder Numa's was the voice in my dreams urging me to find her. "So few even remember us anymore."

"The gods?" I breathed.

"I am nature and natural magic," Elder Numa explained.

"I am the physical and the wills of man," said my sword instructor with an introductory bow.

"And I am the space between," finished the witch.

"But you've," I began, and I swallowed down a lamenting whimper as my focus bounced between them, "you've come to me. You've interfered."

"As much as we could allow ourselves, yes," Elder Numa confirmed.

The witch made a proud sweep with her hand. "A potion for you and Ava."

Elder Numa gave a soft smile. "Sending the wolf when you most needed purpose."

391

The sword instructor's lips curled too. "*Trying* to make you a swordsman." I let out a teary laugh. "Hazlitt went unchecked for far too long. It was imperative that his life end."

At the reminder of life ending, I couldn't help but start sniffling all over again as my mouth curved into a deep frown, and the witch was studying me with something like curiosity. "You don't cry for the reasons most mortals do when they come here."

Fresh tears spilled down my face, and I risked a look behind me to see that Nira had knelt at Ava's side, but not even Nira could comfort her. "This is the most selfish thing I've ever done," I wept. Ava's shoulders were shaking with heavy sobs, but her entire body was trembling with grief. "I couldn't watch her die," I inhaled a stuttering breath, "and now I've made her..." I was so overcome with despair that I couldn't stay straight. I squatted down, setting my elbows on my knees so I could bury my face in my hands as I broke down crying. "Is this the afterlife?" I sobbed to myself. "Am I bound to watching the misery I've caused her?" I'd been so careless that maybe I deserved it... but not Ava. Ava never deserved this.

"This is the entrance to the afterlife," Elder Numa answered.

The witch added, "But it's not the end of yours."

It took a long moment for what the witch had said to sink in. Then I swallowed down another sob, removing my hands from my face so I could look up at them. Did she mean what I thought she did?

Elder Numa gave another smile as the sword instructor strode forward, offering me his hand. "You've played your part in helping Ava fulfill her destiny," he said, helping me to stand. "But it's not your time."

"Ava?" I repeated, my forehead creasing with surprise. "She-" I turned to look at her in the dungeon again, feeling my mouth tighten with the smallest of proud smiles, even though my bottom lip was still quivering with emotion. "It was her all along? All of this was about *her*."

The sword instructor nodded. And they truly meant what I thought they did. They were going to send me back. Back to life. Back to *Ava*, and I was so instantly overwhelmed by their generosity that I had no other reaction in me. I started crying all over again. I sobbed for an entire minute, murmuring every word of gratitude I managed not to choke on while the gods simply watched me.

I thanked them on my behalf, and on Ava's, until Elder Numa said gently, "You've been hard on yourself, Kiena, but you've done so well."

"I do believe we owe you another chance," the sword instructor said, his eyes flicking past me to the dungeon. "You've both earned it."

"But you," I recalled, pointing at the witch. I took a deep breath to keep myself composed, even though I was still quivering with emotion and astounding appreciation. "You told me to go home. You told me to forget this."

"We're not above playing favorites," she replied with a raspy laugh, "gods or not."

"We'd have found another way," Elder Numa added, "and spared you all this suffering should you have been less determined."

"And Ava?" I asked, wiping the remaining blur from my eyes. "Did you make me fall in love with her?"

"There are many things we can control," the witch answered. "The range of human emotion is beyond our reach."

I nodded, taking a moment to collect myself. To absorb what all of this meant. "What now?" I asked shakily. "Ava's killed Hazlitt. What do I do?"

"Now," Elder Numa said, "you fulfill *your* destiny."

"What is it?" I asked. "What is my destiny?"

All three of them simply smiled at me, refusing to answer until the sword instructor motioned beyond me toward Ava, and said, "Perhaps you can give her the love and the peace that we so gravely owe her." My cheeks flared with an embarrassed blush at the expression of my private thoughts.

"Not even *we* can restore life freely, Kiena," Elder Numa said, and in the blink of an eye, we were no longer in the dungeon, but outside beyond the walls and the war. I could see the castle and the battle going on in the distance, but as I watched, Night Phoenix landed in front of us.

The dragon touched down with its heavy thud, and stretched its head toward me in such a deliberate way that I knew it to be requesting touch. "Can it see us?" I asked in shock.

"Dragons are beasts of many talents," the witch answered.

"Hello, friend," I said, reaching out to stroke the dragon's snout. But then I realized why we must have come here, and what Night Phoenix had to do with Elder Numa's statement about life. "If life isn't free..."

The sword instructor nodded. "The dragon you call Night Phoenix wishes to give its remaining years and memories in exchange for your life."

I looked at Night Phoenix as my eyes blurred all over again. The dragon didn't have to do this. It was giving up so many years, so much time and life and energy, and all for me. I was nothing compared to this magnificent creature. It was one of the few remaining dragons in the world, and I was so small. So insignificant. But it cared, and I cried, because I could hardly comprehend the sacrifice Night Phoenix was making solely for me. But at the sorrow and gratefulness on my face, all the dragon did was press up against my hand, as if to assure me that it was fine. That this is what it wanted.

"Will it be reborn?" I asked through a sniffle.

"As it has been countless times before," Elder Numa confirmed. "Retrieve the egg laid in its ashes, and in three years time, it will hatch."

"Will Night Phoenix remember me?" I asked, touching my forehead to the dragon's large nose, and though I'd felt nothing since being killed, I felt the warmth of its mystical breath.

"Not the way you wish," the witch said. "But as you've learned before, some memories live on in blood."

For what felt like the hundredth time, I broke down crying. "You beautiful, selfless creature," I said, pressing a teary kiss to the dragon's snout. "Thank you." I wrapped my arms as much as I could around it, hugging myself over the bridge of its nose while water spilled from my eyes. "*Thank you*. Maybe we'll meet again in your next life." And Night Phoenix chittered its agreement.

"Goodbye, Kiena," said the collective voice of the gods.

There was a flash of light from the dragon, a light of which I felt the warmth and the comfort flowing into me even though it was blinding. It filled me, coursed through my skin and bone and blood. After a few long seconds, it was gone, and the dungeon came back into focus as it faded, and I could hear and see and feel again.

Ava had pulled me into her lap and was hugging me to her, her face buried in my neck, still sobbing with despair. I could look over her shoulder just enough to see everyone else except Nira, who was hugging Ava on the other side. Rhien was shielding her eyes with one hand, but I could see tears slipping down her cheeks from underneath it. I'd hardly known

Skif and Denig long, but Skif's eyes were watery as he rubbed his hand across Rhien's back, and the now human Denig was shaking his bowed head. And even the prince and his parents, who'd been unchained, looked woefully disappointed. Ava was trembling against me, and her tears had soaked the shoulder of my tunic under my armor, but for a minute I just stayed there. Letting her hold me. Knowing exactly how close I'd been to never feeling it again.

"Don't cry," I whispered hoarsely, and Ava froze like she was unwilling to believe she'd heard correctly. "I've never made a girl I fancied cry before."

Ava gasped and drew back just enough to look at me, and when her eyes met mine, she broke down all over again. But they were tears of joy, and relief. She squeezed me to her and then let go to plant kisses all over my face, and then squeezed me to her again as she laughed through the tears. She hugged me and kissed me and cried for minutes, muttering over and over again that I was alright and alive as if she had to convince herself it was true.

"That's a damn lie," she said eventually, laughing and sniffling like she didn't know which to do, but she leaned back to look at me, helping me to sit up. "If I had a copper for every tear I shed over you..."

The moment I was upright, I wrapped my arms around her, holding her tight so she could feel that everything would be fine now. That I was here. "I'm sorry," I told her, wishing she knew just how much I meant it. "I love you. I'm sorry."

It took a minute for me to let her go. She refused to release me entirely, and kept one hand on my shoulder while the other landed on the hole in the chest of my armor. She was still looking at me like she couldn't believe it. There was awe and confusion and still some disbelief in her expression, but she also didn't look like she was about to ask what happened. It didn't seem like she could bring herself to. Didn't want to ask for confirmation of just how near she'd been to losing me forever.

"The gods," I told her, watching a fresh flow of tears fall down her cheeks as she traced the hole with her fingers. Everyone else leaned in too, intent on hearing what I had to say. But I couldn't say it, not entirely. I was too weak, and tired, and I wasn't certain I could explain without breaking down again from my lingering gratitude, but I mentally thanked the gods again so they'd know I would never take this for granted. "They spared me. They sent me back." I'd tell Ava about Night Phoenix. Later, when we were alone and had some rest and I didn't have to worry about a million questions from the others. For now, whether they took what I said literally, or put it down to luck, nobody appeared about to press me with inquiries, and for that I was thankful.

My focus was briefly pulled elsewhere as Nira knelt down by my legs. She still had tears in her eyes, and she brushed the back of her hand over her cheek to wipe away an escaped one. "You're a right asshole, you are," she scolded, her voice wet as she lifted my knee to tie a strip of cloth over the wound in my calf. While the hole in my chest was gone, my arm and leg were still bleeding, and I could feel a throbbing in my cheek. "Lucky the gods saved you, or I'd cross over to kill you once more for scaring us like that."

"I'm sorry," I repeated, reaching out and giving her forearm a grateful squeeze for bandaging my leg, but I couldn't look anywhere but at Ava for long. Her deep blue eyes were still full of relieved tears. "You did it," I told her, reaching up to cup her face, and I thumbed away another stray droplet. I finally used the opportunity to get a complete idea of her injuries. She had cuts and bruises from different weapons, as did all of my companions except for Denig and Skif, but she was alive. We'd *all* made it. "You ended the war," I said. Ava's gaze fell, and I recognized the guilt in her expression when she passed a look in Hazlitt's direction. He was the only person she'd ever *truly* killed, but even after everything he'd done to her, I don't think she'd have wanted it that way if she had a choice. It was a burden I'd have gladly carried for her. One I wished I could because she was finally, completely free of him, and she didn't seem ready yet to rejoice in it. "Will you be alright?"

Ava leaned her forehead against mine, shutting her eyes tight to squeeze out the remaining moisture. After a moment she nodded and pressed a kiss to my lips, saying in a soggy whisper, "I want to go home."

"Let's go," I agreed, giving her one last kiss.

She stood and offered me her hand, Nira doing the same on my other side, and they helped me to my feet. I was hardly standing again when Rhien finally paced over, curling her arms around my middle in such a tight hug that it almost knocked me down again. I laughed, grateful that Ava set her hand on my back to help me balance as I returned the embrace. Once Rhien let me go, we all started up the stairs of the dungeon.

Ava and Nira helped me walk with my arms over their shoulders. Denig and Skif supported the king, and Destrian and Rhien aided the queen.

By the time we reached the castle yard again, the sun was setting beyond the wall. There was victorious shouting filtering over the stone a short distance away, and a handful of horses appeared between the buildings, a mix of the Vigilant green and Cornwall's blue and gray. Kingston was amongst these riders, with Haunt following after him, and he jumped off his horse the very moment they came to a stop. His armor was scratched and dented and in desperate need of repair, there were spots of blood all over the shimmering steel, and his helmet was missing. Even Haunt's gray fur was tinged red, and she was limping from a gash across a front limb, but they both appeared as healthy as the rest of us.

"We've done it?" I asked him. Though I could stand just fine on my own and Nira let me go once we'd stopped walking, Ava's arm was still clutched firmly around my waist. I knew that it wasn't as much to offer me support as it was simply to feel me, but I wouldn't make her let go even if I didn't need the help. Not ever.

Kingston nodded with a massive grin on his face, noticing the king and queen and bowing at them. "Your regions' armies arrived just in time," he told the royals. "What's left of Hazlitt's army has surrendered."

Though still weak, the king left Denig and Skif's support to stagger forward, offering his hand to Kingston. "We couldn't have survived this without you." And as Kingston shook with him, he passed a look around at the rest of us. "Without all of you. Thank you."

"My King," one of the horse riders prompted, hopping down to lead his horse forward. It was pulling a cart. "The physician is waiting for you."

The king nodded, said another thanks, and then went with the queen to sit on the cart and be taken for medical aid. The prince stayed behind, and as his parents were driven away, there was a swift shadow from over the wall. Pine Shadow came swooping into view and thudded down next to Denig, but the dragon didn't slither beneath his hand for affection. It had something curled in its tail. Something that it set gently on the ground in front of us.

"What is that?" Nira asked, squinting at the scaled oval that was a familiar swirl of black and blue.

"A dragon egg," I answered, but I didn't have the energy to explain. "Night Phoenix."

Denig strode forward, picking up the egg that was twice as large as his head. "It needs to be returned to the mountain..." It seemed obvious that it was he and Skif who should return it, and their home was merely a short dragon ride away. Still, he studied the egg for a long minute in deep consideration, looked from it to us, and then extended the egg to Skif.

"Why are you giving this to me?" Skif asked. "You'll get closer to that cave than I will."

Denig shook his head. "I'm not going back. Not yet." His lips pursed apologetically at the confused look Skif gave him. "Nira was right when she said that our way of protecting the dragons was shortsighted. People know now that they're still alive, and we need to do more than hole up on the mountain." He reached out to put his hand on Pine Shadow's head. "At least one of us needs to stay... as an ambassador for the dragons and Dragonkin."

Skif's expression softened with understanding, and it was clear by the way he stared back and forth between Denig and the egg that he was torn on whether or not he wanted to stay too. "Well that's a lot to think on, isn't it?" he said eventually.

Kingston laughed. "I think we all deserve a rest from just about everything for the night." He motioned to the two remaining horsemen who were pulling more carts. "Volunteers to take you back to camp."

"Here, here," Nira agreed, eagerly passing us to plop onto a cart. "I hope we're feasting tonight." And Rhien, Denig, and Skif followed after her, and they were wheeled away just after sitting.

Kingston looked down at my wounded leg, seemed unsure of what to think about the hole in the chest of my armor, and then scanned Ava for injuries. "I'll send Sevedi to your tent as soon as she has the time," he said. We both nodded, and he hesitated for a long moment before setting a hand on each of our shoulders. "Not sure I'd have survived going home without you," he chuckled, giving my shoulder a fond squeeze. "Your mother certainly would have killed me."

"Lucky for us both," I laughed, not having the heart to tell him just how near that fate had been.

"Get some rest," he said with smile. "I'll see you in the morning."

We watched him get back on his horse and ride away toward the wall, and then I realized that the prince was still here. He clearly had something to say, and came to stand in front of Ava and me to get our attention.

"You saved my parents' lives," he said, looking at both of us. "And mine. Thank you." He inhaled a deep breath, his gray eyes falling seriously on Ava. "I don't know what your intentions were last summer, but I don't care. Whatever it was, it's forgiven. I would like to think that though your affections may not have been true, your friendship was." He paused, scanning Ava's face after that last part as though he was wildly unsure of himself. For such a strong, noble-looking man, he appeared rather self-conscious, and I tried not to smile at the boyish hope in his eyes.

"You're a good man, Destrian," Ava said, and though the prince's opinion of her had never been much of a worry amidst this war, I could hear her relief. "And a kind friend."

He held out his hand palm up, and when Ava set hers in it, he lifted it to his lips to press a kiss to the back. "I wish you all the happiness in the world." He let her hand go and turned to me, bowing deeply. "Take care of her," he told me with a friendly smile.

"I promise," I said, bowing in return.

He passed a final, amicable look at both of us, and then headed off in the direction his parents had disappeared. Ava helped me limp over to the cart, and though Haunt had a difficult time climbing up into it because of her injury, I knew better than to try and help her. She managed on her own, and Ava and I sat down too. As the cart started carrying us off toward the wall, Ava wrapped her arms around my torso to hug herself to me, resting her head on my shoulder. We were heading toward the tents, and tomorrow we'd likely be heading home, but in the few minutes of silence as we sat there, I realized that I didn't have a home. There was no need to stay in the Vigilant caves anymore, and I wouldn't be surprised if the caves emptied as everyone really *did* go home, but Ava didn't want to be queen at Guelder, and my cottage had burned down.

"Ava," I prompted, wrapping my own arm around her to set it on her waist. "I don't have a home to take you to…"

All she did was hug me a little tighter. "Tonight, home is a war tent in a battle camp."

"And tomorrow?" I asked.

She angled to peck me on the cheek. "Wherever we should find ourselves, so long as we're together."

I nuzzled against the top of her head when she set it back on my shoulder, and for the first time since I'd met her, I truly understood what she meant when she said that I felt like home. "Can it be somewhere we could hide away for a while, just the two of us?"

Ava laughed one of the lightest, easiest laughs I'd ever heard from her. The kind of laugh that let me know she already felt happier than she'd been in a long time. "Wherever you'd like."

Chapter 26

s we rounded one of the final bends in the road on our journey to Ronan, the castle of Midsummit came into view. It was a beautiful fall day, the cloudless sky painting a picture of serenity over the capital that made my heart swell. It had been just over two months since the end of the war, for a total of eight since Ava and I had been to Ronan, and the exciting circumstances of our visit would make our first journey back a rewarding one. In two weeks' time would be Nira's coronation ceremony, for her not just to act as queen of Ronan, but to *be* queen. A brief glance at Ava, who was on her own horse at my side, let me know that she was just as delighted to be arriving as I was.

Nilson had been chattering away behind us from the saddle of his own small horse, but in the midst of his talking, he caught sight of the castle. He stopped midsentence, drawing in a long overdue breath. "Look!" he yelled to our mother, who winced at his volume because she was riding right beside him. *"That's* where Akamar lives?"

"And where you will too," I told him over my shoulder, "for the next month."

Ava glanced back at him, adding, "That's one month to eat all the sweets you can get your hands on."

Nilson's eyes widened, and his heels kicked back so his horse would go a little faster, taking him ahead of us. "Come on, then." He pointed a mile into the distance. "Race you to that crossroads."

I glanced back at my mother to see if she was up for it, but she waved her hand. "You lot go on, I'll catch up."

I looked ahead at Nilson, preparing to tease him and tell him I'd give him a head start because his horse was smaller than mine, but before I could, Ava went galloping by us. "See you there!" she hollered back.

Nilson's jaw dropped with offense, and as he kicked his heels again to take off after her, he called at me, "She's a worse cheater than you are!"

I simply laughed, watching as they both got farther and farther ahead of my mother and me. After a few seconds, my mother asked, "Aren't you going to race them?"

Pulling lightly back on the reins, I slowed my horse enough to ride at her side. "I've already got them beat," I told her, and to further my air of nonchalance, asked, "what are you most excited for about staying at the castle?"

She hummed, thought about it, opened her mouth to answer, and then set to thinking about it again. While she did, however, I watched her eyes go from me to down the road to check where Ava and Nilson were at in the race. She hummed again. "I think..." She paused, glancing once more at the road. "Well..."

It only took another moment for me to realize what she was doing. "You're trying to make me lose this race!" I laughed. "I'm not sure who's the biggest cheater of the lot." I climbed out of my saddle to dismount, and handed my reins to my mother so she could keep track of my horse for a few minutes. "See you at the crossroads," I told her, taking a few steps back.

In a snap, I was gone. Shot on a flash of sparks a mile ahead and landing at the end of the race while Ava and Nilson still had a quarter of a mile to go. To tease them even more, I sat down at one corner of the crossroads, folding my legs beneath me to make it look like I'd been sitting there for a while. Ava was the first to reach me, only a few seconds ahead of Nilson.

"You!" Ava exclaimed, trying not to let her amusement show as she pulled back on the reins, bringing her horse to a stop.

"What!" Nilson yelled, halting next to her.

"Took you long enough," I said, rising to my feet. "Been waiting for ages."

"You're the absolute worst," Ava accused, but she was laughing and teased right back, "I think you owe one of our horses a ride for that lazy display."

"Lazy?" I chuckled, striding up to her and tapping her foot so she'd take it out of the stirrup. "Magic is hard work, you know." Once she'd removed her foot, I pulled myself up to sit in the saddle behind her, wrapping my arms around her waist. "Or perhaps I just wanted an excuse to ride with my wife."

"Oh, is that it?" she asked, twisting enough to look at me, and she set her forehead against mine. "You could've just said so." I didn't say anything to that, but took the opportunity to kiss her for the first time in *hours*, which was surely far too long to go without kissing her.

"MUM!" Nilson shouted up the road, even though she was still too far away to hear him. "THEY WON'T STOP FLIRTING!" Ava's lips curling into a wide grin pulled her away from me, and I could feel my cheeks heating with a blush even though I was laughing. "*You two*," Nilson addressed, his voice playfully stern, "admit that I won the race because I'm the only one who played fair."

"Alright," I said, smiling. "All hail the champion, Nilson!"

"Take your victory bow," Ava instructed with a giggle.

Nilson didn't just bow at us from his seat in the saddle – he rode his horse around us in a victory lap, waving his hand and saying proud 'thank you's while trying to keep his face serious because of how amused Ava and I were, however unsuccessfully. We waited there at the crossroads for another few minutes until my mother reached us, and then we continued the rest of our short journey to Midsummit. It didn't take long with how close we were, and soon we were riding through the gates, being greeted by a small welcome party of staff who led us to the stables. Our horses were taken by some of those staff, and the few others began to lead us into the castle.

Unlike our first time arriving here, we weren't taken into a tower and upward, but rather were led through a large entrance and to a place that we'd never been to before at Midsummit – the throne room. Our guides pushed open the massive, decorated doors, revealing the long room, at the end of which was a group of people. Nira was the first one I spotted, standing just in front of the large throne and discussing something with an important looking woman in green robes, who was gesturing toward another robed man who was holding the crown on a pillow. Akamar was nearby, staring up at the ceiling with his hands folded behind his back, looking bored out of his mind. He was the first to glance over at our entrance, appearing desperate for a distraction, but his entire face lit up when he saw that it was us.

"They're here!" he shouted, leaping down the stairs the throne was set atop and sprinting toward us.

He reached Nilson first because Nilson had gone bounding forward, and they met in such an eager hug that it knocked them straight to the floor, where they lay in a giggling heap. Nira had started over too, leaving the robed people behind – and looking somewhat stressed about the delay – as she bypassed the boys to pace to us.

She threw her arms around Ava's neck. "You're here!" she said happily, giving Ava an overly enthusiastic kiss on the cheek and then squeezing her all over again. "You're finally here!" After a long moment of hugging her sister, she let go and threw her arms around *my* neck. "It feels as though it's been years." She let me go, turning to my mother with outstretched arms. "Bibbey," she grinned.

At the mention of my mother's name, Akamar finally stopped giggling with Nilson and looked up, as if realizing for the first time that he'd not yet greeted the rest of us. "Bib!" he exclaimed, jumping into my mother's arms not a moment after Nira let her go.

"Hello," my mother laughed, smiling wide as she hugged him back. "You're both looking so well," she told Nira, so overjoyed about it that there were almost tears in her eyes. For those six months in the caves, she'd looked after Nira and Akamar as if they were her own children, and I could tell that she was as pleased to see them again as Ava and me.

"You've arrived on time," Nira observed, setting one arm over Ava's shoulders, leaning against her just to be near. "I take it your journey was fair."

"Indeed," Ava agreed. "It was..."

"Leisurely," I provided, because a ride to Ronan was much more enjoyable when soldiers weren't chasing us, and Nira laughed knowingly while Ava nodded her amused agreement.

"And the horses?" Nira prompted. "How are they? And your cottage, is it luxurious?"

After the war ended, Kingston took the throne in Guelder, and he and Nira had gifted Ava and me a sum enough to last us the rest of our lifetimes. They'd said it was for our services to the kingdoms, but we both knew it to be a generous result of their love. We didn't use it to rebuild the burned down cottage I'd lived in with Mother and Nilson. We'd moved farther outside of Wicklin Moor instead, and bought a few hundred acres so we could make our living doing something simple, and fun, and *safe*. So we could raise horses.

"Our cottage is comfortable," Ava answered, reaching out for my hand, and I knew the gesture to be a reassurance that she wouldn't have it any other way. That not even being back in a castle could make her want anything other than the life we'd begun to build in our comfortable home.

Nilson, who'd come back over to stand at our mother's side with Akamar, beamed up at Nira. "Kiena's teaching me to train the horses."

"Is she?" Nira asked, glancing between him, Ava, and me. "I'll bet the three of you will turn out the best horses in the kingdom."

"In the world!" Nilson exclaimed.

"Forgive me," Nira laughed. She reached out to grab him, pulling him to her so she could ruffle his hair, because he hadn't yet given her a hug hello. "Best in the world."

We wouldn't be doing it alone, however. It was a tremendous job looking after horses, and would only get bigger as our stable grew, and so we'd hired some help. One of these individuals was Silas. Most of the soldiers who'd survived the battle were now soldiers under Kingston's rule, and some others were given punishments comparable to their status and crimes. Silas had been stripped of his knighthood and relieved of his service to the kingdom – a punishment he'd accepted readily and dutifully.

Though our relationship wasn't what it used to be, I couldn't leave him in his newfound situation to wander in search of work, or to potentially find none and be doomed to a life of homelessness. He'd always been a soldier, so he knew no other labor and thus wouldn't have easily been hired by anyone but myself. So I allowed him to build a small cottage on our land and gave him a job. It was an offer he'd accepted as stoically as he could, but with revealing tears in his eyes. We'd left him behind to care for the horses when we'd left for Ronan, along with Haunt, who'd decided to stick around even after the war, but who'd have never survived staying in a castle for a month.

"Your Grace," said a soft voice, and the robed woman gave Nira an apologetic smile for interrupting our reunion. "We still have so much to rehearse, and you'll have hours to converse soon at their-"

Nira made a loud shushing noise, cutting off the rest of the woman's sentence. Then she looked specifically at Ava and me, explaining, "We have a surprise for you tonight," but she cast a look at the robed woman on the word 'surprise,' chuckling amicably when the woman blushed.

"We're here for *you*," Ava protested, and I nodded my agreement.

Nira waved it off with a flick of her wrist. "These last weeks have been more about me than I can stand." She gestured toward the staff members that had brought us here, and who were still standing at the entrance of the throne room. "They'll take you all for baths and refreshments." She hugged us again, pressing another kiss to each of our cheeks. "I'll see you soon."

We turned to follow the staff members out of the throne room, but Nilson ran off after Akamar, both giggling mischievously and yelling about sweets, and my mother and another woman went chasing after them. Ava and I followed our own guide to the upstairs of another wing of the castle we'd never explored before, and were led into a bedchamber. We were assured that our bath was already being drawn, and told that someone would come and get us shortly. As Nira had promised, there were re- freshments laid out on the table in our room, and I went over to have a look.

"Hungry?" I asked Ava, taking in the various fruits we'd been provid- ed, grabbing a particular piece of green melon. "I do believe this is your favorite."

Ava strode over, holding her mouth open so I could drop the fruit in it while she looked over the food too. "Ah," she grinned, swallowing as she grabbed a specific red berry, "we've been provided your favorite as well."

I laughed, narrowing my eyes at her because I remembered perfectly when she'd tricked me into eating that sour berry. Twice. While I reached for a cup to fill it with water, Ava wandered away from me to explore the room. She felt the covers on the large bed and examined the landscape painting on the wall, but it wasn't until she'd reached the dresser and ran her hand over it that I recognized the wistfulness on her face.

Ava had been excited about returning, about seeing her brother and sister again after being apart for a couple of months, but she still had less fond memories attached to this castle. We were in an entirely different wing, and a different room than we'd been in on our first stay here, but everything was similar – the furniture, the colors, the smells. In our nights before leaving home to come here, she'd expressed an anxiety beneath her excitement, a fear that being back here would be too painful for her to enjoy herself as much as she wanted to.

"Is it as difficult as you thought?" I asked. "Being back?"

Ava paused in her tour, standing at the dresser for a moment before turning around to lean back against it, staring at the floor. "Yes," she answered, so quietly that I almost couldn't hear her from the opposite end the room, "and no." When she paused again, I strode across the empty space to where she was, and leaned back against the dresser at her side. "I thought I'd be afraid... terrified, like that day, to think of what happened."

"But you're not," I guessed as I wrapped an arm around her, and she leaned closer into my side.

"No," she confirmed. "Being here already, I'm finding that I'm finally able to separate myself from what happened. From everything *he* did." She looked up at me, a sense of surprised wonder in her eyes. "I don't know when it happened, Kiena, but... I think I've mostly forgiven myself." I pressed a kiss to her forehead, to tell her that I was glad for it without saying it out loud, and felt her arm go around my waist in gratitude. "I do feel some sadness," she admitted, leaning her head on me, "but it's that my father's not here to see how happy we are, or how great a queen Nira will be."

"He knows," I assured her. If there was one thing that my brush with death made me certain of, it was that death wasn't the end. That those we'd lost to this war weren't entirely gone. "He sees."

Ava's arm squeezed me a little tighter, and we stood there for a few moments in silence. "I think," she began eventually, hesitating before taking in a deep breath. "I think I'd like to go back there at some point during our stay. To that room. To face it and let go."

"If you think it will help," I agreed.

She glanced up at me again. "Would you go with me?"

"Yes," I answered, nodding. Ava had forgiven me long ago for leaving her that day, and she'd never so much as hinted that she blamed me at all for what happened to her father and stepmother. I'd have gone with her anywhere, no matter what, but I also believed that she wouldn't be the only one to benefit from facing what happened that day. "Of course."

"Thank you." She stretched upward to kiss my cheek, and we both stood there for a bit longer before she turned toward me. "You know what

I'm looking forward to?" she asked, appearing ready to be in brighter spirits.

"What?" I prompted, and because the tone of our conversation was lighter, I pushed myself backward and up to sit comfortably on the dresser.

"I'm looking forward to making new memories here," she said. She moved to stand between my legs, and set her hands on my knees. "It'll be even better with your mother and brother here, though, I am suspicious of Nira's surprise..."

"Knowing her," I chuckled, "it's probably a party."

"For us?" Ava asked in confusion. "She said the surprise was for us, but we don't know enough people here for a party."

I shrugged. "I suppose we'll have to wait a bit and see."

Ava hummed with further suspicion, but glanced around the room to change the subject, her eyes falling on the bed. "I wouldn't mind remaking some old memories too..."

I thought I knew exactly what she was implying, and began to ask smugly, "Old ones like what?" Only, I hardly got out half the sentence before she reached up and threw a small red berry into my mouth. I don't know how she always timed it so perfectly, but it stuck between my teeth and spilled sour juice over my tongue, and Ava burst into laughter at the way my face puckered up. "Were you holding that this entire time!?" I asked through a laugh of my own.

"Perhaps," Ava snickered.

"Oh, you're in trouble now," I teased, swallowing down the rest of the fruit. She immediately tried to back up, but I hooked my legs around her hips, holding her where she was. "You're not going anywhere," I said, taking her face in my hands. "Not before you kiss me."

She let out a giggling squeal as she tried to squirm out of my grasp. I leaned forward, attempting not to laugh too hard so I could keep teasing while I aimed for her lips. "Kiena!" she shrieked with half-hearted protest, leaning back away from me.

But I wasn't holding her hard, nor was she really trying, and she was laughing so thoroughly that her mouth was hanging wide, making it perfectly easy for me to take her in an open-mouthed kiss. I only kissed her for a few moments, feeling the vibrations of her laughter against my tongue when I licked briefly into her mouth, just enough for her to get a taste of the sour berry. I let her go then, and she was still giggling even though her nose was crinkled with dislike at the taste.

"Are you quite satisfied?" she asked.

"Aye," I said with a grin, leaning forward again to press a kiss to that crease in her noise. "Extremely."

There was a knock on the door then, and one of the staff who'd brought us here opened it and stepped in. "My ladies," she greeted. "Your bath is ready."

Ava and I followed her out the door, through the castle and to a familiar room where the bath was drawn. Like our first time here, the bath was a large area that was bigger than two of the bed in our room, where the floor was indented and filled with water. The wonderful scent of oils reached my nose the moment we walked in, and the steam rising from the surface of the hot water was calling to the travel-fatigued muscles in my body. Unlike our first time here, however, I was no longer hesitant about bathing with Ava. On the contrary, I was rather looking forward to it.

After asking if we needed anything, and then telling us to call out if we did, the woman who'd brought us here left us alone. We both undressed, hurrying to tie our hair up and then slipping toes first into the warm bath. Ava let out a heavy, content sigh as she sat down on the lip underwater, her eyes drifting closed and sinking in up to her chin. I couldn't help smiling at the pleased look on her face while I waded to the deeper center.

"Why have we decided to raise horses when we could live here?" I teased, running my hands over the surface of the water, stirring up the color of the oils floating there.

Ava smiled, opening her eyes to look at me. "You couldn't live in a castle," she said. "You'd miss the woods." She swatted a soft splash of water at me. "And the dirt."

"Maybe," I laughed, bending at the knees enough for the water to reach my chin and wading toward her. "I'd do it for you, though, if it was what you wanted."

"I know you would," she said, "*if* it was what I wanted." I neared where she was sitting, and she curled her arms around my neck so I'd stay in front of her. "But I like our cottage. I like our barn, and our horses." I lowered myself to my knees, and the bath was just shallow enough here that it put us at eye level. "I like going hunting with you," Ava continued, setting her forehead against mine. "I like our nights under the stars."

I felt a smile pull at my lips. I wanted to kiss her, but I held off, sliding my hands up her thighs instead and asking, "What do you like most about our nights under the stars?"

Ava let out a thoughtful hum, and though I wasn't looking at her mouth, I could see the smirk in the sparkle of her blue eyes. "How you keep me warmer than the fire does."

"You know what I think?" I asked, bringing my lips in close to hers to prepare for that kiss. She murmured her curiosity. "I think we should start remaking those old memories right now..."

Ava smiled, giving me a chaste peck on the lips. "Do you remember when you were afraid to even kiss me? And now you'd like to do more than that right here?"

"No, actually," I teased, "I don't recall such a time."

"Sure you don't," she said sarcastically, but she returned it openly when I kissed her. I used the opportunity to slide her off the edge of the seat, and she was light enough in the water that it was easy to guide her legs around my hips. All it did was make her smile a bit wider and pull away from my lips. "You really can't wait until we're alone tonight?"

"No," I replied, and the simplicity of the answer made her laugh. "But," I added, "I have every intention of making love to you again tonight. So it's not as though you're missing anything."

"Well," she said with a mischievous grin, "in that case..."

She kissed me, and we enjoyed the rest of our bath alone, undisturbed until we were well finished with our memory making and so much time had passed that our fingers grew wrinkled. Then a couple of staff members opened the door, pushing in a tall cabinet, which had two doors that opened to the closet within, and one drawer beneath them.

"My ladies," the woman, a different one than who'd brought us here, greeted. She gestured to the wardrobe, the doors and single drawer of which had been opened by the other woman who'd helped push it in. "Queen Nira had these made specifically for tonight. After you're dressed, we'll escort you to dinner."

We nodded, and they retreated out the door again to wait outside. Ava and I left the bath, brushing as much of the water off our skin as we could before patting dry with the towels we'd been provided. The only thing I retrieved from my pile of travel clothes was my dragon pendant, and I slipped it over my neck and then got dressed with what had been brought in the wardrobe. For me, there was a nice white tunic and a pair of brown leather trousers and boots, all of which fit perfectly. For Ava, there was a blue dress and slippers, not nearly as elaborate or sophisticated as the dress she'd worn to the party last time we were in Ronan, but still beautiful.

"What's that?" I asked, nodding toward something in the drawer as I helped tie the string at the rear of Ava's dress.

She reached out to grab the rectangular box, about the size of my hands if I put them side by side. The box itself was adorned with elaborate carvings that intertwined in a circular pattern all over the surface of the lid.

I'd never seen anything like it, but Ava must have, because she whispered to herself, "She didn't..."

"Didn't what?" I asked, and moved to stand at her side. "What did Nira do?"

Instead of answering with words, she flipped up the lid of the box, revealing what was inside. There was a folded up letter, which she set in the inside of the lid so she could show me the pair of rings underneath. They were solid gold – one was slightly larger than the other – and the inlay of each was carved with the same elaborate adornments as the wooden box.

"Are these for us?" I asked in shock.

"It's Ronan tradition," Ava murmured, sounding as surprised as I was. She put the box back in the drawer so her hands were free, and pulled the larger ring from the cushioned lining. "They're wedding bands," she explained, "the twisting lines carved into them represent all the intricate ways our lives are intertwined, but they wrap around the ring, see?" She spun the ring so I could follow a single line, which never ended. "They go on forever, to symbolize our eternity together." She then held the ring so I could look at the inside, pointing to the letters there. "My name is carved into the inside of your ring, and yours in mine, and that's what makes each pair unique."

"I see," I said with a smile.

"You wear it on your dominant hand," she said, reaching for my left, "on your first finger, so even when you're not paying attention, it's always in view." She slipped the ring onto my index finger, and it fit just right, and she lifted my hand to her lips to kiss my knuckles.

I reached for the second ring, and took Ava's right hand to put it on the same finger as she'd put mine. She was positively beaming by the time it was in place. I bent down to press a soft kiss to her cheek, and then motioned toward the box. "What does the letter say?"

"Let's see," Ava said. She picked up the letter, broke the wax seal, and unfolded it. There were two separate pages of parchment, and Ava looked at both for a moment before saying, "There's one for each of us."

"You can read yours first," I told her.

She nodded, holding it up to begin reading it aloud to me. "Dearest Ava, my beloved sister, you're likely thinking that I didn't have to do this, and I want you to know that I know it. This is the best way I could think of to express my wish that you and Kiena find a lifetime of happiness together, as I know you will, and because I expect that I may never see another love like yours so long as I live. Accept these rings as a gift because I wanted to, and because I have no doubt in my mind that our father would have done the same. He was a happy man by nature, but believe, Ava, that I'd never seen him so joyful as the day he finally met you. He loved you all his life. I know he loves you still. You were the piece of our family that I'd never known was missing, and I love you just the same. Nira."

Ava met my eyes with tears filling hers, but she was smiling, and it didn't look like she knew which to do. She sniffled, wiped the back of her hand over her cheek to brush away an escaped tear, and then gave a soggy laugh. Despite the moisture in her eyes, she looked so happy, and grateful, and... at peace. After all this time, she *was* forgiving herself, and Nira's words seemed to have been more of a comfort than Ava was expecting.

"I'll read yours now," Ava said, sniffling once more.

I moved behind her to wrap my arms around her waist, hugging her to me to offer comfort of my own, and so she felt no need to rush. "Whenever you're ready."

She inhaled deeply as she wiped at her cheeks again, taking a few moments to reread her own letter and reflect on her emotions. After a minute, she shuffled that piece of parchment behind the second one and read my letter. "Dear Kiena," she read, "first, I wanted to thank you for everything you've done for me and Akamar. You found us a home when we didn't have one, and we wouldn't have been able to return home if it weren't for you and Ava. You are my dearest friend, and though you've always felt like family, it brings me indescribable joy that your marriage to my sister makes it official. I would tell you to take care of her, but I've seen the ways that you care for each other, and there's not a worry in my mind that your union won't be one of profound comfort and pleasure. Know that I love you too, and that I thank the goddess every day for sending you back to us. Nira."

Ava and I both just stood there for a long minute in silence, absorbing what was read. It had been easy to understand Ava's tears when she'd read her letter, but I felt it more myself now too after hearing the heartfelt words that Nira had written specifically for me. I was beyond grateful for her letters and her gift, and as Ava folded up the parchment again, I could feel in the content stretch of silence between us that she was too.

"Should we go and find her?" I asked, letting Ava go so she could return the letters to the box. Once she'd set them down, she nodded, but turned toward me and wrapped her arms around my waist to hug me tight. "Are you alright?" I asked, squeezing her in return. She released me just enough to look up, and nodded with an unmistakable smile on her face. "You're happy," I observed with a smile of my own.

"Yes," she said, moving her arms around my neck and stretching upward to kiss me. "The gods have been so good to us. Every day I think I can't get happier, and every day I'm wrong."

"Well, Little Will-o," I said, leaving one arm around her back and lowering the other behind her knees, scooping her up in my arms, "let's see if this other surprise of Nira's can't make you even happier."

Ava grinned her eager agreement, and I carried her out the door of the bath chamber to where the two women were waiting for us. I set her down once we reached them, folding my hand with hers instead so we could follow the women wherever they were supposed to take us. They led the way down the stairs to the first floor of the castle, down a long hall through which the savory scent of food was wafting, and to a heavy wooden door. The door was pushed open, and Ava and I motioned in. It was a large room, with a massive table at the center that still didn't even take up half the space, but the moment we crossed the threshold, we both stopped in our tracks.

My mother and Nilson were already finished bathing and dressing, and seeing Kingston here was no surprise. Not only did we all consider him a friend, but as the king of Valens, he'd also been invited to Nira's coronation as a public show of the newfound peace between our kingdoms. The surprise was the other guests. Denig and Skif had been traveling all over the kingdom to educate people about dragons, and I hadn't expected them to be here at all, but they stopped talking to my mother and the boys to turn and grin at us. Even Rhien was here, and though it wasn't a long journey from the Duskford Monastery to Midsummit, I hadn't expected her to come to the castle for another couple of weeks until Nira's coronation. But she stopped conversing with Kingston and Nira, and squealed and sprinted over.

She reached me first, throwing her arms around my neck. "Congratulations," she said, letting me go and moving over to give Ava a tight hug. "I'm so happy for you!"

"Thank you," Ava giggled, returning the embrace as Denig and Skif wandered over.

"Hello, cousin," Skif beamed, wrapping his arms around my shoulders and pinning mine to my sides so I couldn't hug him in return.

"Hello," I laughed. He let me go so I could greet Denig, who held out his hand. "You're looking well," I told him, shaking with him as I took in his outfit. Both he and Skif were no longer dressed in their plain trousers and tunics, but in more elaborate clothing that portrayed a much higher status.

"I'd say the same of you," he said, passing a wink over at Ava, "married life suits you."

While I smiled gratefully, he and Skif both turned toward Ava, bending slightly at the hips in a shallow bow. "Ava," they both greeted with warm smiles.

"Ambassadors," she grinned, giving a small curtsey.

But Skif dropped the formality, reaching out to grab her and hugging her like he had me. "You're family now too!" he exclaimed, spinning her around.

She was laughing when he set her down again, but she stopped in order to smile at Kingston, who walked over with Nira at his side. "Your Majesty," she beamed, curtseying more deeply at him.

Kingston chuckled, bowing at us and then laughing when Nira brushed past him to hug us both at once. Then she let us go and reached for our hands. "I see you got the box." Instead of saying anything, Ava pulled Nira into another tight, grateful hug that lasted almost half a minute. They both had watery eyes by the end of it, and Nira shook her head while she blinked it away. "Don't thank me," she said, reading the looks on our faces. "There's no need." And because she didn't want to hear it, I gave her a grateful hug too. "There's one more surprise," she announced. "For you, Ava, from Kingston."

Ava looked at Kingston in surprise, waiting for him to say what it was or to present it, but in that brief moment, somebody from the doorway behind us cleared their throat. Ava spun around, meeting the eyes of a familiar young woman and drawing in a deep gasp.

"Ellie!" Ava exclaimed, springing forward and nearly knocking Ellie over in the eagerness of her embrace.

Even after all these months, I remembered perfectly who this woman was. She was the lady-in-waiting I'd met at the castle in Guelder the night I'd gone searching for Ava. The dear friend of Ava's who made me swear that I'd hear her side of things before making my judgment.

Ava released Ellie from the hug enough to grab her face, looking at her like she couldn't believe it. "How did you- Where did you-" She hesitated with a world of disbelief and shock and question in her eyes. "I'm glad you're alright!" she said, drawing Ellie to her again.

"Me?" Ellie asked. "Of course I'm alright, but you! Worried me half to death, you did!"

"But," Ava breathed, pulling away and looking back at Kingston, "how did you know?" She looked again at Ellie. "Why are you *here*?"

"Word's got around about our heroines of Valens," Ellie answered, passing a brief but knowing glance at me. "It took me quite some time to work up the nerve to ask His Majesty if he knew what happened to you after the war, or where you were, but when he found out we were friends, our gracious king invited me here. Said you'd gotten married!"

"I did!" Ava laughed, hugging Ellie one more time. "Oh, I'd have written if I knew for certain where you were."

"I'm here now," Ellie said, and she was just as unmistakably excited about this reunion as Ava, "and you can tell me all about your adventures later."

Ava nodded, finally turning to slip an arm around my waist. "Do you remember Kiena?"

"The hunter," Ellie said, with a smile that let me know she remembered me positively. "And..." she added questioningly, "your wife?" Ava

415

gave an eager nod, which widened Ellie's smile to a grin. "It's a pleasure to see you again," she said to me, bending her knees in a curtsey.

"And you," I agreed, bowing in return. "I'm glad you're well."

Before either of us could say anything else, Ava turned away from the door, hugging Kingston tight around the middle. "Thank you, Kingston," she said, sniffling because there were fresh tears in her eyes.

He returned the hug, patting her gently on the back. "You're welcome."

While we'd all been greeting each other, a handful of staff had been loading trays of food onto the table at the center of the room. Now, one of them came forward to Nira. "Your Grace," he said, "dinner is served."

We were all buzzing with excitement as we walked to the table to get seated, but once we'd found our places, Nira stood from her chair. She grabbed her goblet of wine and held it out in front of her, waiting until we all stopped talking. "Because *you two*," she began, pointing teasingly at Ava and me, "decided to get married without inviting any of us, something needed to be done. We can't marry you all over again, but we *can* celebrate." She raised her drink a little higher, each of us raising our own. "To Ava and Kiena, a couple who not only belong together, but who fought so hard to *be* together that they deserve every moment of happiness life brings them. Cheers."

We all drank to that toast, and set to feasting and drinking and talking and celebrating. Everyone had so much to say about what they'd been doing since we'd been apart. Denig and Skif had stories about their travels so far as Dragonkin ambassadors; Rhien would soon be twenty and graduating from the Duskford Monastery; even Ellie had stories about what had been going on at the castle in Guelder and how much better things were already under Kingston's rule.

We talked and laughed and told some of the better stories about the war to those at the table who hadn't been there. Like when Nira had first been learning to shoot a bow and nearly put an arrow into the armorer's backside, or the time Nilson and Akamar had traded Nira's bowl of stew for a cold one with a live frog in it. When we'd talked ourselves out, Nira had musicians brought in to play us music, and we danced and drank some more. We taught Denig and Skif both Ronan and Valenian dances, and they taught us dances from the mountain, and not a one of us was paying any mind to the hours that flew by.

But the best part of the entire night, better than any surprise or joke, was the smile on Ava's face. Not once since I'd met her had I ever seen her look *that* happy. There was no looming of uncertainty or danger, and all the loss she'd suffered didn't so much as cast a shadow on her features. Her eyes were bright, and her cheeks were rosy with energy and mirth. For the first time since I'd met her, she didn't have a care or concern in the world. She was free to smile and laugh and be as joyful as she wanted, because no one or anything was going to stop her or give her a reason not to. And that look – that freedom and bliss – that was what I'd given my life for. It was what I'd build the rest of my life around, because I couldn't imagine I'd ever feel as content as when Ava looked like that.

War History

The Start of War:

Raised in a family devoted to Valens's Caelen religion, Thydric Cieren II took the throne after the passing of his mother, the queen, Marcil Cieren. Under the influence of his deeply religious father, Thydric had grown to fear mindsets and customs that didn't coincide with Caelenian practice. This fear was most directly aimed at Ronan. Though Ronan had long been a peaceful neighbor to Valens, engaging in trade along an open border, Ronan customs and beliefs were more flexible than Caelen instructed. Ronan's religion, Deacantian, allowed for the nearly unrestrained social, political, and romantic movement of class, race, and gender, placing certain restrictions solely on its royals. Because of Ronan's radical way of living, Thydric's rule commenced with unease.

A great addition to this unease was the magical aspects of Deacantian. While only some twenty percent of people were born with an aptitude for magic, Ronan stimulated these numbers by sending them to specialized schools, institutions, and monasteries, where they could foster these abilities into great skill. Although Ronan showed no signs of weaponizing its abled for the sake of military practice, Thydric feared what would happen if Ronan grew too powerful because of its flourishing magic culture.

Furthering that fear was the open trade that Valens had long been conducting with Ronan. While a majority of imports were simple goods like fruits and silk, it didn't escape Thydric's notice that other things were seeping into the kingdom as well. The most concerning to him were the trade of religion and magic. Some of Valens's abled began seeking Ronan knowledge to discover their own capabilities, and others, including those without the ability, sought potions and artifacts for use in every day life.

History

While Valens was a kingdom of religious freedom, Thydric was outraged that so many of his subjects would abandon the standard practice and engage in something he saw as dangerous. Previous rulers, including the former queen, Marcil, were unconcerned about the cultural exchanges happening with Ronan. Thydric, however, wouldn't have it. He outlawed the import of magical items and restricted religious freedom, and began waging a local war against the damage that had already been done.

Thydric's greatest weapon in this home war was a propaganda campaign against magic, through which he spread fear about those who practiced and about the consequences of practicing. With it came a warning of his own: anyone caught doing magic, or with magical artifacts, would be punished by death. Under the advisement of councilors, Thydric gave his campaign years to become successful, and in many ways, it did. For plenty, the growing fear of magic and the penal consequences weren't worth the risk. For others, fear became so great that they turned in friends and neighbors who they knew were still practicing.

Even though Thydric had taken a developing culture of magic and turned it into a society that feared the ability, his campaign wasn't as successful as he wanted. Some towns resisted, and a few individuals had become skilled enough in magic to make imparting punishment difficult – one of these individuals killed eight soldiers and four innocent civilians in his attempt at escape. While this served to further the people's fear of magic, Thydric himself feared that he would never be wholly successful with such a close and practicing neighbor, and his concern that Ronan would invade with its abled developed into a fear that Ronan would invade from within, by enabling Valens's own citizens.

Ronan had been warned about the outlawing of trade of magical items in Valens, but it was clear that trade was still happening. Ever more anxious about the liberality continuing to influence Valenians, Thydric threatened to end all trade with Ronan unless the rulers took drastic measures. He demanded that Ronan also outlaw magic. The king, Adrikon Ironwood, knowing an end to trade would be far more devastating to Valens because of Ronan's more plentiful neighbors, refused Thydric's demand.

Thydric was furious, but his councilors advised him not to go through with ending trade, as Valenian citizens were already at unrest, and furthering the restrictions already in place by cutting off access to certain goods would likely cause uprisings. Thydric took their advice, but not long after, his daughter was caught with a book of magical practice. In his frenzy of panic and rage, all caution Thydric had about provoking his neighboring kingdom was gone. He sent a force of soldiers beyond the Ronan border to attack the closest magical institution to Valens – the University of Healers – determined that King Adrikon would take his threats more seriously.

King Adrikon Ironwood took it seriously. Ronan declared war on Valens, following through on Thydric's threat to end trade by ending it themselves, and stating that any Valenian caught beyond the Ronan border would be put to death. Having brought about the thing that he feared, and more alarmed than ever that Ronan would use its magical inclinations to invade, Thydric decided that he would invade first, and took a highly offensive position in the war. Ronan would spend the next thirty years defending its magical institutions from attack, and fending off invading Valenian forces in the Black Wood.

Those Thirty Years:

Even though Thydric's campaign against magic had succeeded in making his kingdom afraid of it, not everyone agreed with the war. One of these most prominent figures was Sir Nilan Thaon, a knight in one of Valens's regional capitals – Ocnellio – and born ten years after the start of the war. Ocnellio's ruler, Lord Tithian, was one of the few regional lords throughout Valens who refused to fight in King Thydric's war, as he was reluctant to sacrifice his people to something he deemed pointless. King Thydric tried twice to force Ocnellio's soldiers to join the fight, but lost more troops to the civil battles than it was worth for enlisting the well-defended township.

Nilan Thaon, however, took his township's refusal to fight a step further than Lord Tithian. Having been born with an extraordinary gift for magic that was passed down by his father, a Dragonkin, Nilan wanted his people to be free to practice magic and religion without fear of being punished. Because of Valens's fear of magic, Nilan kept his gift a secret from all but his closest friend, the son of Lord Tithian, Kingston Tithian. Nilan built his movement instead on the basis that the war was petty, and that the people were suffering because of it. The people were losing friends and family to battle, and had felt the heavy increase in taxes needed to fund the war, and so Nilan gained support for a rebellion in Ocnellio and the surrounding towns and villages. All that remained was convincing a reluctant Lord Tithian that rebellion against King Thydric was best for the kingdom.

That push came when someone else caught wind of Nilan's rebellion. Hazlitt Gaveston, son of Lord Gaveston who ruled over the Grimeadow region of Valens, had been fighting in King Thydric's war since he was old enough to enlist. Also with a remarkable gift for magic, Hazlitt subtly utilized his abilities whenever he could get away with it, and created a grand reputation for himself as a war hero, leading his father's Grimeadow army to victory in every battle they fought in Ronan. While fighting in Ronan, Hazlitt came across a history book of Ronan magic, and learned of an elixir hidden away in the kingdom, which would bestow so great a power that even the Ronans feared it. Ambitious and willing to do whatever was necessary, Hazlitt was determined to elevate himself as high as he could, starting with the elixir.

Having heard of the growing rebellion in Ocnellio, Hazlitt traveled the distance to see it for himself. Satisfied with what he found, he used his reputation as the heir to Grimeadow and as a war hero to help Nilan sway Lord Tithian's support of the rebellion. All Hazlitt wanted in return for his support – and the support of his father's army – was to take Thydric's place as king. Although hesitant and with an instinctive distrust of Hazlitt's motives, Nilan was willing to set aside his skepticism if it would end the war with Ronan.

For the next five years, King Thydric delayed a large part of his war on Ronan in order to quell the combined uprising of Ocnellio and Grimeadow. With Hazlitt's support, Nilan's rebellion was enough to defend against Thydric's army, as well as against the armies of other regions in support of Thydric. It was not, however, enough to overthrow Thydric's rule. Not only that, but during those five years, Nilan's distrust of Hazlitt grew. Hazlitt was aware of Nilan's skepticism, and did everything he could to hide his magical affinity, but their brewing rivalry culminated in the moment Nilan found Hazlitt's annotated history book of Ronan magic.

Now aware of Hazlitt's true motive, Nilan took his findings to Lord Tithian, hoping to have Ocnellio's army withdraw its support. Lord Tithian, however, was bound to the war's outcome, as withdrawing support from Grimeadow would mean that Ocnellio would face both Hazlitt and Thydric's army. Unable to gain Ocnellio's public support, Nilan used the loyalty and influence he had and started another uprising in the shadow of this civil war, a force that he called the Vigilant. For two years, the Vigilant battled Grimeadow's army under the nose of Lord Tithian, who was furious about Nilan's change of loyalty, as well as his son's loyalty to Nilan – something Kingston Tithian was disowned for.

Daunted by a double-fronted fight, Hazlitt was forced to take drastic measures. He reached out to Ronan, vowing to end the war with them if they sent aid to help put him on the throne. Ambitious and cunning, Hazlitt also appealed for a wife from one of Ronan's most respected families, hoping a blood tie to Ronan nobles would give him an avenue for future political victories. King Adrikon Ironwood, along with the support of Ronan's second-wealthiest family, the Fyshers, agreed to Hazlitt's terms.

Knowing his fight was lost, but hoping that in a last-ditch effort he could defeat Hazlitt in battle, Nilan persuaded his wife to flee Ocnellio with a trusted friend, Leon Leventhorp, who was more concerned with the life of his infant son, Silas, than with his allegiance in war. With the help of Ronan forces, Hazlitt left Ocnellio and the Vigilant in ruin, and in order to set an example, Nilan was stripped of his title and surname and executed on treason. Within three months, Hazlitt had also conquered Guelder and overthrown Thydric's rule, trying and executing the former king for crimes against the people.

A New Rule:

Under the new king, Hazlitt Gaveston, religious freedom was restored on the sole basis of Hazlitt's apathy toward the issue. Thus, the Caelen religion remained the Valenian standard. Despite being in the practice of magic himself, Hazlitt refused to lift the ban on magic and kept his own talents hidden. If his new subjects weren't satisfied with his rule, it would be easier to defend against rebellion if those rebels were without magic.

So, too, did Hazlitt betray the agreed upon terms with Ronan, as he refused to end the war after he'd taken the throne under the guise of distrusting Ronan's magic. Hazlitt knew his kingdom was too fatigued to continue a full-fledged war, but he was still determined to find the elixir he'd read about. Hazlitt proposed a new set of terms: he would end the war on

History

Ronan if Ronan allowed Hazlitt to send Valenian scholars to oversee each of its magic institutions – which would give Hazlitt an unrestricted means of searching for the elixir. Stuck with some misfortune, the King of Ronan died just before Hazlitt submitted these terms, and Adrikon's son, Akhran Ironwood, took the throne.

Seeing Hazlitt's terms as a dubious means of infiltration for future invasion and conquering, Akhran rejected them. He was, however, as unwilling as Hazlitt to engage in the full-fledged war of their predecessors. For the next nineteen to twenty years, the Magical Defense War went mostly stagnant. Hazlitt sent spies into Ronan territory to search for the elixir's location, and every few years, when he thought he'd found it, he'd send part of his army to battle. Some of these battles were successful, though the elixir was never present. Many of these battles, on the other hand, were not, and the Valenian kingdom's people and troops grew wearier with every passing year.

During that time, Hazlitt distracted himself from his growing impatience and frustration by devising plans and strategies, and his ambition grew. He decided that no longer would he be satisfied with its power once he had the elixir, and that after devoting so much time and energy to finding it, he would expand his reach. Hazlitt's new goal was to establish himself as the first High King, taking control of the continent and searching its every corner for whatever magic he could acquire.

Finally, after decades of searching, the location of the elixir was confirmed. It was in Ronan's capital, Midsummit, and there was no way that Hazlitt could get to it without conquering the castle. But Ronan, having been on the defense for the entire war, had lost less of its army than Valens, and Hazlitt's troops were too tired to go against Ronan's full strength. Knowing he needed additional forces, Hazlitt appealed to the neighboring kingdom of Cornwall, but Cornwall wouldn't get involved. Cunning as ever and undeterred, Hazlitt devised a plan in which he'd ally himself with Cornwall through the marriage of his daughter, Avarona, to Cornwall's prince. Once married, Hazlitt would frame Ronan assassins for Avarona's death, and force Cornwall's hand to get the support he'd need to conquer Ronan.

Timeline

Magical Defense

King Thydric attacks University of Healers, the closest magical institution to the Valenian border.

Valenian war hero, Hazlitt Gaveston, hears of growing uprising, enlists help of leader, Nilan Thaon.

58 B.Bl

27 B.Bl

59 B.Bl

57 B.Bl

King Thydric Cieren II threatens to end trade with Ronan if Ronan doesn't outlaw magic.

King Adrikon of Ronan refuses.

Ronan declares war. Ronan spends next 30 years defending institutions and cutting off invasions in the Black Wood.

War Timeline

Hazlitt makes deal
with Ronan - troops to help
win throne and wife
to solidify treaty.

Hazlitt betrays treaty.
Sends troops/spies to
search for elixir.

Ava runs from castle.

20 B.BL

0 B.BL

22 B.BL

1 B.BL

Nilan realizes truth
about Hazlitt. Starts
another uprising.
The Vigilant

Hazlitt discovers elixir location.
Asks for help from Cornwall
to end war 'Ronan' started.

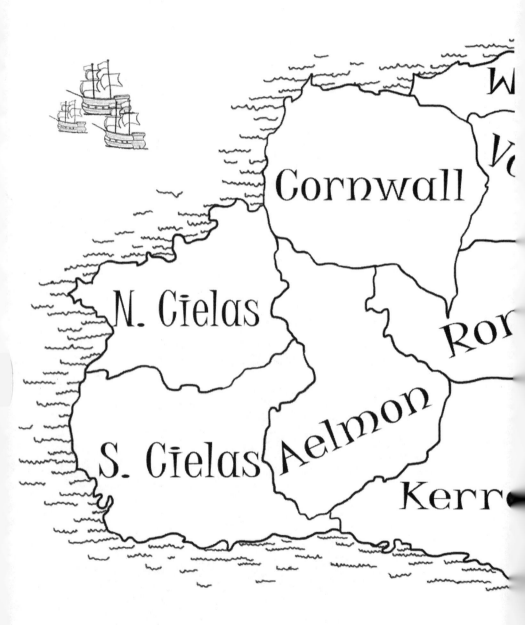